VOODOO
DREAMS

VOODOO
DREAMS

A Novel of Marie Laveau

Jewell Parker Rhodes

ST. MARTIN'S PRESS NEW YORK

ACKNOWLEDGMENTS

Grateful acknowledgment is given for permission to reprint from:
  Foods of the World: American Cooking: Creole and Acadian by Peter S. Feibleman and the Editors of Time-Life Books. Copyright © 1971 Time-Life Books.
  Voodoo in Haiti by Alfred Metraux. Copyright © 1959 by Alfred Metraux. Reprinted by permission of Shocken Books, published by Pantheon Books, a division of Random House, Inc.

An early version of Chapter 2 was previously published in *Feminist Studies* Volume 16, Number 2 (Summer 1990).

Design by Judith A. Stagnitto

Library of Congress Cataloging-in-Publication Data

Rhodes, Jewell Parker.
    Voodoo dreams : a novel of Marie Laveau / Jewell Parker Rhodes.
        p.   cm.
    ISBN 0-312-09869-3
    1. Laveau, Marie, 1794–1881—Fiction. 2. Afro-American women—Louisiana—New Orleans—Fiction. 3. Mambos (Voodooism)—Louisiana—New Orleans—Fiction.
4. New Orleans (La.)—History—Fiction.
I. Title.
PS3568.H63V6   1993
813'.54—dc20   93-24283
                                                                                   CIP

First Edition: October 1993

10 9 8 7 6 5 4 3 2 1

Deep appreciation to Edwardo, my husband Brad, and the National Endowment for the Arts

This novel is a fictionalized account of the life and times of Marie Laveau, a nineteenth-century Voodoo Queen. Many New Orleans residents claim that Marie Laveau, the "Widow Paris," lies in a tomb in St. Louis Cemetery No. 1, where to this day the faithful bring offerings and prayers. In St. Louis Cemetery No. 2 there is a crypt covered with crosses scratched in red brick by followers who believe Marie rests there. Others claim that Marie Laveau never did die.

THE MIDDLE:

Eighteen Hundred and Twenty-two

~

"A story should begin at the beginning. But in this story, the middle is the beginning. Everything spirals outward from the center. Lies, pain, and loss haunt the future as well as the past. The only protection is to become disembodied—to see the self as other. Immortal.

"Grandmère, my mother, my daughter, and myself—we were all named Marie.

"This story is all of us.

"Be sure to write everything down, Louis. Voodoo is worth passing on."

•

—MARIE LAVEAU, JUNE 12, 1881, EARLY EVENING
(From Louis DeLavier's journal)

Three hollow knockings of gourd disturbed the night. Each resounding signaled all was in readiness, all was safe. Then began the timbre of drums, and with each blow Marie sighed and swung her hips, causing her yellow skirt to flare gently.

"Marie," she heard whispered from myriad directions, across swamps, across heavy air. Night creatures, the new moon, and currents of water trapped beneath gritty soil were still. The only movement was the incessant rustling, like bees about a hive, of her followers drawing closer until drums and voices merged into a syncopated beat.

"Marie."

She surveyed the torchlit, low-ceilinged shack. Ribaud was tapping his palms down on dead cats' skins. On the ground behind him lay brick dust, candles carved like men, jeweled crucifixes, and a bantam rooster cocking its speckled head between slat bars. Incense swirled between *gris-gris* charms of stale sweetmeats, flattened insects, and abscessed bone. A statue of baby Jesus, cradled in the Virgin's arms, smiled sweetly. Raised higher, on a small platform, was a crate packed with straw and ornamented with half-moons, herb seed, and an uncut ruby.

"Marie!" Slaves, their backs stooped from the fields and scarred by the lash, pressed in upon her. Mulattoes who barked praline wares in the Market Square caressed her. Veiled *aristo* women mumbled blasphemous prayers, while quadroon whores bowed their coiffured heads.

"Marie." Her followers frightened her. They expected more than she was willing to give, and tonight she was especially fearful; tonight she mustn't fail them. Tonight she'd lose her soul.

"Marie."

She hesitated. Even Christ had felt apprehension before His labors on the cross. He doubted the need for His suffering to save those who pounded the nails in His hands and pressed thorns upon His head.

Marie touched her eyes. Christ gave . . . no, *lost* His body so His soul could live in paradise. She would lose her soul so her body could die. She'd slip into death without caring how she was judged. There would be no resurrection, and so she'd triumph. She'd no longer mirror what her followers needed to believe in, and what they needed to believe in was most often violent, petty, and hateful.

Marie looked at John. He stood in the back with his legs spaced well apart, his arms dangling. In the past, his gaze had calmed her; when she no longer heard the voices, his confidence soothed. But tonight, staring at his dark, bemused face, she didn't feel any ease.

"Marie!"

Her audience was waiting.

Extending her arms, snapping her neck forward and back, she yelled, "Je suis." I am. Then, more huskily: "Je suis Marie Laveau."

Mouths—some flat and broad, some painted red, some white, and some a rainbow spectrum of browns—roared, "Marie . . . Marie est Voudon . . . Voudon."

Bodies humid with sweat swayed in time to the drums. A man whipped his torso, cracking the whip through the air while spittle foamed down his chin. A woman pinched and slapped her buttocks. A youth banged his head against walls.

John came toward her. Marie shifted her gaze. The crowd sang:

> *"Marie est Voudon, Blessure Marie,*
> *Marie est Voudon."*

She arched her spine. Followers moaned while John passed *tafia,* barrels of molasses and rum. Her body segmented into separate rhythms—her feet shuffling, her trunk turning, and her arms motioning side to side while her head rolled free. Moments like this, she so believed the *power* again, for spirits *did* seem to descend. *Possess.*

Followers joined the dance. Men tore off their shirts, flapping them in the hot air. Women flung away dresses, and fat mammies fanned themselves with palms. Marie kept her skirt and cambric blouse on. John wore his black suit and collar of white lace. She was clothed out of decency; John was clothed out of obstinacy.

Marie opened a flask. Brandy flooded her mouth. She spat, and those she sprinkled reeled. Draining the rest of the alcohol into a bowl, she flinted it alight. Twirling three times, she sent beads of flame scattering, singeing pieces of hair, skin, and clothing. *The power spread.* But the crowd's rejoicing didn't satisfy her. Squatting like a Choctaw, Marie felt empty.

John was trembling, his eyes dilated. "Ai-yee," he bellowed, jutting a stick in on each side of the rooster's jail. He lifted the bird by its neck. The bird dangled. John had once trapped her just so, pressuring her neck until she hung, whimpering.

The neck snapped. John's teeth sank into skin.

He ambled toward her—one hand carrying the animal's heart, his other hand rubbing his crotch—exclaiming, "Le roi. The King." John extended his hand, knowing she hated this part of the ritual.

For the first time, Marie took the rooster's heart. It was impotent, warm. "I've grown accustomed," she said. John's brow furrowed. Turning away, Marie held high the offering and cried, "La reine. Glory to the Queen," before swallowing the muscle whole.

Why had she ever been afraid of John? He was only a man. A carnival schemer.

Marie wiped blood from her mouth. The crowd praised her. John retreated. A blond grabbed his hands and smeared her face with their blood. Marie watched John shrug, then throw his arms around the girl. Her resolve grew stronger. There would be no mistresses for John tonight.

She began to chant:

> *"All make way for li Grand Zombi,*
> *Make way! Make way!"*

The heralding echoed through the room. Even the dead ceased wandering at the coming of li Grand Zombi. Swamps and cicadas stilled. Fireflies hovered unblinking.

The ornamented box shifted slightly. Brushing away straw, Marie lifted out the python. "The Zombi is coming. Coming to weave spells." She exhaled and the crowd exhaled with her, as scales wrapped around her waist and up her arm. Vibrations rippled down the python's spine; its smell was the dryness of fallen leaves; its head, the flat curve of an S.

"Dahomeyans worshiped the serpent," she chanted. "For first life came into the world blind. A snake gave them sight." The python licked her cheek.

Worshipers rolled themselves in dirt—secure that each time the animal kissed, it verified their faith in her, her destiny as Queen of the Voudons. Clasping the wedding brooch Grandmère had given her, Marie was filled with yearning. "Come, believers, and receive the vision too."

The drums faltered. "Marie," Ribaud warned.

The followers glanced at John. Angry, Marie noted even now they looked to the King, not the Queen. Yet women were the visionaries, men merely healers. Women, she wanted to shout, handed sight down through the generations.

John gripped her arm. "What trick is this?"

She winced. "No trick."

"The Zombi is for the Queen."

"Tonight is different. Don't you feel it?"

He let her go as the snake's head swung around. It had been John who insisted she use the snake, just as he insisted on the animal sacrifices, the drinking of blood. "Theatrics are expected," he'd said; nonetheless, John was afraid of the snake.

"New gods are eager to descend," she whispered. "Would you deny them?"

Marie enjoyed John's uneasiness. All these years he'd manipulated her, but she'd finally learned his lessons well. "With the weak, you simply demand," he'd instructed. "With the strong-willed, you pull one way and force them to pull the other way. With the proud, you dare."

"Are you afraid, John?" All her life she'd been weak. John would find a dare from her doubly insulting.

"Are you threatening me?"

"Don't deny Damballah, John."

Nodding at her, John encouraged the believers: "Yield. For Marie Laveau is Voudon."

Ribaud slowed his beats.

John murmured, "It won't work."

Marie closed her eyes, assumed trance.

"Whatever you're planning, I tell you it won't work."

The snake spiraled about her; she kept still. "Spirits make *gris-gris*. Spirits make spells." Tonight it was true—though how many would guess her spirit wove this spell?

Opening her eyes, Marie saw a pale child with pigtails and eyes that threatened to swallow her face, watching her from outside the window. Marie wished the child wasn't there, but her rite had begun and she couldn't risk losing her courage again.

"Receive vision." Marie moved among the crowd. "Risk life for belief." Bodies nervously withdrew; superstition claimed the python was poisonous. "Risk, and become a vessel for a spirit god."

"How?" asked a cocoa face which reminded her of her Grand-mère.

"By accepting the serpent's kiss."

Without hesitation, the old woman caressed the animal. The return touch was light. The woman shook as thunder and fell to the ground.

"She's dead," someone shouted. "Blessure mortelle."

"Stupid woman." John sneered. "You've ruined us."

"No. She lives," Marie said, sliding her hand down the snake. With each stroke, she seemed to calm all; except John; herself.

The woman must rise believing a god had touched her; Marie's hopes depended upon it. She smiled wryly. The old woman needed more blind faith than she, the great Voodoo Queen, had ever had.

Marie studied the woman's chest. She could see the outline of deflated breasts beneath coarse cotton. The woman's rib cage didn't move. Perhaps her fall had been too hard.

The woman stirred. "Je suis bénie. Je suis bénie," she said wonderingly. Her face and eyes alight, rocking her body to and fro, she repeated, "I am blessed." Clasping her hands together, tears curving down her chin, she screamed joyfully, "I am blessed."

"By me," Marie exulted. "Blessed by me." The trap was sprung. John's pride would finish him.

"Saint Marie," the crowd shouted, begging to be infected with the spirit. "Saint Marie." They pressed forward, stumbling heed-lessly, trying to touch Marie and be part of the miracle. They clamored for the snake's kiss. Marie felt the old panic, the desire to flinch from sweat-scented palms and outraged neediness. She shouted "Enough," and turned away. Her lack of sympathy, her unwilling-ness to concede one more "blessing," pleased her followers all the more.

Marie headed toward the altar. Would Grandmère have been pleased? Or would she still disown her? *She closed her eyes and felt Grandmère's presence like a wisp of firelight, a curl of smoke.*

"Marie."

With hooded eyes, Marie watched John swagger toward her.

Clutching her hair, causing her chin to tilt upward and back, he kissed her. "How does it feel to be a saint?"

"You may join me."

"I'm already joined with you."

She thought of all the nuances—joined by his plunging into her, by the fears he inspired. Following John's lead, she'd made Voodoo a religion of lies and horror.

"Yes," she said demurely.

"Then why should I want more?"

"Not more." She stared at the scars on his face. "As much as due you."

"I'd rather be kissed by you."

"Why not two kisses for my King?" She offered him the snake.

John edged away. "You're trying to trick me, aren't you?"

Smiling, Marie flicked her hand, calling a slave out of the group.

Awed, the slave fell to the floor. "Hoodooed," he said. "A spell's on me."

"Why?"

"Don't know."

"By whom?"

"Don't know."

"Idiot," cursed John, stubbing the man with his boot. "Cures aren't for the ignorant."

Protecting his head, the slave moaned, "Don't know. Can't eat. Can't sleep. Don't know why or who."

Marie lifted the slave up. "What do you know?"

Reverently, he murmured, "Marie is all. All power. All spirit."

She blew air across his face. "Come to me tomorrow; I'll undo your curse then."

John turned to her. "You can't fix what you don't know. Tomorrow isn't time enough—," he whispered.

—isn't time enough to discover who frightened the slave, isn't time enough to coerce them into stopping. "I'll know," she said. *Once it was true; she would have known.*

"How?"

"By how it drops out of the sky."

"Foolishness." He caressed her cheek. "You believe too much."

She let the weight of her head fall into his palm. "Once you believed in my visions."

"A child's fantasies."

"But I had them, John." Then, softly, "Why not again?"

"It's dangerous when the conjurer believes she conjures."

"Or perhaps"—she cradled the snake—"the gods taught me more than you know."

John paused. "I don't believe you."

"Try," she crooned, offering him the snake.

He opened his arms. "I'm not afraid, Marie." *The snake slid across her arms to his.* "Not of this. Not of you. Any power you have still comes from me." *The snake's tail drifted down his chest.*

Marie sucked in air, hoping the Zombi remembered its trade well—remembered it as well as she remembered the murder of Grandmère, the abomination of Jacques.

John was trembling, fighting his own nervousness. Marie didn't know his secret. She only knew that the snake haunted him, pricked and frayed at the seams of some personal nightmare.

"I made you," John said harshly, "Queen of the Voudons."

"Thank you," she said, *as the snake squeezed, choking him.* His nostrils flared in surprise; his hands clutched and unclutched as he tried to untangle the animal from his lace collar. Lovers from hidden corners gazed in amazement. Some made the sign of the cross. Others rushed to John's aid and Marie hollered, "Let him be. It's a test of his faith," and respectfully, fearfully, they merged back into the crowd. Even Ribaud's drums were quiet.

Marie remembered John saying, "Spells work because people believe." Did John believe?

She turned to him: the snake, a tight fist-sized spring, was wrapped about his chest and throat. His raspy breathing unnerved her; spasms racked his body; his arms were pinioned to his sides.

Though he couldn't speak, she anticipated his question. In a voice only he could hear, she answered, "Because of what you did to Maman. To Grandmère. What you did to me."

He fell with one leg twisted beneath him, his tongue swelling, his eyes popped wide.

Her head lifted. *Marie saw the child's wide-eyed face and fingers pressed against the windowpane.* Marie was sorry the child was witnessing John's death. She stared intently. *The child's face seemed extraordinary, simultaneously young and old, smooth and scarred. The little girl was both smiling and crying.* Stunned, Marie realized she was seeing a ghost. No mother had come to claim her; Damballah was sending her a sign. What did it mean? Was the spirit a ghost of who she had been, or a glimpse of who her baby would be in ten years? Seeing the ghost, she saw her daughter; she saw herself, ten years old.

The child ghost opened her mouth and began a high-pitched wailing. Marie wanted to cover her ears, but no one else heard what she was hearing so clearly. The audience was silent. Marie realized John had ceased struggling.

Reluctantly, she turned to her audience. In a loud, clear voice, she began the chant again: "Dahomeyans praised the serpent. For Eve came into the world blind. A snake gave her—a snake gave me sight. I am," she added vehemently, "Marie Laveau."

The slave and the old woman screamed, "Saint Marie." Chanting again syncopated the drums. Marie looked up. *Grandmère, eyes averted, was floating across the ceiling.*

Followers bowed before Marie; one by one, they shyly kissed her hem. "Marie . . . Marie est Voudon . . . Voudon." She felt like crying.

Marie touched her nails down on the cat-skin drums. "Stop, Ribaud. No more spirits will come tonight." Her spine erect, she watched the numbed crowd file out of the shack.

Tomorrow there'd be new stories about her scandalous power, new weavings of half-truths and lies. People would say she'd raised a woman from the dead, killed two men, sucked poison from a snake's jowls, and fornicated with the devil. In truth, she'd done something far worse; she'd betrayed both Damballah and Christ.

What god would excuse her for killing her child's father? Yet John, alive, would have destroyed their daughter—the fourth Marie—as surely as he'd destroyed all the others.

"The blood is alive," Grandmère *whispered.*

"Yes." Marie closed her eyes. There wasn't any way to stop the coursing of blood. As penance, she could try. Wasn't it her choice to lie willingly with the beast? No Savior had changed the beast into a lamb; John had devoured her. Partly, she had allowed it. Her daughter might still survive. Marie chewed at the corners of her mouth. She was so far from Teché and childhood wonders. She'd been happy in Teché until she turned ten.

When the room was quiet, her followers dispersed, Marie lifted a candle and crossed to the pane. Red mosquitoes banged against it; the startled ghost child was gone.

"Assassine."

"Yes, Ribaud. Murderer."

She saw his reflection grin.

Soon afterward, she heard him slide a heavy weight across the packed earth floor while she stared into a night alive with owl squeals, wind moans, and her own whisperings.

"Women hand sight down through the generations. Mother to daughter."

THE BEGINNING:

Eighteen Hundred and Twelve

~

"I am my mother's daughter. She is in me. I, in her."
"I have always been a good Catholic. Grandmère never understood this."

•

—MARIE LAVEAU, JUNE 13, 1881, EARLY MORNING
(From Louis DeLavier's journal)

M arie could recall a time when all that was required of her was to sit on her Grandmère's knee. She in her yellow-striped bloomers, letting her legs swish against her Grandmère's skirt. On hot summer evenings when breezes wafted light with moisture, they would rock together on the front porch. Amaryllis, peonies, and the pastel of magnolias surrounded them. Scents blended into a cloying sweetness that tore into their nostrils and cloaked their skin.

The land was threatening, yet beautiful. Prickly bark contrasted with willow-leaved jasmine. Cattails ran along blunt edges of rock; sawlike sedge hovered over water-cushioned grass. Sounds overwhelmed them: the lazy, far-off slope of alligators, bat wings interspersed with evening squalls, and the vibrating shrill of cicadas. Off the coastal shore, anxious hurricanes fed.

Ivy camouflaged the house. Grandmère confessed to liking it.

"Solitude est liberté," she said. And Marie piped an echo, though she wasn't sure what it meant. But she sensed pleasant lonesomeness while she and Grandmère sucked crayfish wriggling out of the sides of their mouths like worms. Pleasant lonesomeness as Grandmère sang melancholy tunes while Marie folded her chest against her knees and clutched her skinny ankles with her arms.

Grandmère was huge and fat. Every Sunday after prayers, she'd tuck Marie, squealing like a piglet, underneath one arm, carry her to the stream, and drop her in. When she was clean, Grandmère would sing—about heaven and the Virgin . . . about flowers closing and dying, about innocence and salvation. It was her songs Marie loved most. Grandmère could shape ordinary words until she wept. Hum and make her laugh. Her alto conjured dreams.

"Our home is Teché," Grandmère whispered, "bayou of snakes."

And Marie listened to everything her Grandmère said, taking it in like a thirsty sea sponge.

"We're mixed bloods." The voice was melodic as Grandmère stooped, pressing their faces side to side. "Creoles veined from the line of French royalty. Mulattoes veined from the line of an African queen. And Muskogean warrior veined to make the stew wield power." Grandmère stood, her arms akimbo, her chubby cheeks breaking into a grin. "Happy birthday, ma petite."

Marie squirmed, for beyond Grandmère's she couldn't connect any faces to the blood. She'd never seen Africans or French royalty. Indians flitted past occasionally on hunts. Once each year, she felt an unusual loneliness.

"What's the matter, ma petite?" Bushy brows met. "Don't you feel well this birthday morning?" Grandmère's hand reached out. "You got fever?"

Dodging the rough hand, Marie slipped deeper between the sheets. "Go 'way," she muttered. "Leave me alone."

Grandmère snorted. "You feel the sun streaming in here? God's sun. Don't you know how special it is to feel the sun and be free?"

Marie rolled her eyes. Grandmère was always insisting she be grateful for things. Yet it bothered her that the only face she knew well was Grandmère's.

16

"I used to slave in Master's kitchen. Even on birthdays. Hot. Not enough air. Work. Slicing, stirring, hauling. Always work."

"You told me before."

"So I did." Their gazes held. Grandmère lifted the rosary attached to her skirt and scratched the crucifix across her thumb. "Yet you always seem to forget that in this land you're the first of the line to be free." There was a thin rising welt of blood. "Three generations of slaves."

Grandmère sucked the juice from her thumb. "Mixed bloods. Our history and power." Red speckled the coverlet. "The blood is alive. Always."

For hours, Marie had stared at the squiggly veins in her hands, trying to imagine where the crazy quilt of blood all went. In the mirror, she couldn't see Creole or mulatto. When she pinched skin, she couldn't feel Indians stirring in her veins. Tales of slavery were as distant as Grandmère's Bible characters.

"Why do you mope?" Grandmère demanded. "You should laugh and sing. Why do you ruin such a lovely celebration day?"

Marie knew everything yet nothing about herself. Being "mixed blood" didn't matter; it was what Grandmère didn't say that did. Her most important question (the one she prayed to the Virgin about) still lurked behind her eyes. History was faceless.

On her tenth birthday, Grandmère clanged pots, spoiled rice, and ruined the beans by adding too much pepper.

On her tenth birthday, Marie waited for a sign. All day she waited for something magical to happen, and when it did, they were on the front porch, the moon glowed yellow, and Marie commented how fireflies gleam-blinked like crazed lanterns in the sky.

"So now you speak. Silly child's got a tongue after all." Grandmère leaned forward, swatting the air. "Damn fireflies. They're burning up their lives' blood."

"Oh"—she exhaled—"then why do they do it, Grandmère? What for?"

"Ain't got no sense is all."

"Like Maman?" she asked, her head jerking up. But it was more of a statement than a question. *She had heard this before. Heard it, her body curled tight while shadows fluttered across her bed as two women fought.* They fought *until the front door slammed and one was gone.* Somehow she knew that the two women fighting were Maman and Grandmère. It was Maman who had no sense. Maman who was burning up her life's blood. But instead of asking where or why Maman wasn't there, she asked what she always needed to ask—

"Do I look like my Maman?"

Grandmère stopped rocking. Her hands and lips trembled; her body grew rigid like Medusa's stone. Frightened, Marie wanted to take back her question. She'd been told never to ask about Maman, and until tonight . . . until a firefly, she hadn't.

She stole toward Grandmère, purring against the old, soft bosom. Grandmère didn't hug or caress her. Instead she said flatly, "Lots of God's creatures have no sense."

Marie leapt down the steps, trying to catch fireflies. She caught one and found the erratic glow surprisingly cool.

"Marie. You come back here."

She snipped off the lighted abdomen. There was no red blood. After she threw away the head and the wings, the light stuck to her palm. She snapped her wrist, shook her hand, and finally wept as her nail, like a knife, scraped the double-ribbed flesh onto the ground.

"Marie." Grandmère's shrill call rebounded.

She ran, her hair flapping at the back of her knees. The moon was full. She pushed through willows, feeling her head would burst, tumble off her shoulders, and roll into the grass. Grandmère talked about the blood being alive, but never about people. Wasn't Maman flowing beneath her skin?

She plopped down on a petrified stump. *At its base was a snakeskin, the shell curled as if it were alive.* She rested her head in her hands.

Breath bounced from her hands to her face.

Grandmère said she'd been born with a caul, a skin netting that almost suffocated her. Feeling her twice-warmed breath, she knew what it felt like as a babe, drowning in her own air.

Gasping, she snatched her hands down. *Rainbows swirled in her palms. A kaleidoscope of blue, red, and yellow danced, shifting into forms. She saw herself, bloodied, slipping out of her mother's body, and Grandmère's frantic fingers, ripping the caul away.* Crying out, she clapped her hands. This wasn't a dream. It was something else. Did Grandmère see them too? She skipped down the bank like a ghost. And Maman, whom she'd been forbidden to speak about—did she see them too? Air pockets bubbled the swamp's surface. Her stomach quivered against the damp ground. *She couldn't feel herself breathing. Or hear the piercing call of the owl.*

Marie touched a hand to the water then snatched it back. *Color sprang from her fingertips. A snakelike form rippled the surface.* Then she wasn't sure, for the water became a mirror and she saw her own pursed lips and stricken gaze. Tentatively, she touched the stream again.

The surface glazed. *Three bodies. Three women. Grandmère was stretched as dead. Another woman was crucified on a tree, her face and breasts pressed against the rotting wood; scars lashed her back.* Maman? *Then she saw herself—older, rising out of the lake, three lighted candles waxed to her head and palms.* The vision held. Then it changed. *Four. A baby girl sucked at her teat while chubby fingers grasped the candle's flame.*

There was a rush of sights and sounds. She saw an eel in the muddy water; a single cricket sounded like ten thousand. Marie felt a *whoosh* of air cracking through her lungs.

A snapping twig startled her. She turned, thinking it was Grandmère.

"Grandmère, I've seen things. Strange things." But it wasn't Grandmère.

Marie saw a man so black he blended into the skyline. There was a ruggedness to him, and odd scars raced from his forehead to his chin. She tried to scream as he hunched down toward her, sprinkling her with narcissus blooms. *He smelled of ash and withered leaves.*

Marie closed her eyes, hoping this vision too would disappear. But his fingers smoothed her shut lids, caressed her cheeks, then, gently, teased the dark cores of her breasts. Her eyes flew open. "Who are you?"

"Father. Husband. Son."

He cupped the valley between her thighs, rubbing her in slow, even movements. She sighed; a sticky dampness blended with her bloomers. He laughed, and without knowing why she felt ashamed. His lips covered hers, sucking the air out of her mouth. It felt like the time when she was sucked up by the swamp. Grandmère had rescued her, fingering the mud from her nose and throat. She'd felt painfully alive.

"Grow, ma petite."

Her fist punched through air. He caught it. If he wanted, he could shatter her hand, break her skinny arm in two.

"Hurry and grow," he said.

She swore she never would.

Then he was gone; stars formed new patterns; her troubled breathing slowed.

Awakening, Marie was startled to find the moon was dying. Wiping away flowers, she raced through the jungle forest. *Had anything happened?* Somewhere a dog barked. *Or had she been tricked? By nonmemories? Sleepy dreams?* Sweat layered her skin.

Grandmère sat in the rocker, her jaw slack. Marie wanted to fling herself into her arms. But then she remembered Grandmère was angry at her. Hadn't she run when Grandmère called? Hadn't she mentioned Maman? So she held her breath and crept like a Seminole. The first step creaked. Grandmère didn't stir.

When her hand pressed the doorknob, Grandmère roused and said, "No sense trying to fool me."

"I wasn't."

"Don't lie," she said harshly. "Where have you been?"

"Woods."

"What did you see?"

Marie longed to tell her everything. But shifting from foot to foot, she knew, as surely as she knew fireflies didn't spill any blood, Grandmère didn't want to know the answer. "Nothing," she murmured.

"Come here, child." She ran, and fat arms surrounded her. Grandmère smoothed her freckled nose. "You smell sweetly."

"Flowers," she said hurriedly. "I picked them for you."

"Then where are they, ma petite?"

"I left them." Never before had she told such lies. But it was all Grandmère's fault—it was Grandmère whom she couldn't tell about the man, whom she couldn't ask about Maman. She scrunched her lips into a pout.

Grandmère hummed a note which tore inside her, sharpening her guilt. "No need to hurry and grow," Grandmère sang. Then, abruptly, she rocked forward and asked, "Are you hungry?"

Marie nodded and scrambled onto the waiting lap. She burrowed her head into rose-scented skin. Chuckling, Grandmère added, "My stew's too hot. It'll burn your tongue off. What can we have that's better?"

"Pig's Ears, please?" her voice squeaked, excited by tasting curly-shaped pastries. And Grandmère smiled so lovingly that Marie swore that to please her she would forget everything. Forget turning ten.

Inside, the house was cool. Paneless windows lined three walls of the square one-room house. A ceiling fan whirred from crosswinds. During storms, Marie and Grandmère lashed the windows with palms; nonetheless, the rain would drizzle in.

A table and chairs centered the room, and across from the entrance was the altar with the Virgin serene in blue. On the left were two beds with feather mattresses. On the right were shelves lined with grains, pots, and utensils. A scrub bucket was propped in the corner. Grandmère boiled water on the wood stove.

"I'm glad my girl isn't sad," Grandmère said, shuffling about the small space. "I'd be a bad Grandmère if my baby girl was sad."

Grandmère unwrapped Marie's favorite treat: molasses and nut pastries, resembling the corkscrew twists of a pig's ear. Eagerly, Marie grabbed the sweets, laying them on the table in a neat row. Grandmère snatched one away.

"Three. Never take four."

"Why?"

"Heartache comes with four." Grandmère tugged her hair. "Smile, birthday girl. You can have more. Another set of three."

But Marie didn't want any more. *Hadn't the vision of the candles been four?* As Grandmère admonished her to say grace, she nearly cried.

A porcelain cup was placed in front of her. Loose tea floated like dazed worms. Grandmère always said, "Drink tea when it's steaming, when the worms are knocked out, or else—" what? Gripping the cup tight with both hands, she concentrated on remembering the rest of the maxim. Feeling the heat spread up her arms, she heard Grandmère chatter, "Or else they'll make your intestines grow."

The cup crumbled in her grip. Hot leaves splattered her lap and a slash of blood stretched across her palm. "Marie," Grandmère clucked while bandaging her cut, pulling off her damp clothes. "You're too tired."

She wasn't tired, only scared that Grandmère could read inside her mind. She stared at her in wonder. The old woman didn't seem like Grandmère at all; in the candlelight, her white hair streaming, her face seemed filled with mysteries, her shadow ten feet tall.

Marie shuddered. She didn't understand anything. A flannel gown shook down over her head.

"Mon pítí bebe. Go to sleep. Fais dodo." The lilting Creole overpowered the four walls. Marie was certain Grandmère could charm a bird from its nest, lull a fish to shore, or, if she wanted, sing a body back to life.

"Go to sleep, my kitten. When fifteen years have fled—"

Someone else had sung this song to her.

"—my kitten will be wed."

As Grandmère bent to snuff the lantern, she hollered, "Do I look like my Maman?"

"No," Grandmère said sharply. "You look like me. Go to sleep."

Marie smothered her face in the pillow.

Grandmère clutched her shoulders and turned her about. "Who's my baby?" she crooned, cupping her face. "My oh-so-pretty baby?"

"Me," Marie said. But she knew she didn't resemble this mournful, flat-nosed broadness. She was Maman's baby, not Grandmère's. She caught hold of Grandmère's skirt, pleading, "When will I know about Maman?"

"When you're older." The light went out.

"Then I'll grow," she shouted.

Grandmère stared at her. She stared back.

Like a sentinel, Grandmère stood by the window, blocking out the moonlight. Twisting the black-bead rosary, she began her litany, begging her Virgin for forgiveness, for deliverance from evil.

In the darkness, her head and arms stuck outside the cocoon of the bed sheet, her cut throbbing, Marie watched her. The prayers sounded like irritating bees. Grandmère said God watched over her, but Marie didn't believe it. "The Virgin answers every prayer." Except hers, she thought resentfully.

Near dawn, she saw Grandmère tense. *The man was hidden among the willows and the flowers.* Grandmère huddled and embraced herself. She made the sign of the cross.

"What do you see?" Marie hissed, sitting upright in her bed.

"Nothing." A dull, aching sound.

And hearing "nothing," Marie knew the man could tell her all about Maman. Why else would Grandmère lie?

Later, after Grandmère was asleep, Marie went to the window. The sun was edging out of the ground. *The man was already gone.* She pressed her feverish brow against the cool frame.

So she grew—her hips, soft and rounded; her eyes, slanted and dark. Marie couldn't decide whether anything had ever happened that summer evening, whether she had in fact turned ten.

There weren't any more visions.

She'd lie for hours beside the swamp with her eyes closed, trembling, waiting for magic. She stopped when Grandmère caught her.

"Child, that's the devil's game," Grandmère shouted. "Don't you know eyes are meant to see?"

Touching the water, she didn't see any rainbows.

"What's the matter with you? Sleeping your life away?" Grandmère snatched her to her feet. "Crazy child."

But that summer evening, something *must* have happened. Grandmère's face, normally placid and gentle, closed like a shutter. When Marie tried scrambling onto her lap, Grandmère waved her away, complaining, "You've grown too big." Soon, before she knew it, it was true. Marie felt awkward inside her new skin while Grandmère, day and night, rocked in her rocker alone.

Marie mourned, for that summer evening (dream or not), something was lost between them. Grandmère was moodier, despondent at times; she prayed with greater fervor. In the middle of the night, Grandmère woke up screaming; by day, her songs were dissonant.

Marie did her best to please her, learning all the lessons Grandmère insisted Creole virgins had to know.

At twelve, she learned the ordering of a home—how to bank fires until sparks licked the air, how to snap a chicken's neck and simmer its giblets.

On this birthday, she asked, "Am I old enough?" Grandmère grabbed her wrists and shrilled a knifelike tune. She shook free, ran, and hid beneath leaves to dull the lingering melody.

At fifteen, she learned medicine roots. Bay leaf for stomach troubles, sarsaparilla roots for fevers. She asked, "Am I old enough?"

"You're old enough to know birthing babies is hell." Grandmère smacked her gums. "God cursed us. A woman birthed you just as I birthed her and my momma birthed me. The line goes back to Eve—a woman who sinned."

Marie stalked away. Each year she hoped Grandmère would tell a single simple truth. But she didn't. The lessons intensified. Marie was surprised. She thought Grandmère wanted to slow her learning, slow her growth. Nonetheless Marie wove fishnets until her fingertips bled, wondering if she ever knew Grandmère.

Maman, the man, and her visions were a circle and Grandmère lived in the heart of it, while she was on the outside, disconnected, looking in.

She never heard the history of "mixed bloods" again.

* * *

24

On her sixteenth birthday, Marie escaped her lessons. There wasn't any celebration.

That morning Grandmère murmured, "The only birth worth celebrating is Mary's birth of Jesus. Do you hear? Why don't you listen to me?"

Marie plucked another catfish out of the pail.

"I say a lot more than just my words. I talk all the time. With my hands, my eyes, my songs. But you never listen. You don't respect me. Not enough." Slamming the door, Grandmère went inside the house.

Marie stopped scaling catfish, ripping their innards, and drifted into the woods. Grandmère would chastise her for leaving a task undone. But she hated dead animals. A fat, oily smell trailed after her; the fish were left rotting in the sun.

By afternoon, Grandmère found her sitting cross-legged beneath an oak, watching a ladybug crawl between the creases of her arms.

"Ladybugs are made for wishes." The voice was airy and light; the face crinkled into a grin. Grateful Grandmère didn't berate her, Marie didn't say aloud what she truly wished, but she thought it.

"Say something, ma petite."

"I haven't any wish."

"We all have wishes," Grandmère teased, sucking her toothless gums. "Me, I wish my catfish weren't ruined." Comically, she scowled. "I wish I were two tons thinner. Delicate like you. But I've always been big. Big hands. Big feet." She wriggled her toes, sighed dramatically, then shook a finger at her. "Maybe you wish your Grandmère wasn't so mean sometimes. Wish she was as sweet as a honeysuckle vine."

Marie blushed.

"Ah, I told you so." Grandmère laughed, a deep, gurgling sound. "We all have wishes. Even some we won't admit to." The folds beneath her neck shook.

"I wish you could live forever." The sun hid behind clouds, and it occurred to Marie: if she had any sense, she'd wish she was nine.

The grin faded. "No, birthday girl. The spirit is always more willing than the flesh. And sometimes I wonder"—she massaged the area over her heart—"how much longer I'll be willing."

"What's wrong?"

"I want Mary to mother me," Grandmère said nervously, touching her rosary. "I want to rock in the same cradle as Jesus. Wish, ma petite."

The ladybug rolled onto Marie's finger.

"Wish while you can. Opportunity shouldn't be wasted."

Marie could feel Grandmère hovering over her, her good mood lost. "What should I wish for?" The animal's red and black markings became a blur.

"For someone to love you. You won't always have me. You won't always love me."

"Not true." Marie tried to rise, but Grandmère was pressing her shoulders down. The ladybug crawled into her palm.

"Wish for someone to protect you when I can't."

"You'll protect me," Marie said stubbornly. "Your Virgin can protect us both."

"Wish for a husband."

"I don't need—"

"Do it," Grandmère commanded. "Then blow the ladybug into the air."

Marie wished. As she inhaled, the ladybug flew high, disappearing among tree limbs. Grandmère snatched at her gray hair.

"I'm sorry. I didn't mean for it to fly away."

"Stupid." A hand swung back.

"I'll search for another and wish." A stinging coursed through her head. Holding the side of her face, Marie whimpered, "I don't want a husband."

"You won't have me for long."

"No. Always." If she didn't have Grandmère whom did she have? She wasn't certain Maman was even alive.

Grandmère's back slid down against the oak. She looked like a ragamuffin doll.

"I'm happy," Marie lied, "with the way things are." Air was dense in her lungs. Even the ground beneath her feet was softer, shifting with moisture. Her legs felt weak; mosquitoes were drawing her blood. Marie wanted to go back in time. Yet part of her wanted to rush time forward. She'd changed too much to remain in the bayou. Her head fell forward wearily. Marie closed her eyes and wished for a vision of the future.

Grandmère stirred. Her own voice sounded far off to her ears. "I can barely remember when I've been happy," she said, pinching the folds of skin on her forehead. "I've done what I've needed to do." Protected her daughter, her granddaughter. Yes, she'd always been strong.

Grandmère pressed her fingers to her eyes. Visions of the past rose like dead souls. So long ago. An Indian. Tall, Muskogean warrior. Sachwaw, he was called. She barely remembered how he looked. She remembered best what it felt like having him loving her. What better legacy to give Marie? A legal husband. Not to have to hide in the woods like she did, escaping a vengeful Master and the eyes of jealous slaves who'd rather have seen her whipped than loved.

She wiped sweat from her brow.

An old maid, Grandmère thought ruefully. She shouldn't have become a wasted and dry old maid. Hadn't her body warmed to loving? Sachwaw had always loved her outdoors—beneath a hot sun or a cool moon, in a field, beside a riverbank. They had loved wherever they felt the urge to love.

Sachwaw had never said he loved her. But he'd shown love with caresses, kisses, and fierce stroking between her thighs. Grandmère had responded with all her youthful passion. She could still blush about her behavior. Her body had responded to love, not lust. Her body had understood what Sachwaw couldn't say.

Who told? Grandmère wondered. Who alerted the Master? It could've been any number of men who'd wanted her. Or any number of women who'd envied her and her mother, Master's mistress. Perhaps it had been the overseer. Or maybe Master himself somehow guessed. Though Master had never touched her, Grandmère could still recall how his probing gaze had unnerved her.

Who told? Someone must've told. She'd never discovered who. She'd awakened from loving dreams only to discover her mother bending over her, tranced, staring at her, yet staring beyond her, saying, "Dead. He's going to be dead."

Her heart had nearly stopped. Sachwaw, she'd thought. Her mother had nodded. She'd dashed from a sweet sleep into a run. Stumbling, barefoot, her soul had ached as she raced through fields and swamp. She'd arrived too late.

Grandmère could still hear the coarse shouts. She could still see the group of white men taunting, beating Sachwaw while Master sat imperiously on his horse. Her pleas meant nothing. A black was property, but an Indian's life was worthless.

She could still see Sachwaw dead: twisted, tangled in the rushes—a Moses in reverse. Drowned in but a few feet of water. As she'd screamed her grief, the men flipped Sachwaw over and gelded him like a stallion.

"Marie," Grandmère screamed, her arms flailing. "My eyes are going blind. My bones are tiring. Marie! I'm blind." For an instant, daylight turned to dark. Memories faded.

"I'm here, Grandmère."

"There's so much I don't want to see. So much ugliness I've already seen." Grandmère shuddered and fell back against the oak. Oh, Sachwaw, she cried out within herself. To Marie, she said, "Soon I'll stumble and fall."

"I'll help you, Grandmère. Always."

She shoved Marie away. "Hear it? Don't you hear it?" Grandmère stood, clawing the bark; moaning, she clamped shut her ears.

Marie cocked her head. She saw the sky darkening, saw a rabbit scamper into a hole, and saw Grandmère escaping a sound which wasn't there.

"One crow's caw. My death is coming. Quick." Her swollen feet turned. Grandmère imagined she was running toward Sachwaw. *But the figure ahead was a skeleton surrounded by a flock of crows.*

"Where are you going?" Marie yelled.

Grandmère stopped and swayed.

Marie stopped too, wondering if Grandmère's ears were playing tricks again, if she was losing her mind. "Home, Grandmère," she said plaintively. "Let's go home."

"No. Tomorrow we go to New Orleans." She'd find her child a husband.

Stunned, Marie watched her. Grandmère told tales of New Orleans, where men slit each other's throats, where women sold their bodies and slaves were beaten. The receding bulk grew smaller. Showers fell. Palms screeched, and off in the distance she heard Grandmère ranting:

"Ladybug, ladybug, fly away home,
Your house is on fire and your children are gone."

That evening, for the first time, blood raced out of Marie's womb. The almost-black clots were resilient when Marie pressed them between her index finger and her thumb. The taste reminded her of mangoes.

Grandmère brought her squares of linen. *How did she know?* She undressed her. "It's a sign. A good sign," Grandmère said, rubbing Marie's body with oil. Grandmère's strokes felt like fine silk. "You're ready to marry now." Her crotch moist, Marie thought about the man. Grandmère whispered, "I'm ready to die."

Marie tried to say no but her mouth wouldn't open. Between strokes, Grandmère chanted, "Some say the rivers of blood are dirty. Innards crying. Some say the blood will curdle milk. Devils hide in the blood. Some say a man could die"—she pressed the swab between Marie's thighs—"from a single sip."

Marie was terrified. She could feel the blood rushing down and out of her body. What had seemed natural she now wanted stopped.

"Being a woman is a curse, child." With effort, Marie opened her eyes. "Blood ties—not the blood itself—cause the hurt."

Marie couldn't hear her words. She was staring at eyes. Grandmère was crying. *Marie stared until, beyond dull hazel, she saw rainbows. Snakes were weaving over and out, under and through rainbows.*

She was inside a cathedral. Marie could tell because Grandmère had often described God's house, especially the gold altar aglow with tiny candles and a statue of Christ crucified. She was bewildered because the snakes were inching up Christ's limbs. Grandmère had told her of burning incense, holy water, rosewood pews, and of stained-glass images so lovely they'd make you cry. But she'd never mentioned snakes breeding in God's house.

Where was Grandmère? Marie turned and saw no one. She turned again and in a mirror saw herself dressed in white silk and lace, pinning a gold brooch of a sleeping snake onto her bosom. A black-robed priest was coming toward her. Panic overwhelmed her. She wasn't prepared. She gathered her hair into a chignon. In the mirror, she saw a handsome young man standing beside her, tickling her ribs. When she turned to speak, he was gone. His image was trapped in the mirror. He reappeared when she covered her head with a veil entwined with roses. He smiled sweetly and offered her a ring. As she reached out to touch it, his yellow face faded and was replaced by black skin, scars, and a grin. Her wedding dress turned red.

Christ fell off the crucifix. Blood pooled at her feet. The priest removed his hood; snakes crawled out of his skull. The man with the scars was laughing. He spun her around. The mirror shattered, splattering like brilliant, twinkling stars in her menstrual blood.

"But the blood is also life. A link to all the dead."

"Grandmère?" It'd been six years since her last vision, and this one, like the others, scared her. "I see things." Marie could barely breathe. "Strange things." The grip on her hand was tightening. Her bones would break. "What's happening to me?" she yelled.

Grandmère dropped her hand. Bending over her, her eyes bulging, she said, "Get dressed. Tonight, while the weather's cool, we leave for New Orleans."

"Why, Grandmère?" Marie begged softly. "Tell me why."

Cradling Marie to her bosom, Grandmère murmured, "I've been counting moons for the moment when you would become a woman, when your blood would flow. How long it's been!" she sighed. "I looked for the blood on your twelfth . . . thirteenth . . . fourteenth birthday. Your body was defying me. I imagined the blood pooling, collecting in your body and purposely holding itself at bay.

"Children, Marie." She stroked the dark head. "No man would marry you without knowing you carried seeds for children. No man would ever protect you after I'm gone without bloodlines.

"A woman's safety is her womb's blood. She labors for a child.

A child made and born amid blood. Blood for a legal husband. It makes all the difference."

Grandmère settled Marie against the pillows. Marie looked a child still, innocent of unhappy dreams. She was beautiful—her damp hair fanning over white cotton, her chest gently rising and falling. It was glorious to have a granddaughter.

"Who's my pretty—?" Grandmère stopped. *In Marie's eyes, she saw shadows walking.* The old woman's fingers clutched at the bed sheets. Shadows trapped within eyes meant a violent death for the beholder. Her daughter—Marie's Maman—had complained of shadow figures stalking her. Months before her murder, Marie's Maman said she saw death whenever she looked in a mirror. Grandmère had never seen anything beyond her daughter's brown eyes.

"Grandmère, what is it? Are you ill, Grandmère?"

Grandmère reached overhead for the mirror. It was small, sharp about the edges. "Do you see anything? Anything at all?"

Marie looked at Grandmère, at the mirror, then back to Grandmère. "What should I see?" she asked, bewildered.

"Look again." She thrust the mirror toward her. "What do you see?"

"Nothing."

"And in my eyes, what do you see there?"

"Nothing, Grandmère. Nothing at all."

Grandmère was relieved. Death wasn't stalking Marie.

Yet, with certainty, death was stalking her. Yea, though I walk through the valley of the shadow of death. Grandmère's shoulders drooped; air escaped from her chest. What new sign was this? Her African mother had taught her that death tiptoed about in eyes and mirrors, catching the looker unawares. What did it mean that Marie's eyes mirrored her death? Marie must be connected to the violence that would kill her. How unfair it was! What evil could cause Marie to hurt her?

"Grandmère. Are you all right?"

The shadows were gone.

Premonitions teased, taking months, sometimes years before fulfillment. She'd known folks who'd gone crazy from premonitions, some killing themselves before the warnings were done. She'd see to it that Marie was safely married; afterward, she'd wait for the inevitable. Suffer to come unto me. Jesus would love her. And before she laid her body down, she vowed to see her baby girl safe.

Marie was frightened by Grandmère's stillness. It was as though her spirit flew away, disconnecting from her body. Without spirit, Marie didn't recognize Grandmère. She seemed ghostly and oddly vulnerable.

"New Orleans."

Marie jerked forward, startled.

"New Orleans," Grandmère wailed, her voice lowering to a moan as the vowels rolled through and echoed from her mouth. "New Orleans." The words held joy and pain, promise and despair, hope and hopelessness. Marie wanted to block out the singsong. "New Orleans. New Orleans." Then, incredibly, Grandmère giggled, the sound jarring. Her face jutting forward, her eyes bulging, Grandmère said solemnly, "Can't find you a husband in Teché. No man dares to come here."

Marie pushed away the thought: *except one.*

They piled their belongings into a wagon. Grandmère was testing twine, making sure her rocker was safe. Marie made a last visit to the house. Soon she'd be leaving the only home she'd ever known, Marie thought. No, the only home she remembered.

Her lower back ached. It was as though the blood from her womb enjoyed cramping her stomach and flowing from between her legs. How many days? How much blood could she lose?

She didn't want a husband. She wouldn't like New Orleans. She closed her eyes, trying to imagine her mother's face. Did Maman ever hold her, sing songs, or braid her hair? She hit her fist against the stark walls.

Marie stepped outside, pausing beneath the full moon. A bat flew over the roof. She heard an owl mocking her. Would there be rainbows in New Orleans? She plucked a branch of ivy, shredding it between her teeth. She sucked in air. If Grandmère thought her old enough to marry, she must be old enough to know about Maman. Excited, she ran toward the wagon.

Grandmère was straining to tie a knot. Marie touched her shoulder. The old woman jumped. "Child, you startled me," she exclaimed, placing a hand over her heart.

"Grandmère, I'm old enough."

Grandmère stilled. Slowly, she turned back to her rope, her face and eyes shadowed. "I still can't get this rocker secure. It's too awkward and big. The twine's too fine." She jiggled the rocker. "See, it's still not safe."

"Grandmère, please. I said I'm old enough."

"I heard you." Grandmère spun around, her face ugly. "But after I'm dead and gone, after you've got grandchildren of your own, you still won't be old enough to know about your Maman. She was a stubborn, disobedient child. Just like you. Had to have things her way. A selfish child. Nothing good ever came of her ways. She never listened even when I warned her—," Grandmère stopped, pressing her rosary to her lips. She began mumbling prayers.

Outraged, Marie wanted to squat down and weep. Six years, and she hadn't learned anything. Six years. Grandmère's promises were dust.

"You never planned on telling me anything," Marie said disbelievingly. "You lied to me, didn't you? Didn't you? Just planned to keep lying," her voice rumbled, increasing in volume. "You've never loved me. If you'd loved me, you wouldn't have lied."

"Be still, child."

Marie stumbled forward. "You lied." Now she'd never discover who she was. Marie wanted to make Grandmère hurt, to punish her for raising her hopes. It wasn't right that she should feel all the pain. She wanted to pluck out Grandmère's eyes. Grandmère's eyes had seen more of her Maman than she would ever see. All she had was vague memories. Dreams.

"I hate you," Marie screamed, and with a hard thrust she sent Grandmère's rocker spilling from the wagon top.

"No!" yelled Grandmère.

The rocker's spine cracked upon impact. An armrest skittered into a willow. Grandmère fell to her knees, lamenting over the broken, splintered wood. Even the trees shivered from her song.

"I'm sorry," Marie said softly.

Grandmère looked up. She studied Marie, recognizing that the child, her chest heaving, looked exactly like her Maman. Life was a damn shame. How did she explain she kept secrets because it was best to keep them? Best to keep Marie safe. Or was it? Crickets rattled. Shaking her head sorrowfully, Grandmère said, "Forget about your Maman."

"You drove her away, didn't you?"

Grandmère caught the hem of Marie's skirt. "Who's my baby? My oh-so-pretty baby?"

"That man will tell me."

Grandmère flinched. There was no need to ask who. Marie's intuition was right; that night Grandmère had seen the man, and Grandmère, who wasn't afraid of anything, was afraid of him.

"Who raised you?" Grandmère argued, pounding her fist against her chest. "Who's been your mother, if not me?"

"I'll find him in New Orleans."

"Do so and 'sorry' won't be enough. I won't forgive you."

Grandmère tucked a piece of the rocker in her pocket.

Marie shuddered. How did she explain that the man with the scars scared her too? But it scared her more not to know who she was.

She was sorry for everything. Sorry Grandmère grew her for a husband, when she grew for Maman. Marie climbed aboard the wagon, wondering why all she ever felt was sorry.

Marie held on to her vision. *In New Orleans, on her wedding night, the man would come.*

Grandmère, feeling unbearably old, her hand inside her pocket, felt the pain in the rough edges of the wood. It had its own memories: rocking her and Marie on the porch and, before that, herself and the child in her womb, Marie's Maman.

Her slave mother had taught her there was life in things: African spirits in wood, iron, and the sea. But she prayed to people now. White saints. Statues with eyes, noses, and mouths. Why not? Whites had always been more powerful—like the rough, vengeful men who'd chased her into the bayou swamp, like the white men who'd hurt her daughter. The same kind of men who'd destroyed Sachwaw. She gripped the wood.

There was a sore inside her, festering, waiting to explode. Grandmère couldn't sing this pain. She sang around it. She looked at the sky. The darkness was terrifying, almost as terrifying as Marie.

She'd managed the child poorly. Hiding in the bayou while the child grew restless. Marie needed a husband to calm her. Then they'd all return to Teché. If she was lucky, she'd live long enough to see her great-granddaughter born. Only then would she know the chain was broken. History wouldn't repeat. Perhaps she'd have pleasant dreams again. Pleasant songs. She'd stop feeling she was being punished. Stop feeling sorry for being born. She'd die in bed, resting comfortably, while Mary rocked her in Her arms as Jesus stood by.

ANOTHER BEGINNING:

Eighteen Hundred and Nineteen

~

"After our first meeting, it was hard to recall your face," she said.
"I fell in love with you at once. I was trying to save your precious
Jacques when all I wanted to do was to save you."
"You did, Louis. Many times over."

•

—MARIE LAVEAU, JUNE 13, 1881, LATE EVENING
(From Louis DeLavier's journal)

The trip took five days and four nights. The first day Grandmère and Marie didn't speak. They endured nagging heat and mosquitoes. They thought resentful thoughts.

The second day, Grandmère would only utter omens and warnings. Marie exclaimed over a wounded crow that nonetheless managed to fly. Grandmère promptly replied, "A bird with a crooked wing means sorrow." When they bypassed a dirt path, Grandmère pointed: "A cracked gate means you'll leave and never return." And when Marie was awestruck by the grace and beauty of a huge old willow, Grandmère said snidely, "A willow weeps for women's sins."

By nightfall, Marie thought she'd go crazy if she heard another saying. Relieved, she settled herself for sleep. Eyes shut, her sore head resting on a makeshift pillow, she heard Grandmère say, "A yellow moon means death."

Marie gritted her teeth as Grandmère honored the Virgin with twenty prayers. "Twenty," Grandmère said, "is a good number."

The third day Grandmère saw more omens: dung in the middle of the road, a three-legged cat. That night Grandmère sang: "Lord have mercy, Christ have mercy."

As a contrast to the day, the evening campfire barely kept them warm. Heat still lingered in the air, but the damp ground chilled bones. As she lay on her back, trying to sleep, Grandmère's bones felt as old as the Earth. If Marie had snuggled beneath her bosom, Grandmère would've told her everything. Told her about sores as painful as the calluses on her feet. Told her about her Maman, about the heartache that comes from loving too much. But Marie stared at the woods like there were other secrets she could see. Grandmère stared at the sky. And with each falling star (the sky seemed filled with them), she felt more guilty.

Grandmère knew she was driving them toward trouble. But she couldn't calm herself enough to figure out *why* she was doing it. He'd be waiting for them; like he'd been waiting for her and her daughter, Marie's Maman, when they arrived in New Orleans over thirty years ago. Was she trying in some backward way to punish herself? Punish Marie? Was it worth finding Marie a husband no matter the cost? Grandmère only knew she didn't like being cornered. Staying in the bayou was no answer, for he'd eventually come for Marie. *John.* Why didn't she name him? Like John the Prophet, John the Baptist saint. Judas would've been a better name. Arriving in New Orleans would show him—*John* (say it! think it!)—that she wasn't afraid. And if John believed she didn't fear him, maybe he'd think twice about harming them. Bravado would be a talisman. Maybe John would wonder if she still had her power.

Grandmère searched for the North Star. Christ's star.

The day her daughter died she'd converted to Catholicism. Maybe by going to New Orleans she was trying to prove Christ loved her. Prove He'd defend her in New Orleans as payment for her years of faith. And if Christ wouldn't save her, surely His mother, the Holy Virgin, would. Surely a woman would understand and protect her virgin granddaughter.

Father Christophe had warned her that conversion to escape disaster wasn't real. She remembered staring at the thin priest and feeling she'd do anything to share her troubles with someone real:

not a Voodoo spirit but a man of flesh a.
someone else to share her burdens.

When she confessed, Father Christop.
Christ—the white male God. He said He had t.
and forgive her, and for a moment she *had* felt b.
entered her soul and cleansed her of hurt. She ha.
mind to join those whom she couldn't destroy.

Her poor daughter was dead. Tree spirits must've.
child slowly dying. Why didn't spirits keep her baby aliv.
to African gods didn't do any good. Black gods, like blac.
didn't have any power. You couldn't touch them like you di.
Christophe. You couldn't speak to them through confes.
screens. You couldn't hear them answer, "Nomine spiritus san.
You couldn't watch them baptize, cleanse, and bless your daughte.
body for burial. How lightly Father Christophe had handled he.
baby girl!

Would Father Christophe still be in New Orleans? Would he
explain why for eleven years, though she'd doggedly practiced the
Catholic faith, the Christian light had never entered her soul again—
the light for which she'd given up her power, her magic?

Grandmère stuffed a blanket beneath her head. She *had* to go
to New Orleans to find Marie a husband. Her conscience told her
there were men elsewhere in the world. She'd heard of Kentucky,
Virginia, Boston. Grandmère shook her head and plumped the
blanket. New Orleans was home, she told herself, while another
voice said she lied. She'd never had a home. Not since slavers
discovered Africa.

Before closing her eyes, Grandmère glanced at the squatting,
statuelike Marie. The dying orange and yellow cast of the fire made
her seem unforgiving. Fireflies darted at her hair. The child was too
stubborn for anybody's good.

Grandmère crossed her heart as another shooting star fell from
the black, silent sky.

The fourth day traveling, Marie thought neither the horse, its sides
flecked with foam, nor Grandmère, her skin sallow, would survive

.p. Several times Marie offered to drive. Yet each time Grand-
complained about fools having no place to go. "Fools," she
.bled, "wander like idiots." The wheels spun and clacked.

When did Grandmère grow so old, so slight? wondered Marie.

Marie didn't know how to tell Grandmère that she loved her
.ymore. It'd been easier to show "I love you" when they were both
.ounger, happier. She and Grandmère could rock for hours on the
porch. They'd hunt twigs and roots for medicines. She'd imitate
Grandmère's songs. Even laughing together at a pompous owl had
told Grandmère she loved her.

Now, with each passing mile, Marie sensed Grandmère rapidly
and unnaturally aging. It was as though Grandmère's flesh was
intentionally betraying her, intentionally sagging, pulling her and her
spirit down to the ground. Marie felt helpless. There seemed nothing
she could do to break the silence between them. And the one action
that could break the silence—refusing to search for Maman—Marie
felt she couldn't do. Heartache rose between them.

From the wagon top, from every angle of vision, Marie saw
willows. How many willows were weeping because she couldn't say
"Grandmère, I love you"? Things would be better when they found
Maman, Marie consoled herself. Everyone would be happy. She'd
prove to Grandmère that the joy of being a family again—three
women together—was worth any pain. Marie crossed her hands over
her waist and rocked forward and back.

What if Maman couldn't be found? What if Maman didn't
want her? Marie rocked her worries away; her thoughts were too
destructive to contemplate. But worry, like a restless ghost, stayed
perched on Marie's shoulders, ready to overwhelm her.

By noon, Marie's foreboding transformed into excitement as
the wild landscape of home gave way to narrow roads bypassing
tenant farms and pillared plantations. Interspersed between the
miles, Marie saw people: dozens of rows of black men and women
hoeing, picking in cotton-speckled fields. Farmers shouted orders
while maneuvering wagons. White children climbed trees as black
children rolled bales of cotton. Marie began to realize how isolated
and alone she'd been in Teché. She smelled hints of sea salt.

Naive, Marie liked the view of people working in the fields

best. She liked the symmetry of the cotton rows and of black hands plucking colorless white. She especially liked when the workers lifted their voices in melancholy song. It was like hearing Grandmère's voice echoed by a hundred.

If Marie had asked, Grandmère would've told her that the workers were exhausted and that the sweet "River Jordan" song was about longing for freedom in Africa and peace in the afterlife. But Marie and Grandmère, both stubborn, kept the wasting silence between them. Sea salt grew more pungent.

Finally, on the fifth day, their travels ended. Marie and Grandmère were on the wide roadway leading down into the city at sunrise. Grandmère felt apprehensive; the city seemed a glittering trap ready to ensnare them. To Marie, New Orleans unfolded like the striped tissue on an All Saints' Day gift. People were furious patterns of movement, brisk colors dotting the landscape. A never-ending expanse of blue-green sea hugged the shore. Marie couldn't recall ever seeing such marvelous sights.

Women's voices rose, sounding like a calliope:

"Brocanter. *Buy. Orange peels.* Les chandelles.
Candles. Coffee. Pois de senteur. *Sweet peas.*"

There were stalls of bananas, oranges; baskets overflowing with ice, headless shrimp, catfish, and buzzing flies; carts filled with marigolds, pralines, and sugared *beignets*. The mixture was tart yet sweet, repelling yet seductive, as chocolate women wearing scarves, their ears clicking with golden hoops, persuaded passersby to buy.

Admiring the kaleidoscope of skirts, Marie felt dull in her beige shift and with her unbound hair. The cloth inside her bloomers itched.

"What is this place?"

"Market Square. People don't till land," Grandmère complained. "Don't catch fish. Just buy and sell."

A woman shoved a bowl of dry rice and herbs beneath Grandmère's nose. "Please buy. Finest Creole rice." Grandmère slapped at her, but the woman deftly ducked away.

Giggling, Marie swung her eyes to the Gulf. Ships jammed the

Mississippi harbor, their planks encrusted with algae, their rigging like a spider's web. Women dominated the square. Men dominated the wharf, scurrying barefoot on decks, unloading bales of puffed cotton, rum, and squealing piglets.

"If Christ was on earth"—Grandmère cackled—"He wouldn't visit New Orleans."

Feeling blasphemous, Marie wondered whether anyone would notice if Christ visited New Orleans. The activity was astonishing. Marie guessed there were over a thousand people. Figures flowed from the avenues, converged, and swelled in the Market Square. Bodies mixed as easily as the ingredients in a gumbo stew.

Skin hues astounded Marie: swarthy sailors, olive gentlemen tapping canes against the boardwalk, and white women twirling parasols while black boys carrying baskets trailed behind them. A dozen uniformed men, carrying bayonets, were marching lackadaisically in front of a garrison. "Who are they?"

"Soldiers," Grandmère answered. "New Orleans has always needed soldiers to govern her. If they were Spaniards, they'd be more brown, less tall. If they were Frenchmen, they'd be lean and handsome. These must be Americans. They look like mules." Grandmère spat on the walk. "Barbarians."

Barbarians or not, Marie found the blue-coated men fascinating as they marched in and around the Place d'Armes. The entire world sailed into New Orleans. Marie's spirits lifted; she would find the man here, maybe even her Maman.

Marie relaxed her grip as traffic brought the cart to a halt beside a cayenne stall.

A curly-haired seaman was tickling a market girl, his fingers running along the curves of her breasts. Marie frowned as the girl pushed the sailor away. Cajoling, his arms encircled the plump waist. The girl now encouraged him, alternately giggling and batting her lashes. He caressed the girl's face.

Marie rubbed her hand against her own flushed face. The sailor turned toward her. Marie snatched her hand down, pressing it safely into her lap. The young man flourished a bow. Marie blushed. The market girl threw her arms about the sailor's neck while softly imploring, "Jacques." Marie averted her eyes, but not before she saw the girl glare at her.

The cart rumbled forward. Marie twisted around. The sailor was waving. She smiled shyly, then turned herself about. His name was Jacques.

Up ahead, a dark man was beckoning people nearer. He wore a tattered shirt and patched pants. Garlic and camphor hung around his neck. A hat stitched with parrot feathers and birdseed covered his skull. Beside him was a bucket of wriggling snakes. Marie nudged Grandmère.

> *"Cure for souls. Come and buy my cure for souls.*
> *Soothe devils. Soothe demons.*
> *I got de spells. Powerful spells. Spells from the spell man.*
> *Come and buy. My cure for souls."*

His hoarse call seemed meant for her—or was it meant for Grandmère?

"Who is he?"

"No one." Grandmère ruthlessly whipped their horse. Women shrieked and men shouted curses as the wagon lurched dangerously through traffic. The horse galloped forward. Grandmère struggled with the reins. Marie screamed. The horse reared and the wagon buckled to one side. Marie's head hit the wood backing. Grandmère moaned. The frightened nag kept stomping, pawing at the side of a carriage and the gold crest painted on its side. Beneath the crest was the letter D embellished with vines and a rose with thorns.

"Damn." Antoine DeLavier leapt out of the carriage, moving forward to quiet the animal. His shoulders and thighs were muscular. His lace collar added a dissonant note of femininity.

He moved efficiently and precisely, jerking the horse's bit and patting its heaving ribs. He didn't spare any soft words but rather ordered the horse to be still. When the horse didn't respond, he added several vicious tugs on the reins.

Antoine swung open the carriage door. "Brigette. Louis. Are you all right?"

"Yes," answered Brigette, leaning heavily against Louis' shoulder.

Marie marveled. Brigette was Grandmère's Virgin statue come to life. Dressed in pale blue, blond curls falling to her shoulders and breasts, she seemed extraordinarily lovely. She seemed vulnerable, too, cornered between two men—one with his arm wrapped about her shoulder, the other grasping her hand. Antoine gently kissed her fingertips. Marie wondered which man was her husband.

"Louis, see to her," Antoine said. He turned and scanned the scene. He shouted vehemently, "Vite. Away with you," to the onlookers, then caught hold of Grandmère's arm.

"How dare you interfere with our passage? Don't you realize my sister could've been hurt?"

Grandmère bowed her head.

"Are you deaf?" demanded Antoine. "Answer me."

"My apologies," said a subdued Grandmère.

"Who's your master?"

"We're free."

"I don't believe you." Antoine's voice lowered. "Maybe I should restrain you? Imprison you until your master posts a reward? Or perhaps a beating would serve you better." Sun and clear sky outlined his riding crop.

"No. Stop." Marie thrust out her arm, clenching her teeth as the crop struck her hand.

Angrily, Antoine reached up and caught Marie by the waist. He lifted her, kicking, down from the wagon.

"Let me go," Marie screamed. "Someone help me. Please." No one would aid her. Women laughed behind fans, men raucously encouraged her taming, while the coloreds about her kept their heads bowed. Grandmère prayed.

"Grandmère, please. Help me."

The old woman was clutching her rosary, fervently muttering over her black beads.

Anger burst from Marie. Against Antoine, she fought every grievance of the past five years; hitting him, she imagined she saw her Grandmère's face. She scraped and scarred him with her nails. Blacks in the crowd gasped at her courageous folly.

"Fiend." Antoine shoved her away and, stumbling backward, Marie fell, sobbing.

Antoine traced the cut on his chin. Between his index finger and his thumb, he massaged his blood. "You should've run away," he murmured.

Marie felt nauseated by fear. She struggled up and tried to run as Antoine moved toward her. She darted to the right. Just as quickly, Antoine gripped her hair and drew her in to his chest. Marie squirmed.

"It will be a pleasure to tame you." He pressed her face close to his.

Marie glared. Antoine had the same blue eyes as his sister, the same ivory skin. But the features that were lovely on Brigette were ugly on him. He jerked her hair again. She cried out.

Antoine's free hand caressed Marie's throat and breasts. "Coloreds aren't usually so bold." He lowered his head toward her mouth. Marie screamed.

A voice shouted, "Maman, sister, what's happened? There's been an accident, no?" Marie strained toward the sailor, Jacques. Antoine held her tight.

Jacques bowed. "DeLavier. Your"—the sailor hesitated— "reputation is known throughout the city. I'm sorry if my family has caused you any harm." His hand swept toward the carriage. "It wasn't intended."

"Who's this black who pretends to be a gentleman?" Laughter rose from the crowd.

"Jacques Paris, at your service." The sailor clicked his heels. "Of late from Santo Domingo."

"A bastard quadroon."

"I shouldn't have left my family alone. They're new to New Orleans. But"—Jacques opened his palms expressively—"business couldn't wait."

"Your business is to feed on manure." The words were almost casual. "To lie among pigs with your lovely whore of a sister and mother." Antoine shoved Marie at Jacques. "I wouldn't be surprised if you pricked them both with your black cock."

"Hurry," Jacques whispered, pulling Marie back toward the

cart. "Get away quickly while we fight." Marie let him lift her up beside Grandmère.

"Coward," Antoine shouted at Jacques' back.

Marie's hands were on his chest, Jacques' hands just above her waist. Fleetingly, Marie thought of the market girl. But now the sailor's face was sad. He flicked her nose. "I'll be all right. I'm like a cat with nine lives."

"You don't even know me."

"Sssh," Jacques said, pressing her hand. "I have two lives left." He grinned cockily, and as he did so Antoine spun him around. Off balance, Jacques fell face forward in the dirt. Before he could recover, DeLavier kicked him repeatedly. Groaning, blood dripping from his mouth, Jacques tried desperately to shield his head and abdomen from the flurry of blows.

"Grandmère, help him, please."

"There are ways, child," Grandmère said softly, remembering. "A cry to the gods, a charm of hair, linseed, grave dust. . . ." She'd managed a slow death for the Master who'd killed Sachwaw. She could do it again: kill another white man. Why not? If her power was still there. . . .

Grandmère breathed deeply. Fortifying air rushed through her mouth into her lungs. A hum rumbled in the back of her throat. "Guédé, Guédé, Guédé . . . come, hear my plea . . . Guédé, Guédé, Guédé . . . your servant needs you. . . ." Grandmère concentrated on seeing the death gods. Her vision would make them real.

Her eyes rolled back in her head.

Grandmère was standing, arms outstretched. Wind ceased blowing across the Gulf into the square. Seagulls swooped silently across the clouding sky. Grandmère could feel the ancient spirits hovering near, rejoicing in her call. She was surprised at how readily they answered her after all these years. A rush of confidence filled her.

The Guédé were laughing like three raucous boys. Her fingertips itched. All she needed to do was point. The Guédé were ready. If she pointed, the process would begin. Her hand was shaking. Point and say "him" *and it would be over. The Guédé would destroy him.*

"Do it," *said the Guédé in unison.* "Do it now."

"I can't. I can't." Grandmère collapsed. Warding off sin, she pressed her rosary to her eyes, mumbling, "Thou shalt not kill. Thou shalt not kill." To Marie, she said hoarsely, "Spells. I don't dare use them. It's too hard on the soul to kill a man."

It was over in a matter of seconds. Marie blinked and saw a Grandmère she'd never seen before. Standing atop the wagon, her face contorted, the whites of her eyes visible, Grandmère had personified violence. It was crazy, Marie knew, but for an instant she believed Grandmère could kill anything. Anyone. Then she blinked and Grandmère was once again sitting beside her—a weary, sad-eyed woman.

Antoine kept beating Jacques. Upright, the two were locked in an embrace. Jacques was holding tight, trying to recover from his pain. Antoine was pushing Jacques away, thrusting ineffective jabs at his sides.

"What's done is done," pronounced Grandmère. "It's better that we leave." She gathered the reins.

"No. I won't go," said Marie.

"We must."

"I won't."

Marie glanced at the crowd: delight shadowed the white faces, a passive horror haunted the blacks.

The two men were apart. Jacques was swaying, his eyes were bruised and swelling, and his cloth shirt was torn. Antoine still seemed impeccably dressed, a gentleman. Jacques was wiping blood from his mouth, grinning strangely. "If you allow it, sir, we can duel at sunset."

The blow was unexpected. Jacques fell, clutching his abdomen.

"I don't duel with blacks."

Antoine lumbered forward, cursing Jacques to get up. The sailor rose to his knees. Antoine's boot slammed into his stomach. Jacques groaned. Cursing, Antoine turned toward his saddle for his whip. It was a large cord, knotted with supple and biting leather.

Marie yelled, "Get up. Get up, Jacques."

Sprawling in the dirt, Jacques murmured, "Run away. Get away." He tried but couldn't get up.

Louis DeLavier was furious. His cousin Antoine represented everything he hated about the South. Brutal, unfeeling, and arrogant about his own power, Antoine was the epitome of a southern gentleman. Louis knew he was no match physically for his cousin. But there had to be some way he could stop Antoine from murdering a man for sport. He shouted, "Antoine, I insist you stop this."

"Go to hell, Louis."

Louis jumped down from the carriage, moving quickly to block Antoine's path. "You know he can't strike you."

"He would if he had any guts."

"It's death for a black to hit a white. The law forbids it. You know that. You can't just whip him to death."

"Why not?"

"Haven't you any honor?"

"Not your northern honor. We don't tolerate insolence from coloreds." Antoine uncurled his whipcord. "Get out of my way or I'll whip you too." He smiled. "Believe me, it would be a pleasure."

They stared at each other. Louis was taken aback at seeing so much hate. He had no doubt that Antoine would enjoy killing him. "It doesn't matter that we're cousins and soon to be brothers-in-law, does it?"

"No. If anything, it makes it worse."

"Damn you," Louis said, turning, feeling ashamed that he couldn't rescue an innocent man.

He heard the *whoosh* and snap of the whip parting through air and falling upon Jacques' back. Jacques' cry was heartrending. Many in the crowd applauded.

Louis looked up and saw his cousin and fiancée, Brigette, staring out the window, her breasts pressed against and ballooning over the carriage door. Her lips were parted and her expression reflected pleasure. Louis was revolted. The whip fell again. Jacques screamed. Louis knew the only person Antoine ever listened to was Brigette. She had to help him. He moved forward quickly, placing his two hands over hers. "Stop him. You've got to stop him, Brigette."

Brigette's eyes flickered. It irritated her that Louis was so unmanly.

"If you love me, stop him."

Brigette didn't love Louis but, seeing some flicker of distaste, she was suddenly afraid that Louis had seen something in her that made her less desirable.

"Antoine." Brigette posed in the window, looking elegant and slightly bored. "This upsets me." Her cool voice stilled the scene. The crowd focused on Brigette as if she were a sainted virgin.

"It can't be helped." Antoine's face was petulant.

"I say it can." With the black coachman assisting, Brigette stepped gracefully down from the carriage. She opened a white parasol to deflect the sun's glare. "It's rude to be threatening one's visiting cousin. Louis already thinks we're barbarians as is."

"He shouldn't interfere with southern ways," said Antoine, playing to his audience, striding cocksure. He snapped the whip's tail in the dirt, creating swirls of dust. The audience cheered.

"You shouldn't be embarrassing us in front of a common crowd. Father wouldn't have approved." Twirling her parasol, Brigette stared at Antoine, a pout curving her painted mouth. Her gaze was steadfast. "Do as I say, Antoine."

Marie was amazed that Antoine's eyes shifted first. Antoine glanced everywhere but toward his sister. His boots scuffed the earth, making him resemble a scolded boy. Reluctant, he walked toward Jacques.

Jacques was lying face down, his legs sprawled to the right. Blood was bubbling to the surface of the deep scores on his back.

Antoine was furious that he hadn't finished what he'd begun. He stooped, vowing, "Another day, sailor. Your whore of a sister too." Bypassing Louis on his way back to the carriage, he whispered, "I won't forget this, Louis." With exaggerated grace, Antoine escorted his sister back to her seat. Louis helped Jacques to his feet. Disinterested, the crowd dispersed.

Once at the wagon, the exhausted sailor slid out of Louis' arms onto the ground. Gingerly, he rested his back against the wagon wheel. His shoulders ached. His lungs felt small.

"Easy," counseled Louis. "Breathe slowly and easily."

"I'll be all right." Jacques doubled over in a fit of coughing.

"I'm sorry," said Louis, feeling awkward and helpless.

Jacques waved his hand dismissively. "I've survived worse."

Louis looked up at the slip of a brown girl. From the wagon

perch, Marie was smiling, bending toward him, her dark hair cascading and smelling of hyacinths. Louis was struck by her loveliness. He ignored the old woman jiggling beads and focused on the simplicity and wonder of Marie's face. He felt as though he were drowning in sensation. Marie seemed the fulfillment of dreams he'd never realized.

"Thank you, sir," Marie said.

Louis smoothed his prematurely thinning hair. "It's nothing. I wanted to do more."

Marie noted the clipped, nasal twang in his voice. He didn't sound like anyone else she'd ever heard. "And that lovely woman. Thank her for me too."

Louis winced; then his hands shot up toward Marie's face. She tensed. He gently drew her head down, closer to his. He closed his eyes. Like a blind man, Louis traced Marie's chin, nose, and brows. His fingers paused, memorizing the surface of her lips.

Marie was too startled to move. His touch wasn't threatening; she could feel her own breath warming, escaping through his fingers.

Louis' eyes opened. They were brown and vague. Marie had the distinct impression that, while touching her lips, he'd traveled somewhere else. "I'm sorry," Louis said, stuffing his hands into his pockets. With quick steps, he scurried away.

Louis couldn't imagine what had come over him. Ever since coming to New Orleans, he'd felt disoriented. It was as though he'd left America and was visiting some far-flung foreign city. New Orleans released inhibitions and, like the city, the girl aroused his senses. He was almost drunk with the smell, sight, and touch of her. Louis took a deep breath and swung himself into the carriage.

"Are you calm now?" Brigette asked archly. "Mulatto women have been known to stir the staunchest Puritan."

"I'm fine." As always, Louis was uncomfortable with Brigette. Though she looked demure, she never acted demure. He found her strangely exciting too.

"You've shocked our cousin again," drawled Antoine, lounging calmly against the cushions, a boot propped on the window ledge. "What must he think of southern womanhood?"

"Or of southern manhood?" countered Louis.

"At least I'm not a cowardly Puritan," replied Antoine.

"Protestant, not Puritan. Northern DeLaviers are Protestants. But I've told you," said Louis, "I don't subscribe to any faith."

"There, Brigette." Antoine sneered. "A godless cousin."

"No. I think I still believe in God. It's religious hypocrisy that appalls me."

"Convert to Catholicism," said Antoine, digging his thumb into Louis' chest. "You might find salvation."

"And be like you?" Louis said mock-seriously. "So I could drink, whore, curse, and gamble all week. Confess on Sunday, say ten Hail Marys, and become pure enough to begin my sinning all over again on Monday. Amazing. Your religion would be too exhausting."

Brigette giggled. The carriage jolted forward.

Louis looked out the window. Marie was bending toward Jacques.

Louis felt an inexplicable jealousy as Marie's hand stroked the sailor's head. Sun made her brown skin seem luminous. He'd forgotten to ask her name.

Marie lifted her head. Shading her eyes, she watched the carriage race by. She saw the strained white face in the window.

Louis was thinking only a god could create a face as lovely as Marie's. An Eve amidst the temptations of New Orleans, the modern Sodom and Gomorrah. He released a small sigh.

It would be almost a year before Louis saw Marie again. Nearly sixty years before she would again seem so vulnerable, so sweet.

Marie was struck by how ordinary the Market Square now seemed. Business resumed. Traffic crisscrossed the space where the fight occurred. Nothing changed. Everyone continued doing what they did before.

"Can you climb up?" Marie asked Jacques.

The sailor nodded and stood, using the wheel frame as a crutch. "Are you certain?" he asked, gesturing toward Grandmère.

"As certain as I should be about any man who saved my life."

Jacques, unexpectedly shy, lowered his head. Marie extended

her arm and helped him swing himself up onto the wagon seat. Their hips and legs touched.

Grandmère sat on Marie's left, her head bobbing nervously, her fingers tapping sporadically. "What's done is done," she said. Her hum was disjointed, her breathing shallow.

Marie turned to her. "Grandmère, are you all right?"

"Leave me alone. Tend to your man, I'm no use to you."

Gently, Marie slid the reins from Grandmère's bruised hands. The old woman closed her eyes on the world.

Marie drove them to a side trough. Jacques got down and tethered the horse. The nag drank greedily while Marie pulled a rag from the stockpile she used for her menstrual blood. She raised the lever on the pump, causing water to gush onto the rag. After wringing the excess moisture, Marie pressed the cloth against Jacques' brow.

"You don't have to do this," Jacques said, staying her hand.

"You didn't have to protect me."

"What are brothers for?" He grinned, then winced at the pain in his jaw.

Smiling, Marie dabbed once more at his cuts. Jacques' eyes in his yellow face were brown flecked with green. She wiped blood from the corner of his mouth. She turned to his back, cleaning the wounds, applying cool water to offset the pain. Jacques groaned a little and paled.

"I need salve to dress your wounds. You must come with us."

"Might I know my sister's name?"

"Marie. And that's Grandmère." She pointed to the slumped figure. "Excuse her. But Grandmère is . . . we're both grateful." She lowered her hand, allowing the red-speckled rag to float listlessly in the trough.

Jacques touched her arm.

Marie looked up. "You're kind."

"No. You are." Watching her closely, his fingers caressed her chin. "Why didn't you run away?"

"Why did you fight for me?"

Suddenly exhausted, Marie sat beside Jacques on the trough edge. The passing scene was hectic. Vendors were still hawking wares: "Sweet potatoes. Yams." Children were begging coins: "One penny, please. A penny for dinner." Women were haggling: "Sweet potatoes. Five." "Too expensive." "Collards and yams."

Across from Marie and Jacques was a livery stable where a sturdy blacksmith pounded metal shoes against an anvil. Two men were loudly arguing whether a saddle was of a finer quality than the sway-backed horse beneath it. Sailors, soldiers, gentlemen and ladies, black folks, white folks, were riding, strolling, laughing, buying, and selling in the Market Square. Some bold citizens were even loving in the dirty, mud-blotched street. A soldier stroked his girl. Prostitutes struck suggestive poses. Marie felt innocent and ill prepared.

She'd never seen storied buildings before. Marie was startled when a door opened and a woman screeched from a wrought-iron balcony, "Two pounds. Catfish." The city was wondrous, but Marie knew it was also dangerous. She scrutinized some of the white gentlemen and wondered whether any of them could be as brutal as Antoine DeLavier.

Grandmère, breathing through her mouth and with her head cocked back, was apparently asleep. Marie now knew not to rely on Grandmère's protection. But as soon as she thought this, Marie remembered Grandmère looking fierce and powerful. What was it Grandmère had said? She could kill a man if she wanted. Had she killed before? Marie shook her head. She must've been dreaming.

"Are you always so quiet?" asked Jacques.

"What? No, I mean—"

"I'm not used to women ignoring me. I might not be the most handsome of men—"

"Oh. But you are. The most handsome, I mean."

Marie blushed furiously as Jacques laughed.

"Grandmère . . . I'm . . . we're awkward with strangers. There aren't many people where we come from. Sometimes it's months before we see anyone besides ourselves. And the people we do see are usually Indians or a lone trapper. Mostly birds visit us. Egrets, flocks of robins, hummingbirds, and crows. We sing to them; they sing back. You don't worry about anyone hurting you. There's no one like DeLavier."

"Where is this heaven?"

"Teché. Bayou of snakes."

"Are you sorry now you've left?"

"I'm not sure." In the bayou, days were predictable. Here, it was somehow thrilling to be frightened, ill at ease. Marie stared at Jacques' blunt hands. "I'm not sure at all."

"I am. I couldn't be happier that I've left. New Orleans is far better than Santo Domingo." Jacques leaned against the rail; the nag nuzzled his neck. "Hot island sun." He pointed to the sky. "Much · hotter than this. And more humid. Field upon field to hoe. You could work all day and see no progress. If you weren't planting, you were harvesting. Your back bent with pain, the cotton seemed endless. Always cotton. Masters there were a thousand times worse than here." Jacques smiled ruefully, remembering. "DeLavier was nothing compared to those men. Luckily, I escaped."

"Escaped?"

"A vessel picked me up. Near dead, they said I was. I worked hard and later bought myself free."

"Free?" Grandmère said, "We're free." Her brow furrowed. "DeLavier thought we were slaves, then." For a moment, Marie was overwhelmed with grief, overwhelmed by her own ignorance. Grandmère had told her about bondage, about people being treated as possessions. "I've never seen a slave," she murmured.

"Look there." Jacques pointed at a dark woman trudging with a basket. "And there." A boy in ill-fitting clothes was squatting in the street. "And there." A man in gold livery was aiding a portly child into a carriage. "Most of the blacks in New Orleans are slaves. A few are free. The less black, the more likely you're free—a sailor, perhaps, a market girl . . . or a mistress."

"Whore?" Marie asked. Antoine had called her such.

Jacques nodded, lifting the rag out of the trough. "The lighter your skin, the less they hate you." He held the rag to the back of his neck. "Some masters will set a price in years of service or else in gold for the freedom of a light-skinned black. Usually, it's because the master has fathered the slave. The ole white massa," Jacques drawled, "feels guilty seeing white peeping out of his darky children. It makes him nervous seeing his eyes, his hair and coloring, his features blended with black ·skin." Jacques' lids lowered, his tone

56

became less flippant. "Or else his white wife can't stand the children and insists the bastards be sent away. Preferably sold, not freed."

"How could white women be so heartless?"

"Not all white women are heartless," he said honestly.

"Like Brigette DeLavier. She stopped the fight."

Jacques shook his head: "Mad'moiselle DeLavier and her kind are only interested in their own pleasure. I've heard rumors about her. She stopped Antoine because she was jealous of his attention to you.

"Never underestimate the hardness of a woman's heart," Jacques continued. "White or black." He touched the tip of Marie's nose. "No more than you would underestimate a man's. Mad'-moiselle's late father was one of the cruelest slaveholders. If a slave's words offended him, he would cut out his tongue. If the eyes were offensive, he would pluck them out. I've even heard he kept slaves in a basement for torturing. He bought them regularly from the slave ships. New Orleans honors the DeLaviers. I doubt if Mad'moiselle DeLavier is cherished for liberal kindness. Like father, like daughter. Like father, like son."

Marie shuddered. Jacques spoke so matter-of-factly about horrible things.

"Besides, white women who insist on selling bastard children are being practical and economical. Light-skinned blacks command a high price. Whites believe they're perfect as house and body servants. They believe darker slaves are perfect for field work."

"But you were in the fields."

"My white father reversed the trend. He liked seeing his children whipped. He raped my grandmother and his daughter, my mother, as well." Jacques laughed lightly. "He made slaves of everyone, his legitimate and illegitimate children. His poor wife had no power. She used religion to distract her from her husband's infidelity. I sometimes think she was the most abused person on the plantation."

"I can't believe such cruelty is possible."

"What of DeLavier?"

Marie frowned. "I don't know anything anymore."

"You need to know to survive in New Orleans." Jacques gripped Marie's hand. "Come."

"I shouldn't," she said, beginning to feel nervous. Grandmère had taught her about thyme, bark roots, and the seasons of the moon, but nothing about people. Perhaps Jacques had harmful motives of his own.

"It'll take but a moment."

"But Grandmère—"

"Trust me," said Jacques.

Grandmère shouted, "Go with him, child. He's the one we came for."

"I thought you were sleeping."

Jacques laughed full out. "Trust me. Your Grandmère knows."

"Go on, child. He'll not harm you. That I know."

How did Grandmère know?

Curious, Marie reached for Jacques' outstretched hand.

"You'll be going with him soon enough," Grandmère muttered to no one. "A perfect husband."

Marie and Jacques skirted traffic; they drew nearer to the ships in port. The smell of plankton, rotting fish, and bait assailed Marie. There was a vile odor she couldn't place. They'd rounded a corner and entered a different, less elegant world. Men in coarse dirty cotton strutted on the wharf; a few cried out to her, obscenely gesturing.

"There."

There were hundreds of them—filthy black men and women, legs manacled together, stumbling out of a ship's bowels. The rank smell of excrement caused Marie to bow her head low.

Several bodies, emaciated and near death, were carried on litters. Others walked, shading their eyes and whimpering in the sunlight. They were urged forward with whips.

An adolescent girl, her hair matted and lice-ridden, was crying. She seemed to be entreating the earth. She dropped to her knees, her hands cupped in supplication. "Damballah," she wailed.

Was it God she called? But God was in the sky, not the earth, Marie thought. She tasted the strange sound: *Damballah*. Marie sensed the ground trembling. She felt a sympathetic stirring in her soul.

A whip fell across the naked girl's back. She arched and screamed. Marie almost cried out.

"Africans. They come from across the ocean."

"What?" For the second time she'd forgotten Jacques was there. "Where will they take them?"

"There."

The cage was unshaded in the harsh heat. Nude bodies were lying in the dirt. Some vomited phlegm. Some, too weak to rise or change position, had urinated on themselves and on others. Swollen stomachs, bleeding gums: the slaves were jammed like crabs in a trap. The adolescent girl was stumbling forward.

"At noon, they'll be sold. To work, fetch, and carry for whites."

Marie began to understand. Grandmère had complained about slaving in Master's kitchen, but the image had always been vague. Her history was faceless. Shrouded. Marie had never sensed, like now, the brutality of slavery. She hadn't seen, smelled, or heard the misery.

Yet Grandmère must have endured and lived with slaves such as these. Had Grandmère ever felt the despair, the loneliness, the starvation these Africans felt? Maman, too, had been a slave. How old had her Maman been before she was set free? As old as this African girl?

"Color makes them slaves?" Marie asked tentatively.

"Color is the excuse. Just as color was the excuse for DeLavier to attack you."

Pinching her tan hand, Marie realized more secrets Grandmère had never told her. Color, not just the blood, defined her. "Don't saints protect them?"

"Did a saint protect you?"

Marie stared at the milling bodies. Arms stuck out through wooden slats.

"I've given up religion," Jacques confessed. "I was baptized Catholic because my mistress was Catholic. She baptized slaves to earn a place in heaven. It made her feel important."

Was it because the Virgin's skin was white, her eyes blue, that blacks were slaves? Was it because of color that she still didn't know about Maman? Marie felt she was being watched.

"Slaves have their own religion. They pray to *loas.*" Jacques rubbed his hand against his chest. "I've seen things, Marie. Strange things."

She inclined her head. Between two cotton bins, she sighted the market girl, her arms crossed over her breasts, staring jealously. "Is she your mistress?"

Jacques' stance became rigid, but he whispered, "Aye."

So a woman could be both—market girl and whore. Inexplicably, she felt disappointed. "Take me back." Marie wanted to say, Back to Teché.

They covered the distance in minutes. Marie felt all sorts of odd thoughts and feelings rushing through her. Only a few hours in New Orleans, and her heart and mind were chaotic and confused. She couldn't imagine when she'd feel at peace again.

The spell man they'd seen earlier with the bucket of snakes was gesturing wildly at Grandmère. The two were arguing.

"Voodoo," murmured Jacques. "The slave religion." Reflexively, he sketched a cross.

Marie hurried forward, her chest contracting with guilt. She shouldn't have left Grandmère alone.

"Keep away, old man," Marie shouted. "Get. You're not needed here."

"Be sure innocent," he said in a high-pitched whine. "All have need. I'm only here to serve." He began hopping from foot to foot, dancing crazily.

Jacques shoved, sending the old man sprawling. "Dance elsewhere."

"I'll dance on your grave, brave one." The spell man nimbly scrambled up. "Dey'll say de earth has swallowed you up. But I'll know where your bones'll be scattered"—his spindly fingers swept the air—"where your restless soul be wandering." *You'll leave a fine widow. The Widow Paris.* Lips stretched across golden teeth. Marie shuddered. "Fear me. Fear Ribaud." His voice filled the square. "All of you, fear me."

A heavyset mammy screeched. A child hid beneath a wagon. Even burly whites avoided the gaudy man's commotion.

"I will conjure a spell dis evening." The plumes on his hat swayed as he placed a hand on Jacques' shoulder. "Give me a sliver of hair, a sliver of nail. Even a piece of clothes will do."

The sailor paled. He was more frightened of this man than he'd been of Antoine.

Grandmère straightened, her brittle limbs emanating strength. "May God strike you down. Be gone, I say. Get out of here."

The spell man cackled gleefully. "Wid pleasure." He threw dust at her. "But I shall dance atop your tomb."

"Will you dance on mine?" Marie demanded. The spell man shuffled; it was her imagination, Marie was sure, which saw him cower. In the next moment, his eyes flared wide and he barked, "Perhaps not, mademoiselle. But, my master, John, will."

Dignified, the bony man clutched his bucket of snakes and departed, seesawing from side to side.

Jacques lifted Marie into the cart and looked expectantly at Grandmère. She nodded, and he swung himself up beside them. The three were subdued. The sun was high. Market business thrived as hawkers called, voices chattered and bartered, and a slaver boasted about the quality of his merchandise. Church bells and a steamer's whistle toned in counterpoint. Grandmère's hum soared into song:

> "Dear Lord, these days I'm growing old.
> Full of haunted dreams am I.
> Dear Lord, only You can ease my soul."

~

"The night she died, Grandmère sang to me.

"I don't remember the song, I only remember seeing Grandmère for the first time as a whole person—a woman with passion, yearning, and sorrow. In the melody, I felt her regret for not having lived her life well.

"Grandmère's heart had been broken. I helped. I'll never forget Grandmère's last song. I heard her singing it to me, though we were miles apart. I was birthing my baby and Grandmère was dying."

•

—MARIE LAVEAU, JUNE 14, 1881, MORNING
(From Louis DeLavier's journal)

Marie didn't like her new home. She felt estranged and sad because the world beyond the bayou was so disappointing.

She lived in Haben's Haven. It was really Heaven's Haven, but someone had misspelled the name on the signpost. No one changed the sign. It was simpler to accept the mistake, just as blacks had been taught to accept any number of things—especially poverty and their downtrodden ways.

Haben's Haven was a small community beyond the city boundaries, on the shores of the Mississippi, occupied by free people of color. There were immigrant islanders from Haiti, some ex-slaves, and some Creoles, French-black bastards freed by sympathetic fathers.

"These are your people," Grandmère declared daily. "A part of your heritage. A part of your skin."

Marie now knew the significance of shared color. She'd learned black skin could make you a slave or encourage a white man's assault. Yet she couldn't feel any intimacy with these strangers. She didn't have the knack of conversing. In Teché, she'd spent time with plants and animals who'd accepted her and were never threatening.

"These are your people. A part of your blood," Grandmère insisted.

But only Maman's blood seemed significant to Marie. Only Maman was she certain she could trust.

Everyone was kind. Indeed, the villagers embarrassed Marie at times with their kindness. Shad, a toothless fisherman, winked, told tales, and made silly faces, causing her to smile. Ziti, sixteen like her, gave her ribbons and marveled that Marie's hair was as fine as any white woman's. Children drew stories in the mud, made garlands for her, and sang outside her bedroom window about a mischievous spider named Asanti. Young boys staged mock battles and escorted her everywhere.

The villagers were neither cruel like Antoine DeLavier nor indifferent and cynical like the city folk who'd watched her struggle against him. Nonetheless, Marie couldn't help feeling there was something sinister and secretive behind the villagers' smiles, some motive behind their gifts and kindnesses. They wanted something, but Marie couldn't figure what. Toward Grandmère, the villagers were deferential; toward Marie, they were expectant. Expecting what? Marie lay awake nights, worrying. A restless energy overcame her. One morning she confessed to Grandmère.

"They frighten me."

"You're being silly."

"They're always watching me. Waiting for something to happen, for some change in me. As if I'll grow wings like a caterpillar or shed my skin like a snake."

"You know nothing about people."

"Then tell me about people. Why do they watch me from the corner of their eyes? Why do their heads turn when I pass by? Why do they look at me when they think I'm not looking?"

"They're curious," blustered Grandmère.

"They make me feel like a monster. Like something is wrong with me. They mean ill."

"You wrong them. It's in your mind."

"It's not," Marie said. "None of it is in my mind."

Grandmère turned slowly, and Marie thought she saw sympathy.

"What do they want from me?" she asked, her arms clasped about herself.

"You know nothing about people," Grandmère scolded gently. "They're only being good to you. They pay attention because they care about you. You're part of their blood." Grandmère left Marie alone in her bedroom.

Marie sighed, stretching her belly down on the feather bed. Why did her anxiety persist?

Nattie, who claimed to be Grandmère's friend, made her especially nervous. The woman always seemed to be hovering when Marie least expected or wanted her to be.

Marie flipped herself over. Outside the bedroom window she could see blue sky and a thin snakelike streak of cloud disturbing the horizon.

Grandmère was right. She didn't know people. She'd rarely thought about the world beyond the bayou; and when she did, she'd imagined wondrous, godlike people in it. Gentle, generous people. Beyond the bayou she'd expected to find another Eden with Maman waiting patiently for her. Now Marie knew most people were ordinary, subject to the same faults and tempers as she was. Some, like the slave traders and Antoine DeLavier, were simply brutal.

It seemed, too, as if God had abandoned Haben's Haven. Life was unreasonably hard. Even with the Gulf air, Marie found the days and nights sweltering. People sweated dirt as humidity dampened clothes, bed sheets, and puckered wood.

The Mississippi was majestic. Yet when Marie stood beside it, its length, breadth, and relentless currents made her and the entire community seem insignificant. The river was aggressive, mocking. Its surface calm belied a brown undertow that could drag a body down within minutes. Already a child had died. When it rained heavily, the water was menacing as it rose above the shoreline. A twisting tide could belly-up a boat or split it against rocks. When storms passed, poisonous water snakes were beached. Haben's Haven was certainly no Eden.

Teché was dangerous, yet the absence of people made it seem somehow less menacing and more holy. Marie missed the lush tangle of vines, the cooling and comforting greens, the startled and startling animals.

In Haven, practical realities dominated; people had cleared away trees, set fire to bush, and left the shoreline flat and exposed. Haven was gritty mud that sucked between your toes and caked your legs and arms. Rabbits and squirrels, wary of traps and bird shot, wouldn't feed from Marie's hand.

But it was their poverty that hurt Marie most. Though the blacks in Haven were free, they appeared in many ways like the slaves she'd seen on the squalid Orleans dock.

More than a dozen cottages were clustered a quarter mile from the shore. Inside the cottages were large families of eight to twelve. Between each house was a garden plot. But the soil wasn't like the soil in Teché; the mixture of rock, damp sand, and mud stunted growth. Kale wilted and yams were pockmarked and puny. Even scavenger crows disdained the crop. At first, Marie wondered why the women bothered planting seeds, but later she realized the food was needed. She'd seen mothers often splitting a too-small sweet potato between their children. Ziti, scrawny and superstitious, said the land was hexed.

In Haven, livings were made as best one could. After claiming a reluctant catch from the water, men and boys competed to sell eel, shrimp, and whiskered catfish in the market. Some stole; some begged. Others trudged the miles to town and offered themselves as "penny servants." Young women, late at night, coupled with white strangers.

Marie learned the value of money. In Teché, nature provided; in Haven, everyone needed silver and gold from New Orleans. No one ever had enough money, and when they thought they had enough, prices in the city went higher.

"All the money in Haven," Jacques had explained, "wouldn't equal a tenth of the wealth of the DeLaviers."

Jacques told unending tales of rich whites with city and country houses. During yellow fever season, aristocrats retreated to their plantations. "This August for certain," Jacques had said, "half the folks in Haven will die choking on black vomit. They'll catch the sickness from working hard in the stifling city. If you're rich and white, most likely you'll escape the fever. You'll rock on an expansive porch sipping mint juleps while complaining about the country heat." Marie wondered if Jacques was capable of hurting someone simply because they were white. His bitterness was greater than hers.

"Where in the world can a black man go and be free?" Jacques always wanted to know.

Marie stretched and leaned outside the window frame. She heard the desultory twang of a banjo. Someone, despite the heat, was frying catfish. The sharp, blackened smell of grease and fish made her throat hurt. The Mississippi was swollen, and naked children were dancing in mud. Somewhere an infant was crying; angry shouts and whimpers were spilling outside a nearby cottage. Part of her expected Maman to walk by; yet Marie couldn't believe Maman would visit so ugly a place. God had deserted Haven and she felt sorrowful. She felt frustrated too, because she was trapped in a shantytown with no chance to find the one person she needed the most.

Marie wept. Her world hadn't gotten larger; it had only gotten smaller, uglier. Grandmère wouldn't let her visit New Orleans, and without a doubt her Maman would be there.

"What's this, child?" Grandmère entered, a basket of herbs slung on her arm. A rose-colored bandanna was wrapped about her head. "You sick? Or moping?"

Marie dried her eyes; she couldn't bear it if Grandmère scolded her again for missing her Maman.

"There's nothing to do here," she said quietly. "Why must we live here?"

"This is a fine enough place."

"The city would be better."

"The city is expensive."

"I could work." Marie hadn't planned on saying 'work,' but

she *could* work, couldn't she? Surely there was something she could do. She could comb white women's hair like Ziti.

"I didn't raise you to work. I raised you to be a good wife," Grandmère grumbled, clicking her gums. "Besides, I like it here."

Marie had to admit, since moving to Haven, Grandmère was happier than she'd been in years. She was teasing fun again. She kept busy making medicines and root stews for the women. She talked gossip in kitchens, on the riverbank, and in the stunted gardens.

"We can't be ungrateful," said Grandmère, lowering herself into a chair. "Nattie has given up rooms for us. She's accepted us."

"I don't like Nattie."

"Marry then and live where you please."

Marie slyly stuck out her tongue. Nattie had been the only villager who had the luxury of living alone. When Marie and Grandmère first arrived (with the battered Jacques in tow), Nattie had given up both her bedrooms. Grandmère accepted this as her due; Marie had protested: "I can sleep with Grandmère."

"Never be no mind," Nattie had responded, glaring at her. "You insult my friendship. I knew your Grandmère since before you be born. Or be pretty Miz Marie afraid to sleep alone? Simple foolishness," snapped Nattie. "Girls afraid to sleep alone ought to have a husband. Menfolks meant to soothe nightmares."

Marie blushed.

"You want a husband, don't you?" Nattie pointed at Jacques, who was busily helping Grandmère heat water for the evening baths.

"No, I don't want a husband," Marie said guiltily, and the matter of the bedrooms was closed.

Nattie now slept on a pallet in the kitchen. The kitchen separated the bedrooms. Marie wondered whether Nattie had some motive for dividing her and Grandmère. If she cried out at night, Marie wasn't certain Grandmère would ever hear. Likewise, if Grandmère needed her, she'd probably never know.

"Stop woolgathering," Grandmère insisted.

Marie blinked and came back to the present.

"Ziti, Halo, Annette, they all admire you. You could make friends if you tried. Nattie feels a particular kindness."

Marie scowled. "I don't like Nattie."

"Don't be stubborn, child. Give of yourself. Don't spend days hiding in this room. Nobody's keeping you lonely but yourself."

Marie was lonely, but not for what Grandmère imagined. Head lowered, Marie knelt before Grandmère. Placing her hands in the old woman's lap, she felt knobby bones beneath Grandmère's cotton skirt.

"Ah, ma petite. I feel the Virgin has finally blessed me." The old woman gently stroked Marie's hair. "I'm among friends again. I'm needed."

Marie raised her head. "I need you."

"I know. But it's nice to have others need me too. I can do much good here, curing sickness, salving wounds, birthing a baby or two. When we go back to Teché, I'll have fine memories. They'll warm my bones when the cold stalks by."

"I'll never go back. Not without knowing Maman."

Grandmère forced a smile. "Jacques will be by tonight," she said brightly. "Cleaning the ship's hull will take three days, he said. On the fourth day, he promised to come. The fourth day is here."

Marie stood, turning away from Grandmère.

"He's just the man for you, ma petite."

Marie nervously twisted her fingers.

"Don't undervalue a good man's love."

Marie felt guilty for not discouraging Jacques. She didn't love him. He was pleasant enough, but she didn't love him. Many times she'd been about to tell him to leave her alone, but each time he'd tell a story about New Orleans or his travels to the islands or about New York and Boston. His eyes became her eyes, searching for Maman. Once, she'd asked, "Have you seen a woman who looks like me?" He had answered, "I'd remember a woman who looked like you."

"You be nice to Jacques." Slapping the armrest, Grandmère punctuated her sentences. "Saved your life, he did." *Slap.* "Handsome as the day is long." *Slap.* "He doesn't deserve any hurt."

"Yes," Marie murmured.

"Take him, child."

Sunlight pierced Marie's eyes. Tonight she would tell Jacques to go. If she worked in New Orleans, she'd find Maman herself.

"Come," said Grandmère, rising from the chair, pushing the weight of her belly forward. "I must see Annette." Gripping Marie's shoulders, Grandmère turned her around. "Such beauty." Grandmère stroked and pulled her hair to the front of her chest. "Pure black hair," Grandmère murmured. "Heavy like the best blanket. A man and child would find much pleasure touching such hair."

Marie winced. She understood marriage meant lying with a man and making babies. She didn't want babies. She wanted to know who she was first.

"Come with me. If only for a little while," Grandmère cajoled. "Annette's baby is due in a month. You can cheer Annette. Annette can cheer you."

Marie searched Grandmère's eyes. She wished Grandmère would read her mind now and try to understand her pain.

Marie wanted to ask, How did you free yourself from slavery? Was your master harsh or kind? Did Maman suffer much as a slave? There was so much she didn't know. But she'd be a fool to think Grandmère would answer these questions any more than she would answer: Do I look like my Maman?

"It's hard waiting for a birth," said Grandmère. "But any child is well worth the wait."

"Even a stubborn one?" Marie smiled slightly.

Grandmère nodded, her lips stretching over pink gums. She squeezed Marie's arms. "Don't forget you are my special child. My greatest blessing. Your happiness is mine. Do you understand?"

Marie's spirits plummeted. It was hard enough living for herself; Grandmère made it much harder by insisting she live for two.

"Come. Let's go, then," said Grandmère.

Annette's was the last house on the right, the one nearest to the shore. As they walked diagonally toward the cottage, children skipped, jumped, and cut across their path. False angry, Grandmère shooed: "Go on. Get. Crazy, crazy children. Get out of my way."

Marie laughed as one boy did a cartwheel, another walked on his hands. Shad, who was patching a hole in his dinghy, hollered, "How do."

Grandmère graciously inclined her head.

"Sure is hot," remarked Shad.

Two women washing clothes in the Mississippi hushed him. "Any fool knows it's hot," said one long-legged gal. "Madame Laveau don't need you to tell her it's hot."

"Just being polite."

"Being stupid, more like," said the other woman, slapping a dress hard against the rock.

Grumbling, Shad went back to patching his boat. Marie and Grandmère, burying laughter in their hands, kept walking. They stepped onto a deserted porch.

"Knock on the door, Marie."

Marie stepped forward, amazed the door was closed against the heat. They heard a brittle voice cry out, "Shuey, let them in."

A girl, no more than eight, opened the door. Bedraggled, she wiggled and watched her dirty toes.

"Is your maman home?" asked Marie.

The little girl nodded and stepped back, allowing Marie and Grandmère to enter. Heat smacked them. The home was dark and windless; the windows were shut.

"Why doesn't Annette allow in any light? Any air?" whispered Marie.

"When a woman's with child, some folks try to make their house like a womb. They think if the house is dark, the windows shut, no dead spirits can steal the child. Some women claim spirits have flown through open windows and ripped their babies from their wombs." Grandmère shrugged. "I've told Annette it's not so. She won't listen."

Marie felt as though she'd walked inside a grave. She smelled camphor and rancid tallow. Sweat cloaked her body, and she could barely breathe. Eyes straining, she saw Shuey and four other baby girls circling Shuey like frightened birds. Annette was in a corner lying naked on a straw bed, her stomach grotesquely protruding.

"Madame Laveau, Miz Marie."

Marie had never seen a pregnant woman up close before. Gingerly, she touched her own stomach. She couldn't imagine her body holding a child. She didn't want Jacques or any man, if it meant her body would bloat and stretch till it was ready to burst.

"I and my husband, we so grateful you come," said Annette with solemn dignity.

A thin, grinning man stepped into the circle of candlelight.

"This is Bébé."

Marie let out a small cry. Bébé's face was skull-like, his eyes too white. Marie couldn't imagine him as either a husband or a father. He seemed like a lost child.

Bébé's head bobbed while he patted Annette's stomach. "She's doing well, no? I'll have me the finest son." Bébé, gurgling excitedly, cocked his head at Marie. "I already have five daughters. Good pretty girls. But I say to Annette, with Madame Laveau as midwife we be sure to have a son. Nothing like a son. A son makes a man proud. I say Madame Laveau cast a spell for us. She call on the great snake god."

Marie looked quizzically at Grandmère.

"She make miracle. She call on the snake, li Zombi, Dambal—"

"Stop this blasphemous talk," Grandmère demanded.

Bébé looked stricken, his eyes dimmed. He glanced at his wife, who was clutching her abdomen. "Sorry," he said mournfully. "Bébé didn't mean it. I didn't mean anything. Nothing. Bébé didn't mean nothing. I forgot I mustn't tell."

Marie looked from Bébé to Grandmère.

Grandmère was staring at Bébé, looking as if she wanted to strike him. "You'd do better to say prayers to the Virgin. To open this house to air and sunlight, if you want a healthy son."

Bébé looked terrified. "Yes, yes," he said, bowing.

"Leave. There's women's work to be done."

"Bébé will leave." He scooped up two of the babies, who'd been startled into crying by Grandmère's shout, then shooed the others into a line before him. He opened the door. For a moment, sunlight illuminated the one-room house and Marie could see Annette and Bébé's modest belongings. A few chairs. A series of straw beds for the children. Against one wall, Marie saw what she thought was an altar. There wasn't a Virgin or Christ figure; instead, clay snakes were propped against unlit candles and sticks of incense. The door closed, and the room darkened again.

Marie looked to Grandmère for an explanation. Who was the snake god, Damballah? The threatening man in the Market Square had carried a pail of snakes. The slave girl had prayed to Damballah. Bébé believed Grandmère could make sure he got his son.

Annette was struggling to sit up. "Forgive us. Please. Bébé didn't mean—"

"It's all right, Annette," Grandmère said, stroking her arm. "You have a child to worry about."

"You won't hurt—?" Annette stopped, too afraid to finish her question.

Marie wondered if Annette was worried more about her child or her husband. In either case, fear was silly. Grandmère wouldn't hurt anybody. She was the gentlest, sweetest Grandmère, wasn't she?

Grandmère bent her ear to Annette's stomach. "Good, strong heart. Listen to the heartbeat," she said to Marie, motioning her closer to the distended stomach.

Embarrassed, Marie staggered backward. Annette's docile gaze settled on her. " 'Tis wonderful," she said, shyly smiling. "You'll have your own baby one day."

Marie clasped her hands across her waist. Grandmère was humming. The tune wasn't any tune Marie had ever heard before.

Inexplicably, to Marie's eyes, Annette grew lovely. Like magic, Marie could feel a languor overcoming her. Annette, caressing her abdomen, seemed like Grandmère's Madonna, except brown-toned and far more beautiful. The sweetness of her smile, her gentle eyes, chased from Marie's mind any questions or anxieties.

If she listened carefully, Marie could hear a lyric in Grandmère's simple, haunting melody. It was as if words were embedded in the humming. How could that be? One sang a song or hummed; it wasn't possible to do both. The tune echoed in the room. Marie felt she was being coerced—some small battle was being won by Annette and Grandmère.

This moment, marriage and babies seemed almost lovely.

* * *

"Heh, look here," Nattie hollered from the porch, pointing at the man beside her. "Look who's come. It be Mister Jacques. So handsome Mister Jacques has come." Nattie rested her hands on her sprawling hips. Otherwise she was a thin, wiry woman, but her hips and buttocks fed on beans and rice.

Grandmère rejoiced. "Jacques said he'd come." She tugged Marie's arm.

Marie felt reluctant; she wanted to slow her steps. Jacques was grinning.

"Life be filled with surprises. Miz Marie said today she be missing her man Jacques. 'Where he be?' she wanted to know."

Marie looked up sharply.

" 'Tis true," Nattie said emphatically.

Jacques looked warmly at Marie.

Marie wanted to call Nattie a liar. She would've if it wouldn't have hurt Jacques, if it wouldn't have caused Nattie to laugh at her. A crow. That's what Nattie reminded Marie of, a crazy black crow.

"Mister Sun be going to bed now," said Nattie, slapping Jacques' back, motioning toward the dusky horizon. "That be good. Mistress Moon likes lovers better. Likes them lying"—she flattened her tongue, producing an elongated sound—"d-o-w-n before her."

"Nattie!" exclaimed Marie.

" 'Nattie!' she say. Simple foolishness. No need for shy. Not when you have such a handsome man. He must lie down pretty well." Nattie winked. "In Haiti, everybody knows the Moon be lovestruck. The Moon likes life, love. When the Moon be yellow, love and life be suffering in this world. With Jacques, I bet there be plenty love. Plenty of white, lovely Moons."

"Please, Nattie."

"Simple foolishness. I no say what don't be true." Nattie turned and went inside the house, her rump swishing fast and furious.

Marie blushed.

Grandmère hollered, "Be back in time for dinner."

"But we're not going anywhere."

"Yes we are," said Jacques, taking Marie's hand. Marie felt flustered. Jacques' hand was burning, rough.

Grandmère stayed Jacques. "Be safe."

"I wouldn't hurt her."

"It's not you I'm mistrusting." Grandmère clicked her gums and pressed her lips. For months, she'd felt safe and content in Haven. Now, without warning, she felt ill at ease, like a bad wind was teasing her. Nothing was wrong, she told herself. Seeing Jacques clasping Marie's hand should be enough to convince her everything was all right. Her plan was working. It had to work.

"Madame Laveau?" Jacques' hand darted out to steady her.

"Be back in time for dinner," she said softly.

"Soon as Mistress Moon has smiled on us," Jacques said, laughing, pulling Marie toward the shore.

Grandmère could feel Nattie stealing behind her. "They're a good couple," Grandmère said forcefully, watching Marie and Jacques jostle and weave.

"Who you be trying to convince?" Nattie chuckled. "Who really cares but you?"

Marie was planting her feet into the earth, trying to slow her progress. "Let me go."

"I've been waiting days to see you."

"I don't care." Marie jerked her arm away. Jacques snatched it up again.

"All I think of is you," Jacques boasted. "I don't eat. I don't sleep. All because of you."

"That doesn't give you the right—"

"Hush," said Jacques.

"I won't hush."

"Lovely girls don't need to talk."

Mud sucked at her dragging feet, splattering her legs. "Everybody orders my life but me."

"You need looking after. See," he said, pointing to a rock and jerking her sideways. "You almost fell."

"I can look after myself."

74

"Like a chicken at slaughter."

"Oh!"

"Like a minnow swimming into a whale's mouth."

Marie stumbled, splattering her dress with mud.

"Like an infant child." Jacques helped her up from her knees.

"I am not a child!" Marie screamed. Jerking her hand from his, she abruptly faced him.

Jacques carefully surveyed her body. Mud-soaked, the front of her dress emphasized her hips and thighs. "You're right. You're not a child."

Her fist punched through air. Laughing, Jacques caught it.

It wasn't fair that men should have such strength. Jacques could crush her hand, Marie thought. No matter which way she moved, it would hurt her arm, not his. Frustrated, she wanted to cry.

Jacques tenderly placed her hand on his chest. "I'm sorry."

Marie sucked in air. She knew Jacques would never hurt her. Not intentionally.

Pulling her closer, Jacques draped his arms around her waist. He kissed her temple; his lips drifted down to her neck.

She stirred nervously.

He held her face in his two hands and brushed his lips against hers. "Let's watch the moon," he said.

Marie twisted out of the circle of his arms. Her feelings were jumbled. When Jacques grabbed her, she felt passion, recalling memories of the dark man who'd caressed her in the bayou. Jacques wasn't threatening, but the man in the bayou was. Even as a child she'd known that after a touch from him she'd be ready to yield everything, even her soul. Jacques was sweet; the man in the bayou was desire.

"There's one advantage to watching the moon with me," said Jacques.

Marie lifted her brows.

"You don't have to listen to crazy Nattie anymore."

"She is crazy, isn't she?"

Jacques grinned. "No doubt."

Marie felt a release of tension. If she closed her eyes, maybe she could pretend Jacques was the stranger in the bayou.

"Marie," Jacques murmured. He gathered her hair, kissing it and inhaling the aroma of hyacinths.

Marie wanted to arch her neck backward and burrow her head on Jacques' chest. She stumbled forward. What was the matter with her? She was supposed to tell Jacques she wouldn't see him anymore.

It was twilight. The Mississippi was at its most beautiful. Marie squatted, letting her hand drag in the river. Ripples upset the reflected sunset. Stars were overhead; the moon was rising. Candles were lit inside the cottages. Children were being called to dinner, and stews were stirred with onion and pepper. Across the water, Marie could see fireflies flickering along the willow bank. Mosquitoes were biting.

"Marry me."

Marie felt both thrilled and frightened.

"You must marry me."

Marie squinted her eyes. Jacques, still standing, looked magnificent in the fading sun. In his sailor clothes, he vaguely reminded her of Christ's apostle Peter. So clean and honest.

"I don't love you."

"You like me. Isn't that enough?" He stopped beside her, clutching her hand over his heart. His earnestness made him young, like one of the village boys who paraded and did cartwheels before her.

Then Jacques kissed her. His tongue forced its way inside her mouth. He was demanding a response. His hand slipped beneath her bodice, stroking her breast, causing her nipple to harden. Marie moaned. Jacques' other hand moved to her thigh.

"Marry me." He maneuvered Marie backward and laid his body down against hers.

Her body seemed foreign to her. Her crotch moist, her breathing ragged, Marie wondered, Is this love?

The moon was halfway overhead, and Marie was split between mind and body. She wondered whether Mistress Moon sensed her ambivalence. Over Jacques' shoulder, sighting the rounded moon, she sighed at its stark beauty—white against the black night sky. She kept staring. *The moon's surface seemed like shifting clouds.* Vaguely she heard Jacques' endearments, vaguely she felt his caresses.

Mistress Moon seemed to be beckoning her, expanding. The sky overflowed with moon.

Marie saw the outline of a familiar yet unfamiliar face. Eyes, nose, mouth. Three diagonal scars on each cheek. The black skyline was bleeding through the white. The laughing man of her dreams was watching. The bayou stranger.

Marie cried out, her hands pounding, pushing Jacques away.

"Marie. Marie." He gripped her flailing hands. "I'd never hurt you."

She struggled to sit up. The moon was plain again. Innocently, it hung in the sky; it had shrunk to normal size.

"I've offended you."

"No," Marie said, trembling.

"I couldn't resist—"

"Never mind."

"You can't know how much I need you."

"Shut up. Just shut up." Marie clapped her hands over her ears.

Jacques crouched back on his heels. "I meant no harm. You know that."

"I don't know anything anymore. Everything confuses me. I don't know you. You don't know me."

"I *do* know you. For years, you've come to me in my dreams."

"You believe in dreams? Visions? Nightmares?" Her voice pitched higher. "Haunting signs that make you wish you could drift deeply into sleep and sleep till you never bothered waking again."

Jacques' finger twisted a tendril of her hair. "I've never dreamt terrors. Only pleasant dreams. And you are my most pleasant dream." He paused. "Your Grandmère, she wants you to marry."

"Don't use her against me."

"I'd use anything to keep you."

"You don't have me."

"To get you then." Jacques slapped his palm against his chest. "Aw, Marie. Just tell me." His head lolled to one side. "Tell me what you want."

"I don't know. I don't know." She shrugged helplessly. "Sometimes I think all I want is to please Grandmère. Other times, I only want to please myself."

"What would please you?"

"Finding Maman. No. I don't know." She pressed her fingers against her eyes. She felt herself on top of a cliff, ready to slip off the edge. "When I was a babe, my Maman left me."

"For where?"

"I don't know."

"Surely your Grandmère knows."

"She does, but she won't tell me." Marie slapped the water, then rushed on, afraid that if she stopped she'd never speak the truth again. "I do and I don't want to find my Maman. Sometimes I'm glad Grandmère forbids looking for her. I'm glad I don't have to bear all the blame for not finding her. But I swear by the Virgin and all the saints, I do want to find her. I want to ask Maman why she left. Why she never returned. But what if she says it was me?" Horrified, Marie stared at Jacques. "What if Maman left because of me?" She broke into tears, burying her face in Jacques' lap.

Jacques saw Marie stripped of all her bravado. He identified with her misery, her inarticulate longing. He understood how the child Marie could blame herself for being abandoned. He stroked her hair.

"I was six, maybe eight," murmured Jacques. "I don't know which. Slaves don't celebrate birthdays." He inhaled and began again. "I was six, maybe eight, when my mother left me. For years I didn't cry, I just hated her. I believed she hated me. Why else would she leave?

"It wasn't until I was eleven that I realized she'd been sold. I still can't forgive myself for having hated her."

"Oh, Jacques." Marie sighed, sitting up, watching his sad face.

"Even now I think if she'd loved me better, she would've found a way to stay. But I know there was nothing she could do." He paused, looking intently at Marie. "Your mother would never have left because of you. No mother could be as cruel as that. She must've had a reason."

"Then why won't she return?"

"Maybe she can't. Look," Jacques said. "In the water."

The Mississippi was a mirror. Marie saw herself, the moon, and Jacques peering over her shoulder.

"See how beautiful you are. I'm sure your mother wants to be with you very much. At least as much as I."

The picture in the water was disturbing. Suddenly, Marie realized, Jacques was the other man in her dreams. In Teché, she'd seen Jacques' face before she ever knew him.

"Marry me. We'll find your Maman."

"We'll search in New Orleans?"

"Wherever you like."

Marie knew she should be overjoyed, but happiness didn't come. The world was slipping beyond her control. Staring at the Mississippi's reflection of herself and Jacques, she realized images guided her. She blinked and saw a vision in the water. *She was in a cathedral dressed in white silk and lace, pinning a gold brooch of a sleeping snake onto her bosom.* It must be Maman who was guiding her. *Jacques was standing beside her, tickling her ribs.* Maman and the bayou stranger. *Jacques' face faded and was replaced by black skin, scars, and a grin. Her wedding dress turned red.*

In New Orleans, on her wedding night, the man would come.

Jacques was stroking her hair. "When we marry, you'll wear a white dress. And your hair will be pinned up," he said, lifting her tresses, mimicking a stylist slipping in pins. *She was gathering her hair in a chignon.*

In the river, Marie saw the same image she'd seen in Grand-mère's eyes. *Jacques was replaced by a man with three scars and a grin. Her wedding dress turned red.*

"I've never loved anyone as I've loved you," said Jacques.

Marie stared at him. Could she stand deceiving him? Inadvertently, Jacques' presence reaffirmed the signs she'd been waiting for. What if Jacques was harmed because of her? *You'll leave a fine widow. The Widow Paris.* Impossible. Jacques wouldn't die because of her. Her vision, Marie was certain, came from Maman. Maman was everything good. But what if the prophecy didn't come true? What if she remained married for a lifetime to Jacques? She'd spend years heavy and swollen, bearing child after child. Annette and Bébé. Marie and Jacques.

Marie knew if she turned and looked at Jacques now, she'd cry out, unable to go through with the marriage. If she looked at him now, she wouldn't be able to stand seeing him loving her. She wouldn't be able to stand seeing herself reflected in his eyes, not returning his love.

What a fool she was!

Collapsing her shoulders, burrowing her head into her chest, Marie tried to squeeze herself small.

"Will you marry me?"

"Yes," she said.

She felt herself falling over a cliff, into a river, a destiny shaped by pictures. Images in the water, in a mirror, in Grandmère's eyes dominated her. But they never seemed to reflect *her*—never allowed her to see herself more clearly. Rather, she was following an indirect trail. Pursuing the mystery of Maman, she hoped she'd uncover herself. Why else would Maman be tempting her with visions? Who else besides Maman would send them?

"Yes," she said again. "I'll marry you."

Jacques jumped, whooped, hollered, and danced like an Indian. Hearing the noise, folks rushed, gathered outdoors.

"She'll marry me," Jacques shouted, slapping his hands against his thighs. "She'll marry me."

Shad set aside his plate of catfish and lifted up a candle to wish them well. Ziti, who'd been wiring ladies' combs, twirled and flitted about, exclaiming, "A party. There's going to be a party." Mistress Halo, having halted her baking, wiped flour-crusted hands over her bosom and demanded of Ziti, "When will you be next? When will some man want you?" Mother and daughter squabbled like starving chickens. Ziti, Halo insisted, would become "a hollow old maid."

Marie tried to disappear as villagers circled and commented upon her good fortune.

The three women who'd earlier been washing linen in the river put their heads together and gossiped about "how fine," "how handsome" Mister Jacques was and about "how pretty," "how sweet" was Miz Marie. Bébé kept to the sidelines with his flock of children, though he flashed a smile whenever he thought Marie was looking.

Villagers darted forward to shake hands, congratulate, and sigh enviously. Ziti did her best to look nonchalant. The well-wishers stepped aside, hushing expectantly as Grandmère and Nattie arrived. Feeling fraudulent, eyes downcast, Marie said a soft "Hello." Jacques kept a proprietary arm about her shoulder.

Grandmère said nothing, her head cocked to one side.

Marie peeked at her. Did Grandmère suspect dishonesty? Would she guess the confusion and lies in her heart?

Grandmère hesitated for only a second; then she smiled, opening her arms wide. Marie stepped inside the comforting circle. Marie relaxed, feeling the warm hug engulfing her as Grandmère whispered, "My baby girl. Blessed be the Virgin."

Grandmère turned to Jacques and holding his hand aloft, she proclaimed to each and every member of the crowd, "My only son. My one and only son."

There were shouts, excited roars. Many of the villagers carried torches. Night had fallen with a blanketing suddenness. Flames and shadows heightened the sense of festive unreality. The Mississippi, unperturbed, flowed in the darkness. Owls began the hunt for rodents.

"Sing, Madame Laveau," someone shouted. And the chant was taken up by the crowd. "Sing. Sing, Madame Laveau."

"Sing a song of love," called Halo, poking her slow-top daughter Ziti between her ribs.

"Yes, do, Grandmère," urged Marie. "Your voice is so lovely."

Grandmère shook her head.

"Do it for me."

"No," Grandmère said sharply, while Marie, hurt, stepped aside. "I don't sing for crowds. It's sinful. Against God." Grandmère strode purposefully toward the house, her rosary beads clicking against her skirt. She hadn't meant to hurt Marie. But the request for a song reminded her of times she preferred to forget. Blasphemous audiences once worshiped her songs. And she hadn't sung a love song since Sachwaw died.

"What did I do?" Marie called futilely after Grandmère. "What did I do wrong?"

The villagers were silent. Jacques held Marie's hand, and she squeezed his gratefully.

Nattie, covering the awkwardness, sang, "I know a pretty girl named Marie." Her shrill voice was absorbed by the trees. Nattie gestured at Shad.

"I know a pretty girl named Marie." Shad's deep bass complemented Nattie's soprano. Shad extended the song: "She plan to marry a handsome sailor called Jacques."

Jacques slapped his chest and cried, "That's me."

Bébé sang out, "They live happily and make pretty babies."

"No!" shouted Marie. But no one heard her. There was enthusiastic applause. Impromptu dancing began, surrounding the engaged couple. The villagers adopted the made-up tune and forged a lively harmony:

> *"I know a girl named pretty Marie.*
> *She plan to marry*
> *a handsome sailor called Jacques.*
> *They live happily and make pretty babies."*

Soon all the villagers, including the children, were dancing and singing. "I know a girl named pretty Marie." Jacques' voice carried the loudest. "She plan to marry. . . ."

Marie, ignoring the merriment, watched Grandmère trek across the mud plain and enter the house. Never once did Grandmère look back. Why was it, wondered Marie, even when she aimed to please, she managed to displease?

Marie stared at the cottage; in the candlelight glare, she could see Grandmère's shadow moving behind the curtainless windows. Unexpectedly, bile rose in her throat. Why couldn't Grandmère sing for her? The marriage was Grandmère's dream, not hers.

Nattie slipped behind Marie, murmuring, "I be surprised. I never suppose you be marrying."

Marie was startled. She thought a devilish spirit had cornered her. She tried to turn, but Nattie's grasp kept her still.

"You must be afraid to sleep alone," Nattie wheezed. "They say menfolks be made to soothe nightmares. I hope 'tis true. 'Cause some nightmares don't go away, Miz Marie. Some nightmares walk around in the day. Some nightmares even have a name."

By the time Marie had spun around to demand what Nattie meant, Nattie had lost herself in the rollicking crowd. Before Marie could search for her, Jacques sauntered up, demanding his betrothal dance and kiss.

Marie woke from a nightmare. Snakes were walking on two legs, chasing her through alleyways behind the Market Square. The sun was high, yet the avenues were deserted of customers and hawkers. Black snakes, green snakes, adders, and poisonous snakes trailed her.

Marie felt physically and emotionally worn. It was Nattie's fault, Nattie with her silliness about nightmares walking. The room was somber. Marie felt disoriented and groggy. She could hear the ghostly rush of breezes in the trees, the twisted, roaring currents of the Mississippi.

She saw a light beneath her door. Someone was still awake, sitting in the kitchen. Grandmère and Jacques? Sleep was settling into her eyes again. Marie felt heavy, weighted to the bed. She struggled to stay awake.

"Teché," she heard Jacques say. "I'll take her there and keep her safe."

"She mustn't know what we've agreed."

"She'll never know."

Something was wrong. Jacques had promised her New Orleans. Marie's head fell back onto the pillow. She felt hazy, unnaturally lethargic, like the time she'd sucked too long on an elder root. Disoriented, her body seemed to be floating beyond the bed. New dreams were calling. A huge snake lay curled in the middle of her path. No matter which way she turned, the snake appeared—behind her, to the left and right of her, above and below.

Marie needed to discover Maman herself. She was drifting asleep. Jacques wouldn't lie, would he? There was no sense marrying if they weren't going to search for Maman. Marie's last thought was that she was still in the grip of a nightmare. *The snake was hissing her name. A singing Grandmère was barely alive and Jacques' tongue was split and bleeding.* Jacques was too good to lie. Wasn't he?

She sank deeper into sleep.

~

A journalist's job is to be objective, to investigate truths without hindrance by emotions.

What am I doing then? Obsessed by a young girl's face and form, in love with a ghost.

If she was substance, I would've found her. I've searched for her for more days than I care to number. I've haunted alleyways, the wharf, the Market Square. I've visited the free coloreds' meanest clapboard shacks. No avail. I don't believe she's real anymore. Even Dante could gaze upon his Beatrice.

What truth am I pursuing?

•

—LOUIS DELAVIER, JUNE 30, 1819, AFTERNOON
(From Louis DeLavier's journal)

Louis, you haven't been listening to a word I've said."

"What?" Louis looked up from his desk, his eyebrows pinched by a frown. Reflexively, he closed his journal.

"You see. You aren't listening. Are you trying to offend me?"

Pouting, Brigette slipped onto his lap and wrapped her arms snugly about his throat. Her breasts flattened against him.

Louis wasn't aroused. Brigette looked and felt like cool porcelain; she smelled of heady rose talc. Once he'd been attracted by Brigette's fair charms, but that was before he'd met a brown girl who was warm, inviting, and smelled of hyacinths. Such lips she had, tender, soft, and naturally pink. Brigette's lips were always painted red. They flirted and promised but, finally, preferred not to be disturbed.

"Louis, listen to me!" Brigette tugged his cravat.

Louis looked at her vaguely.

Brigette was mystified. Louis had been considerate and pliable, but since the altercation in the Market Square he'd taken to wandering the city streets, only to return home distant and preoccupied. Brigette couldn't get him to confess where he went on his nocturnal jaunts. If she didn't know better, she'd suspect some black auntie had worked lovesick magic on him, had hexed him with a Voodoo spell.

"You promised you'd attend Madame Bijou's with me," Brigette said sweetly, anticipating the trip to the expensive modiste since Louis was paying. "I'm to be outfitted for my traveling dress. The cream satin with Brussels lace, yellow rosettes—"

"I'm sorry, I forgot. I've made other plans for this evening."

"How could you?" Inelegantly, Brigette scrambled to her feet. "How could you forget? You know how important this is to me!"

Brigette paced, her wide skirt swishing from side to side to show a delicate expanse of ankle. She tossed her curls and fanned herself furiously. Her cheeks heightened in color. A display of temper made her attractive. Any number of men had told her so. Any number of men had complied with her wishes. Besides, she was wearing one of her more provocative dresses: a rose silk with a low square-cut bodice with white satin ribbons flowing down from her bosom's center. By the end of the day, her breasts would ache from the unnaturally tight upward pressure. But a few naughty gentlemen once whispered they were transfixed, waiting for her to overflow her gown. Some said they were tempted to pluck her breasts like peaches. The last remark had been particularly off-color, but Brigette had been pleased when she'd heard it. Her new colored maid, Clara, told her she looked particularly desirable today. But Louis didn't seem to care, Brigette thought; Antoine would've noticed.

Louis thought Brigette looked out of place in his study. She was too brilliantly colored for his brown-toned room, too illiterate for his room of books. Brigette's favorite reading consisted of fashion plates from Paris. He wondered if, even in the schoolroom, she'd read anything else besides the society column and tales of gossip and fashion. But why should he blame her? She was no different from any other privileged New Orleans mademoiselle.

"You've ignored all my attempts to engage you in our wedding plans. One would think you didn't care we were being married next month."

Louis smoothed his thinning hair. "I do care."

"Then I don't see why you can't make this fitting with me. Madame Bijou has new silks from Paris. You promised you'd come." Brigette leaned forward, allowing him to catch the heady rose scent rubbed onto her breasts. "Doesn't it matter to you how I look on our honeymoon?"

"It matters." Louis thought his fiancée was a vulgar tease. But all the women he'd ever met had been taught to tease. Nervously, he tapped his journal. Southern women made teasing an art. Brigette knew how to convey a dozen different messages with a ballroom fan. She once explained the code to him: a fan tilted to the right meant "yes" for either a dance or a kiss; a light tap on a beau's wrist meant "later" for a dance, but if it was accompanied by a soulful glance it meant "later" for a garden rendezvous. His journal was filled with scathing comments about such feminine nonsense. Yet his own emotions had been no proof against them. He'd found himself engaged to Brigette with remarkable speed.

"I sometimes think that journal," Brigette said, pointing, "is the only thing that matters to you. If you're not out walking, you're scribbling in it."

"I'm a journalist."

Brigette advanced. "Let me see it. I want to know what you find so interesting to write about."

"No!" His vehemence startled both of them. "I'm sorry. I didn't meant to shout." Staring at the desktop, Louis cleared his throat. "I prefer to keep my writing private."

"I never considered publication in a newspaper private," Brigette hissed sarcastically. "The *Daily Picayune* would resent your slur against its circulation. Or was your last antislavery article private? If it was so private, I needn't have worried about what my friends thought. I was never so embarrassed."

"Some. I prefer to keep *some* of my writing private. Does that satisfy you?" Louis slid the journal into his desk drawer and locked it. "And I don't give a damn what your friends think. Beyond that, I will not discuss politics with you. Slavery is a barbaric custom."

Brigette pasted a trembling smile on her face. She shifted strategy; honey pots collect more flies. "I'm sorry," she said, wiping a lace cloth across her eyes and moving haltingly toward the fireplace. "It's just that if Father was here, I wouldn't so selfishly demand all your attention. Father was especially considerate. He was so good."

"Yes, yes," Louis sighed, smoothing his thinning hair again. Brigette could spend hours lamenting her orphan status and discussing her dead but "charming and handsome" father. He went to her and hugged her awkwardly. "I've been the selfish one. I haven't been paying enough attention to your needs." He held her at arm's length. "Now have I?"

Brigette nodded. Her face was tear-streaked.

Louis felt guilty. It wasn't Brigette's fault he no longer loved her. Still, he was honor-bound to marry her. A gentleman's code was strict. Having once proposed, he was obliged to marry. Only the bride-to-be could change her mind.

The situation was his fault entirely. He'd been escaping a wintry North and an even colder father.

His father, Henri DeLavier III, had married a staunch Puritan for her family's fortune. Could Louis blame him? The younger son of a rich Louisiana family, his father had no inheritance, since the plantation and slaves were entailed on the elder son, Brigette's father. Southern belles wouldn't marry Henri, knowing his prospects were so dim. So he'd gone north to seek his fortune.

Fortune had meant breaking down the reserves of a plain, unaccomplished woman. When she'd become pregnant, her family had to choose between scandal or marriage to a penniless outsider.

Louis' mother, plagued by guilt and images of hellfire, had chosen celibacy and prayer after marriage. His father had spent his days acquiring money and his nights acquiring mistresses. Louis, an only child, had been constrained by a fervent, zealous mother.

There had never been any light or laughter in the house, only repentance and kneeling to a strict, demanding religion. Louis' mother had seen her only child and son as proof of her licentious sins. She'd insisted he be cleansed and purged.

Louis' father had demanded nothing of anyone. He hadn't even demanded love from his son. The only time Henri DeLavier was passionate was while reminiscing about New Orleans. Louis was attracted to New Orleans because he was jealous of the emotions the city aroused in his father. He'd visited New Orleans knowing that his father would disapprove officially but would be secretly pleased. Having once given the city up, his father had never returned, perhaps fearing that reality would contradict his memories.

Initially, New Orleans didn't disappoint Louis. Its sensuality overwhelmed him. To the warmth-starved child in him, New Orleans had beckoned with open arms. Sunsets over the Gulf, bourbon and mint, and music filtering through the city streets had lulled him. Wide, friendly smiles and the open pursuit of pleasure had released his suppressed needs. For one summer he'd become the perfect gentleman—an inebriated, inveterate gambler who disdained work. But New Orleans' crowning achievement was the southern belle—an aristocratic white woman versed in the rituals of flirtation.

Louis had been mesmerized by Brigette. Attractive and lusciously foreign, her drawling Creole French had tantalized while her sighs, bare shoulders, and nearly exposed breasts had excited him.

Louis had taken advantage of their kinship by rushing them into an official engagement. He should've insisted that they wait. Now, half the time he hated Brigette, while all the time he hated her friends and culture. New Orleans' loveliness was superficial; rot and decay festered within. Slavery was but one example.

The memory of the first time he'd seen the unloading of a slave ship still haunted his dreams. It had been early morning, and he and Brigette were just returning home from a ball. A companion couple had been with them. He couldn't remember their names. But that morning they'd all been great friends and very drunk, very cheery. They'd taken the harbor route because Brigette had thought it more romantic. And it had been. Brigette never looked lovelier. She'd glistened like the shimmering new dawn on the bay.

The man had shouted for the coachman to stop. He had an open magnum of champagne, and he'd wanted to toast the unloading of a ship's cargo. He'd invested in it and stood to earn a tidy fortune.

"By all means," Louis had agreed, standing up in the open carriage, cocksure in his evening wear and taking his turn at the bottle. When the unloading began, however, he'd been revolted. He'd seen filthy, diseased, weakened, and dying bodies. He couldn't even think of them as people, their humanity had been so thoroughly stripped. But he'd known the cargo *was* human. His mother's Christian abolitionist teachings came to the foreground. Up until then, he'd accepted the southern rationale that blacks were happy as slaves. He'd never seen evidence to the contrary. But that morning he caught a glimpse of the black coachman's face contorted with grief. The poor man, stylish in a silk hat and uniform, had been forced to witness the degradation of his racial family. Brigette's blithe comment that blacks were used to hard work, hot sun and "don't feel as we whites do" had capped Louis' disgust. Afterward, he'd begun writing again—feverish abolitionist prose. Yet even though Louis now saw New Orleans in a clearer light, he couldn't overcome his need to be part of her decadence. Disillusioned, he nonetheless didn't want to live anywhere else beside New Orleans. He hated this part of himself. Hated the part of him that needed to feed in a passionate, alluring, yet destructive world.

His disillusionment with Brigette had occurred more gradually. As with the city itself, Brigette had made him confront his passions. She'd blatantly attracted him, and he just as blatantly had responded. In the past, he'd visited painted prostitutes but now found these trips distasteful. Brigette acted the whore but was also a lady. And because she was a lady, he'd proposed. He'd allowed himself to confuse sexual desire with romantic love. During the engagement, he'd discovered Brigette was quite cold, a dishonest and fashionable tease. But she was only what her culture had made her. And knowing all he knew about her, he couldn't quite forgive himself for wanting to treat her like a whore. He still found himself occasionally dreaming of deflowering her and using her body as he would a prostitute. Only his memory of the brown girl in the Market Square had kept him from acting on this impulse. Whenever he thought of the brown girl, he thought of himself as a rescuing knight. He could still feel her lips quivering beneath his fingertips. Attracted to her innocence, Louis had felt his own honor restored. Ironically, it was honor that kept him tied to Brigette and made his need of a brown girl hatefully dishonorable.

Louis tightened his hold on Brigette's small waist. Her too-heady rose perfume irritated him.

Brigette felt restless. She tried to relax. She stared at Louis' collar, the side of his neck, the trail of hair on his chin. It was Antoine's fault she was wrapped in an abolitionist's arms. Free the slaves. What a foolish and naive thought! Everyone knew blacks were more ape than human. It'd been proven by scholars, her father once said. Brigette sighed. Her brother Antoine misspent. That's why she was in Louis' arms. "Bad investments," Antoine had said. "Gambling," she said.

It was her fault, really. Antoine didn't ask her to sacrifice herself. Far from it. Antoine hated Louis. But since losing their parents to fever, Brigette felt responsible for Antoine. His comfort was hers. Her wealth would be his. What was wrong with marrying Louis? A wealthy, manageable cousin.

Brigette didn't think Louis would notice or care she wasn't a virgin. She'd heard northern gentlemen weren't particular. Southern gentlemen, on the other hand, liked their wives pure. Most of them preferred their mistresses pure as well. They spent thousands supporting the Quadroon Ball to attract young virgins. But, once bedded, the colored mistresses were expected to be passionate whereas the poor white wife was expected to be aloof.

Brigette planned on being cool in Louis' bed. That is, if she ever reached it. She was nervous about the wedding, nervous that Louis seemed less pliable than she'd expected. Already he'd succeeded in delaying the wedding by six months. The DeLavier household was desperate. Silk was astronomical, and the price of beeswax kept rising. Antoine hadn't backed a winning horse all summer. It was hot and uncomfortable in Louis' arms.

"Dearest, didn't I agree to postpone the wedding till August?" Brigette asked in her most soothing voice. "Though Lord knows why. My friends will have left town to escape the fever. But you see how obedient I am? I try to please you in all ways while you displease me in all ways. What's so important that you can't attend my fitting? What's so important that you don't care how I dress or look on our wedding day?"

Louis half heard her. He kept looking at her, hoping to dispel the vision of another face. "Kiss me, Brigette."

"Why should I?"

"Kiss me."

Brigette angled her face slightly; his kiss brushed the side of her mouth. Louis twisted her head and kissed her fiercely. He could feel Brigette resisting. He kept kissing her, hoping desire would well in him. Why was it that when his fingertips had merely touched the brown girl's mouth, he'd been moved beyond measure?

Brigette thought she'd swoon. Louis' mouth on hers, his palms stroking her back and neck were disgusting.

She broke away as the study door opened.

Antoine paused on the threshold. Brigette, unable to restrain herself, ran to her brother. Louis, embarrassed, turned toward his desk.

"Charming, cousin," said Antoine, cradling Brigette in his arms. "I didn't know Northerners were in the habit of frightening young women."

"She's going to be my wife."

"But she isn't yet."

"Antoine, please," said Brigette, furious at her lack of control. She was acting like a schoolgirl, not a young woman of twenty-three. She took deep shuddering breaths.

"I'll try not to overset Brigette's nerves again." Louis sought calm by touching the writing implements on his desk: his inkwell, his leather mat.

"See to it, cousin. Else I might withdraw permission for the marriage."

Louis pressed his quill pen backward, splitting it in two. His head ached. His problems would be solved if Antoine forbade the marriage.

"Since Father's death, I've been my sister's unofficial guardian.

I wouldn't want to be derelict in my duty. A woman's reputation is sacred. Do you understand me, Louis?"

Louis felt out of control. He'd give anything if Antoine would deny permission for the marriage.

"Do you understand?" Antoine shepherded his sister from the room.

Antoine and Brigette paused in the hallway, far enough away from the study door. Antoine feathered Brigette's face with kisses. The two of them held each other, breathless and expectant. Neither cared about the two black footmen standing tall and still at each end of the hallway. Slaves were sightless and unfeeling as far as Brigette and Antoine were concerned. Nonetheless, their behavior was rash. Antoine pushed his sister a little aside.

"You needn't marry him, you know."

"What will we live on if I don't?"

Antoine scowled.

"We need money."

"Then marry someone else. They're certainly enough gentlemen calling. What about Claude Montrachet? Or Duclair? Armand would be glad to have you. He wouldn't be overly demanding. He already has more whores and boys than he can manage."

"How long would it be before Armand or Claude suspected us? What would they think of our time, let alone our nights together?"

"Damn you." Antoine ruthlessly gripped her arm. "You're never to speak of it. I told you never to speak of it."

"But it's true, Antoine," she said, raising her voice to a hushed whisper. "We're not suspect now because I'm engaged. If only you'd married the Piètre girl—"

"I couldn't go through with it," Antoine blustered. "Too damn eager. Something suspicious about Anne-Marie. She left town, didn't she? She must've birthed a light-skinned nigger." Antoine flushed with an uncommon guilt. Anne-Marie had confessed she loved him, and that scared him more than anything. He'd taken her maidenhead and then had told her he never wanted to see her again.

"We have no choice. One of us must marry." Brigette stroked her brother's chin. Antoine could be childish at times. With Antoine, she needed to be the practical, responsible one. Sometimes she thought it would've been better if she'd been born the boy and he the girl. Truthfully, she was the unofficial guardian.

"Antoine, listen to me," Brigette said coaxingly. "Louis will be the most manageable husband. He's family. He'll understand our desire to be together. Hasn't he accepted living in New Orleans? He'll not separate us. He feels sorry for us poor orphans."

"I won't take his pity."

"Think, Antoine. One of your gentlemen friends would surely ruin us."

Antoine's body seemed to deflate. Here was a problem he couldn't conquer with physical strength. There seemed to be no way he could protect his sister. Just as there seemed to be no way to deny their need to be together.

"Antoine," Brigette murmured. Disarming him with caresses and a warm smile, she said, "Look."

They turned and saw themselves reflected in the gilt-rimmed mirrors lining the hallway walls.

"Nothing matters except this," Brigette murmured.

Arm in arm, they were a perfect complementary set: Twins. Same height. Same eyes. Male, female. One dark, the other fair. Mirrors reflected them on all sides. Their images echoed down the length of the hallway.

Antoine let out a shout. Pleased by their beauty, brother and sister hugged.

The two slaves exchanged glances. With a flicker of their eyes, they commented on the whims of white folks.

As soon as the wide oak door closed shut, Louis wanted to call Antoine back. He wanted to rain curses on his wastrel uncle and on his cousin, Antoine, for gambling the estate to bankruptcy. Because they needed his money, Antoine and Brigette would think twice before rejecting him. Just as his dead uncle altered his father's life because he wasn't the heir, Louis felt the same uncle reaching from his grave, altering his life because he had more than enough money for the DeLaviers to spend.

Louis sank despondent into his chair. Eyes glazed, he saw nothing. But he felt self-hatred, cynicism. He felt disgusted with himself because he was a man who needed a woman. Not just any woman but a colored woman.

Louis scorned white aristocrats who seemed addicted to brown-skinned mistresses and the perverted gentlemen who enjoyed sodomizing black boys. Yet he wasn't much better. He was already contemplating adultery and the betrayal of his soon-to-be wife.

He touched the drawer that held his journal. A chivalric vision was restored in his mind whenever he thought of his brown girl. His beloved was sweet, good, and honorable. If he believed in it, he'd say he'd fallen in love at first sight. Had his brown girl been fair of skin with the bluest of eyes and the most golden hair, he still would've loved her. It wasn't her skin color but a sense of wonder and innocence in her that he loved.

Louis sat at his desk. He retrieved his journal, selected another quill, and tried to recapture his brown girl with inadequate words.

M*arie heard drums. She tossed fitfully but the sound crept inside her, her heart matching the rhythm of the drums. She jerked awake, then laughed nervously, for she heard nothing. Silence.*

As her head touched the pillow, she heard the drums again. Someone was calling.

"Marie."

She threw off her covers. At the window, she saw an eerie moonlit beach, waves lapping incessantly against the shore and smoke rising near an inlet cove. "Marie." The man was calling her. Like a sleepwalker, she tiptoed through the house, past Grandmère's closed door (Nattie's pallet bed was empty), and out the front.

Breezes curled the edges of her gown, and as she floated across the sand her chill and dread were replaced by a certainty that she was heading toward home. Voices, disembodied, swirled. She stopped. Inside her head, she heard clearly and distinctly, "We're waiting." She couldn't have turned back if she wanted to.

Drums lured her until she saw a crowd dressed in stately white, swaying about a bonfire, their hands clasped together, singing, repeatedly, a single note, "Voudon." It was the loveliest sound she'd ever heard. Peaceful, cloaked in darkness, her body swayed.

Outlined against the water she saw him. His chest above his white pants was muscular and broad. She felt an urge to drown in his arms. Behind him, she saw the spell man, his feathered cap beating in time with his hands on the drums.

There was Nattie, leading a she-goat to the circle's center. She recognized more of the faces—men, women, and children from the village. Ziti. Shad. Bébé. All of them turned expectantly toward the man, who had his arms raised, a blade in his hands.

Mesmerized, she watched him slowly turn, the blade reflecting rainbows, and she saw his three scars—it was the man from the bayou, the one in her visions.

Spirits descended, drifting down through the top of her head. She felt numb; her soul, lost. The blade fell and rose again and again, each time barely missing skin and rousing the crowd to frenzy. Something pushed her toward the circle's center. The crowd parted to form a path. The man glanced at her triumphantly; then, lifting the blade again, he severed the goat's head.

"Marie." Grandmère was beating her with a stick. "Damn you. Damn you." Everyone was watching. The spell man was resting his head on the drums. Nattie was stroking the goat. The man stood, angry and defiant, the blade tip spilling blood. She couldn't feel anything.

Grandmère pushed her forward, the stick cracking across her shoulder blades. She looked back.. The crowd, Nattie, and the drummer were skeletons. Sticks of bone. The man seemed a demon. She screamed, and spirits, gray curls of smoke, flew out of her mouth.

The next morning Marie awoke, hot and headachy. Welts lined her back. The villagers were taciturn, mumbling hasty good mornings. When she asked Nattie about the night, Nattie replied, "Nothing happened. Why would I be prowling about the night? I be asleep all night in my bed."

But Marie knew something real, not make-believe, had happened. Her skin was raw from Grandmère's stick. She remembered vividly the man compelling her forward. Nattie was lying.

In the afternoon a rooster in a black hat, tie, and tails was found on the porch step. Grandmère sang a tortured melody. She ripped the cock apart with her hands.

By evening, Grandmère claimed she was blind. She stumbled into chairs. Twice, she fell.

Marie asked, "Why, Grandmère?"

Grandmère said, "A disobedient child stole my sight. I don't want to see."

At first Marie didn't believe her, but as Grandmère stumbled about the cottage, Marie came to believe she had indeed stolen Grandmère's sight.

Marie spoon-fed Grandmère dinner, undressed her, and tucked her tired body into bed. Afterward, Marie curled herself between sheets and prayed to the Virgin that sweet Grandmère would wake with her sight restored and she, a worthless granddaughter, would die by morning.

But she didn't die. Lingering in the air like a mocking nursery-rhyme curse, Marie thought she heard, "Obedient children don't ask why. Obedient children do or die. Obedient children rest in their beds. Obedient children never hear ghosts!"

"Miz Marie, come away from the window, now, hear?" Nattie rested her hands on her sprawling hips.

Marie shook her head, trying to rid herself of the memory of the haunting. *She'd felt elation when the goat was dead, wonderment and beauty. Why should drums entice her so? Why should spirits fly from her body?* In the weeks since the ceremony, she'd learned to keep her own secrets. Nattie would call her foolish, Grandmère blasphemous.

"Staring at the sun won't make it set any faster."

"I know," Marie said, turning from the window. "It's simple foolishness."

"That's right. Simple foolishness." The black woman looked up from her sewing. "You mock me, girl?"

"No, Nattie," Marie said wearily. Tension always sparked between them. "It's just, for you everything is 'simple foolishness.' If I pick flowers, you say—"

"Simple foolishness. They should stay in the good earth where they belong. A flower picked and a good child cries."

"If I don't burn shedding hair—"

"Foolishness. A bird find it, use it for its nest, then your hair fall out."

"If I sleep facing the wall—"

"Somebody die." Nattie pinched the material with her needle. "Simple, simple foolishness."

"How do you know such things are true? How do you know who dies?"

"Don't matter who, just matters that it's so. You try and it be—"

"Simple foolishness." Marie sighed. Nattie and Grandmère were alike: full of odd sayings and never answering questions. But Nattie's eyes were sly. Her words were wedged between insult and sincerity. Marie could never tell whether Nattie hated her or, oddly enough, loved her.

Marie's nails scraped the puckered wood on the sill. She'd been in Haven for months now, only three miles from New Orleans, and she hadn't discovered anything about her Maman. Grandmère's blindness crippled her like chains. Voices inside her head replaced her visions, and at times she felt insane.

"And here you be simple foolishness about this man, Jacques."

"Jacques's a good man," Marie said defensively. She couldn't admit she was marrying him to fulfill a vision.

"I no deny that. Whole town knows how he makes you coo. 'Tweet, tweet.' Even in your dreams his arms must hold you. Well, foolishness won't kill you, but it sure makes you sweat. You'll find out so tonight."

"Nattie!"

"Nattie! she say." The black woman shrugged. "I no say what don't be true. Ooo," she exclaimed, "I should hide these away. Scissors opened during a wedding mean the groom won't raise his pretty stick. Won't be able to stroke away nightmares. Won't be able to make pretty fat babies. Don't want Jacques," Nattie said wickedly, "to have such a problem. Else the marriage be no good."

Exasperated and embarrassed, Marie turned back toward the window.

Tonight everyone would celebrate her wedding. Shad was in the Gulf trying to net jumbo shrimp. Children were stringing flowers into garland chains. Women were shelling peas and slaughtering chickens.

August 4, 1819. It was the start of yellow fever season. Already some city folk were dying. It didn't seem right to be marrying in a month known for death and disease.

99

It was funny: Despite the ladybug, Grandmère had gotten her wish. But Marie felt dishonest. She was accepting Jacques so on her wedding day the dark man would come. He was the spirit who'd haunted her in Teché. He would tell her who she was. Tell her about Maman, Voudon, and the voices. When her menstrual blood first flowed, he was the one whom she'd envisioned replacing the groom. She prayed her vision wasn't false. But if it was false, she'd make Jacques take her to New Orleans. He'd promised.

"Big festivities make for big heads."

"Why do they do it, Nattie?" Down on the beach, Halo and her daughter, Ziti, were stirring gumbo stew.

"Plan feast? Simple question. Most people need an excuse to celebrate." She smacked her hips. "You. Good excuse."

"But Halo should be working in the square. Ziti, combing her fine ladies' hair. Even Shad—"

"Lazybones," grumbled Nattie about her long-suffering beau. "He wakes with the moon."

"—missed a morning's work. Five days you've been sewing on my dress."

" 'Tis so. Try it on."

Marie quickly slid off her shift. At Grandmère's request, gold crosses were stitched along the bottom. "To protect her," Grandmère said, "from evil."

"It's beautiful," Marie said, dancing about the room, watching the material billow. *The gown was exactly as she had envisioned it.* She stopped.

"I'm not worth such honor. This dress. The feast. It isn't for me. It's for Grandmère, isn't it?"

"Yes," said Nattie bluntly. "A good woman."

Marie glanced at her sharply. Something in Nattie's tone was false. *Marie pressed her fingers to her temples. She held her breath to better hear the whispers. If only she could be quiet enough, she would understand them.*

"They always honor her," Nattie shouted.

The buzzing stopped. "But it's more than that. A kind of—"

"Respect," concluded Nattie. "And shouldn't they do so? Respect one's neighbors? Respect the old?"

Marie recalled how strange it was that, in New Orleans, Grand-mère had known precisely where to go. Strange, almost magical, how a crowd had greeted them at the Haben's Haven cottage. People had bowed, given gifts, and, as Grandmère accepted them, each had responded as joyfully as though they'd been blessed.

"Everyone reveres Grandmère. Like a goddess. Or a saint." Villagers left offerings on the doorstep: a piece of string, a twig, a lock of hair. When they were ill, they begged Grandmère to lay her hands on their wounds and sores. They swore she had the power to heal in her fingertips. "Why, Nattie? Why do they worship her? People don't do such things."

"What you know of people?" The vehemence was startling. "What people live in Teché? Birds, animals live in Teché. Sometimes I think you be one. 'Tweet,' you sing for your lover. But you be goat when it comes to understanding. Be not your Grandmère a good woman?" Nattie paced, her hips furiously shaking. "Well, people pay debts. Always 'tis so, else there be no dignity." She stopped, tapping a finger into Marie's chest. "Be not your Grandmère a good woman? Who goes among them and heals? When sickness comes, who keeps the spirit in their bodies? And Annette's unborn child, who brings that life into this world?"

"Grandmère."

"Yes." Her anger deflated. "It be only right to respect her. She be a woman of great power. Only right that people pay debts." Nattie sat, her lungs wheezing.

Now there were no sinister nuances to Nattie's words, only love for Grandmère. Marie felt confused. She'd misjudged Nattie. Ashamed, she plucked imaginary threads from her bodice.

"What has Grandmère done for you?"

"Ah, Marie." Nattie's voice was distraught. "I wish I could tell you all she's done. Then you know how great she be." Nattie stared at her calloused hands. "When I traveled from Haiti, she took care of me. Fed me, clothed me. Taught me wondrous mysteries."

What power did Grandmère have? Why should Nattie and the villagers honor her, a tired old woman? When they looked at Grandmère, they saw someone else. If only Marie could see what they saw, maybe she would see part of herself.

Marie inched forward. Nattie raised her hand in warning. "No. No more questions. Time not be right for you to know the answers."

"When will the time be right? When will everyone stop treating me like a child?" she demanded. "I deserve to know who I am." Feeling helpless, Marie collapsed before Nattie's chair.

Silence had been more comforting, Marie thought. If only the firefly hadn't provoked her into asking, 'Do I look like my Maman?' Was she burning her life's blood? Like Maman? Yes, and there didn't seem to be anything she could do to stop it. Marie had a foreboding that her future was meant to be unhappy.

"Always I thought of you as my child too."

Marie roused from her reverie.

"When you be little, no more than four, you'd scamper like a demon through the streets. Yes," Nattie answered the upturned face, "you were a village girl then. You lived in this house. A house full of women."

Here, then, Maman and Grandmère had argued.

"When you be in trouble, you'd squat beneath my skirts. Nobody," she said forcefully, "nobody found you there. Not your Grandmère, not your Maman. I was hurt when you didn't remember me. Hurt when you looked at me suspiciously."

"I didn't know."

"There be lots you don't know," Nattie said roughly, then murmured, "I was your Maman's friend. When she and your Grandmère were travelin', doing their business in New Orleans, I watched over you."

"What business?"

Nattie shrugged. "Same business your Grandmère do now," she said with studied nonchalance. "Roots, herbs, and such. Delivering babies, animal or human. Preventing sickness. Your Maman and Grandmère be well known in New Orleans. They cured many people."

"Tell me, Nattie." She stroked Nattie's fingertips. "Tell me about Maman. Grandmère. About Voudon." She watched expressions flit across Nattie's face: anger, doubt, then resolution. Expectant, Marie sucked in air. She could almost hear Nattie thinking in the quiet. Nattie would tell her everything.

Grandmère crossed the threshold.

Nattie snatched her hand away as though it'd been burnt.

Grandmère carried an herb basket; her other hand tapped a cane. "Annette's doing fine. Just fine. Labor's slow, but fine." Grandmère gazed vacantly, blindly, about the room.

Another five minutes and Nattie would have told her everything. Marie wanted to scream I hate you, at Grandmère, to break Grandmère's blind man's cane in two. But she loved Grandmère. More than anything. She ran to her and burst into tears.

"Child, why are you crying? Sssh, let me see this face." Grandmère edged her head up from the burrow of her shoulder, her fingers exploring, wiping away tears. "What? No smile for me?"

Marie stared at her eyes. Sometimes they would flicker and she'd feel certain Grandmère could see. Other times, like now, she saw only darkness.

"I've got a gift for you."

Marie barely glanced at the brooch. "Grandmère, I'm begging you. Tell me who I am. Tell me about Maman. Tell me." She clutched Grandmère's sleeve. "Please. I need to know who I am. I need to know about Maman. Tell me," she said, her voice dropping to a whisper. "Tell me about you."

There was the sound of three women breathing. Nattie hugged her hips; Grandmère rocked her body. Marie focused on the point where Grandmère's cane merged with the dirt. Grandmère didn't say a word.

Finally, Nattie said, "No more long face." Then, more heartily, she added, "Today be a day for grand celebration. Now slip off this dress. It'll be bad luck for Jacques to surprise you so."

When Marie was dressed again in her old shift, she quietly slipped outside the house and examined the brooch. *She knew before she saw it, it was the one to be pinned on her wedding dress.* A snake curled about a rose's thorns. The latch had opened. Blood trickled across her palm. "Damn her," Marie exclaimed. Grandmère should be the one to tell her about Maman, not Nattie—nor a stranger whom she wasn't sure wished her good or harm.

Was Maman so terrible? Did she kill? What was it about

Maman, about all of them, which made it so difficult for Grandmère to speak?

Three generations. Three women. Were parts of them monsters? Marie shuddered. Grandmère was right. Something horrible must have happened.

In frustration, she threw the brooch into the weeds and started toward the beach. *A persistent roar in her head said, "Listen."* "No," she screamed. With a force pressing against her chest, she stumbled backward and sagged against the wall of the house. *"Listen."*

Eavesdropping, Marie wasn't sure she wanted to know any answers.

"You're killing her."

"Better she die in ignorance than become like her Maman."

"But what happens when she discovers answers? What happens when she discovers her Grandmère lies?"

"She knows all she needs to."

"Does she know who you be? Does she know which traditions mark her family? Nothing, I tell you. She knows nothing. Do you hide the truth because Marie can't bear to see it? Or because you can't?"

"Don't threaten me, Nattie."

"She not even know about Voudon." *Marie stirred at the word, feeling a kinship she couldn't fathom.* "She see the snake pin as a trinket. She no see the god of it, her mother's spirit in it." *Marie wanted to weep; she swore she would hunt for the brooch.* "You think Damballah, the snake god, takes this kindly?"

"I need to rest, Nattie."

"But you no rest."

"I need to raise Marie in my own manner."

"But you forget your manners. The manners and customs of your people."

"How dare you say so?"

"Then why you no practice them? Everyone waits for you to praise Voudon. We wait for you on the beach. 'Marie,' we call." *Marie had forgotten Grandmère was also named Marie.* "But you no listen. John call your granddaughter. She listened. And you came beating her with a stick."

"That man is evil."

"I no understand you. You let John lead us in the faith when, by right, a woman should do so. You should do so. But you no longer give to your people."

"I gave them my whole life."

"Marie's fate is to serve Voudon," Nattie went on relentlessly. "To be priestess just like her mother and her mother's mother before that."

Marie rested her head on the windowsill.

Nattie and Grandmère were collapsed on the floor. Nattie seemed the mother, Grandmère the child in her arms.

"Who loved your daughter as well as you? Who would do anything to spare her heartache? Yet your daughter's *fa,* her fate, was to practice Voudon. You can't prevent Marie from knowing. Three generations of women. Three generations of Voodooiennes, all named Marie."

"I'm old, Nattie. I can't die knowing Marie is in danger." Grandmère's eyes were pathetically wide. "You've seen the signs, Nattie? Seen my death crawling across the room? Three Fridays the moon has been tainted yellow."

"Damballah is ill at ease," Nattie said, rocking her. "Annette's labor be too slow."

"Yes, yes, my friend." Grandmère stroked Nattie's knee. "I've been hard worried. I think it might be twins."

"Better to kill them then. Twins be cursed spirits reborn."

"But more than this, Damballah caused Marie's blood to flow too late. Sixteen years, and she's just now ready to marry. But I can trust Jacques. He's God-fearing. He's promised to take her back to Teché. He'll keep her safe."

Nattie stood in disgust. "In Haiti, there be woman like you. She neglected her gods. First they warn her with illness; then her chickens died, and she had to go begging in the market. Still she no listen. Finally, she went mad, tearing her clothes and skin off." Cruelly, she bent down and pulled Grandmère to her feet. "You have become that woman. Because of you the village's plants die.

105

Because of you Annette labors too long. Because of you, the faith is dying."

Grandmère moaned, twisting in her arms.

"You've stolen nothing from Marie." Nattie's voice mocked Grandmère. "Do you dare say that? You, who ripped the caul from her face. You, who know better than anyone else. You, who sinned by baptizing her Catholic. You, who know Damballah's need of her, sentence her to what, faith in white saints? The same saints who tormented her mother?"

She snatched Grandmère's rosary and it burst, the beads scattering like pebbles.

"Marie will never go back to Teché. The calling is upon her. She sees visions, you know that? Or have you been," she added sarcastically, "too blind?" She shoved her away. "You don't fool me like you fool that child."

Grandmère's head, almost disjointed, fell backward onto her shoulder.

Nattie saw Marie's horrified face framed in the window. "If I don't be mistaken," Nattie said softly, "Marie hears the voices too. Why else would she stay behind to listen?"

Grandmère spun around. Marie and Grandmère both screamed as the old woman's eyes focused. *She could see.* Grandmère sang a note, conjuring wounds. She hissed at Nattie, "You've betrayed me." She lunged, beating Nattie with her fists.

Marie rushed through the door, tugging, pulling Grandmère from behind. "Leave her alone. Leave Nattie alone."

"You've betrayed me." Grandmère sank to her knees, scrambling after pink rosary beads. If she restored the rosary, Grandmère felt she'd restore the Virgin's power. The Virgin would protect her from this evil.

Nattie touched her cheeks, feeling them bruise and swell. "I try to do you a favor. Spiteful, crazy woman. Try to bring you to your senses. But my debt to you is paid. You can hit a child. Not me."

"You betrayed me."

"You betray yourself."

"The Virgin will punish you," Grandmère shouted.

"Your Virgin be nothing compared to Damballah. I serve Him

faithfully, and after tonight I serve Marie as well." Nattie looked at Marie. "Marie named for her Maman, the Voodoo priestess."

Awed, Marie reached for her outstretched hand.

"Marie," cried Grandmère, "let me explain." The pleading wail crested and hung in the air.

"No. Maman will explain."

Grandmère wanted to shout, Your Maman is dead. My baby is dead. But she couldn't. She kept seeing her daughter's battered body strapped on the tree. She couldn't undo the lies and false hopes she had stirred in Marie. She couldn't admit her own guilt in not preventing her daughter's death. Besides, Marie wouldn't listen to her anymore.

Looking back, Marie saw a defenseless old woman. She felt pity, but then she remembered Grandmère's sins and her lies. On the ground, the cane blocked her way. It had been a weapon of guilt. Marie lifted the thin white cane and splintered it against the door.

Grandmère's song was silent.

Marie wanted to cancel the wedding. But Nattie urged her to go through with it, to fulfill the vision. "Damballah wants you to bleed in marriage." Afterward, Nattie promised, John, the leader of the Voodoo cult, would come.

Marie was thankful Grandmère didn't come to the church. Annette's labor had intensified. Thankful, too, that the white priest, Father Christophe, didn't counsel her and Jacques before the Wedding Mass. Entering the cathedral, she felt assaulted by relics and symbols. Dozens of gold crosses, inlaid with pearl, hung upon the walls. Basins of holy water flanked the entrances, and frankincense burned in every corner. Hundreds of candles flickered before life-sized statues of John the Baptist, Saint Peter, the Virgin, and Christ. Velvet covered the pews and pathways leading to the enormous marble altar, encrusted with gold, rubies, and diamonds, on which the Communion Host was prepared. The atmosphere was hushed, reverential, and Marie felt intensely the power and wealth of the Catholic church.

Both Grandmère and Jacques had insisted that the marriage

take place in St. Louis Cathedral. They wanted "the living saint," Father Christophe, to perform the ceremony. New Orleans hailed the priest as a healer. It was said he had cured a thousand fever victims and never once fell ill.

As Marie knelt before the altar, a statue of Christ stared down at her. Red stains marked where the nails were pounded into His hands and feet, where the thorns were pressed against His head. Marie's vows to love, honor, and obey were mortal sins. The alabaster Christ knew she lied.

She had wanted a village wedding. To "jump the broom," as many slaves and ex-slaves did, so she and Jacques could pronounce themselves man and wife. But Grandmère had said such a union would be sinful, "heathenish." To Marie's mind, her marriage in the church was the greater sin—if you believed in God, that is; she wasn't sure she did anymore. She felt intimidated and nervous, but she didn't feel an overwhelming stirring of faith. She knew white saints must be powerful; Grandmère wouldn't honor them without reason. But Marie was interested in other types of spirits—spirits who might listen to the pleas of a black girl needing her Maman.

The cathedral was nearly empty. A few parishioners were praying in the back. Another priest was hearing confession. A drunk was sprawled in a pew.

None of the villagers were with Marie and Jacques. It was yellow fever season, and the villagers avoided the city when it didn't entail making a dollar. Though August had just begun, Marie couldn't help noticing that black satin sashes decked several town doors. She wanted to curse Grandmère for hastening the marriage. She was likely to catch fever on her wedding day and die.

It was a lonely wedding. Marie's gown felt oppressive. It was hot. Jacques was annoying. Her veil provided no protection from his triumphant eyes.

Marie coolly watched Father Christophe's delicate hands readying the sacrament. He believed her soul to be unblemished, untainted with sin. Marie had lied when she said she'd recently confessed. She trembled when the good father gave her the communion wafer. It stuck to the roof of her mouth. The blood wine wouldn't wash it down.

Father Christophe pronounced them man and wife. Jacques kissed her boyishly. "J'taime," he said. "I love you very much."

Conscience-stricken, Marie murmured "J'taime" and turned to leave.

"Madame Paris."

Marie stumbled, upset by the sound of her new name.

"A moment. Please."

Jacques paused with her, his hand supporting her elbow.

"I'd like a few words with you. Alone," said the priest.

Marie panicked. She could feel her heart racing, her lips becoming dry.

Jacques smiled, unaware of the strained current between his wife and the priest. "I'll untether the horse."

Marie wanted to beg Jacques not to leave. Had the white priest divined her plans? Had his gods whispered of her defection? Clasping her hands, Marie forced herself to face Father Christophe.

His hands—the same hands that soothed yellow fever victims—were outstretched.

"You won't catch the fever from my hands. You won't sicken from my touch."

Marie blushed.

"Heed the faith of Christ. There is one truth. One light. Your Grandmère discovered this nearly eleven years ago."

"But she believed in something else first, didn't she?" The priest's words failed to shock Marie. She knew now that Grandmère had secrets, another life. New Orleans proved there was a great deal left unsaid.

"If you're intent on learning about darkness, about evil, it may destroy you."

The priest seemed compassionate, and Marie felt an urge to unburden her cares. She wanted him to explain the world to her. She asked, "How can darkness be evil if your God made the universe? Didn't He make darkness too?"

"He dispelled the darkness with the light."

"But darkness existed. He had to have made it. Just as He made me." Marie paused, wetting her lips, trying to frame what she needed to know. "Don't whites think me evil just because I'm dark? Isn't that why there are slaves?"

"You're confused."

"Explain, then."

Father Christophe sighed. Marie saw tiredness etched in his face; the lines creased his eyes and mouth.

"It's not easy accepting the wisdom of God. He sends trials to all of us, so we may eventually see a clearer truth." The priest gazed steadfastly at Marie. "The diseased, condemned men and women sentenced to hang, all God's accursed children, share the potential for finding an unheard-of peace. The accursed, the persecuted, most easily gain heaven. Suffering becomes a blessing."

"I don't understand."

"Being dark is no different. The colored races are the children of Ham, cursed long ago."

Marie's brows arched in disbelief.

"Ham, Noah's youngest son, looked upon his father's nakedness," said the priest, quoting scripture. "When Noah awoke, he knew his son's sin. Noah cursed Ham, the father of Canaan, and all descendants from his blood. He said, 'Cursed be Canaan; a servant of servants shall he be unto his brethren.'

"Black people share the burden of Ham's curse. But the burden is edged with great potential to see and feel God's blessings. Slavery and servitude are tools of God."

Marie vaguely remembered Grandmère's tales of Noah's ark and the covenant of the rainbow, but she'd never heard of Ham or Canaan. She spoke bluntly. "Why should I bow to a God who has cursed me and others like me? There must be a faith where darkness isn't evil. I know there are other gods."

Father Christophe shook his head. "There's one faith. One true God."

"Who did Grandmère believe in before she believed in Christ?"

"It's blasphemy to speak of it." The priest walked forward toward the altar. He genuflected and made the sign of the cross.

"Did Grandmère ask you to speak with me?"

"No," he said, turning. The crucifix, forged in gold, loomed behind him. "I fear you'll lose your immortal soul."

Marie felt fear. The priest in his black tunic robes, surrounded by the lavish and bejeweled altar, seemed all-knowing, all-powerful.

Would she go to hell? When she was a small child, Grandmère taught her the Catholic catechism and the Ten Commandments. "I am the Lord thy God. Thou shalt have no other gods before me." Marie trembled. The gold crosses stitched on her hem glowed, or was it candlelight that made them seem alive?

She looked closely at Father Christophe. Pale skin, a shaved circle on his head, a coarse tunic. He was remarkably unintimidating. It was the setting of painted saints, gold filigree, and custom and ritual that made him seem more powerful. But a man is all he is, thought Marie. A man like DeLavier. Like Jacques. Why should he, or any man, have the power to condemn her? Even Christ had been a man once.

"It's a wife's lot to obey her husband. Be good and charitable, Marie. Honor your husband. Have children."

"I don't want children." It was true. She wanted to receive a mother's love, not give it. At least not yet, not now.

"Then you're intent on destruction."

"I'm intent on finding myself."

"Christ said lose yourself to find perfection. It's the only way to reach heaven."

"I don't wish to be perfect," Marie whispered. "Heaven is too far away. I need a way to live my life now."

They were at an impasse. Priest and sinner. Marie thought they might've liked each other if she was less questioning of the Catholic faith.

"Walk with God," Father Christophe said sadly. His hands blessed her. "If you like, assist me in my work. I minister and nurse fever victims, even prisoners awaiting death. They've a great deal to teach. You might learn why the suffering instead of the healthy, the impoverished instead of the rich, have the better chance at salvation. Besides," he said, slowly smiling, "it's practical, good, honest work."

Marie smiled back. The priest was another good man—like Jacques—trying to help her. But she had to find her own path. Marie

111

regretted saying no to him. Soothing the dying would be an easy path to salvation, if salvation were what she was looking for.

"Goodbye, Father," she said, turning down the aisle. The train of her wedding skirt rustled about her ankles, slowing her progress.

"If you need me," the priest called, "I'll be here."

On either side of her, Marie saw painted murals of the Stations of the Cross. Christ's trials were displayed: His condemnation before Pilate, His crowning with thorns, the abuse as He dragged the cross through the city streets, and, finally, His crucifixion.

Why did faith have to be based on pain? She didn't really care about faith. She just cared about Maman. But Maman was Voudon. She wondered: did Voudon have more joy and less pain?

Near the church exit, she saw a hand-drawn sign: BLACKS AND COLOREDS UPSTAIRS. Marie smiled grimly and walked out into the night. Father Christophe must have married her downstairs as a favor to Grandmère.

Jacques was smiling broadly. Waiting for Marie, he'd woven fantasies of their future life. He'd imagined Marie kissing him hello and goodbye between his sailing trips. She'd be worth coming home to . . . she'd be worth all his loving. Jacques realized that until now he'd never let himself fall deeply in love. Slavery had proven that loving someone meant extra hurt, extra pain. But having Marie made him willing to be vulnerable again. He had to remind himself that she couldn't be sold. She wouldn't ever leave. He gently kissed her.

"Let's away, then," he said, clicking his tongue at the horse. "Giddyup."

Marie felt guilty and sick. She was going to hurt Jacques.

The wagon moved at a clipped pace through the crowded streets. Modern gas lamps were spaced throughout the French Quarter. The city streets were bathed in artificial daylight. Marie was attracted to the brightly lit miracles. She couldn't imagine the process of containing fire in glass. Would a thousand fireflies caught in a jar give off as much light? How long would they last before burning themselves up?

Jacques maneuvered the wagon between whores, drunken, elegantly dressed gentlemen, and slaves doing illicit errands. Nighttime New Orleans illuminated strong passions. From the wagon perch, Marie could see a fistfight through a saloon's windows, two bare-breasted women walking hand in hand, and a sailor urinating by the wayside. Down an alley, she saw a market hawker's cast-offs—rotted heads and fish bones—being scavenged by a score of cats.

"What's that?" Marie asked, pointing at a cart stacked high with heavy packages wrapped in black cloth. The driver wore a kerchief over his face. Street revelers scurried out of his way, some shouting obscenities, others yelling, "God protect me!" Others made the sign of the cross.

"Fever victims," said Jacques. "Those are whites who couldn't afford or else foolishly preferred not to leave the city. They'll be buried in a common tomb."

"How can you tell they're white?"

"If the victims were black, they would've been piled together, coated with lime, and taken to be burned on the edge of town."

Marie shivered. In her mind, she could see a mountain of bodies bursting into a hot white light.

Jacques kissed her ear. "No unhappiness. It's our wedding night."

"Yes." Driving out of the city, Marie's mind juxtaposed images of dead bodies and flames, the church with its white plaster saints, and Father Christophe's probing, light-filled blue eyes.

Soon Marie was back among her own kind, among dark faces, and as they celebrated the wedding on the beach, Marie felt bound to every man, woman, and child by Voodoo secrets. She was certain all the villagers knew what would come later that night. The shy smiles, the occasional touch on her shoulder, the murmured best wishes.

On her wedding night, the man would come. Only Jacques, sweet Jacques, was oblivious and enjoying himself.

"Where's Grandmère?" Marie asked Halo. The old woman hadn't met them returning from the church.

"Birthing Annette's baby," answered the Creole woman.

Marie expressed surprise. "Shouldn't the babe be born by now?"

"A hard labor. Most strange. After five babies, one more ought to slip right out." Halo, shrugging, scratched her chubby arms. "A baby born is a good sign for a new marriage." Halo winked. "If only Ziti would marry," she muttered, stirring a pot of black beans and rice. "Dat girl is going to end up a whore like me for sure."

Marie murmured a few words and stared in the direction of Annette and Bébé's cottage. She shook off her worry as two men began beating drums held fast between their legs and feet. Tonight was for celebrating. She was going to find herself.

The unmarried males surrounded Marie, removing her shoes, throwing off her headdress and veil. They blindfolded her with a tassel of silk. The young women, Marie knew, were dancing, stealing toward a blindfolded Jacques, slipping him a kiss, then hurrying away before he had a chance to capture them. Marie fended off the men.

She'd be a Voodoo priestess. She'd make Maman proud. Maman would say, "You look . . . you *are* just like me."

Marie and Jacques were spun around and around at dizzying speeds and shoved toward each other. Like reeling drunks, they clung together, fell, and rolled in the sand.

Marie could almost imagine her mother smiling, beckoning her. She leaned her head back and laughed. Villagers applauded and smiled benevolently. Marie laughed again. She found it unbelievable that the villagers had ever made her anxious. They were part of her skin, part of her blood.

"Come and eat," Halo hollered. Villagers scurried forward to the pots of gumbo, black beans, and rice.

Everyone except Marie lay groaning from too much food. Jacques rested his head comfortably in Marie's lap. The drums were silent, the moon glowed yellow, and waves collapsed against the shore. Now was the time for the telling of tales. All turned to Shad, the sometime dockhand. His dull face lit up as he began. "There once was a Rabbit who met a Lioness with fur golder than the sun. He fell in love straightaway."

Jacques brushed Marie's cheek. "Like I did," he said. "I fell in

114

love straightaway." Marie felt sorry for him. Felt herself a cheat as Shad talked of a "sweet honeymoon."

"Stop it. Stop it. Everybody go home." It was Grandmère, cutting across the beach, her voice ragged, her white hair flying. "No more celebration," Grandmère shrilled, plucking her hair, beating a fist against her chest. "Everybody go home." Nattie trudged behind her, carrying a dark bundle. "Go home, I say. Go on. Get."

Marie watched Grandmère, like a woman possessed, trying to shoo the villagers away.

Nattie was cackling, her black face sparkling from the fire. "You all want tales? I'll tell you a tale. Grandmère neglected Damballah. Voodoo and the black gods. Look at the curse she's brought among us."

Screams rent the air. Villagers were running like crazed dogs. Grandmère was yelling. Jacques blessed himself with a cross. An ill-featured baby—not twins—dangled from Nattie's hand. Its heart had grown outside its body; its head was formed without a mouth or nose; its limbs were shriveled and blue. Nattie laid the babe at Grandmère's feet.

There were gasps, shrieks, then a deafening silence as the villagers pitied the deformed babe.

Looking across space as if no one else but Marie existed, Grandmère asked, "Do you condemn me too?"

Marie looked at Grandmère and tallied up all the harm she'd done. Grandmère had driven her Maman away, then raised her ignorant of Maman and Voodoo. Grandmère had accepted Ham's curse and favored white saints. Now she'd cursed Annette's baby with her sins, her blasphemies against Voodoo, against dark people. Grandmère's selfishness had crippled a newborn baby boy.

Marie strode toward the house. Jacques followed. He sympathized with Grandmère, but Marie was his wife, and he dared not challenge the signs of Voodoo power.

The wedding bed was strewn with flowers. Good children everywhere were crying.

Marie undressed and laid herself down. Jacques caressed her arms and thighs, sending the flowers scattering. Only after he kissed her neck and shoulders, only after she caught his hair while his mouth nursed her breasts, did he plunge. Marie cried. For what, she didn't know. Innocence? Jacques murmured, "It's all right. Everything is God's will."

But which god? The Voodoo god? "Damballah," the slave girl had cried. "Damballah," she'd heard Grandmère and Nattie say.

Marie wriggled from underneath Jacques' arm. He was snoring slightly, his spine curved like a garden snake. Jacques had courted her sweetly, offering her English tea and oranges. She still loved him like a brother or a friend.

On the sheet, she saw the stain from her hymen. Her wedding dress lay in a heap on the floor. Quietly, Marie slipped it on. Without looking back at Jacques, she walked out of the house. *John . . . and someone else . . . were calling.* She walked easily, the salt air whipping her hair. She felt certain Maman was near.

She saw three figures outlined against the shore—a stark trinity.

"Marie," said Nattie. "This be Ribaud." The spell man removed his feathered cap and, with a mocking grin, bowed. "And this be John."

John's eyes were slate gray. He smiled, and the scars on his cheeks reached the edges of his eyes. Marie hesitated. *There was a feeling of age about him—ancient secrets and death.*

"You've grown lovelier than I thought. You resemble your Maman." His voice was husky and, to Marie's ears, reassuring and gentle. John didn't seem as threatening as he had in the bayou. He held open his arms. She went to him, feeling more his wife than Jacques'. Off the coast, the wind was churning up a storm. His hands locked about her.

She whispered, "I know who I am."

"Do you, child?" Grandmère emerged from the shadows.

John tensed, tightening his grip about Marie's waist. Marie noticed Grandmère's beaded rosary was gone.

"Good evening, John. It's been a long time, hasn't it? Twelve years." Grandmère was calm and dignified. "Each morning in the bayou, I woke knowing you were waiting. Waiting for Marie to grow.

116

Waiting to snatch her from me. You think you've won, don't you?"

"Marie's won."

"Yes," Grandmère said softly. "She's a woman now." Marie flinched as Grandmère stared. "I longed to keep you a child. Can you forgive me?"

When she didn't answer, Grandmère edged closer, and Marie felt Nattie and Ribaud creeping behind John as they would behind a shield. Grandmère's frailty had disappeared.

"I warn you, John. I'm not dead yet. Nor am I so stupid not to realize when a pregnant woman's been poisoned. When her child's been hexed." She cocked her head. "I've been afraid of you. But I think you're more afraid. Why else would you curse me with a rooster? I destroyed its power by swallowing its heart. Didn't Nattie tell you?"

"Did you swallow your saints?" Nattie taunted.

"Shut up," said John.

"But you'll pay," Grandmère shouted. "Tonight I'll curse you to both God *and* Damballah. My power to conjure isn't gone." The old woman rocked back on her heels, satisfied she could still worry him. She opened her arms. "Come home, Marie. Jacques will miss you. I will miss you." She crooned a lullaby.

Marie covered her ears. The song would break her heart. So she concentrated on how ugly Grandmère had been murdering the cock. She, not Grandmère, had swept away the rooster's scattered bits. Conscious of the missing heart, she'd scrubbed the floor and walls.

John captured Marie's hands, earnestly pressing her palms with a kiss. "Like your Maman, I'll teach you your faith. I'll make you Queen of the Voudons." She let him guide her away.

"He's lying, Marie. There are things he'll never tell you. If you go with him, one day you'll hate him enough to kill him."

How stupid Grandmère was. She felt safe in John's arms. He would tell her about Maman.

"Marie!"

As they drifted down the beach, Marie dreamed of a sacrificial goat sprinkling her wedding dress red.

*"When I saw him, it occurred to me that I'd been waiting for my
life to begin. All I had to do was step across a gap of sand, place my
trust in him, and be reborn.*

"History does repeat.

*"From the moment I entered his arms, I started to die. Just like my
Maman."*

•

—MARIE LAVEAU, JUNE 14, 1881, EVENING
(From Louis DeLavier's journal)

Incense and the stench of tallow clung. John insisted on
keeping the doors and windows shut. A haze cloaked the room and,
sitting demurely with her hands clasped in her lap, Marie waited.
From the corner, she'd be called to perform a part she didn't know.
The crowd frightened her: knowing women who brushed their hips
against John; leering men who didn't touch her but looked as if they
might.

For weeks, John had kept her inside the small city house,
preparing her, dedicating himself to her lessons like another Grandmère. "Be calm," he had said, and when he looked at her she felt
calm. The same intense calm which had caused her to sigh in the
bayou. With John, she felt painfully alive. Her senses were heightened. Like the time when the swamp almost swallowed her up. She'd
been caught between life and no life. She'd nearly regretted it when
Grandmère dragged her from the dark, welcoming soil.

"At the right moment, I will call," John had said, letting his finger dance lightly across her chest. "Damballah will send both you and me a sign."

Damballah, the favored and most powerful of the spirits. Damballah, who inched across the earth hissing life into the first creations. A fertility god: ruler of both land and water. A god who birthed and rebirthed Himself.

On the altar, between candles, hexagons, and a circle, was a crude drawing of a snake. Arching over the snake was a rainbow. At the base of the altar was a box filled with the gods' clothing and adornments; the possessed would dress to make the gods feel more at home. Ezili wore a red silk dress. Ogu had his spear and shield.

John wore his costume, a tailored black suit with a white lace collar and cuffs. Majestically, he raised his hand. Nattie shook the gourd rattle, and Ribaud bent to his drums.

Tonight she'd discover if Damballah was worth leaving Jacques and Grandmère. Not a moment passed when Marie didn't worry about Grandmère. Was she doing well? Did she eat enough, sleep enough? And Jacques, had he gone to sea? Had he already forgotten her?

It wasn't fair that she should have to choose between Maman and Grandmère; it wasn't fair to choose between Jacques and John.

John had said Damballah would return her Maman if she would return to Damballah. Marie had felt both pleased and dismayed. She'd never known she belonged to Damballah. Never known her visions and imaginings were linked to a snake god. *Your home is Teché,* Grandmère whispered, *"bayou of snakes."* Had Grandmère secretly hoped her quest would lead her here? Grandmère had given her the snake brooch which she had so carelessly lost and never found among the weeds. Grandmère must have known Maman's life was entwined with a snake.

Maman! Marie thought with joy. She imagined Maman aglow with smiles, walking through the doorway, exclaiming how pretty Marie was . . . explaining how she'd never forgotten her daughter. Then Maman would hug and envelop her with overpowering love. Their reunion would persuade Grandmère they belonged together. They'd live happily ever after—Maman, Marie, Grandmère.

119

"Yes," Maman would say, "you look just like me."

It never occurred to Marie that she could *resemble* and *be* only herself. She felt thrilling anticipation; her anxiety became birthing pains. Tonight, with Maman, she felt she'd be reborn.

Thirty followers shifted into a circle: the men were bare-chested and wore white pants; the women wore kerchiefs and dresses. They swayed and stepped in unison. Ribaud played a dull, repetitious pattern. Marie reminded herself these were ordinary people. She saw folks from Haven: Shad, the fisherman and tale-spinner; Ziti, who'd braided her hair with blue ribbons. There were others whose names she didn't know. Ordinary people. Yet in their dancing Marie sensed elegance and beauty, in John a macabre dignity. She closed her eyes, gently rocking. The beat was hypnotic:

> *Legba, remove the barrier for me*
> *So I may pass through to the spirit world.*
> *Remove the barrier*
> *So I can visit the* loa.

Legba was a feeble old man in rags, carrying a crutch.

John had taught her there was life in every living and nonliving thing. Spirits to be conjured. Each god had its own personality and function. Legba guarded the spirits' gate.

"Legba, remove the barrier for me. Let me pass through." John led the chant. With dust, he drew symbols at the foot of the altar.

The drums changed rhythm. Masterfully, Ribaud was heightening tension, coaxing the gods to come. Nattie passed tankards of rum. She pressed a rim to Marie's mouth, forcing her to sip. Across the room, John was smiling and encouraging her. Marie could almost hear his caution to relax. She drank more deeply, though the spirit burned her throat.

Time collapsed.

Suddenly spirits were everywhere. Legba was inside a young boy; he sucked on a pipe and walked painfully. Agwé rode a hefty slave who kept shouting, "Agwé blows, the storm roars. Agwé, he blows. He roars." His body jerked; his lips puffed and spluttered the sounds of a storm. Ezili, goddess of grace and beauty, twisted the hips of a mulatto girl and paused now and again for a kiss. Ezili was a coquette. John caressed her. Ezili moaned and moved on.

Damballah would only enter a priestess.

John towered over her, appearing out of air. Marie tried to speak. *Deep, gurgling sounds caught in her throat. She couldn't recall how long she'd been sitting. She felt her arms merging with her knees, her legs fusing into one. She felt weighted, pulled down toward the ground.*

> *Serpent, serpent-o,*
> *Damballah Queen,*
> *You are a serpent,*
> *Serpent, serpent-o.*

"We will call the serpent. The serpent does not speak."

Marie slithered down from her chair. She moved through forests, crawled, and felt the earth tremble beneath her belly. So cool she was. She had lived . . . always. Hundreds of millions of years. She saw humans born. She would watch them die. Damballah survived, hoarding secrets . . . seeing beyond futures.

She was the center of the natural universe. Wind, water, sky, and sun all made obeisance to Him. She was the seed-giver, fertilizing the universe with life. Marie felt a harmony as wide and as deep as never-ending dreams filling her soul. It was like Grandmère's singing. Sometimes, listening to Grandmère's song, the beauty was so much, Marie would break down and cry. In Damballah's world, the peacefulness was so great, Marie felt it had the power to unhinge her mind. But it didn't; that was the thrill of it. There was great comfort knowing Damballah could elicit feelings almost beyond her capacity to feel them.

Marie shuddered, fell limp and unconscious. John helped her to her feet. Her gown was gray. Dirt speckled her mouth. "You were beautiful," he said.

She shivered; her limbs burned. Stunned faces watched her. "You were a snake."

Marie tried to imagine what she looked like in Damballah's grasp. She'd felt regal, uplifted, but now her dress was covered with dirt from crawling on her belly. She didn't want anyone to see her unclean and without control.

Followers closed in upon her. "Touch me, Miss Marie." "No, touch me," each demanded, grasping at her skin. They wanted to be blessed.

"Tell them to go away," she screamed, "to leave me alone!" Marie cowered against John.

"Get used to it." Nattie, hands on hips, her feet solidly planted, exuded scorn. "I've seen Damballah ride your Grandmère, your Maman, and now you."

Beneath the disdain, Marie sensed a threat. Why was Nattie angry?

"Allow them to fawn a bit." Nattie was a monster; flailing arms parted about her like water about a stone.

Unrelenting cries of "Touch me; no, touch me." Ribaud's laughter counterpointed his beats. She'd swoon.

"Nattie's right, Marie. You must accept this. Stand up straight."

Because John asked, Marie did as she was told.

Hands rubbed the length of her body. Fingers tangled in her hair. Ringed and braceleted hands, calloused and blunt-tipped hands, poked at her breasts, waist, and thighs. She kept still. Each follower wanted their square of skin to take home. She was their charm. Several dared to caress her nose and mouth. She'd suffocate. How did Maman stand this?

John was singing:

> *"If you see a snake*
> *You see Marie Laveau,*
> *If you see a snake*
> *You see Damballah;*
> *Marie Laveau is a snake."*

Bodies threatened to knock her down. She tried to escape. John caught her. "Call the gods, Marie. They'll help you." He shook her. "You must get through this. Everything will be ruined if you don't."

She gulped air.

"Marie. Call Damballah."

"Damballah." She heard a hiss and trembled.

"Good, ma petite."

She felt vulnerable, lost. "Damballah." Mucus clogged in her throat. She whimpered, "Send my mother to me. I need to feel her, please." Crouched in John's arms, she recalled a woman playing hide-and-seek with her, helping her to cast animal shadows on the wall. She stared at the door; surely Maman was just behind it. Never in her life·had she more needed a mother's love. Maman would enter through the doorway and hold her. "Maman." *A rainbow hovered.* "I need to see her . . . have her now."

She was Marie. Damballah blessed her.

The door didn't open. *Instead, floating above the sea of hands, she saw a figure wearing a dress the color of lemons. The cotton back was in tatters, and welts crisscrossed her bare skin. The spirit turned. "Je suis Marie."*

Marie felt both panic and fright. She couldn't quite grasp why Maman had appeared in the air like a wounded angel . . . why she hadn't walked through the door, why she floated and seemed so insubstantial. Nonetheless, Marie opened her arms.

Maman dove inside her, possessing, fitting neatly into sinews, bones, and blood. Maman took glory where Marie couldn't. So this, Marie marveled, is what Maman felt like.

"I am Marie." *My mother reborn.* Transformed, Marie strode through the room, touching the tops of heads.

"Miss Marie, touch me."

"Yes, I will touch you." *Maman laughed.* Then Marie laughed, spinning on the balls of her feet. Unafraid, Marie felt the equal of John.

Maman moved gracefully, head high, and paused before Nattie. Pointing at the tankard, Maman murmured, "I can get used to this very well." Breathing, feeling, tasting. She easily swallowed the rum.

"Marie." John caught her by the waist.

"I've returned." *Two minds in one body.* To both of them, he seemed lovely. His darkness was a haven. Marie ran her fingers through the grooves on his cheeks. He bit her ear.

Turning toward the crowd, his hand clenched hers. "This is our new Queen." John imagined proclaiming this fact to sixty, ninety, a thousand followers. "Damballah has brought her home."

"You did," Marie said, amazed by her boldness. "You brought me home."

Nattie slouched against the wall. Ferretlike, Ribaud's gaze darted between Marie and John.

Three times they circled the room. Stroking the outstretched hands, Marie was conscious of John watching her. Marie smiled. *Maman accepted her due reverence.* She brushed the drawing of the snake.

"Maman-*loa* Marie," the crowd chanted. "Maman Marie."

John slit a goat; its bowels tumbled out. Followers tainted their mouths with blood. John held her, burying his face in her hair. Marie exulted. Compared to the two of them, the others in the room seemed frail, human. *Maman thought them worthless.*

John lifted her up, her skirt cascading over his arms. The ceremony was ending. One initiation was complete. As he carried her, Marie heard the strain:

> *Legba, remove the barrier for me*
> *So I may pass back to earth.*
> *When I come back, I will salute the* loa.

Her feet never touched the ground.

Marie undid his lace collar, he the drawstring on her blouse.

She sucked the depression at the base of his neck, then arched as he kissed her breasts and torso. *Maman groaned.* His hand slipped between her thighs. She was already warm.

"Together we'll be famous." He plunged his hand inside her; she writhed. "All of New Orleans will beg at our door. Dear Marie." He nuzzled her neck. "We'll finish what we started."

Maman already knew his contours, where his buttocks rose above thighs. Positioning her on her hands and knees, John entered her from behind. She cried out. He pulled her down onto his lap, gently rocking. Jacques had not made her feel this way.

Marie wept. Turning, she ran her tongue along his while stroking the backs of his legs. John sucked her breasts and she felt explosions inside her womb. Loving him, she felt a healing of old wounds. Her mouth surrounded his scrotum. Loving him, she nudged the woman out of herself. Everything sensual.

Marie lay atop, shivering as they melted into one. *Maman preferred to ride him.* Marie tried to separate feelings. Something in Maman wanted to hurt. *Maman dug her nails into his sides. She slapped at his chest. Maman played the coquette, lifting her torso.* Marie preferred loving more sweetly. *Maman forced him to move beneath her while her hips remained still.*

He flipped on top. Marie moaned his name. Then, opening her eyes, she felt him come; his eyes were closed and his facial scars twisted into a grotesque grimace.

"Marie," he yelled, and she could feel contractions, deep, somber waves, rushing to meet him.

Maman fled. Marie edged her hand up beyond the pillow and grasped his.

His elbows locked, he looked down upon her. Marie felt shy, disoriented at losing part of herself. She reached up. She wanted to be held; she wanted memories between two, not three.

John slipped out of her. He sensed she was alone. Disappointed, he turned away onto his side.

The possession had ended.

Her head turned toward the window. A full moon hung in a cloudless sky. *Which Marie had he called? Who was she? What was she?*

She was in love.

She didn't sleep. Wind howled outside the window. Marie couldn't understand why she felt—no, *was* rejected by John when Maman was gone.

In the morning, Ribaud found her curled tightly in a ball. He burst into the room and tipped his feathered hat at her nakedness.

Dreaming, John had wrapped himself in the sheets like a dead man. Marie wished she could disappear.

"Master John." Ribaud edged round the side of the bed. "Master John. Mademoiselle Brigette wants you."

His eyes didn't flutter; they opened, instantly alert. "Tell her I'll be there. Now get out."

Ribaud easily avoided the blow. He grinned at her, and Marie thought: conspirators. Why did she think that? How did she know Ribaud wasn't moved by her nakedness? Ribaud felt a kinship with her, she could feel it. For one brief moment, during the ceremony, when she'd heard his drums, she'd felt he, not she, was responsible for bringing Damballah.

"Get out," said John, swinging his legs to the floor. The spell man shrugged, flashed another quick grin, and scooted out the door.

Cradling his head, John seemed older. Marie thought he didn't remember she was there. His hair lacked luster; his face seemed ashen. As he walked to the dresser, Marie thought his skin looked flaccid rather than firm like the night before.

He lifted his case of *gris-gris* charms and measured powder, seaweed, and oil. He swallowed the mixture three times a day. Like a trick of the light, color flooded his skin. His breathing became more regular. Marie watched his morning tiredness fade. Preening in the mirror, John saw her. He wasn't pleased.

John preferred his women more full-blown. Marie's reflection was still too angular. Last night he'd loved the mother, not the naive child. He ran his fingers over his face, turned, and smiled pleasantly. "Good morning, ma petite."

"I'm a woman now."

"Ah, yes, I forgot. When you're as old as I am, everyone seems young." Striding lightly, he came toward her.

Marie wanted to throw her arms about him.

He touched her stomach but without desire. "You did well last night. And next time you'll do even better. Damballah's ride will be longer. He'll infuse you with new powers."

Marie slipped her hand down toward John's crotch. He gently lifted it away. "I have to go out."

"Where?"

"Does it matter?"

"Brigette's?"

"Jealous?" Putting both legs into his pants, he pulled them up. He splashed water over his face and underneath his arms. "If you want influence, you court it. It's one of the requisites of our profession."

"Profession?" she murmured.

John hesitated. He'd have to remember the child believed in magic. She hadn't yet learned Voodoo was a business. Profit. Manipulation. Power. Her Grandmère had never understood this either. The daughter Marie had understood: that's why they'd made the best of allies. Lovers.

Drying himself, his eyes carefully hooded, John said, "I'll be gone all day. Nattie will teach you your lessons."

"I don't want Nattie."

"You'll do as I say," John said harshly. With her legs stretched into a V and with her hair fanning across the pillow, Marie reminded him more of her Maman.

John could curse the history, the *fa,* which brought him here. Why did he have to rely on a silly child to achieve power? His due wealth? There wasn't much time. Funds were scarce to rent this house, to dress and eat.

He massaged his brow. Forever, he'd been chasing dreams. John had thought he'd won when he met an aging Voodoo Queen and her lovely daughter. He never dreamed the daughter, Marie, would get herself killed.

For twelve years he'd been waiting for this Marie—selling medicines and spells throughout the South but always coming back to New Orleans. Sweet, expensive New Orleans. He'd sent spies to Teché to monitor his future. The reports had always been the same: "The girl is growing. The old woman doesn't suspect we're watching."

It had been degrading, selling penny powders to illiterate slaves. Only his dreams kept him alive. Now his future was bright again, but it all depended upon this . . . *girl.* John scowled. He couldn't quite forgive Damballah for favoring women with His powers.

He stared at Marie. With long coltish legs, she was sweet bait. She had no false modesty in bed. Or maybe that was the mother's influence? Maybe not. Marie was appealingly earnest. He didn't want to love her. He didn't want to make the same mistake he made with her Maman. He threw the sheet at her.

"Next time, cover yourself. I don't want Ribaud to get ideas. I don't share what is mine." Then, to make peace and mitigate his harshness, he allowed Marie to kiss him.

Marie could feel John growing aroused. She couldn't fathom why he held part of himself separate. Or why he didn't seem to want her as much as she wanted him. In her, John awakened intense sensual needs—taste, touch, smell. The sight of him stirred her.

Her hands caressing his back, Marie pulled him down on top of her body. She rubbed her hips against his. Loving was surrendering, wasn't it?

Marie practiced exploring his mouth with her tongue.

Wasn't a woman supposed to give all of herself? Be a vessel for a man's seed just as the Virgin was for the Holy Spirit? Just as she was a vessel for Damballah. And if she surrendered, gave up all the parts of herself, what about him? When a man was well loved, did he return the loving equally well?

A knock sounded.

John pulled out of her arms and quickly slid on his shirt. "Yes. Come in."

Surveying the disheveled room and a disheveled John, Nattie's face was a mask. "Brigette wants you."

"I know. I'll be leaving in a few moments."

Exposed, Marie lay, stomach down on the bed, her hand dangling off the edge.

"Be a good girl, Marie." John pinched her nipples. Nattie and Marie both winced. John turned, pausing in the doorway. The room smelled of herbs, semen, a woman's heat and tension. He knew Nattie was furious with him. He smiled.

"Nattie, take care of the little one for me. See she learns her lessons well." He chuckled low. "Maybe she'll become as skilled as her Maman. Or maybe as skilled as you," he said more softly to Nattie.

"You no-good whore of a man," the dark woman cursed. "Fall in a plot of dung. Fall backward down a flight of stairs. Thief of hearts." John whooped triumphant and shut the door. "Damn the man." Nattie rested her hands on her ballooning hips. "No more sense than a rutting hog. May his cock drop off from too much use."

"Shut up," Marie shouted. "You're making it ugly."

"You be Miz Innocent?" Nattie hastened toward her. "Your Grandmère be shocked to see you so. Naked and with no shame."

"Shut up." Marie covered her ears.

"Did you have to give him everything? You don't give your flower away to any man who asks. You hold something back. Couldn't you hold something back? Any little bit of something?"

"No."

Nattie slapped her hips and sighed. Back slouching, lips pressed, she lowered herself down onto the bed. "No one ever holds John," she said dully. "He's one bee who doesn't like honey. He sucks, tastes a little here, a little there. But he never be satisfied. Never ready to stay for a good long while."

Nattie's face was arresting. Strangely, sadness made her almost beautiful.

Marie had a curious thought: Nattie was in love with John. But that was stupid. Everybody knew Shad, the fisherman, was Nattie's beau. Besides, Nattie was as old as Grandmère.

"So many others have tried to hold him." Nattie kneaded her arms. "Black skin, white skin. It don't matter. So many still hope. Simple foolishness. No one held John. Not even your Maman."

Maman? Last night, Maman had held John—John had held Maman. They had used her body to love each other. Maman was spirit! Marie's mind balked. If she was spirit, then Maman was dead.

"Maman," Marie cried out. Now she'd never know if she looked like her Maman, never know who she was. Did she even want to know? Maman's spirit had been cruel, ruthless, and hadn't spared a thought for her daughter. Would Maman alive have been any different?

"Maman is dead."

"Of course," said Nattie. "Can't have mother and daughter

rutting for the same man. Be disaster. Sharing the same cock. Your Maman would've killed you."

A scream was tearing up from her gut. Marie tripped forward. Nattie lunged to save her, but Marie's temple hit the bedpost. Nattie staggered from the unbalanced weight. Both Nattie and Marie fell to the floor.

"Marie," Nattie moaned.

Marie was losing consciousness, falling into chaos. Maman had never loved her. She wasn't worthy of being loved. No wonder John disdained her. How ugly and vile she was! Hadn't she spent the night trying to prove that she could use her own body better than the spirit possessing her? No matter that Maman was dead. She was jealous that in John's arms, Maman could feel through her his lips, his chest, his arms. Worse, John loved her Maman more than he loved her.

If Maman was alive, would she like her?

She'd hate her.

Marie's guilt was torturous. When John's cock had slid inside her, it had made her feel new again. Virginal. His sex had stirred her like a drug. But it was wrong of Maman to share her sensations. The dead should stay dead. It was wrong, a mother loving through her daughter. And given the choice, Marie knew she would do anything to betray Maman and keep John's love. She was just as selfish and perverse. Like mother, like daughter. She tumbled further into sleep.

She could hear Nattie calling her, demanding that she wake, but Marie refused. She deserved punishment. She deserved to stumble into nightmare dreams.

In her dreams, she saw herself nine years old, traveling an endless corridor lined with doors. Behind each door, there were monsters—creatures who fed on frailty, gigantic insects eager to suck the blood from her veins, and plants that could cause her bones to break. Maman appeared, floating along the ceiling, carrying a potion that could make the doors and monsters disappear. The nine-year-old Marie was crying. Maman stared at her blankly, then briefly laughed before abandoning her and disappearing with the precious vial.

* * *

The next ceremony, nothing happened. No visions. No rainbows. Marie resisted any possession, afraid that Maman would use her to get to John.

John was frustrated. "Try," he urged.

"She needs more time," said Nattie.

"There isn't any." His jaw rigid, John concentrated on controlling his emotions. "She'll ruin what I started."

Feeling lost, Marie cried alone in her sleep. Self-hatred swallowed her up.

Awake, Marie fixated on the idea that Grandmère had always known Maman was dead. And if Grandmère had known, why had she allowed her to go on searching? Marie would've been spared rejection by her mother. But maybe that was the point. As long as she was searching, she could believe the lie that Maman had loved her and that she was worthy of being loved. Having found Maman she'd come face-to-face with her own pitiful self, her own reflection in a ghost. There was very little difference between her and Maman. "Two women rutting for the same man." They both deserved rejection. But she was worse, even more hateful than her mother; she'd abandoned Jacques and Grandmère for a dream, when everything about herself was a nightmare.

There wasn't any real Marie Laveau.

~

I can't find her. I can't find the woman Antoine accosted in the Market Square. I swear I've asked every slave, every servant—even strangers upon the street. No one knows the colored woman I describe. A too-hot summer has become an unseasonably cool fall. Could it be almost a year since I met my brown girl in the spring?

My butler, Charles, says Voodoo can help me find a "lost one." It's nonsense, of course. Voodoo is a primitive religion. And yet I am tempted to try.

Through a peephole, I watched the house slaves perform a modest ritual. It was hardly intriguing: dancing to drums, a little bloodletting, drinking gallons of wine. I was unimpressed. The slaves appeared to be raucous children playacting at possession. Charles says they have "no leader, no Queen. So no important gods visit."

Perhaps it is my own narrow-mindedness that labels Voodoo primitive. (I'm suspicious of all religions. I believe they're all riddled with hypocrisy.) Yet are the trance states of a Voodooienne any different from a Shaker speaking in tongues? Isn't Voodoo dancing analogous to singing in a Protestant church?

Voodoo certainly sounds less complicated than Catholic ritual. I admit I've an especial prejudice against the papal faith. I find my wife's need to make confession astounding. I also find it interesting that she consults with a Voodoo Doctor named John. How she reconciles both religions, I can't imagine.

"Every Louisianan is Catholic," says Charles, "and every Catholic believes in Voodoo spells."

Writing a series of articles on Voodoo might prove interesting. Wasn't America founded for religious tolerance?

Charles tells me there are rumors of a Voodoo Queen. Someone

132

*powerful enough to call upon and be visited by Damballah—a snake god
of considerable wisdom, I am told.*

I believe in no other God besides rationalism.

I wonder—is it rational what I'm doing now?

*Is it rational to marry a Catholic whom I don't love, to live in a
southern city where the majority of the population is enslaved, and to
make excuses to speak with a Voodoo Queen in order to find another
woman I don't know but do love?*

My search is surely doomed to failure at the start.

•

—LOUIS DELAVIER, OCTOBER 1819, MIDNIGHT
(From Louis DeLavier's journal)

Anxious, Marie tried to keep still as Nattie hemmed her
skirt. Waiting was hard. It seemed she was always waiting. Waiting
for ceremonies to begin, waiting to disappoint John again.

Even now, as John, Nattie, and Ribaud scurried frantically to
prepare for the coming night, Marie knew it was useless. She would
hold herself apart, closed to possessions, and the ceremony would
have no climax. No miracle. Damballah would not come. But neither
would her Maman, and that was what she wanted.

John was mixing powders for good luck, good health, and a
good man or woman's love. Ribaud was slicing worms, burying them
inside bottles with sand.

Any second, Marie felt she'd giggle hysterically. It was raining.
Thunder rumbled. Lightning stabbed the sky. The sparse salon they
all occupied was ghostly, without warmth.

"This is your home," John had said. "Maison Blanche." The
white house on St. Anne, a short block from the French Quarter. Yet
Marie never felt at home. Her emotions ran too deep. She considered questions that were better left alone; she wondered if John
loved her.

The salon held a few random chairs, a table, and an altar.
During ceremonies, the salon became the meeting place, and the
dining room and hall doors were thrown open to accommodate the

crowds. The house was larger than the one in Haven. She had a small bedroom, all pinks and greens; John, another. Nattie slept on a cot in the kitchen, Ribaud on the floor.

She was a city girl now. But New Orleans had little appeal since she had discovered Maman's death. Her world was as small as ever. John and Nattie never encouraged her to go out. If she had wanted to go out, they probably would've forbidden it. She was almost a recluse. But the world never stopped coming to her. People requested favors and prayers. They left money and gifts.

Tonight everyone would come. John would proclaim her wondrous powers, proclaim her the hope of the Voodoo cult. And the crowd would be disappointed.

"Stop fidgeting," said Nattie, snapping, tugging at the yellow material.

"I'm sorry."

Disapproving, John looked up. He was mixing his own special potion: seaweed, black powder, and oil. He refused to tell Marie, or anyone, what it was or what it cured.

"I'll try to be good," Marie stammered.

"Do that," said John. Marie winced. John was always moody, irritable, and tired before his *gris-gris* drink. But lately he'd been worse. Last night he paced, cursing, between sips, the gods who didn't come. He stopped short of damning both her and Damballah.

"Nattie, I'm scared," Marie whispered. "What if nothing happens?"

She wanted to confess to someone—a woman—why she kept Maman's spirit at bay and how she didn't know any way to ward off Maman without also excluding Damballah.

"Something will happen. Sooner or later, it always does."

"What if we've made a mistake. What if I'm the wrong one?" Furtively, Marie glanced at John. The grainy mixture slid down his throat.

"If you don't have faith, the gods won't come." Flashing scissors, scooting about the hem, Nattie grumbled, "The first time you be lucky. Damballah rode you gently. But next time he may make you shed your clothes, stuff yourself with dirt, and coil your body

134

about a post. Ass-up, he may inch you out into the streets. Make you hang from a tree as a warning to disbelievers."

"Stop it, Nattie."

"But if the Guédé, the death gods, mount you, they'll ride you till your spine arches like a cat . . . till your heart threatens to burst." Scissors sliced the air. "Till you twist, shout, and sway with the power."

Shuddering, Marie imagined dancing like a marionette.

"The Guédé make life seem death, make hell and glory one, and the poor Marie in you will be forever lost. In her day, your Grandmère be the Queen with the greatest power," said Nattie, her voice tinged with a vague lust.

Marie couldn't reconcile the Catholic Grandmère with a blasphemous Voodooienne.

"You should be more like her," Nattie snapped. "Not a nervous, twittering soul."

Why hadn't Grandmère told her this history, *her* history, about the blending of religions as well as of blood?

"Grandmère's visions lasted from dusk to dawn. The gods loved entering her. People from all around came to see. They saw her walk on water. Saw her touch the clouds.

"After your Maman died, your Grandmère deserted Damballah and started to sing. People came for that too." Nattie frowned. "Sinful. Came to hear her magic misplaced. She won't thank me for letting you know it, but your Grandmère," Nattie said slyly, "gave John his start." Ribaud squealed. "Without your Grandmère, John wouldn't know the little he knows."

Ribaud squealed again and received a sharp blow to his head.

"Get out," John shouted. "Take your stinking self off. Have the candles been carved? Get out," he yelled again. "Finish tonight's preparations."

From the doorway, the spell man glared at John's back.

Nattie laughed. "Ribaud be too slow to escape that one." Nattie smiled too sweetly at John.

There were undercurrents among the three: strong, violent emotions which unsettled Marie. Exiting, Ribaud rubbed his melon-shaped skull.

"What did Grandmère teach you?" Marie murmured to John. She wasn't certain he had heard her. His jaw slack, John seemed to stare through her. She shifted from foot to foot.

"Come here, Marie," he said, moderating his tone. "No, I won't shout at you." His scars narrowed as he smiled. "You, unlike Nattie, don't disappoint me with silly gossiping."

"Humpf," exclaimed Nattie.

Marie felt a bit of revulsion. Besides licorice-flavored herbs, she smelled acrid rum on John's breath.

John lifted Marie onto his lap. "You see, Nattie's a crow. Picking up bits of tales like rice."

"I be the prettiest crow you know, then," said Nattie, sashaying her hips.

John roared. Tentatively, Marie touched his chest. Everything about him was outsized. No matter what he wore, how he acted or spoke, there was a magnetic grandeur which made Marie accept his authority. When he was sweet and charming, he was irresistible. Irresistible because she couldn't imagine why someone so grand would care about her.

"Now, ma petite"—John kissed her fingertips—"I don't make mistakes. You are not a mistake." His tongue stroked her palm. "What your Grandmère was or wasn't has nothing to do with you. If she cared at all, she'd be here. If Nattie cared, she'd stop frightening you. But Nattie's a jealous old crow."

Marie buried her face in his hair, tight coils cushioning like down.

"Trust me," he said soothingly. "The *loas* will come tonight. You and the serpent will exchange souls. Don't believe Nattie. Nothing you do when you're possessed is shameful."

"Has the serpent ever been in you?" Marie blurted. John's jaw tightened; his hands about her squeezed. Marie refused to cry out.

"Tell her," prodded Nattie.

"No," he said. "The serpent's never been in me." Scathingly, he added, "But Damballah's never been in you either, has He, dearest Nattie?"

Nattie stabbed the yellow remnants with her broom.

"How old are you?" John lifted her chin. Marie squirmed,

conscious of the warmth of his hand, of his legs beneath her bottom, and of Nattie, pausing between sweeps of the broom to listen.

"Sixteen."

"Same age as your mother when Damballah took possession. She was beautiful then." John retreated into himself, his breathing becoming shallow, his eyes lowering to his chest. Marie felt a stirring of jealousy. She brushed his cravat. "There was nothing your Maman would rather have been, do you understand me? Nothing other than a Voodoo priestess."

"Yes." She understood. Only John could explain her history, teach her all she needed to know. She'd become a Voodooienne because it was what John had loved best about her Maman. Yet how could she explain her jealousy of Maman—that she didn't want to be possessed for fear Maman would be inside her reaching toward John? Her memory of Damballah's ride was peace, freedom. But Maman made her feel unloved and vile.

"John thinks he knows all about Voodoo," sneered Nattie. "Grandmère could teach you better, Marie, ten times better."

In one fluid motion, John lifted Marie from his lap, rose, and cracked Nattie's broomstick. "I'll snatch the tongue from your head. Learn to keep silent, Nattie."

"I be silent enough already."

Marie thought the big-hipped woman was obscene, flirting, touching John beneath his waist.

"I keep your secrets well enough."

John twisted Nattie's arm, straining her elbow and shoulder sockets. Because she didn't beg for release, he seemed disappointed.

"Hurt me too much and I'll tell everything. Don't forget I know more than you want Miz Marie to know."

Abruptly, John shoved her away. Following Ribaud's trail, he stormed out the front door.

Marie chased him to the door, stared at it, then spun around, demanding, "Why do you provoke him?"

Nattie shrugged. "Sometimes he be too full of himself."

"You know Grandmère won't teach me anything."

"I also know without you, John be nothing." Gingerly, she rubbed her arm. "Why you so upset? He's just gone for a walk.

Gone to clear his foolish head." Taunting, she added, "You never acted so with husband Jacques. Never begged him to stay."

Primly, Marie shut her lips. Nattie gripped her arms. "Visions come to special women. The power be passed down through the generations. You were the one born with a caul, not him. The best he can do is a little magic." Nattie spat the word. "A bit of healing. It be him that needs you."

Marie jerked away and flung open the window. Rain and rivulets of mud careened down cobblestones.

"You should listen to me."

Nattie was cruel. Mean-spirited.

"You know what happened when your Grandmère didn't."

Marie looked both ways, up and down the street.

Nattie crept behind her. "Don't worry about John. If I know him—and I do—he's gone to be comforted. I hope he drowns," she said bitterly, "in his blond sweetheart's arms." Nattie spit into the corner. "Brigette DeLavier."

Marie settled down to watch the rain, waiting for John to return.

All her ceremonies failed.

John ranted. He broke chairs and wrecked dishes. Shadows creased his eyes. He drank too much rum.

Marie wondered why John never touched her again as a lover—why she'd so easily transferred her desire to please from Grandmère to him. She felt sorrow and guilt for failing him. The nights John didn't return home, she imagined him loving Brigette.

Days lengthened into weeks.

Marie's identity was linked to John. But so far he hadn't brought revelation or comfort. Was this her *fa?* Could she have chosen *not* to abandon Grandmère—Grandmère who used to rock her on her lap, tuck her into bed, and whisper "love you."

When Maman called, trying to possess her, Marie shunned her.

Sometimes Marie thought she should give in, allow Damballah—and her Maman—to enter her. She wanted so much to please John, to make him proud of her. But it was enough that she had to compete with Brigette DeLavier. She didn't want to compete with a ghost. John's love was hard enough to hold.

She began to feel that the very walls of the house were waiting, waiting for her to do something wondrous, to win John's love, to be the Great Voodoo Queen.

But she didn't know how.

She was still waiting to find out who she was. First, she'd waited for Grandmère to tell her, then she'd hoped Maman would tell her. Now John seemed her last hope—and he never told her anything.

John was thinking he should've been born a woman. He was fashioning a *gris-gris,* a rag doll with snake etchings and stringy hair. A follower wanted to destroy her rival in love. The charm would kill sleep, kill appetite and thirst. In two weeks, the person charmed would die.

Another ceremony would begin in an hour.

"I hope it goes well tonight," said Nattie, sauntering toward him.

"It had better. The first time she was perfect. The crowd believed she was a serpent. But since then nothing—limp as a doll."

"Gods have their own time, you know," Nattie said, flattening her hips onto a chair. "It prevents arrogance. Prevents us from feeling too secure."

"Don't tell me about the gods, Nattie. I'm sick of women who know all the answers."

John thought of Grandmère's curse. Fierce, like a snake-haired witch, Grandmère had vowed to sway both God and Damballah to destroy him. When no one was watching, he made keep-away charms of bark, kelp, grave dust, and purified water for protection. Grandmère was a formidable rival. But she was old now, and he didn't doubt he could kill her if he wanted. But he needed her alive in case he had to use her against Marie.

"Are you sick of women who don't know all the answers?" Nattie gestured with her head.

John stared across the room. His heart raced. Marie, with her hands clasped in her lap, was sitting in a corner on her stoop. She was as frightened as a prairie bird. If he'd been a woman, it would be him waiting for Damballah's call.

"I could be ruined this evening," John said softly.

" 'Tis true. Disciples won't give you another chance."

John recalled snide laughter, recalled how the crowds perversely grew larger each week. They came to see his failure: his Marie, the Voodoo Queen. If he'd been a woman, he wouldn't have failed. He would've assumed power. Expertly. Willingly.

John lowered his head to his chest. He was helpless. He didn't like feeling so exposed.

To Nattie, John seemed mournful yet as vibrant as when she'd first met him. She recalled the first time he'd come to dinner. He'd been too thin, underfed, but handsome. His clothes had been threadbare.

Before the evening ended, Marie had been dancing between the furniture with love and exuberant foolishness. "Her John," she'd said a thousand times that evening. Everyone had to meet "her John." Wasn't "her John" attractive? Charming? Marie raved that "her John" was an African prince. Marie was in love.

Yet to Nattie, John had never seemed in love with Marie. His eyes roamed too often over their comfortable cottage, over the decent good-quality clothing they all wore. She'd thought he was impressed by three black women doing so well. Impressed that they sold services other than their bodies.

Those had been the days! The Haben's Haven cottage had been in good repair and overflowed with gifts from folks Grandmère had cured and counseled with her Voodoo prayers. There'd been live and stewed chickens, smoked pork, crayfish, well-crafted tables and chairs, celebration quilts, and sacks of flour and rice.

When Nattie had met John, her instinct had been to be reserved. She distrusted men. Always had. But John had, even for her, a seductive power. She recalled John tasting her Haitian black beans and rice that night and proclaiming them wonderful. Like an idiot, she'd smiled. Even scuffed up and poor, he'd been powerful; she would've given anything for some of that power to be hers.

Nattie wasn't certain about John's age (perhaps he'd been thirty when they'd met twenty years ago); she was only certain that

John had aged better than she had. Her skin had sagged and spread. Wrinkles dominated her eyes and mouth. Her hair had streaked gray. She knew to John she seemed as old as Grandmère. She was only forty-eight.

Surely John was as old as she was? Yet he looked like a boy.

Tonight, touched by John's sadness, Nattie was as sweet and as yielding as a mother. John, she thought ruefully, never thought of her in any other way. Oh, he'd had sex with her. The same way a rutting hog looked for an outlet, a hole for its mindless passion. John had never showed her any tenderness. But held infrequently, Nattie had learned to cherish what she could get.

And what Nattie received was the leavings. When John had fought with Marie's Maman, spite brought him into her arms. Sometimes Nattie liked to fool herself and daydream about what would've happened if he'd remained angry at Marie. They would've been partners, lovers forever. Ruthless, Nattie reminded herself that John preferred white women or women named Marie. His loving her had been merely revenge.

Nattie shrugged. No sense crying over spilt milk or over hurts that inexplicably haunted her even after twenty years. When John had come to her and asked her help to seduce the grandchild Marie away from Grandmère, she'd felt a rekindling of sexual longing so wide and deep she couldn't have filled it with tears if she cried for a hundred years. One day, though, she'd claim vengeance against John. For after twenty years John had taken her assent for granted. He hadn't even bothered to make love to her.

"Where will you go tonight if Marie fails?" Nattie murmured.

"North."

"Are there fools enough up north?"

John grinned. "You always were a contrary woman. Sassy. Much too smart for your own good. I always liked you, Nattie." His eyes glazed. He took a shuddering breath, then his shoulders rounded and drooped. "I can begin again up north. Fix potions and roots. Charms. Shape Voodoo dolls so frustrated lovers will pound at my door. Half of this"—John pointed at the altar, the caged animals; he shook the limp doll in his hand—"is make-believe."

"So you've said often enough."

"The weak need something to believe in. I provide symbols."

"How do you account then for the other half? Marie's no trick."

Expressionless, John looked across the room. Marie was folding accordion pleats in her skirt. Child's play, he thought. Everything he longed for depended upon her.

"I be jealous too."

John glanced quickly at Nattie.

She smiled ruefully. "And unlike you, I be a true believer. Sometimes I wonder why Damballah chose her. Except for her history, her family blood, she has so little to recommend. Damballah be most mysterious. How can He see any greatness in her?"

"Yet you see it in yourself?"

"Yes. Just as you do."

John scowled. Nattie promoted Voodoo at all costs while he promoted himself. Nattie was a fool.

"You'd whore for the chance to have Damballah inside you," he said scornfully.

"Is what you do any different?"

John plunged a needle into the rag. "I wish her mother was here."

"Whose fault be it that she isn't?"

"Damn you. You helped."

"So I did." Nattie closed her eyes. She regretted a great deal in her life, but nothing so much as helping the second Marie to her death. She and John had goaded Marie into performing Voodoo in Cathedral Square. With someone as impulsive, as reckless as Marie had been, it'd been simple. They'd made certain Grandmère knew nothing about the ceremony. Grandmère would've refused, saying it was too dangerous. It didn't help that John had miscalculated how threatened white folks would feel. Poor Marie had died because a pious Christian mob scared of hellfire had whipped her to death. They'd stopped her in the middle of her dance, in the middle of the cry "Damballah." Nattie still remembered the look of surprise on Marie's face. She'd been young enough to believe Voodoo Queens were invincible and immortal. She hadn't realized the difference between literal and spiritual truths.

"Yes, I helped." Nattie sighed. She could still hear Marie's screams as they lashed her to a tree. "Did you ever wonder why?"

John rubbed his hand through his hair. He was sick of women, sick of their tired charms and conniving. Sick of wide-eyed innocence. "It was a risk worth taking," he said, defensive.

"What a fool I was to have believed you. Believed *in* you."

"But if it had worked, Nattie—"

"Hush. Do you want the child to hear?"

John glanced across the room, then spoke insistently. "If Marie had completed her ceremony, think how powerful we would've been. Think how powerful Voodoo would've become. No more hiding in corners. No more shame for our beliefs."

"Our beliefs?" she asked sarcastically.

"We'd have churches like any Catholic. Freedom and money to practice our faith. Marie took the risk willingly," John said stubbornly.

"Because she loved you too much. Because you badgered her into it."

"That's a lie. Marie wanted power as much as I did. It was Grandmère who lacked imagination. I could see the future better than she ever could. She and her daughter could've exploited the wealth of this city. They needed whites—influential whites—to believe in them, not just slaves. So I miscalculated. But I'm convinced there's truth in my dreams."

"But you knew Grandmère be more interested in faith than money, didn't you?"

"Even a faith healer is entitled to money."

"Marie and Grandmère had all they needed. They ate. They slept in clean beds. You were greedier. Grasping and greedy."

"Weren't you?" John gripped her arm.

"But not for what, John," Nattie whispered scornfully. "For *who*. I was greedy for who?" She snatched her arm from his grasp. "Don't tell me you don't know."

John cloaked his eyes. Nattie watched him thinking. He caressed her thigh. "Nattie, I—"

She slapped his hand away. "Don't tell me lies, John. I only be interested in the faith now. I want to restore the faith. If I could've convinced Grandmère to practice Voodoo again, I never would've betrayed her to you. It be foolishness to give you a chance to hurt me again.

"I want our people to have a Voodoo Queen again, John. Pretty soon we'll all forget Africa."

"What do you know of Africa?"

"More than you claim to know. I be more African in spirit than you be in your bones," Nattie said defiantly.

John slouched in his chair. He hated women. He dropped the *gris-gris* doll and lifted a bottle of rum to his mouth. He drank deeply. Lowering his bottle, he stared at Marie. He would tear her guts out if it meant being free of her.

"She's still Damballah's chosen," Nattie said coolly. "Don't mistreat her, John. I won't help again. There won't be two deaths on my conscience."

Shifting uncomfortably, John felt sorry for himself.

"Marie loves you."

Only one woman had ever understood him, and she was dead.

Marie was thinking she should've been born a man. Maman had birthed the wrong sex. Or was Grandmère to blame? If she'd been properly raised to her faith, would she be so terrified now?

John, with his confidence, ought to be the one awaiting Damballah's call.

Marie didn't understand her new faith at all. Why would Damballah want to visit a reluctant priestess? What was so special about her? She'd been taught women weren't special. Christ and God were special. The Virgin was special because she gave birth to Christ. But could God, the Father, exist if a woman hadn't birthed Him too?

And yet Marie felt the unfairness of life. The unfairness of viewing women as less than men. Women could be powerful. She remembered Grandmère claiming she'd killed a man.

Marie had never felt powerful, except when Damballah had filled her. Damballah honored women as creators. "Damballah, the giver of life." Marie imagined birthing a baby would be painful, thick with blood. She'd seen how snakes rubbed their noses against a rock and squirmed out of their hard, dead skin. How easy it would be if, like a snake, she could birth herself anew instead of birthing a newborn child. Grandmère had said, "Blood ties bind." She'd birthed Maman just as Maman had birthed her. Daughter to mother. Two Maries. Like a snake, she'd been uncovering another layer of her own skin. Maybe that was the secret. Damballah favored women because they could do what men couldn't. They birthed themselves—woman to woman—in a chain as old as creation. The line went backward and forward to Eve. The snake itself was a never-ending circle.

Marie closed her eyes. She might be Damballah's priestess, but it was John, not Damballah, who was the center of her world. It was John who was visible each day, John who had the power to join with her, bringing ecstasy and a different sort of peace.

Marie glanced across the room. Fat and sassy, Nattie was stirring trouble. John's expression was angry and bleak. Marie wished she could hold and comfort him.

John and Nattie had their heads together. What were they whispering? John pulled back and drank. Nattie stood and slithered toward the altar.

Was Nattie jealous because Damballah had come to her? Or because John did? Marie only knew, as a child, she never could've loved Nattie.

She saw John take a deep breath and rise. He was coming toward her. She tried to hide her nervousness.

"Are you ready, ma petite?"

Marie wanted to soothe the scars on his face. She didn't dare. "I think so."

"You should know so," John said, restraining his irritation, maintaining a patronizing calm. "You are Marie Laveau. Your mother's daughter. The gods have selected you."

She plucked at her skirt. To encourage the gods, to please John, Marie had purified herself. For a week she'd bathed in chalky milk and eaten nothing but rice. Damballah liked white foods. John had insisted on celibacy, and she'd repressed her disappointment.

She also repressed her suspicion that he really didn't want to touch her without also touching her Maman.

Why couldn't she admit to John that each time she'd felt Damballah's possession beginning, she'd resisted? She was afraid she'd die like a firefly, burning out of control in Damballah's possession or, worse, in Maman's. She wanted to find a measure of control in loving and in being loved by John for herself alone. Not for spirits who could control her body and share her soul. If Maman took hold of her again, she thought she'd go mad.

John stooped before her, cupping her knees. He wanted to ask Marie to pretend, to make believe Damballah possessed her tonight. He rested his head on her lap. She wouldn't understand.

Marie massaged his neck.

John felt old. Marie's mother would have laughed at his pain; she'd preferred him less assured. But then the mother wasn't so naive. His gut tightened, and a cool sweat broke out along his back. He'd worked hard to build his reputation, and in two months Marie had nearly destroyed it. Tonight was his last chance to salvage his Voodoo business and his dreams for power. He tried a different tack. "Do you care for me?"

"Oh, yes."

John cringed. Marie's innocence was so disarming.

"Your Maman had a premonition of her death."

Marie inhaled. "How did she die?"

John held her hand. "Your Maman was reckless. She wanted to be the best, the most renowned Voodoo Queen. She convinced herself a ceremony in Cathedral Square would bring her glory. I warned her. Nattie too. She wouldn't be guided by us. Your Grandmère encouraged her. So . . ." His voice trailed off. "Your Maman always tried to please Grandmère."

"I think I've seen Maman's death."

"That's impossible."

"When I was younger, I saw visions in the water. Was Maman tied to a tree and whipped?"

"Yes."

"By whom?"

"White men. Catholics. *Aristos.* At the last minute, your

Maman wanted to withdraw from her ceremony. But your Grandmère insisted she finish what she started."

"Yes, that sounds like Grandmère. Grandmère doesn't like tasks left undone." Marie couldn't quite believe Grandmère would've endangered her daughter. But perhaps that explained why Grandmère never talked about Maman. She felt guilty.

"I was knocked to the ground unconscious. I don't know precisely what happened to Marie. The crowd thought she was a devil. I only know I couldn't save her." John weighed the effect of his story. Marie seemed to be accepting it. There was a slight furrow between her brows, a gentle quivering of her lips, but otherwise a calm acceptance.

"Before the ceremony, your Maman told me to look after you. In case something went wrong, she said. She'd guessed your Grandmère might act unreasonably. I promised to look after you. A duty became my act of grace. But Grandmère spirited you away to Teché. I watched you grow at a distance, always in hiding. Remember, our paths crossed once. It was your birthday. You had just turned ten."

Marie blushed furiously. It didn't occur to her to question why a man would touch a child so intimately. She did remember her yielding response.

"It was a pleasure to watch you grow." John thrust for his kill. "Do you love me?"

Disoriented, Marie could only stare.

"I never left you. Even in the bayou, I watched you grow every step." John's hands slid beneath her skirt. Marie tensed, then her legs slightly parted. "Whether you knew it or not, I was always there." He stroked the inside of her thighs. "You must grow another step. My life depends on it." He hated his dependency. Hated Marie. "Sweet love, allow the gods to enter you."

"Nattie," she blurted, "says Damballah decides when to enter, not me."

Marie was being stubborn. Perverse. John smiled charmingly. "Do you want me to fail?"

"No, I—" She was bewildered. How were her failures his?

"I've got a present for you." From his pocket, he pulled a miniature locket. "This is who you are."

The skin in the portrait was brown tinted with hints of gold. Dark hair framed a small face. Soft pink lips. Freckles bridged an upturned nose. Slanted eyes, luminous and hardened. The eyes knew everything. With a flicker, they judged her; they served as a warning.

"Your Maman posed for this shortly before her death."

Marie didn't want to look at it.

"I can make you just as she was. And I can make you greater. In five years, I promise you, everyone will know who you are. But you must"—he wrapped Marie's fingers about the locket—"you must allow Damballah's possession."

John was a magician. He could transform her into something she wasn't certain she was meant to be, or wanted. "Who are you?" she asked.

"Who do you want me to be?"

She drew back.

"Aw, ma petite." His arms caught her by the waist.

Across the room, near the altar, Nattie eyed them like a starving crow.

"I should've been a king. I should've ruled hundreds, thousands. My father lost a tribal war." His face sagged. "I was taken prisoner. Sold to white men. At eight, I was shipped to the Indies."

"You bought yourself free?"

"No, I fought. I waited until I was old enough to kill with my hands."

Marie saw John as a dark, avenging demon.

"I have loved you," he said.

She recalled their one night of love, as well as all the other days and nights when he'd ignored her, treated her like a child.

John had a marvelous capacity for believing his own lies. Staring at Marie's sweet face, he repeated, "I have loved you."

"Oh, John," she murmured. He dotted her face with kisses. Marie loved him better than Maman. They held each other. There seemed to be no one else in the room. No one else inside her body.

"Succeed tonight and we'll make plans."

"Damballah scares me," she lied.

"Just you and I. Succeed, and I'll love you better than anyone else."

"It's not me," she whispered. "None of it is me." How could she explain to John that Maman was not her?

"Fail, and you'll ruin my hopes."

"It's not fair."

"Nothing is fair," John said harshly. "I shouldn't be here. The world isn't just. I should be ruling a kingdom, not living in a country where my skin color makes me less of a man. Help me reclaim my rights. Myself."

Marie imagined John, the young boy, suffering. Would he have needed her then? Did he truly need her now? She was being stubborn. Perverse.

"You owe me," he said.

Did she? she paused, thoughtful. "We could be happy in Teché."

"Rocking on a porch? Watching the moon vary shapes?" John shook his head. "I can't live that way. Neither can you. You have a unique gift. I can show you how to use it. How to build us a future."

Her head ached.

"Succeed tonight, and I'll look after you very well." He curled his fingers in her hair. "Do you understand me?"

Marie understood. To have John, she had to give up herself, give up the little she knew. Ashamed, Marie lowered her eyes. Why should John's need be more important than her self? Yet the one time he had made love to her, there had been a frightening and exhilarating rush of passion. She had a recognition of herself as a woman. She could be touched in places that caused her to cry out with great joy. Marie felt disgusted with herself. Was this it, then? She'd do what he wanted to feel his touch? He had hurt her too. How did she even know that what she'd felt had been her feelings, her pleasure, and not Maman's? She shuddered.

Every fiber in her body said, Hold me. John did. His hands explored the creases between her trunk and thighs. She'd do what he wanted. She'd lose herself to Damballah. But not to Maman, never again. Not if she could help it.

Later, John went to the window and whistled. His shrills were repeated by a boy in the alleyway; then the staccato notes were echoed by a slave in his master's garden, by a coach driver, by a kitchen girl—until all the coloreds in New Orleans knew a Voodoo ceremony was about to begin.

Smiling, John turned from the window. He felt new hope, self-assurance. Ribaud congratulated him by tapping once on the drums. Nattie drank a cup of rum in silent salute.

Marie steadied herself. For love she could manage anything.

~

"On some level, my quest never was about finding Maman; rather, it was about finding love, hope, warmth.

"When I realized I resented Maman, when I realized I hated her and she hated me, I lost the small confidence I'd had. I became a child again and John the punishing father. When he comforted me, I was his willing slave. And when he hurt me, I accepted it as proof that I deserved to be hurt. It made a crazy sense for him to punish the child whom the mother had rejected.

"Strangely, too, in John's bed I learned to be a woman. I was filled with irrational passion. It felt dangerous. Good."

"Weren't you ever in love, Marie?"

"What is love?"

"Conquering selfishness. Wanting the best for someone simply because it's good for them."

"No. Never in love. John was a distraction from the hard work of finding myself."

"Was . . . is Voodoo evil?"

"When I was younger and didn't know any better, I would've answered yes. But Voodoo reflects what is. Maman was evil . . . so it presented her as she truly was. Voodoo had never demanded Maman's death. But it was Voodoo, steeped in ancestor worship, that gave Maman back to me in all her ugliness, with all her spite."

"What of John, Marie? He was Voodoo."

"A religion can't account for its charlatans. I was a charlatan."

"Always?"

"I grow tired, Louis. I doubt if I'll survive the night."

152

"Were you always a charlatan?"
"No. At times, I had the greatest gift. I was a woman with power."

•

—MARIE LAVEAU, JUNE 15, 1881, THE DAY BEFORE HER DEATH
(From Louis DeLavier's journal)

Τ he ceremony had finally begun.

The audience strutted in and around Marie. Skeptical, they scowled. Darting close to her ear, they called her "whore," "false seer," and "defiler."

The women wanted to know what wiles Marie had used to misguide and entrap John. The men were more explicit. What positions had convinced John she was a prophet? She stared at the charcoal painting of Damballah. The followers already had forgotten the one time she had inched and curved like a snake. Silently, she begged Damballah to come.

John moved through the crowd, murmuring "Patience." He cajoled the young men; with the women, he flirted. Ribaud seduced the followers with the sound of his drums. Nattie poured more rum.

With each breath, Marie concentrated on exhaling thoughts and feelings. Damballah would fill her up.

Dancers swayed in slow motion. They called Legba. Candles flickered. A pregnant woman quaked and shouted.

Ogu, the warrior god, erupted. Nattie torched a bowl of rum. The possessed man dipped his hands in the fire; his skin was unscathed. He tied a sash about his head and swung a saber, frightening the others. He cursed and stomped. He drank a jug of rum.

"Ogu drinks, he drinks but he is never drunk." Grabbing a woman's crotch, Ogu kissed her. The crowd chanted:

> *"Ogu drinks, he doesn't eat.*
> *He pays money*
> *To sleep with pretty girls.*
> *Yesterday evening, his girl*
> *   went to bed without supper.*

•

Ogu fights, he doesn't eat.
He bought a dress
To give to his girl.
Yesterday evening, Ogu
*   went to bed without supper."*

The man nicked his skin with the saber. He sucked his blood.

Spirits came and went, whirling about John. If he believed in the gods, he'd say they blessed him tonight. But to John, possession was playacting—dull people performing acts they dreamed about. Loss of memory was convenient. Marie, her Maman, and Grand-mère were the only ones who'd disturbed his disbelief. He did believe he'd made love to a dead spirit. He remembered too well smelling, tasting, and touching her—Marie's Maman.

Marie appeared dead. John flashed his hands over her face once, then twice. Her eyes never blinked.

Marie felt as though there were a war inside her—her heart ready to yield to possession, her mind fearful of the loss of control. To satisfy Damballah, she had to yield completely. Have faith that He would never hurt her. Yet on the edge of consciousness, she could feel Maman's presence. Maman wanting to be her, be inside her, live again through her. She could feel all the frustrated anger of a woman who died too soon. Maman wanted to hurt.

The Guédé, the death gods, arrived. There were three of them: Baron Samedi, Baron Cimetière, and Baron La Croix. The possessed, two men and a woman, flung on their costumes. All three chose a top hat, dark jacket, and glasses. The Guédé were violent and obscene.

Samedi, speaking in a nasal tone, told dirty jokes and made the women laugh. Cimetière demanded food. Nattie handed Cimetière a black rooster. Cimetière plucked the squawking creature, chewed it, then strode about the room, pressing the bloody carcass to his chest.

La Croix prostrated himself in front of the altar. Beating the ground, he moaned, "The world is unjust. I died too soon."

Inside her head, Marie could hear Maman echoing, "I died too soon. I died too soon."

154

La Croix slapped Cimetière, stole the bird, and threw it onto the dirt floor.

Maman was trying to get in. How painful it was. Enormous pressure was building inside her; Maman was battling, trying to scratch her way in.

"No." Marie kept repeating the word silently, "No. You will not come in. You will not destroy me. You will not live through me."

Marie could feel a soul crying.

She wanted to cry. How ironic that her quest would end with banishing Maman. Yet even in death, Maman's jealous desire for John was as strong as hers.

"I died too soon."

Marie's soul contracted. Maman was reasserting herself, pleading, begging to be let in.

"No." Marie ruthlessly rejected Maman as she had been rejected. *For Maman's desire to be substantial, physical again, was too strong. She'd possess Marie again and again until there was no life left for either of them. Their battleground would be John, and Marie would end up burning, being destroyed like a firefly.*

Their minds touched: two Maries. "I need to live my own life." *She could feel Maman's anger and, beneath the anger, a grudging admiration, an awareness that there should have been joy, not hate, between them.*

"Go."

Maman's soul fled.

The woman possessed by La Croix screamed and collapsed. The Guédé disappeared. A man, perspiring heavily, placed his head between his knees. A small girl moaned. The ceremony was ending. John panicked. Frustrated, he wanted to tear apart the altar. Marie, John thought, was still in an uneventful trance.

Nattie covered her face. John was right. Her religion was magic. Illusion.

Only Ribaud kept faith in pretty Marie. Patting his drums, he wooed both her and the serpent.

Damballah took center stage. Marie slid down from her chair.

John wanted to shout and sing. Nattie rushed forward. *Possessed by Damballah, Marie's nails threw up snatches of dirt.* Followers shied. *She dug a shallow pit and curled within it, her tongue darting between her teeth.*

John stroked her. "Damballah. Oh, my Damballah Queen."

"Yes," she exulted. Damballah was filling her up, augmenting, not suppressing, her identity. The relationship was symbiotic. Damballah was the wise one, making her feel powerful, sharing secrets of creation, encouraging her to shed old images of herself and believe it was right for a child to separate from her mother. Everything was a cycle. Time and earth and sky would heal. Everyone and everything would be reborn.

Followers arched their backs, imitating the grace of a snake. Nattie extended a bowl of milk. *Marie licked it clean.* "Maman Marie," followers chanted.

As if John were a tree, Marie curled about him. John lifted her up, believing her triumph was his. *Eyes closed, Marie was limp in his arms.* He held her close.

"Papa John. Maman Marie," followers chanted.

"Do you dare defy and mock me now?" John shouted to the crowd. "Those of you who don't believe, get out. Leave and I'll curse you to"—he kissed Marie's brow—"Damballah."

Marie opened her eyes. *"Do you believe?"*

Startled, he almost dropped her. John had heard two voices merging, blending in unison. There was Marie's soprano, then a huskier timber which made him think *Damballah.* But that was nonsense. None of this was real. Yet some part of him felt fear.

Marie wriggled down from his arms. Damballah was encouraging her to heal. Evading John's grasp, she tapped a young girl's shoulder. *"What is your name?"*

"Clotide."

"Your problem?"

The girl blushed and looked from side to side. "I'm in love."

"He doesn't love you," Marie murmured sorrowfully.

"How did you know?"

Marie brushed the girl's head. "I can feel the sadness in your heart." And she could *feel it. Damballah was showing her the sensitive glory of people's souls.*

"Give her a charm," whispered John. "Have her burn sugar with a lock of her lover's hair."

Marie placed her hand on the girl's chest. "Someone else is meant to love you. You need to keep your heart whole. Light candles to Damballah. A new lover is near."

"Maman Marie." The girl wiped tears on Marie's hem.

Marie could feel heartache subside. The young woman only wanted to believe that someone, one day, would appreciate all she had to give.

"Bless you, Marie."

Marie inclined her head; she paused before an arthritic man. "You dislike your master."

"He beats me." He showed the bruises on his chest. "I'm too old to be beaten."

"Poison. It is the only answer."

"Hush, John. There is a better way. Place your master's name in an empty coconut. Burn a black candle in one of the eyes. Never let the flame die out. In two days, he will begin to ache for every lash he's given you. Thereafter, he will cry even if he dreams of harming you."

"Bless you, Maman Marie. Bless you."

One by one, Marie listened to problems and gave advice. Her energy was unbounded.

John hovered, fuming that Marie had silenced him, fuming that the crowd had turned its attention from him to her. They were all fools, straining to hear the soft voice, nodding, affirming the wisdom of Marie. Even Nattie was slack-jawed, pushing herself forward, mesmerized. Wasn't this what he wanted? His Voodoo Queen was a success. But it was an affront that, in her success, Marie didn't seem to need him. The pale lovestruck girl was now a confident woman. Damballah? He didn't believe it. Marie was playacting and, in her playacting, belittling him just as her Grandmère had done—just as her Maman had done.

Marie exulted. Damballah gave her a new vision of herself. She was helping those without help. Her heart was solaced. For once she wasn't causing anyone any pain.

Marie felt light, without form. Her body suddenly began ascending, levitating. Astonished, Marie laughed a child's laugh, gay and hearty.

The crowd hushed as she rose above them. Some pulled back, frightened. Some dropped to their knees. But they all chanted in the barest of whispers, "Damballah Queen. Maman Marie, our Damballah Queen."

John, his arms locked about himself, kept shaking his head. Marie's feet were merely inches removed from the ground, but it might as well have been miles. Envy was like bitter gall. It was a trick. There had to be some trick.

Marie spun around until her yellow gown was imbued with rainbows. She descended to the ground as swiftly, as smoothly, as an angel. Damballah was gone.

The drums died abruptly.

Marie looked at John. She couldn't tell what he was thinking, and the way his eyes stared as if she were hiding something made her nervous. But then she smiled: how silly she was. With Damballah gone she was already reverting to her old, frightened self. Of course John would be pleased. Hadn't she done what he wanted? For love of him, she had battled Maman—risking her soul—and opened herself to Damballah. She'd taken a step toward a new life, a new self. Surely John would love her now.

Without looking back at the enraptured crowd, Marie entered John's bedroom, and he, following her, gently closed the door.

Marie woke alone. Prism patterns of sunlight decorated the wall. The room was bathed in hot, humid air. She tried to sit up but fell back, clutching her abdomen. Bruises covered her body. Her face felt cracked.

She felt weighted on the bed.

After the ceremony, John's loving had been gentle at first. His tenderness was her reward. Then, for no reason, he slammed her head against the headboard.

"Why? What have I done?" she moaned.

"I am not a fool. Everything you are, you owe to me. Everything you do, you do for me." Straddling her, he punctuated his words with small blows.

"Damballah entered me. Isn't that what you wanted?" Her lips were bleeding.

"Tricks. All tricks." He bit her nipples, then thrust himself inside her. "Remember—I am the King." Marie thought he had pierced her abdomen. "All pleasures begin and end with me."

"And I am the Queen," Marie yelled, furious that he would use her so, furious at herself for ever thinking she had loved him.

John flipped her over and entered her anus. Marie screamed. John murmured in her ear, "I could kill you."

"Do it. Get another Voodoo Queen." All she wanted to do was die. John gripped her hair, pushing her head deeper into the pillow. She was suffocating. Marie could feel herself yielding. Not fighting for breath.

John turned her head sideways. "You'll live and you'll do as I tell you."

"You'll have to kill me."

"I'll kill Grandmère instead."

"No!" she screamed, marshaling her energy, her arms and legs flailing helplessly, as John pressed his weight and cock into her again and again. "No!"

She blacked out and didn't remember anything else.

Marie rolled toward the edge of the bed and vomited. She dragged herself to the basin and submerged her face in water. Drying her face, she saw her reflection, wan and swollen. She couldn't cry.

Frantically, Marie searched for her skirt. Inside the side pocket, she found the locket. The portrait's face was smooth and untouched. Her face was ugly with bruises. Nonetheless the resemblance was amazing.

"I see he seduced you well enough."

In the pinched black face, Marie thought she saw pity. "Leave me alone, Nattie."

There was silence except for the cloth's sucking sounds as Nattie cleaned the vomit from the floor. When the basin was dirty, Nattie dashed the water out the window, showering the cobblestones.

Marie stared at Nattie's back, wondering if she'd come to gloat.

"Your Maman hated you."

"Did she hate you too, Nattie?"

Nattie turned, masking her irritation. "You be upset." She extended a soothing hand.

"Leave me alone, Nattie."

Nattie cocked her head. "You be hard, Marie." Nattie swung her hips and lifted the locket from the dresser. "Your Maman was hard too. And as selfish as the day be long. Always had to have her own way. John was her way. Your Grandmère loved your Maman. Nobody could say a word against her daughter. Grandmère was blind until the very end. Hardened by her own stubbornness." Nattie paused.

Marie's bland expression hadn't changed.

"I think it be too much loving that makes you hard."

"Get on with it, Nattie. Say what you have to say."

"It was your Maman who found John rattling about, hungry. You should've seen him then—claiming to anyone who would listen that the scars on his face made him a prince. Your Maman persuaded Grandmère to take John in, teach him the Voodoo ways. Your Maman loved John like a kitten loves milk."

Dry heaves racked Marie's body.

"But John was unfaithful. He tried to hide it at first. Your Maman was smart and found out anyway. She slept with a white man out of spite. As you grew, so did John's desires. His outside interests. Do you understand me? He no longer bothered to hide his women.

"Grandmère had to tie your Maman down to keep her from ripping you out of her womb. I prepared her food, always careful to see she didn't add a powder to birth you stillborn." Nattie spoke to Marie's reflection.

Marie feigned calm. Nattie mustn't see her vulnerable. "Is that all, Nattie?"

" 'Is that all?' Be that all you can say? Foolishness." Nattie gripped Marie's elbows and shook her. "Who are you? You not my same sweet Marie. I be the only one who can help you. Don't shut me out."

Frustrated, Nattie slapped her hips.

"You think I like seeing you beaten? You think I like the thought of John touching you? He uses you as he used your Maman." She paced, her chin jutting. "John wants you to succeed to make him greater. A prince. Your Maman wants to live again for John. She don't care about you. She never did."

Marie slumped down on the bed.

"A black woman has no power. But you do. My skills be small. But I know spells, Marie. I can mix potions. Together we can rid ourselves of your Maman and John. You and I can restore community. I be sorry to betray your Grandmère. But I had to. Damballah be more than anybody. Even Grandmère.

"All I want is to be a part of the Voodoo world again," Nattie pleaded. "All I ask is to be a part of your grace. I want to feel Damballah's kiss." Nattie closed her eyes, imagining Damballah imbuing her with power.

"When Grandmère left the faith, there were fewer, more paltry ceremonies. Grandmère was the core that held us; without Grandmère and your Maman, there be no priestess worth following. No African faith to claim."

Nattie spoke hoarsely. "You and me, Marie. Two women will share power."

Marie expelled air. Nattie wanted a part of her soul as much as anyone else. Suddenly suspicious, Marie asked, "How did Maman die?"

Nattie's face pinched tight. What version of the truth should she tell? She'd learned long ago that half-truths were better than lies.

"White men," she said slowly, "killed her." Why didn't she tell Marie that John had caused Maman's death?

Yet Nattie couldn't betray John, for he and she were alike— both desiring power, sacrificing anyone to achieve it. Only their justifications were different. Nattie believed that faith, rather than money or fame, was the better reason for committing unpardonable sins. Besides, Nattie loved John. Always had, always would. The pain of loving him was closing her throat. She cradled Marie's face. "Love John and he'll hurt you for sure."

Marie whimpered.

Nattie stroked her hair. "Sssh, child," she said. "Sssh."

Marie pushed her face up against the black bosom. By degrees, she relaxed. Nattie's comfort was a balm. Nattie's comfort encouraged self-pity.

"I'll be your maman."

Marie exploded. "Get out! Leave me alone!" She slapped

Nattie's crowlike face. "You—the gods—everyone—leave me alone!"

"What's the matter with you? You be crazy?" Nattie, mouth open, one hand holding her jaw, looked comic. Any other time Marie would have laughed, but she was hurting. Nattie wasn't sassy, sarcastic now.

"I don't want another mother. Or father. Or anyone," yelled Marie.

"I no take slaps from you anymore than I take them from your Grandmère. You be nobody," Nattie said viciously. "Nobody at all."

"Get out, you ugly crow. Ugly old crow." The door slammed shut. Uncontrollably, Marie's limbs shook. Her body felt cold. Shock was claiming her. Marie staggered.

Grandmère had been the best maman.

Quiet, Marie lay in John's cluttered room, watching the sun set. Grandmère had told her all good things needed their rest, even the red-waning sun. Shadows reminded her of bayou trees shuddering to sleep. Outside there was a summer shower. Mist floated in through the window. Bayou owls would be perching; bats would be swinging upside down.

Marie's body was sore.

If she left, where would she go? If she left, how could she protect Grandmère from John?

In the bayou nothing would have changed, and she had changed too much. She'd wanted someone to love her. Twice, she'd chosen the wrong one: first a mother by blood, then John by desire. Like a stranger traveling through the marsh, she'd been swallowed whole. No one would love her.

The room was dark. *She heard Grandmère singing. The sweet strain brought her peace.*

She sat up, smelling sweat and damp cotton. "John?"

He struck a match. The candle haloed his face. His eyes were weepy and dull. His collar had been turned up against the rain.

Water beads cascaded down his face and neck. Standing there, palms open, John seemed tentative, unsure of himself.

He stretched down and huddled in her arms. Marie stroked his damp head. The victim soothed.

All she could think was that if she didn't do as John wanted, be as he wanted, Grandmère would be hurt. And being with him was surely her penance for betraying Grandmère's love.

"I didn't mean—"

"Sssh." She pressed him closer.

"Poor love," he said, kissing the dark swells beneath Marie's eyes.

She steeled herself to keep from flinching. Yet as he caressed her, she could feel her body responding. Did John use spells? Or was loving always so unwise and heartfelt? John began loving her. His gentleness reminded her of Jacques on their wedding night. She turned her lips toward his throat. Was she really so desperate for loving? How pathetic she was. He moved inside her, and it felt like her first time. Her soul was opening, yielding.

A sound welled from within her.

"Aw, Grandmère," Marie moaned.

"Marie is a slave name. Maman was named Marie. Grandmère was named Marie. I asked Grandmère why we were all Maries.

"She said, 'My mother, Membe, birthed me, but Master gave me his surname, Laveau, and the first name Marie. I didn't keep my name out of loyalty to the Virgin Mary. My conversion to Catholicism came later. I kept the name Marie to remind me of what we've lost, all of us who've had the misfortune to be enslaved in this New World. All of us are Maries.

" 'I sometimes think the African spirits are confused by this uprooting. They might not know which name to call—my slave name, Marie Laveau, or the unknown African name that should've been mine.

" 'When I die, what if the spirits call the wrong name? What if they call a name I never learned? Then where will my soul go?'

"I felt sorry for Grandmère, Louis. She was afraid of dying. I often wonder: When she died, did the spirits call the right name and did Grandmère hear it?"

•

—MARIE LAVEAU, JUNE 15, 1881, NOON
(From Louis DeLavier's journal)

O pen up. Aw, Grandmère. Please let me in." Marie's fists were swollen from knocking. The cottage appeared deserted. But Grandmère was there. Occasionally, Marie saw shutters move.

The day was cold. It was the first day of December. The Mississippi battered sluggishly against the shore. Crows paused in flight, and field mice searched for crevices in the wooden shacks. Marie wrapped her cape more tightly about her. A nasty wind touched her chest. "Grandmère," she shouted.

Neighbors from Haben's Haven paused to watch and listen. They spied from behind doors, poked their heads out of windows, or more boldly stood on porches, gathering shawls and scarves about their heads and throats. They clicked their gums and shook their heads. Marie felt criminal. Shad, who used to doff his cap, passed by without speaking. Halo muttered loudly about sinful, ungrateful children. Ziti simply smiled; but the smile reminded Marie of a bitter, mutinous goat. What hypocrites they were, thought Marie. All of them attended her ceremonies. They praised her for worshiping Damballah but condemned her for abandoning Grandmère. Didn't they know she couldn't honor both? No matter which choice she made, she sinned either against faith or family.

"Grandmère, please." Marie knocked harder.

Glancing to her left, Marie noticed a small black cube on the steps. She stooped low and opened it. Inside the box was white satin and an etching of a heart surrounded by mint. Marie had no idea what it meant. Was it an evil charm or a charm to ward off evil? Carefully, she closed the box and replaced it on the porch.

The villager's stares were making her nervous. Marie looked about and saw Bébé and his daughters. She'd heard a rumor that Annette was pregnant again and shut inside the house. Their eldest girl, Shuey, had died from yellow fever in September.

Marie wasn't sure why she was back in Haven. These past weeks, she'd been happy. Her ceremonies went well. Damballah blessed her. John had been generous and loving. Nightly, she'd dreamed fanciful dreams in his arms: a wedding, baptismal celebrations for a slew of children. Once she'd dreamed they set sail from the dock in New Orleans. They were returning to the African shore as king and queen when a storm erupted. The crew mysteriously died, then rose from the dead and ripped the limbs from John. She didn't discourage them. When she sighted land, she steered the rudder toward the expansive sea. Marie woke, realizing how easily she fooled herself, calling it love when John touched her sweetly, yet hating him desperately, even more so because he caused her to confuse her own emotions.

With Nattie, she had an uneasy truce. By week's end, Nattie'd claimed her bedroom. Ribaud shifted his rest from the kitchen floor to the kitchen cot. Marie found herself permanently installed in John's room and bed. Still she heard Grandmère's song, haunting tones rising from the bayou.

She knocked again. "Grandmère, I need you. Please."

The door opened. Marie sucked in air.

"Marie, is that you?"

She rushed into Grandmère's arms. The old woman's skin was dry; it barely covered her bones. Marie drew back. Grandmère's skirt was stained with urine, her blouse speckled with bits of rice. Her hair hung like tangled yarn, and her nails had curved under and inward. Grandmère looked like a witch.

"Marie, is that you?" The voice was shrill. "I've done told you it's a sin to try and kill a child. Your womb was made for life." Grandmère turned and shuffled back inside.

Holding her breath, Marie saw the disarray. Rotted food cluttered the table. Furniture was tilted upside down. Flies hovered over excrement. For months, Grandmère had shunned the pot and squatted where she stood. Only the altar was immaculate. The Virgin gazed on human waste.

The old woman sat in the straight-backed chair and rocked. "Don't make no sense," she mumbled, "to kill a child who's done no harm. I don't care what John is doing, what women he's visiting. The child inside you means no harm."

Marie was stunned. Grandmère thought she was her mother; she'd forgotten her only daughter was dead.

"Bless the Virgin Mother. She takes care of all babies."

Marie wept. All these months, she'd relied on the white Virgin to care for Grandmère. Grandmère said rosary prayers. Shouldn't white gods have sympathy for someone so good? Marie dropped to her knees. She felt a surfacing of old guilt. It was she who'd done the most harm to Grandmère, the most violence. White gods couldn't be expected to care for an old black woman when her own granddaughter didn't. Why should anyone in Haven—Ziti, Halo, or Shad—care about Grandmère? Didn't the villagers hold Grandmère responsible for Annette's deformed child? Marie almost fainted from guilt. What a sorry fool she'd been.

"I'll take you away," Marie said.

"Where, child?" Grandmère's gaze was unfocused. "Ain't no place to go." Notes floated out of her mouth, precious and sweet. "Things will be better when the child is born. You'll see. Blood ties bind."

"Can you forgive me?"

"Mon pítí bebe. Fais dodo."

"Forgive me."

The song stopped. For a brief moment, Grandmère was lucid. She stroked Marie's palm. "Never no need for forgiveness among family. Among three Maries."

Marie rested her head in her Grandmère's lap.

"Go to sleep. In fifteen years, my kitten will be wed."

The tenor of Grandmère's voice hadn't changed. Her song stirred deep emotions. They could've been in Teché. Marie thought she smelled roses. Then the room's foul odors seeped through the fibers of her clothes.

Marie got up.

Grandmère crooned, "Holy Mary, Mother of God, forgive this daughter of yours, this daughter who's sinned. . . ."

Marie removed her cloak, twisted her hair into a bun, and raised her dress sleeves. The wash bucket was still in the pantry, but it was layered with moldy food. Gripping the handle, Marie went outside the house (Grandmère never noticed she was gone) and dashed the spoiled food out back for crow and opossum scavengers. Calmer, she realized someone must've bought Grandmère food. Who could it have been? Shad? She trudged to the well, with the bucket clapping and bruising against her legs. Eyes watched her. Some villagers, staring, leaned over porch rails; others walked gingerly behind her. Mothers kept their children attached to their skirts. Someone, somewhere, said, "Hail, Marie. Marie est Voudon." It occurred to Marie, had the villagers more faith in her, they would've cared better for Grandmère.

Once inside the house, Marie scrubbed and cleaned and

scrubbed and cleaned again. She did her own penance. The sun lowered. Marie could feel the stirred-up dust and filth filtering downward, layering her hair and clothes. She cleaned the floor, table, and cupboards while Grandmère said enough rosaries to save a thousand souls.

At sundown, Grandmère's litany abruptly stopped. She stared beyond Marie, her mouth puckering like a fish.

Marie turned and saw Jacques in his broadcloth uniform, standing in the doorway. His skin was crisp and brown. It amazed her how, between voyages, his skin faded to yellow. Grandmère hummed. Marie lowered her eyes, avoiding Jacques' gaze.

Jacques felt spellbound. Laying his package on the table, he lifted out bananas, okra, and rice. It wasn't fair. Earlier he'd been ready to meet Marie. But instead he'd found Grandmère, unkempt and alone. He'd been furious with Marie. He wouldn't have left an animal in Grandmère's state. He'd hoped he could forget Marie, using his anger to dismiss her as ruthlessly as she'd dismissed him, his heart and feelings. Now with her hair twisted primly on top of her head, with dirt on her hands and face, Marie was even lovelier than he remembered. He wasn't prepared.

"I thought Grandmère would like fresh food," Jacques said. "Nothing grows well around here. I went back to the city."

"How long has she been—?" Marie stopped.

"Don't you know?" Jacques slapped his chest.

"I haven't seen her in months. John doesn't like me to come."

"Damn John." Jacques shook his fist and felt a rush of color and heat like a cock before a pit fight. He inhaled deeply. Nervously, he pinched his ear.

"I only arrived today too," he murmured. "This morning." He traced the ridge of an okra. "After you left, I shipped to the Indies. Massachusetts Bay." His eyes settled on her. "I returned to find you."

Marie stood behind Grandmère, holding the woman's shoulders to prevent her rocking. Even in a straight chair, the motion irritated Marie; it stirred too many memories of lazy evenings on the bayou porch. She'd been a silly child.

"Why?" demanded Jacques. "Why did you desert her?"

Marie shrugged. "Why does anything happen the way it does? I don't believe I've had much control over anything in my life. I wish I could lie and say otherwise."

"Ladybug," Grandmère muttered, "ladybug. Fly away home. Wish for a husband. You won't always love me."

"Sssh, Grandmère. Please." Marie lifted a banana from Jacques' groceries, peeled it, and handed it to Grandmère. The old woman stuffed it into her mouth and rocked.

Going to the window Marie saw, off in the distance, the quiet stretch of beach where the wedding had been celebrated, where the monstrous babe had lain at Grandmère's feet, and where Nattie had introduced her to John. Jacques hovered over her. "You must've hated me," she said.

His head drooped forward. "Yes. I don't feel much better now that I've seen you. Here." He held out the okra. "You can cook this better than I." Softly, he added, "I've never been left before, Marie. Never."

Nights aboard ship, Jacques had felt he was going insane. His mind had replayed their wedding night, the sweetness of loving her. He couldn't tell Marie about his pain—about his misguided arrogance in assuming that if he loved her well enough she'd fall in love with him. He couldn't tell her about waking from their loving and calling her name, then puzzling when she didn't respond. He couldn't tell her about his desperate search through the house and along the beach, shouting "Marie!" When his despair had peaked, he fell, remembering how only hours before, he and Marie had clung together and rolled in the sand. Gloating, Ziti, the hairdresser girl, had told him Marie was gone. His world was forever changed.

Marie had started dinner. Slicing the green stems, steaming the rice, she wondered why Jacques didn't reproach her more. Candles lit, the house was cozy, brimming with family. A stranger, peering through the window, would've thought them happy. Grandmère was singing with Jacques, a favorite tune of the docks. The song, about a seagull stealing the harbor master's wig, didn't make any sense. But Grandmère loved it. Her rich voice was uplifting. As they sang, Jacques off-key, Marie felt calm. He'd always been a good man.

"I'm surprised no one helped her." As soon as she said it,

Marie was sorry. Grandmère was her responsibility. She set the plates down.

"The charm on the steps keeps the neighbors away," said Jacques. "It's a death curse. I saw such charms often in Domingo."

"Aren't you afraid?" Marie asked, defensive and sarcastic.

"Yes." He sketched a cross. "Yes, yes, I am."

Marie felt shame. She shouldn't reproach Jacques. She knew John must've been responsible for the curse. She was responsible too. The charm was one of John's ways of controlling her.

"I'm a little afraid of you." Jacques stared at his boots. "I've heard tales. But I have trouble imagining you, my wife, worshiping snakes, rising ten feet off the ground." Nervously, he stroked his hair. "You're still my wife."

"Yet you've seen things. Voodoo trials in Domingo. Haiti."

"It isn't you," he said emphatically.

Marie finished the dinner. She measured out portions of beans and rice on the plates. She kept quiet as Jacques tenderly fed Grandmère, the old woman smacking her gums between bites.

"Worms, nothing but dazed worms," Grandmère sighed as Marie offered tea.

"Is it you?" Jacques asked.

Marie shook her head and Jacques, slowly nodding, seemed satisfied.

"Marrying you, I thought I'd have my own family. I never really knew my mother. Or father. In Domingo, they separated slave families. Somewhere, if she's alive, I have a sister. Maybe a brood of nieces. Nephews." He looked wistful.

"There's so much about you I don't know." What did she expect? she thought. They'd met. They'd married—he for love, she to please Grandmère and Damballah.

Jacques threw back his head and laughed. "Remember the time we went fishing?" His curly head bobbed. "I was so surprised that you, a country girl, got tangled in the line. Grandmère, you should've seen her. I had to cut the line to pieces." He popped more rice into the open mouth. Grandmère gurgled. "You were so beautiful, Marie. Shimmying like a grounded fish. I couldn't wait for our own baby girl."

"Marie times four," Grandmère screeched.

Marie retreated into a corner.

"Why don't you talk?" shouted Jacques angrily. "Say something. I haven't seen you in months and you don't talk. Talk to me, Marie."

She turned sharply. "What do you want me to say? I'm sorry. I'm sorry. Talk. Is that enough talk?"

"No, it's not enough."

Grandmère's eyes were wide. The loud noises frightened her.

Jacques wiped stew from the wrinkled lips. "I would've taken our daughter fishing," he said stubbornly.

Marie went about her business. She shielded herself from some of the pain rising in her own breast. Over the open fire, she warmed water to fill the huge metal tub. She undressed Grandmère. Emaciated, Grandmère's body resembled a child's.

Jacques' face was taut. He sat on the edge of the chair, straining forward. "I don't want to love you anymore." He waited for Marie to talk and answer him. Finally, he gathered Grandmère's soiled clothes and took them outside.

"I'm too tired," the old woman complained, splashing and fluttering her toes in the bath.

"Me too, Grandmère." Marie sponged the flabby breasts. "I'm afraid if I talk, I'll talk forever."

Grandmère crowed and dunked her head under water. From outside, Marie could smell Jacques burning Grandmère's garments.

When Grandmère was clean and dry, Marie was soap-stained and wet. Marie tucked Grandmère into bed, feeling certain a step had been missed. Grandmère was the child.

Eyelids drooped and Grandmère slept. From time to time, her lashes fluttered; she whimpered like a dreaming pup.

Marie left the bedroom door ajar.

She paused, watching Jacques resting his brow against the table. He inhaled. Exhaling, he pressed his sleeves to his moist eyes.

Marie stepped forward.

"You startled me." He got up nervously. "Is Grandmère all right?"

Marie nodded.

171

"You look tired," said Jacques. "You look as though you've been dunked in the Mississippi." He pulled a blanket from the cedar chest. "You'll feel better if you put this on. If you let your clothes dry."

Marie stared at Jacques blankly. She couldn't register what he was saying, what he was doing here, why he was trying to be nice.

"Marie—" He held out the blanket.

Weariness was dragging her down. Her body and soul felt off-center. Staring into the hearth, Marie murmured, "Don't." Jacques was unbuttoning the back of her gown.

"What went wrong, Marie?"

"Nothing."

"I must've done something." His hand traced the length of her spine. "Damn you. What went wrong?" He pressed hard on her collarbone. Lightly, he kissed the down on her neck.

Marie was too tired to argue, too amazed that Jacques still desired her. She stepped out of her shift. Jacques enveloped her in the wool blanket.

"Damn you. I'm doing my best not to hurt you." Jacques' head rested on the back of Marie's head, his arms crisscrossed about her waist. "I don't believe it's you."

Marie wanted to tell him it *was* her. Everything she did or didn't do was her. She was a Voodooienne.

He turned her around.

"Did you promise Grandmère you'd return me to Teché?"

"How did you know?"

"I knew."

"Forgive me." His hands slid down the length of her arms, across her back and buttocks. Silently, he asked his question.

"I'm your wife," Marie said simply.

Methodically, Jacques undressed himself, giving Marie a chance to change her mind.

All Marie could think of was that Jacques was so much simpler than John. The fire was crackling in the hearth. Jacques would be hurt if she told him flames reminded her of fireflies . . . reminded her that she was burning . . . reminded her she was too damned contrary to love the right man.

172

Looking vulnerable, almost childish in his nakedness, Jacques said belligerently, "You needn't feel grateful for my help."

His skin smelled good, musty. On tiptoes, Marie kissed his nose. Giggling, she pinched his buttocks.

"Marie." He lifted her straight off the ground. Their lips pressed. "We'll have a pretty girl like you."

"No." She'd be barren with him just as she'd been barren all her months with John. "A child won't hold me."

Roughly, Jacques dragged her down onto the blanket. Marie stared into the fire, feeling his anger wash over her. Eventually, Jacques calmed. She shifted in his arms and faced him. "You're all right?" she asked.

"Yes."

They loved as sweetly as they both knew how.

"Come again." Jacques' voice sounded flat to his own ears, but he couldn't think of much to say after making love to his wife for the second time. Married for over a year, there should've been hundreds of couplings between them. Whenever he recalled their wedding night, he felt an immediate ache in his loins. Liquor and seemingly endless seas had blunted almost nothing of his pain. He stroked his cock, reveling in the aftermath of pleasure.

Marie carefully kept her back to Jacques as she dressed. She slipped her dress up and over her soft shoulders and crooked her elbows and hands backward to button the tiny buttons on her dress.

"Come back if you can, Marie. I'll be here."

She snapped her head, letting her hair swing back, off her face and chest.

Jacques thought Marie had the impatience of a dockside whore, eager to be gone after her work was done. Her body had felt different too. Experienced, yet sweeter, because she knew better how to give back what he needed. He didn't let himself dwell on where and with whom she'd gained the experience. Pressed in the back of his mind was the dream that he might win her back. "I won't ship out for two months," said Jacques.

Her hand hovering above the doorknob, Marie looked back.

Resting on a crooked elbow, the blanket covering his abdomen, Jacques looked humble. A victim. Marie flushed guiltily.

Jacques tried to think of something he could say, something to restrain her from walking out the door. He was afraid if he demanded anything, he'd chase Marie out of his life. Having her some of the time was better than no time at all. He said softly, "I'll watch after Grandmère."

Marie smiled a sweet, genuine smile. "I'm grateful," she said and was gone.

Outside, Marie kicked aside the miniature coffin. She was furious with herself, furious that good people were always hurt. The box cracked apart on the steps.

"You can come out now."

A figure emerged from the cottage's shadows. Ribaud slipped off his cap and smiled his gold-toothed grin. Marie had seen him hiding when she first went to the well. She was grateful Ribaud hadn't interrupted her reunion with Grandmère. Or with Jacques. How much had the spell man seen? If she had it to do over again, she'd still make love to Jacques, not caring that Ribaud was a witness.

Marie hurried forward and Ribaud fell in step behind her. It was late.

Crossing the city boundary, they bypassed a French Quarter bar. Someone played a harmonica. Squealing and whining notes pierced the chill night air. "A colored girl is free game," Shad once said. "White men don't understand 'No.'" Marie was grateful Ribaud was with her. Torchlights hollowed out the eyes of prostitutes; aristocrats placed money in their hands. Eyes cast down, Marie stared at the boardwalk. "Men, both black and white, will leave you alone once they know your name," John had said. "They'll fear you." But she was convinced nobody knew her name. "Marie Laveau, the Voodoo Queen."

What did that mean? Her religion stole over her. It was no more hers than the notion that she belonged to herself.

Marie heard evening matins. She stopped, studying the St. Louis Cathedral, the crucifix steeple shrouded in mist. This was the square where Maman had been murdered. She felt strangely unmoved. Father Christophe would be overwhelmed by her sins. Adultery, blasphemy, filial disrespect. Could he give her absolution?

"Miz Marie, we got to hurry."

If her religion inspired fear, the Catholic church was unforgiving. Blasphemy was a mortal sin. Marie thought it was her own ill luck that she hadn't been solaced by African gods in wood, iron, and the sea.

"Miz Marie. Master John will be angry."

"Who's John?" she shouted, her color high and her eyes flashing. "Tell me that. Who's John? Damballah lives through me." She slapped her chest. "John is nothing without me. Do you understand?" her voice crescendoed as she propelled herself forward, stomping her feet, her hands curled into fists. "Nothing." Passersby turned and stared. A woman shrieked and stumbled out of the way. Angry, Marie was magnificent.

The spell man trembled. He was crouched against a wall, his mouth agape with a terrible wonder.

Marie smiled. There was a kind of solace in fear.

She inclined her head and imagined herself turning like a grand masted sailing ship setting out to sea, her dress and cape billowing. Ribaud trailed after her, skip-hopping to keep pace.

They scurried down Rue Royale, past the merchant shops and musical saloons, and turned left on St. Anne. Marie felt deflated. The small clapboard homes lacked character and substance. Her fierceness left her like a sudden gust.

She looked apologetic. "I'm sorry, Ribaud." He squeezed her hand reassuringly and they walked a few steps more, their pace slowing.

"Ribaud, why do you stay? John seems to hate you."

"Where else would I go?" His face crinkled like walnut skin.

She was home. The white house appeared suddenly like a misshapen skull; its windows were glowering eyes. She turned sharply. "Don't tell, Ribaud."

He caressed the dried garlic hung about his neck.

"Don't tell John where I've been."

Marie held her breath while Ribaud considered. He jerked his head, and Marie bent to give him a quick hug. His slight, birdlike

body leaning briefly into hers gave her renewed hope. They entered
the house in companionable silence, in companionable fear. Marie
knew she'd have to build her strength one moment at a time. She
must be careful. She had to learn enough to protect Grandmère.

That evening, Marie learned to lie well.

"Where've you been?"

She responded blandly, "I visited the docks." She cooed and
called his name. "John. Teach me, John. Teach me about Voodoo."

When John caught the spell man by his neck and Ribaud
answered, "Walking. All she did was walk," Marie relaxed. For now,
she was safe.

When they were alone, Marie massaged John. There was a
terror about him that drew her. She patterned circles on his back.
She desired and feared him.

"You don't worry about your sailor, do you?" he asked.

Marie tensed and said "No," marveling that it was true.
Jacques could take care of himself.

"I worry about you."

Marie felt torn between dreams and the facts. John didn't care
about her. He flipped over on the bed. Marie saw into the cavern
of his mouth. Grandmère had told her about the swallowing of
Jonah. Poor Jonah lost in the belly of a whale.

"Don't ever lie to me," John said. "It's too pleasurable to beat
you."

Marie shuddered, knowing every word he said was true.

John touched her cheeks, her recently blackened eyes. "You're
healed. You'll be able to perform with no marks."

"Perform? Isn't what I do real?"

John sighed and slapped her bottom. "Yes, it's real. But I tell
you, people's fears and desires are more real. Convince a dying man
he's well and he'll live to one hundred. Cast a spell for an ugly
woman, and the next day she'll be beautiful. Even you'll be stronger,
more lovely, once you have more confidence. Once you've charmed
yourself into being powerful."

176

John's philosophy was tempting. She could reinvent herself by just believing in herself. She'd become as strong as he was.

"So what am I?"

"A vessel."

Marie wanted to cry out her disappointment. As a Voodooienne, she was a thing, an "it," a medium for other people's dreams and desires.

John stood. Carefully, Marie watched him measuring and spooning his potion. She knew enough now to memorize the ingredients. "Is that real?"

Gliding toward her, he said, "Everything I do is real." He swallowed his potion, his tongue licking at the stray juice on his lips.

Marie shuddered. With John, she'd been caught by the promise of herself. Who was she in love with, him or herself?

Marie laid her head on his chest.

But it would be John, if anyone, who could teach her about Voodoo. He was the imperfect link. The man she hated and desired, the man who could connect her to a heritage she'd sensed but never known. Other than him and Nattie, who else did she have?

John slowly made love to her. He intentionally hurt her once, to remind her who held power. And Marie, feeling the pain radiating from the deep center of her body, swore she'd remember each hurt against her, until she had enough hurt piled up like sticks for a fire to consume John. Avenging Grandmère's hurt would serve as kindling to make the flame burn brighter.

Well, that's that," said Louis mock-casually, turning, letting his feet hit the floor. He paused a bit, his chin touching his chest, his hands on his knees. He couldn't prevent melancholy.

"We can try again," said Brigette, resting her head against his back. Her fingers drew circles on his chest. "We just need more patience." One hand slipped down toward his crotch. "Please, let's try again."

"I don't understand," said Louis. But he did understand. Sex with his wife was unappealing. He brushed his lips against Brigette's cheek. "Sleep well, my dear."

"No," she said forcefully. "I don't want you to go." She'd spent the day preparing for a successful seduction. Hadn't her body been perfumed, oiled? Hadn't her maid said she looked lovely? Any man would desire her.

Louis looked at his wife. There was something different about her. Her charms were more lush. She looked vulnerable. A bit desperate, perhaps.

"Please don't go." Her lips were parted. Bright curls cascaded down her back.

Louis felt tender toward Brigette. Protective. But that was all. "It isn't your fault," he said.

Brigette lay back, restless in her bed. Her sheets were satin, soft and smooth to the touch. The bedroom was blue and feminine. The top sheet fell across her abdomen, exposing white shoulders, white breasts. Louis was putting on his silk robe. His body was narrow and lean, almost too pale in the burgundy wrap; his flaccid cock seemed bruised by comparison.

Brigette couldn't believe her failure. The Gulf breeze streamed in through the french windows. She could see stars beyond the balcony, sparkling without relief. She'd never imagined it would be difficult getting Louis to make love to her. John, the Voodoo Doctor, had shown her how to simulate the breaking of the hymen. Nonetheless, the honeymoon had been a disaster. Seven thrilling nights of Louis' impotence. Her lack of virginity was never a question. Louis had hardly seemed interested.

They honeymooned at Désire, the drained and dissolving family plantation. At first Brigette was glad to be at Désire, glad to be spared the onslaught of yellow fever season in the city. Only a Northerner would plan a wedding when the weather was sweltering and disease was spreading. Yet she grew bored. There were no parties, no picnics, no scintillating dinner conversations. She grew tired of picturesque slaves singing and picking cotton. Tired of mildewed rooms and a leaking roof. She was impatient with Louis, forever apologizing about his impotence. She missed Antoine.

After a week, Brigette had begged Louis to let them return to town. Oh, how she and Antoine had laughed because she'd rather risk fever than bear another honeymoon night in her dull husband's arms. Louis had never been able to penetrate her. Now she wished he had.

Until two months ago, the marriage had been satisfactory. A success, really, since Louis was generous with his money without exacting conjugal duties as payment. It had been convenient pursuing separate interests; adultery was discreet.

Brigette was certain Louis was unfaithful to her, and a "marriage of convenience" had more than suited her. Like most of his kind, he had a colored mistress. She'd seen how the slave Lil had looked at him. But things were different now. Brigette clutched at her abdomen, feeling bloated and despairing.

Over a year and Louis was still unable (or unwilling) to consummate the marriage. Tonight, like a needy prostitute, she'd begged him to come to her. She'd nerved herself to endure his touch, all for nothing and all because she needed his seed to cover her sin.

Across the room, Brigette could see herself in the vanity mirror. Thick blond hair. Blue eyes. A figure ripe and teasing. Wasn't she supposed to be what every man—white or black—dreamed of? Since she was thirteen, she'd been conscious of men watching, assessing her. She'd never dreamed her own husband would be backward in his attentions.

Repentant, Louis was bending over her. "I'm sorry." He wanted to bestow a good-night kiss. His dressing gown parted, exposing him.

Staring at his limp cock, Brigette was enraged. His penis seemed to taunt and humiliate her. "Get out." She sat bolt upright, screaming. "Get out of here. I don't want you to touch me." Her nails slashed at him. "Pig. Filthy pig."

"Brigette!"

"Get out of here." She battered him with her fists. "I don't ever want you to touch me. Not ever."

Louis captured her arms and held her tightly, paralyzing her arms and fists against his chest. Brigette was frantic.

Louis could feel her ragged breath and smell her rose oil scent. "I'm sorry. I don't mean to hurt you." Lightly, he rained kisses on her neck.

Over Louis' shoulder, Brigette could see the Virgin Mother. Blond hair. Blue eyes. The statue hung upon the wall. A cry rose in her throat. She'd go to hell. Her sins were compounding.

"Forgive me," Brigette whimpered, expecting the statue to come alive and comfort her. "Forgive me."

Louis felt devastated. He'd been able to push his impotence to the back of his mind, but now, consoling the distraught Brigette, he felt responsible for hurting her. "Brigette, listen to me. Please, listen. There's nothing to forgive."

Hysterical, she shook her head no. Only the Virgin Mother had the power to comfort her.

"You're not to blame." Guiding her back toward the bed, Louis covered her nakedness. "I'm to blame. I'm the one who's incomplete. I'm the one who's incapable of loving." He tucked the sheet lightly about her throat. "Should I call your maid?" he asked softly.

Brigette was sick. Nauseous. The Virgin Mother was cruel.

Hadn't she ignored her prayers? Hadn't she stared balefully while Brigette begged for her help?

It had been years since Brigette's soul was clean enough for communion. She couldn't confess to a priest. How could a man understand a woman's need for affection? Romance? How could a man understand a woman's desire to be held, comforted? Finding solace often led to sex. It meant surrendering your body to a man's coarse passions. How could a priest understand all that? But Brigette expected the Virgin Mother to know and understand. She must've been a wife to Joseph.

"It'd be lovely to erase everything," Brigette mused. She'd have no bad memories. Her parents would be alive. The estate would be rich. She'd be unmarried, flirting at a ball, pursuing stolen kisses and no commitment.

"Here. Drink this." Louis offered water from the bedside urn.

"You're almost handsome," Brigette said dreamily. "But not nearly as handsome as Antoine."

"Brigette, did you hear me? Would you like your maid?"

If she could erase the past, she'd be her father's "sweet daughter" again. Father had been the most charming man she'd ever known. Some days he'd bring her bunches of violets, callas, delphiniums. She hadn't quite forgiven him for abandoning her. She'd watched Father in bed, feverish for days, with a personal slave to wrap cool, damp towels about him every half hour. Each second, she'd expected her father to rise and be well. His death had been a willful rejection. Papa would've saved her. "He would've protected me from Antoine."

"What did you say?" Louis gripped her shoulder blades. "What did you say?"

She'd been daydreaming. She'd thought herself a child again. Brigette focused. Louis was watching her intently. "I didn't say anything."

"You did. You said, 'Protect me from Antoine.' You said that."

Brigette's face was blank. She hadn't said anything, had she?

"What did you mean?" Louis was barely controlling his anger.

181

His brother-in-law preferred hurting to kindness. Louis couldn't stand it if Antoine had hurt his wife. "What did you mean?"

"Nothing. Just nothing," she said, twisting from his grasp.

"If Antoine has done anything to hurt you—"

"You're crazy." She pulled away, knocking the water glass off the nightstand.

"I mean it, Brigette. I protect what's mine." It still flashed through his mind, Antoine attacking his brown girl in the Market Square.

"Nothing's yours," she shouted back. "Antoine hasn't hurt me. You're the one who's hurting me. You think you can ignore me while each night you service your whores and sluts?"

"What are you talking about?"

"What is it they do that I won't, Louis?" She pressed forward. "If you tell me, maybe I could arouse you. Maybe I could keep your delicate cock aloft."

"You're talking filth."

"Am I?" She scooted toward him. Breasts and belly quivering, she whispered fiercely, "You've got a darky whore in this house."

"Shut up."

"You think I don't know about Lil? I've seen how she looks at you. Where do you bed her, Louis? In the slave's quarters or in your own bed? How many more are there, Louis? One, three, five?"

"You disgust me."

"You've got some darky whore from the streets. Why else do you stay out all night? You don't know how to touch a clean woman," she said shrilly. "A clean and pure white woman. You need black skin to do your rutting filth."

Louis raised his hand. He wanted to strike her and make her feel some of the pain she caused.

Defiant, Brigette stared. "Prove how manly you are, Louis. Protect what's yours," she murmured sarcastically.

Louis lowered his hand. He should've known better than to feel sorry for her. Brigette was behaving like the selfish, vindictive shrew he'd married. She was only interested in her own vanity.

"Why did you marry me?" he asked.

"You're the only one stupid enough to ask."

"Money?"

"It certainly wasn't your powerful sexual charm," Brigette drawled.

Louis touched his head. He'd been such a fool. He'd ruined not only his own life but Brigette's as well. All because he'd been too honorable to break their engagement.

"Do you prefer free coloreds or slaves, Louis? Which is better for your lust? Have you found that girl you tried to rescue in the Market Square? You didn't even do that well, did you? Her brother saved her. Did you track her down before Antoine got to her? He enjoys darky flings. You two could share the girl. What's her name, Louis? Or did you forget to ask? I bet Antoine knows her name. I bet he knows every inch of her."

Louis turned from her spite. Off-balance, he leaned against the wall. He'd always thought honor was a noble pursuit. Now it seemed futile. Destructive.

Brigette was laughing at him.

He deserved her scorn. He'd be lonely for the rest of his life. He'd always sworn he'd have a different marriage from his parents'. He'd marry for love and companionship. He didn't expect an infatuation to catch him off guard. The girl he thought he could love, he couldn't find. And if he found her, it would be illegal to marry a colored. He didn't even know her name.

"Sleep well, Brigette." Louis didn't face her. He kept walking toward the door, toward his bedroom and escape. "Perhaps we can both act more civilized tomorrow." But tonight he'd go out; he'd drink until forgetfulness. He'd keep himself from imagining Antoine plunging into his brown girl.

"Louis, don't leave me like this." Brigette's fists hit the bed. "I won't stand for it, do you understand? You can't just walk out. I won't stand for it. I won't, do you understand?"

"There's nothing to understand," he answered. "You dislike me as much as I dislike you." He gently closed the connecting door between their apartments.

"Damn you." Brigette threw herself across the bed. "Damn. Damn. Damn." She punched her pillow, tore at her bed sheets, and threw the water pitcher against the wall, where it shattered. She'd defeated herself. Louis would never have sex as long as she berated him.

On her left, another door opened.

Brigette flipped over. Her legs splayed wide. "What do you want?"

Antoine looked admiringly at his sister. Blond tendrils highlighted the space between her thighs.

"Did your seduction work? Did Louis have romantic success?" Drunk, Antoine was leaning against the door. His hair was sweaty, slick against his forehead.

"What do you care?"

"I care that my sister is happy. That she's sexually satisfied in the conjugal bed," he said mockingly. "Were you satisfied today?" He came into the room and raised his eyebrows at the broken glass on the right side of the bed.

Brigette scowled. "I think you've come to gloat."

Antoine shrugged. "Call it what you like."

Two connecting doors flanked Brigette's room: one door led to her husband's room, the other to her brother's. Brigette often found the pressure unbearable, mediating between the two.

Antoine sat on the bed. Possessive, he anchored an arm on either side of her. "Did you think I didn't notice your none-too-subtle preparations for love? Rose perfume." He sniffed at her neck, then lifted a gossamer gown off the floor. "Sheer negligee. Did Louis enjoy taking it off?" His fingers glanced off her breasts. "Your maid must've resented firing and drawing water for your bath. It's not even Sunday."

"I think you're jealous."

"Who am I to deny a husband's rights?" He kissed her cheek. His cravat was disarrayed. Brigette smelled whiskey.

"You look like hell."

"So do you." He grinned impishly. "I thought I heard you shouting like a fishwife. You might have murdered our northern cousin. Was something lacking in his performance?"

Brigette ignored him. "Where've you been?"

"Quadroon Ball." Antoine flushed, thinking of the pale, nearly white, black girls who'd paraded before him. Some had been as fair and as blond as his sister. But none nearly as pretty.

The ball was a respectable whore market, a contradiction in terms but a circumstance accepted by New Orleans society. Lovely light-skinned girls hoped to improve their lives by attaching to a white gentleman. In exchange for sex, a gentleman was expected to offer a cottage, support for babies, and a lifetime annuity.

"You were otherwise preoccupied," Antoine said, defensive. "Thought I'd buy me a mistress with Louis' money. Isn't that why you married him? So I could have all the privileges of a white southern gentleman?"

"You're all alike. You goddamned men are all alike. Can't resist black blood. One would think it was gold. What do you need a black mistress for? Plenty of white women desire you."

"Do you desire me?"

Brigette flounced from the bed. "I'm going to get drunk." She jerked the velvet sash that rang for her maid.

"Running around naked, one would think you were a lady of the streets. With some sun, Brigette, your husband might desire you."

"You beast." She threw her hairbrush at him. Antoine ducked. Sibling rivalry had made their arguments brutal and familiar.

"May I remind you I didn't ask you to marry him," said Antoine. "You needn't have married anyone."

Brigette glared. "How else were we to live?"

"We would've managed. Better than you manage Louis. 'Oh, he's manageable,' you said." Antoine leaned back, laughing coarsely, placing his dirty boots on the blue satin sheets. "Well, I don't see you managing him very well, sister dear. Too often you forget your honey-pot charms. Louis misses the sweet southern belle he fell in love with. If he'd asked, I could've told him she didn't exist."

Brigette stuck out her tongue. "I hate you." She threw open the door to the hallway. "Clara. You black bitch," she bellowed down the stairwell. "I want my brandy. Bring anything. Whiskey. Gin. Clara!" she hollered. "Get up here!"

"Yes'm," said a far-off voice at the bottom of the steps. Clara was Brigette's newest slave. She hadn't adjusted to Brigette's volatile temper. The dark girl scooted down the hall like a terrier, mumbling.

"If you asked me," said Antoine, carelessly resting on the bed, an elbow propping his head, "I think you married Louis for yourself. Not for me at all."

"Why, you're the grateful one."

"Martyrdom seems to be a calling for women. You spend plenty of time telling me about your sacrifices. You're always insisting that I thank you."

"You bastard." Hand upraised, Brigette advanced. Antoine deserved punishment; Brigette recognized more than a measure of truth in his words.

Antoine jerked her into his lap. "No slaps from you, sister dear. Or kicking. Or biting. Don't you know men are stronger?" he murmured, holding her in a tight, intimate grip. One hand cupped her crotch.

"Here 'tis, Madame Brigette. Here 'tis." The slave girl stared open-mouthed at the two on the bed: Antoine in evening clothes, Brigette naked and struggling in his lap.

"Set the brandy here. On the nightstand." Antoine grinned foolishly. "I won't bite you, Clara. Do as you're told."

Brigette squealed in frustration and embarrassment. But trying to wiggle out of Antoine's arms only made her situation worse.

Clara walked slowly, averting her eyes, staring at the colors woven into the carpet. She set the tray down; her hands were trembling. No colored girl, if she could help it, would let her brother see her naked. Let alone touch her down there.

"Your mistress thanks you," said Antoine. He was enjoying himself. "Don't you, Brigette?"

Clara stole another glance at them. She couldn't help her curiosity. She'd seen naked white women before, but none as young and pretty as Madame Brigette. Her skin looked as smooth as a baby's.

Frustrated, angry at Antoine, Brigette roared, "Get out of here, you black bitch. Get out!"

"Yes, ma'am. I'm going. Yes'm." Clara walked backward, mesmerized by Antoine's hand stroking a full, plump breast. She'd been a good girl; yes, she had. She'd never paid attention to kitchen gossip about sinful doings in the house. But now she'd seen it with her own eyes. Her very own eyes.

Struggling free from Antoine's grasp, Brigette threw both pillows at Clara. Seams burst and goosedown filled the air. "You black bitch."

Clara shrieked and left the room.

Squatting, Brigette tried to catch her breath. "No-good black bitch. Antoine, I could kill you. Do you hear? She'll be carrying tales to the slave quarters tonight." Brigette gasped, her hand pressing against her chest. "She'll say awful things. She'll exaggerate. She'll say we were fornicating."

"Weren't we?" Antoine pulled her back into the cradle shaped by his arms and chest.

Brigette slapped playfully at him. "Did you see her face, Antoine?" Mimicking, Brigette stretched her eyes wide and let her jaw hang slack. "Clara was so shocked. What a ludicrous face." Brigette burst out laughing.

"Bug eyes. Big-lipped mouth. She won't be able to face us again without seeing your bare behind in my lap."

"Or your hand on my breast."

Antoine pinched her side. "Clara has an overactive imagination."

"It's all your fault."

Antoine hugged his sister, then flipped on top of her, his legs straddling hers. "Do you hate me? Say you do."

"No."

He was tickling her, causing a crick of pain in Brigette's side. "Say you hate me, sister dear."

She was laughing furiously.

"Say you hate me."

Antoine looked handsome and desirable. "No, I don't hate you," his sister said.

He lowered his head until their lips gently touched. "You've the sweetest breath," he murmured. He lightly kissed her again.

The moment was precious. Brigette luxuriated; swapping breaths, they were in tune. As twins, they'd always been insular, never needing any other friends or confidantes. But as they'd grown older, the world had intruded more. Papa died. They both had social roles to play. She needed to become a wife.

Likewise, Brigette needed to tell Antoine what was troubling her. Though he didn't know it, her secret was as much his as hers. "Antoine, I've—"

He swung back, reaching for the brandy. A light alcoholic sweat dampened his shirt. "Clara's probably going to get some Voodoo nanny to sing a spell over her. She'll swear she's been cursed 'cause she's seen your naked butt in my lap. On a bed, no less. She'll swear she's seen evil."

"It is evil, isn't it?" Brigette whispered, all bravado gone.

"I've told you not to say that," Antoine exploded. He gulped at the brandy. "Here," he said, handing her the bottle. "You said you wanted to get drunk."

"I'd rather confess."

"Damn you. Why be so difficult? You always start in on it. Over and over."

"I need to confess."

Antoine stopped, arrested. "To some twisted boy-fucking priest?" He retrieved the bottle and swallowed. "A DeLavier ought to be able to confess to God directly. Just yell 'Holy Father!' and expect absolution. There must be a place in heaven reserved for decadent yet otherwise genteel aristocrats."

"You're drunk."

"So what." He took off his jacket. "Hot as hell in here." He kissed Brigette lightly. "Drunk or not, it still doesn't mean some half-assed priest can pass judgment on you." He drank. "Or me." He paused, his brow and face puckering. "No one calls my sister sinful."

Brigette put her head on his chest. Why weren't things simpler? She snuggled against him the way she did when they were children. The two of them had spent hours closeted together, teasing each other and taking comfort. It was the comfort that was sinful. The gentle explorations that had brought them both pleasure.

"Have you heard about the Voodoo Queen?" Brigette hurried her words, knowing Antoine would be angry. "John said there's a new Voodoo Queen. Said she could perform miracles. Said she could stop us."

He plucked her chin and said, deceptively gentle, "You think some Voodoo witch can keep me away from you?"

"It's wrong."

"You didn't think so before."

"That's before I knew—"

"Knew what?"

"No. I don't know," Brigette said, unable to say.

Antoine was kissing her. If she told him her secret, what good would it do? He kissed the hollow of her neck. He kissed her eyelids. His hand stroked around and between her thighs. Maybe he'd think she was just playing martyr again. Maybe he'd even stop loving her.

"No Voodoo witch or priest is going to keep me away from you. You tell this John to keep away if he knows what's good for him."

Brigette elbowed him away. "John helps me sleep." Leaning over him, she reached across and sipped brandy from the bottle. "He knows cures for illnesses. Rheumatism. All kinds of pain— whether in the head or the heart. The slaves love him."

"I doubt that," Antoine said dryly, twisting the bottle out of her hand and up toward her mouth.

"He's a man of taste."

"That's what I'm worried about. Sister dear, I don't want him desiring a taste of you. If he comes round again, tell him I'll gladly kill him."

"I need him," said Brigette, staring at the sputtering candles.

How could she explain to Antoine that she needed someone to confess to? Confessing to a black man made her crimes seem less real. Besides, John offered hope: charms and spells and the power of a Voodoo Queen. Father Christophe would condemn her. For mortal sins, the best salvation a priest could offer was a hell-on-earth of continuing repentance and Christian deeds. If you were lucky, purgatory came afterward. Heaven was always denied.

"Don't let this Voodoo doctor hex you." Antoine swallowed another drink. "How did he insinuate himself in our lives anyway?"

"He said he knew Father."

"That I believe. Our esteemed father was always looking for the unusual. I heard he got himself more than a taste of a pretty Voodooienne." Antoine hooted. "The affair scared the daylights out of Mother and Aunt Louisa. They both retired to bed for a month."

"You're lying. Father wasn't unfaithful."

"It's said this Voodooienne hexed the family fortune. She realized that money meant more than life to our good father."

"That's a lie. Nothing but filthy gossip," said Brigette, pummeling his chest.

"How would you know? Don't you think we're cursed? Poor like swamp rats."

"You drunken sot. That's not what I meant at all." Brigette tried to scramble off the bed. "Father wasn't unfaithful."

"Come back, sister dear. You're going to hear the truth for once about our charming father."

Antoine was drunk. He could feel the weightiness in his head, the tremors behind his movements. One arm kept Brigette pinned to the bed. She struggled uselessly. God, she was beautiful. Her thighs, breasts, and mouth were at once sensual and regal. He liked best the curves sloping down from her rib cage to her abdomen. Antoine couldn't stand the thought of Louis touching his sister. It was even worse accepting Brigette's loyalty to their father. It was her one area of naïveté.

He taunted her. "You know how it's done. Marry a white woman, have a dark woman as mistress. Why do you think Father was any different?"

"Because he was Father, damn you. Mother was faithful to him. He wouldn't dishonor her."

"Even after she was dead? You don't believe he was a monk, do you?"

"He adored Mother. He wouldn't have violated her memory. He loved her too much."

Antoine shook Brigette and said ruthlessly, "Father had plenty of mistresses before and after his marriage. Aunt Louisa said he'd left Mother's bed as soon as she was pregnant. Her death only made him less discreet."

"It's not true."

"You were his golden girl. His pretty belle. Father kept you innocent because it suited his ego to keep you innocent. He was particularly fond of untried little girls."

Brigette flushed. "You've a nasty mind."

"I, on the other hand, had to learn proper southern behavior." Antoine sounded bitter. His words were clipped and hard. "Father was a great teacher of the social arts. Of the southern gentleman's code of honor."

"Why shouldn't he have been?"

"It was our twelfth birthday," he said softly, almost to himself. "Two years before our good father's death. How I wish he'd died earlier. Don't you remember the party?"

"I don't understand."

"The ballroom was made to look like a garden: roses, lilies were everywhere. Our birthday party was the social event of the season. Don't you remember? Tell me you remember." Still straddling Brigette, Antoine stared unseeingly at the bedpost.

Brigette felt hot, uncomfortable. Antoine was acting crazed, like a stranger. Her instinct was not to listen to him. Yet she was fascinated by seeing Antoine gripped by some private emotion. She'd thought they shared everything; clearly, there was something she had missed.

"There were miniature fountains, and archways of wisteria and magnolias. The night was cool for once. Soft, yielding breezes. I was dressed in my first evening dress pants. I was so proud."

"I was dressed in my first gown. It had a satin train and ribbons at the neck," said Brigette, remembering.

"Yes. You were lovely. I saw you dancing the quadrille while Father was leading me up the stairs. I wanted you to come with me too. I wanted us to be together always. Father said no. He said you had your own surprises. Said he had special memories designed for me." Antoine swallowed. In his memory, he could see it happening all over again. He could feel his anxiety, taste the wet fear.

"The yellow guest room was crowded. I asked Father what was going on. But he didn't answer. The room was dense with cigar smoke and clove-laced snuff. Clove snuff was very popular then."

"Gentlemen and, I do remember, a woman or two were standing, milling about. They were excited about something in the center of the room. I couldn't see. I wasn't tall enough then. There were too many people.

"But when they knew Father and I were there, the crowd stepped aside, and Father threw me into bed with three black whores. One girl was about twelve, like me, another eighteen or so; the third must've been in her late twenties. Maybe older. They were naked, and their bodies glistened with perfumed oil. The oldest girl, the fairest of the lot, pulled me on top of her and undressed me. She made a great to-do about my long pants. Drawing comparisons between them and my cock. I was frightened out of my wits. I remember screaming and Father yelling at me 'to be a man.' " His gaze lowered. "I had to be intimate with all of them."

"Antoine, no."

Antoine's face was set; his hands trembled. He continued, his voice grim. "At first, I was overcome and couldn't rise to the occasion. The two women played with me, held me, and rubbed me against the youngest girl. I was to have sex with her first. I think she was drugged, for she lay there utterly uncomprehending. I was utterly uncomprehending. All I knew about sex was boyhood rumor. They pushed my mouth between her legs." Antoine closed his eyes and stopped. He could still hear his father bellowing, placing bets on his virility. Helpless, Brigette glanced away from his face.

"Father and his friends watched. I hated Father then. Have ever since. When I abruptly squirted my seed, those dark whores laughed at me. Everyone laughed. I pay back every black bitch I can, for those two laughing." He collapsed across Brigette's body and pushed his face in the pillow.

He still recalled it all vividly. Once he'd come, the older whores kept laughing at him as they'd flipped him onto his back. The girl, eighteen, had ridden astride him, arching his buttocks high and plunging him deep inside her. The older woman had lowered her vagina over his mouth and teased him. The claustrophobia had been overwhelming. Tendrils of hair and damp skin had filled his mouth. The women had never stopped laughing. His father had never stopped laughing. Only once, before the oldest whore forced him inside her, had the laughter stopped and Antoine had thought he saw in the woman's eyes fear for herself and pity for him. He'd been angered by her pity. He'd bitten her breast and drawn blood. And because he'd been the white gentleman and she the dark slave, she couldn't make any complaint. She'd had to go on laughing.

Antoine shivered, stuffing the pillow inside his mouth to keep from crying out. He couldn't admit how wildly fascinated he'd been by the dark women; he couldn't admit that the fear, mystery, and pleasure of that evening had never been equaled since. Except when he made love to his sister.

"Did Aunt Louisa know?"

"Of course," he said harshly, shifting onto his back. "She was the one who called me. 'Come here, dear,' she said, 'your father has a surprise.' You and your girlfriends were given cake and party favors. You opened your presents while I was trapped upstairs, performing."

She did remember. She remembered looking for her brother, wanting to show him her pearl necklace. A single valuable strand with a pinkish ivory glow. It meant she was a maiden ready for courting.

"Aunt should've stopped it."

"A poor relation. She'd no claim on Father. She was pathetically grateful he asked her to stay on after Mother died. Southern society isn't kind to maiden women."

Brigette remembered their flightly, ineffectual aunt, as dull and as plain as Mother was beautiful. Even after her sister's death, Aunt Louisa had studiously avoided any comparisons with the vital, glowing portrait of Mother in the drawing room. She'd always sat in the farthest corner, with only a single candle to light her fingers' frantic knitting. Beyond dinner parties and mandatory social engagements, Aunt had kept to her darkened room. Sensitive nerves had kept her shut away with handkerchief's dipped in lavender water pressed against her temples. It was Father who'd charmed the household. As he'd charmed her. Maybe that's why she loved Antoine; he was a reflection of Father as well as of herself. If it wasn't for Antoine, she would've been lonely between the infrequent times when Father breezed in. Father would allow her to entertain him for only a half hour. She'd never known what to do to make him stay. She'd tried every childish ploy she knew. But tears, clowning or begging had made no difference. Antoine had comforted her. How could she have denied the blood and loneliness linking her to Antoine?

Aunt had died from the fever first. Then Father had died and all the light went out of the house. Fourteen, newly orphaned, she and Antoine had both been seeking solace. What was wrong with that? Now something was wrong. She had to put an end to it.

Antoine tried to shake his maudlin mood. He was an adult now. Time to be philosophical. He downed another shot of brandy.

"Aunt—and I suppose Mother, too—was boring. Conventional. Just as you would've been if I hadn't rescued you."

"Rescue? Is that what you call it?" Brigette glared at him. She was seeing Antoine anew.

"I've always preferred you to black girls."

She couldn't stand Antoine's nonchalance, the self-satisfied tone. "You knew what you were doing, didn't you? You intentionally seduced me."

"Yes." He caught her hand before she could strike him. "Even at fourteen, I'd had plenty of women. Father primed me well. Remember your maid Sal? Same age as you. Fourteen. Hazel eyes."

"I remember," she said tersely. Of all her maids, Sal had been the most like a friend. Sal, with her bright, sunny manners, had known best how to ease her tempers. Sal had made her feel gay and human.

"Why do you think she was sent away? Why do you think Father sold her to that beet farmer in the North County? Walton always did fancy her. Thought she'd be a great breeder."

Brigette winced. How naive she'd been. Sal had never told her the name of the baby's father. She'd assumed it was another slave. Only a month before he caught the fever, Father had sold Sal.

Brigette had never protested. She'd been hurt that Sal hadn't trusted her enough to name the father. She'd also envied Sal for being womanly, while she was still a girl. How she'd teased Sal, asking if she'd enjoyed making the baby. Sal had only cried. She sorely missed Sal. She never had another friend.

"I was always desiring you."

Nausea swept over her. She'd had romantic notions. She'd

believed it was an accident when Antoine first loved her. Mother was dead, Sal was gone. Aunt Louisa and Father had both died. After Father's funeral, Brigette had hidden in the attic. She'd found the trunks of old ballgown silks and childhood toys comforting. The attic had been a second playroom. She and Antoine had spent thousands of hours there, weaving tales of make-believe and chivalry.

Antoine had found her. He'd still been in his mourning clothes. To her adoring eyes, he'd looked handsome, heroic, and mysterious. He'd touched her gently. She'd pressed against him, enjoying the caresses on her face and hair. At first, she'd been shocked when Antoine touched her between her thighs. But he'd made her feel such pleasure. She'd been afraid, too, that if she asked him to stop, he'd stop loving her. Then who would she have? Not Sal. Not Father. Not Mother. Not Antoine.

"You're a monster," she said.

Brigette remembered. The first time it had hurt. Antoine had pressed at her until she bled. Afterward, when she wanted to say prayers, chant her rosary, and confess to a priest, he'd mocked her. By threatening to leave her, he'd seduced her again.

"Don't be puritanical." Antoine kissed her shoulder. "You're a DeLavier. Father was anything but puritanical. I sometimes think he would've approved of my regard for you. My own, belated, birthday surprise."

Brigette wondered if Antoine loved her. Really loved her. Or had he been exacting his own revenge on Father's "little girl"? Exacting payment for the loss of his own innocence.

Her head ached. Five years, she'd deluded herself. She'd thought their alliance had been something special and strangely chaste in its sexuality. As twins, it was more a case of loving one's self, wasn't it? Her infertility had seemed to support it. Five years, and there hadn't been a pregnancy. Brigette had seen that as a sign from God that their relationship was of a different, less sinful nature. But that was changed now. Her glance roamed over her abdomen.

"Who else do you whore with besides me?"

"Don't be jealous." Antoine remembered the hurt he'd felt when his father and the guests had departed. The two older whores had gone and claimed other companions. He'd lain in the sperm-scented bed, alone and not quite alone, for the youngest girl had been laboring for air in her drugged sleep. After a while, one of Father's drunken guests had claimed her. Laughing at the boy Antoine, sharing a joke, the guest had sucked the girl's breasts and pushed a hand up her vagina. Then, on his knees, he'd pulled her upward to meet his cock, erect and hard over the top of his tailored pants. Later, the man had offered himself to Antoine.

Antoine shook his head. "If you were mine all the time, I'd be all yours all the time. You think I like the thought of Louis pawing you? I get sick thinking Louis has a legal right to touch you. One of these days I just might kill him." Antoine stroked her abdomen while she lay still.

Brigette felt dead, displaced outside her body. She couldn't feel the weight of Antoine's hand. John said for four hundred dollars the Voodoo Queen could do everything: remove the babe, remove Antoine, and make Louis love her again.

Antoine nibbled a breast.

She blinked. His face seemed grotesque. "I don't know you at all."

"Why should you?" he said, lifting his head, startled. "We're twins. Two peas in a pod, yes. But not the same person."

"We must stop. You mustn't touch me again."

"If God made us, then He made me desire you. Let Him carry the weight of our sins." Expertly, methodically, Antoine went about the experienced business of making love to her. He knew which places to stroke, tease, and kiss. He knew, too, how to overcome her resistance.

Afterward, Brigette wasn't sure why she'd allowed him to touch her. Perhaps it had to do with her resolve to give him up, to be a good woman and a good wife. As far as she believed, tonight was their last night together. What did it hurt to lie still and be compliant with his whims?

"Blow out the light, Brigette. I'm tired. Let me sleep in your room, please."

It was the boy talking. The same boy who'd visited her after Father's funeral. He expected to get his way.

"Please, let me sleep in your room." His semen was spent.

Listless, Antoine brought his knees to his chest and curled a fist on the pillow.

Brigette got up. With the candle snuffer, she went about the room, eliminating the lights. She paused, listening, at the door leading to Louis' room. She didn't hear any sounds.

"I'm tired, Brigette," Antoine whined, falling asleep.

She climbed into bed and tucked the covers close.

"So tired."

She looked outside, beyond the french windows and the balcony, to the sky. Stars were falling; a shower of them glittered across the sky. Antoine's drunken snores drifted toward the ceiling. Brigette sat upright; her hands covered her belly and the monstrous babe inside. She'd see the Voodoo Queen tomorrow.

"Why didn't I search for my father? Such a silly question."

"No, I mean it, Marie. No one was there loving you. Not your mother. Not John. Jacques was always gone. Your Grandmère was seeing ghosts. I was never given a chance to love you well, though I've always loved you."

"Where do you get these illusions? You've never loved me. You've always loved the idea of love, the idea of rescuing me. You've never loved the woman in me."

"That isn't so."

"I'm the one dying, so I say it's so. I can't believe you think I ought to have searched for my father. What would I have gained? What good would it have done to have another parent reject me? What good would it have done to say, 'Father, I need you. Your approval. Your warmth.'

"Louis, you're such a fool. I'm still torn up with hurt. I'm nearly eighty, and I still recall clearly the pain of learning that my mother didn't love me. She used me. She manipulated me. And John, who 'fathered' me in countless ways, did his best to destroy me. Damn it, Louis, don't you understand anything? What was I supposed to do? Find the white man my mother whored with and say, 'I've come to claim my inheritance'? He'd have only to look at me to reject me. My color would decide it all. And my dear father could enslave me . . . seduce me . . . beat me and still be within his rights as a white man of New Orleans.

"I'm certain by now that my father is dead. I think, 'How wonderful.' How smart I was not to let another parent reject me too."

"I wish I could've been with you, Marie. I wish I could've comforted you."

"I wish I could've been satisfied to let Grandmère mother me. I didn't know how good my life was, when I was nine. Just think, seventy wasted years."

•

—MARIE LAVEAU, JUNE 15, 1881, EARLY AFTERNOON
(From Louis DeLavier's journal)

How did one count days when each day seemed like a month and each month like a year? It was spring again.

Marie brooded. The warm weather didn't stir her. She was supposed to be dressing for another ceremony. John insisted she wear elaborate gowns, kohl on her eyes, and rouge on her cheeks and lips. Looking in the mirror, Marie saw someone other than herself. Each passing day, her face and form changed a bit. She was growing uglier, more theatrical.

Marie reached for her rum. More often than not, she kept a glass beside her. She'd learned to like the forgetfulness it sometimes brought. She needed someone. She was lonely. She couldn't visit Grandmère again. It was too dangerous. Instead, brave Ribaud visited Grandmère and brought back tales.

"Grandmère is doing poorly." "Her feet, dey sore." "She too sad." "She misses you all de time." "She don't clean herself at all."

Ribaud's terse statements told her volumes. Marie grew closer to the spell man. He brought her more solace than imaginable. Weekly, he'd spy on Grandmère through the kitchen window. Once Grandmère had caught him and thrown a pail at his head. The scar was still there.

Ribaud offered money to the village children, who in turn gave it to their parents, and the parents understood they were being bribed to care for Grandmère. The money helped Marie assuage her guilt. Each visit Marie sent word through Ribaud that Grandmère was to receive the best of care.

Often, Marie toyed with the idea of visiting Grandmère herself. She'd plan elaborate strategies to escape the city and John's spying, but she never acted upon them. If she was caught, she knew John wouldn't hesitate to kill Grandmère. So Marie used rum to suppress her worries. She never pried when Ribaud said cryptically, "Money's not enough." What good would it do when she was so helpless?

John jailed her with notoriety. The city's entire network of slaves and free coloreds seemed to know who she was. John was her promoter and, like a good promoter, he paraded her in the streets and spread rumors about her powers. Blacks whispered whenever she passed by. "She's Marie. Maman Marie." Her infamy and recognition were astounding. She couldn't go anywhere without someone knowing her, seeing her, and telling John. John no longer needed Ribaud to spy on her. Even some of the white populace was beginning to know who she was. There'd been complaints.

John insisted on ceremonies twice a week in Congo Square, just off Rampart Street, in the bourgeois area. Voodoo ceremonies were now publicly tolerated. A carnival show in the district where shopkeepers and their families lived wasn't threatening to city aristocrats. Besides, a new tolerance was in the air. The *Daily Picayune* published a series of articles on Voodoo written by Louis DeLavier. Citizens prided themselves on living in the most sophisticated city in the New World. *Aristos* enjoyed slumming, and what did it matter if after a ceremony their gold coins went to tradesmen who owned saloons and genteel bawdy houses? "Money," John said, "makes for strange friends." Lust, thought Marie, made for stranger friends still. She was all too aware that both whites and blacks found sensual and sexual the night air, the pulsating rhythm of the drums, the twisting gyrations of her dance. She'd seen desire in men's eyes, and their gazes made her feel unclean. John either never noticed or never cared how she was made to feel.

Marie gathered her hair back from her face. Shadows from the candles emphasized the dark circles beneath her eyes. She was thin. Spirits used her body relentlessly. When she wasn't conducting a ceremony in Congo Square, she was being possessed in the house on St. Anne. Her only respite was on Sundays. Sometimes Marie wanted to die, just like her Maman.

John promised, when the time was right, she'd perform in St. Louis Cathedral Square. Marie threw her head back and laughed.

Why not? Whites would kill her for it. It was one thing to take advantage of society's leniency in Congo Square and quite another to blaspheme on the steps of the Catholic church. That was Maman's mistake fifteen years ago, and Marie doubted that time had changed anything. She applied more rouge to her cheeks. What better irony than to die like Maman. She deserved it. She'd let Jacques go to sea again without saying goodbye.

Marie's shoulders drooped; she fought back tears. She cried too often and too long. But whenever she thought of her cruelty to Jacques, she was filled with self-loathing. There didn't seem to be any way to recover her self-respect. It was impossible to leave John for Jacques, and part of her shame was that she didn't want to.

"Marie. Look here. This is perfect for tonight."

John stood in the doorway. He carried a crate almost too large for his arms. Rude holes were punched in the top. Dry straw pushed through slats. "This will assure our success. We'll take New Orleans by storm."

John was amazingly attractive: angular, lean, ruthless. Lusting for John, Marie learned to hate herself. Her logic was circular: John was evil—she must be evil too. If she were truly good, she'd stop wanting a man so evil.

Marie stared at John's reflection in the vanity. He was talking excitedly, balancing his box. Something in her must need his viciousness. All Marie knew was that in loving John she'd caused a hardening of her heart. It was difficult to be kind and forgiving. She distrusted kindness. She couldn't even forgive herself.

"Too much loving makes you hard." Who had said that?

John was bending awkwardly, setting the crate down. "I paid dearly for it." He was talking fast, almost incoherently. "Our customers will make it worthwhile. Here. In the house. We'll use it tonight. If tonight goes well, we'll use it in Congo Square. Next time Cathedral Square. Everyone will know your name."

Marie tugged her dressing gown tight. "I'm tired, John. Rouge can't disguise how tired I am." She swallowed rum. "Too many ceremonies. I'm getting sick. My head hurts all the time."

"Gods don't care about your ills. While I care a great deal about the money," John said, without looking at her. "Business is fickle. We earn what we can, when we can." He tapped gingerly at one of the crate's holes. He looked through it, shutting one eye and squinting the other. "I hope it isn't dead. I'll have my money back if it is."

Marie slumped in the vanity chair. She watched John circling the crate. It was old, pockmarked by rot. The wood smelled of swamp, mildew, and bones. John, who normally pushed and ripped and tore at things, kept circling, hesitating to disturb the wood slats. His caution more than anything else made Marie want to know what was inside.

Taking a decisive breath, John tugged at the slats. They fell away easily. Marie gasped. Inside the crate was another box surrounded by damp straw. This box, too, had air holes. John stroked a sweaty palm across his brow. His breathing was harsh, labored.

A spirit moved.

"It isn't dead. Whatever it is you've got there, it isn't dead." Marie shivered. "What is it, John?"

"Our fortune."

John's eyes were unnaturally bright; his entire being was focused on the box. He held out his palm and felt a thin, cool air emanating from the box. The air stirred unsettling memories. He could feel, smell, and sense Africa, recall deliberate cruelties.

John wasn't quite sure why he'd insisted on having the creature. It had been an impulse. He hadn't been fearful of it when it was across the ocean, deep in an isolated jungle, waiting to be trapped and caught. He'd forgotten all about the creature until yesterday, when he was told it had arrived. He'd been caught off guard. The beefy captain had demanded extra payment, since a man had died pursuing it. "Heat exhaustion," he'd said.

John had ordered the captain to show him the box in the dank hold of the ship. John's heart, warningly, had skipped a few beats. He'd shrugged it off.

Standing over the box now, John felt dread. The thing in the box and failure were the only things that scared him. "Open it, Marie. Go on. Open it."

"Why don't you?"

"No, it's your gift."

"I don't want it."

"It's good for business. It'll mean our fortune."

"Your business, not mine. It's your decision to demand money."

"The Catholic church collects money."

"Doesn't mean it's right."

"Open the box, Marie." He was beside her, his voice unnaturally calm. His quiet tone warned of a beating. "You're trying to trick me."

Marie nearly swooned. Like lightning, a hint of madness distorted John's face. He shoved her forward. The box shifted in her direction. John took several steps back.

Something was alive in the box.

Marie feared what she might find: a wild animal, a tormented spirit, a creature from some netherworld. John could've captured any evil and brought it to her. Hysteria rose.

Something deadly was inside the box.

She spun around. "John, I can't—"

"Open the box."

"Damn you."

John slapped her.

Marie whimpered. "Please."

John ignored her; thin streams of sweat were pooling in the hollows of his neck and back. "Open it."

Nervous, Marie placed her hands on top of the box. Rope held the lid tightly in place.

"Open it," whispered John.

"Damn you. Damn you. Damn you." Marie tore at the rope, her nails breaking on the hemp.

She could feel the thing moving, the rope unraveling itself.

"Open it," he hissed.

Marie lifted the lid, screaming when the thing darted its head forward. "Help me. Oh, my God, help me." She fell, scrambling backward on her knees.

John crowed. "This is your Damballah god." He was laughing fanatically, smacking his hand against the wall. "Your great Damballah." His eyes were wet with laughter. Marie, curled in a ball, was murmuring, "Oh, my God. My God."

There was pounding on the door. "Marie? John. You be all right?" It was Nattie and Ribaud. "Open the door. Everything all right?"

"Go away," John shouted. "Nothing but a surprise." He slammed his weight against the door, guffawing loudly. "Nothing's wrong. Nothing but a friendly surprise." His ribs ached with laughter and from the sudden release of tension. It was a snake, nothing but a dumb, ordinary snake. His fears had evaporated as soon as he saw Marie scuttling like a nervous rabbit.

"Where'd you get this?" Marie was shivering with anger and embarrassment. Looking down into the box, she saw huge coils on matted straw. A head, flat and broad, raised itself high. The animal hissed; its tongue was forked.

"Marie, meet Damballah. Damballah, meet Marie."

"It's a snake," she said angrily. "It's not Damballah." Damballah was something more than this—like Christ, like God.

"Who's to know?"

"Where'd you get it?" She'd never seen such a snake. Ash-colored, it stared at her. It looked like a water moccasin but it was much longer, wider, and, Marie suspected, more deadly. "Where'd you get it?"

"Slavers. It's an African python."

"You deal with slavers?"

John shrugged. "They can't capture me twice, can they? I've freedom papers. Forged but effective."

"You disgust me."

Leaning his broad shoulders against the wall, John replied, "I thought I was brilliant to remember the village snake god. A living icon is much better than a plaster statue. We might put the Catholics out of business."

"I don't know much about Voudon"—Marie spoke over her shoulder while staring into the box—"but I do know Damballah is more than this."

"But does anyone else?"

Marie stared at the snake. Head lifted, the snake was still. Wary.

Watching. Perhaps she was wrong. Perhaps Voodoo *was* this snake: ancient, primeval. Marie couldn't rely on what John told her about Voodoo. He was more interested in manipulating effects. He managed a sideshow; she was his actress. Nattie was even more reluctant to talk about Voodoo. During ceremonies, the *loas* never visited Nattie or John. Even the lowliest slave or servant had his or her own moment of possession. But Nattie never lost control, never belonged to any spirit other than herself. John never had spiritual grace.

Marie inched closer to the snake. Studying it, she laid a hand on the box. She was an unlikely priestess—unversed in her religion but nonetheless its guide. She couldn't even tell whether this snake was a sign or a significant symbol. Or was it part of her *fa?*

The snake stretched its neck forward. Its cool flesh brushed against her hand. Marie experienced awe, the same wonder she felt as a child in the bayou. The animal was alive, vibrant, a part of the natural world. Everything in Teché was controlled by nature, a random and yet not so random power. What if nature was nothing more than the collective spirits of plants and animals? What if these spirits were the *loas?* John had once said there were spirits to be conjured in every living and nonliving thing. Maybe this snake was a god, special, extraordinary, like all the other ordinary parts of nature.

"It'll grow strong enough to kill a man." John was somber.

"I doubt it," Marie said softly. Damballah wasn't this snake, but this snake definitely had power. Marie sensed it in the same way she sensed a spirit's presence. She held out both arms.

An understanding passed between them. Marie heard the snake sigh.

"Aren't you afraid it will poison you?"

Marie realized John hadn't moved from the room's outer edges while she and the snake occupied the center. She pivoted. The snake was stretched across her arms.

"Put it down. Do you want to be hurt? Put it down." John swallowed hard.

"It won't hurt me. Are you afraid?"

"No, why should I be?" His tone was belligerent. John squatted, his back against the wall, his hands dangling between both knees.

Marie was amazed. John had lost his patronizing calm, his

supreme confidence. He was on edge like a bantam rooster before its head was sliced off. Slowly she stroked the length of the snake.

"Aren't you afraid it will bite you?" John demanded again. "Poison you?"

"It doesn't have a rattle or venomous jowls. The bayou teaches the differences between snakes."

"I hope no one else knows."

"Didn't you?"

John looked at Marie. "Yes, of course I knew. Remember, you don't control me."

Marie flushed angrily. The snake was cold against her chest. Marie realized it served as her shield. Intuitively, she knew John would never harm her while she held the snake. "Our followers will see what we tell them to see. They'll believe the snake is poisonous, because it thrills them to believe it. Isn't that so, John? Isn't that what you taught me?"

John fixed on the snake's mouth.

"Why do you need me, John? Why can't you leave me alone?"

John eyed her coolly. "You're like the python. You attract paying customers."

"With my performances?"

"Yes."

"Don't you believe something special happens to me? Something beyond belief?"

"Fantasies."

"You claim to be African."

"Not claim." John moved forward, but Marie saw him subtly check himself when she shifted the snake. "I am African. I should've been a king—"

"—and ruled over hundreds, thousands," murmured Marie, the snake making her bold. "Don't you recall the Voodoo of your fathers? Your ancestors, John? Tell me about it. It must be more sacred than what you and I engage in." The snake slid down her arm.

John kept his eyes carefully hooded. How could he explain he lacked belief in any god, black or white? Life was too harsh to justify religion. He hadn't been captured as a slave, he'd been sold by other blacks. Tribal enemies, showing misguided mercy, had spared his

206

life. But his memories were more horrible than any simple death. He knew what it was like to be near starvation, sailing in the hulk of a ship, chained to hundreds of other poor souls, all of them babbling in different tongues. He'd spent over a hundred days trapped in festering darkness, lying in his and others' waste.

How could his ancestors, his family's guardian *loas,* have allowed it? What about all those years when his family made obeisance and sacrifices to the gods and ancestors? The old kings, his great-grandfathers, should've protected his father the king and himself, as heir. In the hold, John had thought it through thousands of times, only to reach the same answer. The *loas* were powerless. There wasn't any justice. Or fairness. Or faith. He'd grown more embittered each time he heard the lapping of a wave against the hull, each time urine had cascaded down his thighs, each time a fly, attracted by dung, had landed in a place he couldn't scratch. Family spirit *loas* were a myth. Ancestors were bones and disintegrating flesh buried in dirt. Nothing more. The others captured had called upon innumerable gods: Ogu, Damballah, Legba, Agwé. He'd almost gone crazy from the unrelenting buzz of entreaties. Cries in the night. Cries in the day, which had passed as night in the oppressive darkness. Cries expelled with the last breath of a dying body. Nothing changed. The ship had sailed on to the auction block and slavery.

Marie wished she could see inside John's mind. His face showed distress, vulnerability. He seemed achingly human. There was so much she didn't know about him. She only knew that during his rare tentative moments she loved him all the more. The snake coiled about her waist. The snake knew she'd never hurt it, and Marie trusted the snake to do the same.

John thought the python was taunting him. Without guile, it calmly explored Marie's body. If he didn't know better, John would've thought it was tame. Curious, his eyes followed its slow upward progress. Damballah, he thought sarcastically. Why should he owe allegiance to anyone or anything? So much better to dominate. Control the universe yourself. He did control his world. The women in it, the religious followers. He made money at it. What else should satisfy him?

"Tell me, John. What do you remember of Africa?"

"Leave me be," he yelled at Marie, his expression pained. John rocked back till he was sitting on the floor, his legs thrust before him like a lame peddler. He couldn't stop watching the snake's hypnotic progress. Uncertainty assailed him. His gut tightened.

He remembered a death from his childhood: a young man had been strangled by a python. Damballah. The two were intertwined. John did, yet didn't, believe in spirits. He'd been seven, perhaps eight, and the slow violence of the snake strangling the man had impressed him. He couldn't remember the man's transgression—perhaps he'd stolen another man's boar or chicken or wife. He vividly remembered the man's refusal to struggle. For years, he'd pushed the memory to an obscure part of his mind. But purchasing the snake today, traveling with it through the city, sensing its movements, and smelling echoes of African woods had made the memory regain its force.

He couldn't begin to guess why the man hadn't struggled. Perhaps the odds had been too overwhelming. As a child, John had thought he could win a struggle against anything. He was a prince. But he'd never known whether it was the unnatural strength of Damballah that killed the man or the man's belief in Damballah that killed him. Enslavement had made him believe the latter. He'd seen how oppression made cowards of men, sapping their strength and initiative. But he wasn't sure. His mind played tricks on him. African memories challenged him.

John rubbed his eyes.

Marie and the snake were frozen in place.

Marie, her hair hanging free, was sitting cross-legged like an Indian. The snake covered most of her body. It coiled about her thigh and waist, and its flat head hovered near her face. He blinked. John thought, The two of them are dead. *Not dead, just somewhere beyond the walls of this room.*

There were moments when John was certain Marie was not herself—when a spirit did, in fact, possess her. Yet his arrogance couldn't let him accept what he hadn't experienced himself. No matter that the three Maries had always disturbed him—Grand-mère, Marie's Maman, and now Marie. He rationalized that their minds tricked them into believing they were possessed. Likewise when he was tired, a bit drunk, his mind shaped illusions.

Most of the time John succeeded in convincing himself there were no Voodoo mysteries or miracles. But tonight a child's nightmare and long-suppressed African memories upset him. He recalled the village priest, adorned with beads, feathers, and a mask to ward off evil spirits, ordering that the strangled man's body be left to deteriorate. His father, the village chief, had consented. It was then that the boy John had realized that the man must've been guilty of some serious crime or desecration. For without a proper burial, his soul would wander outcast forever from his tribe and ancestors. Later, John had watched the buzzards who'd tasted the dried blood on the man's lips and torn the flesh from his thighs. He couldn't forget the tattered body. John had blamed it all on the python. Only the first death mattered. Five nights later, hyenas had claimed the body.

Staring at Marie and the snake, John said with certainty, "It'll grow strong enough to kill a man." His head nodded vigorously. "It'll kill a man."

"A small animal. A child, perhaps. A woman. But any man ought to overpower it."

Agitated, John pounded the floor with his fist. "You don't know what you're saying. I tell you it could kill a man."

"Impossible."

"I've seen it happen." He stood up hurriedly. The room spun. He rubbed his brow, then paced wildly, stumbling into furniture. His fate was connected to the snake. Damballah. He was sorry he'd purchased it. There wasn't any god. No miracles. No spirits. Just hard, hurtful reality. "Get it out of here. I want it out of my sight. Put it in the courtyard. Ribaud can get rid of it in the morning."

"What are you saying?"

"Destroyed, damn you. I want it destroyed."

"It's my gift." Marie panicked. She didn't know why, but it was important to keep the animal. If she lost the snake, she'd be losing something valuable. "You gave it to me."

"I take it back."

"No." Marie was standing, the snake suspended like a shawl across her shoulders. "Think, John. It's good to make the gods visible. You said that. There'll be plenty of money tonight. Double what's normal. I'll dance with it, sing to it. Think of the effect."

John paused, wetting his lips. He was behaving irrationally. He'd had too much to drink. He looked at the snake strung about Marie's throat. It was perhaps eight feet in length, the thickness of his fist. Perhaps it wouldn't grow any larger. A knife could still slit its throat. Yes. A man could fight it.

Marie held her breath.

John went to the vanity and finished Marie's half-filled glass of rum. "You can keep it," he said, adding hoarsely, "But I want lots of gold, Marie. Lots of money. Else it goes."

She nodded.

John examined her from head to toe. Her dressing gown was open, fraying at the hem. The snake seemed at home with her, touching her soft, exposed breasts.

"Put it away and get dressed. I don't want to see it until I have to. We've a guest tonight."

"Who?" Marie said dully, hiding her happiness. She was glad she'd won the python. Carefully, she lifted it from her neck and returned it to its box.

"An *aristo.* If Voodoo cures ills, solves heartbreak and trauma, there's no sense in discriminating. Rich and poor are entitled to your services. White as well as black."

"Yes, you're right, John." Her hands spanned his waist.

"What's this? You've never agreed with me before."

"I get afraid sometimes. I grow weary." She buried her face in his shirt. She could feel and taste his moist fear. Her hands began massaging away the tension in his shoulders and neck. She said, "I love you," amazed that she could say a lie and a truth at the same time.

John enveloped her in his arms. Marie sighed. She was aroused, overwhelmed by a wealth of feeling.

She was lifting her head for a kiss when John slapped her. She screamed and John gripped her jaw, twisting her mouth off-center. "Don't manipulate me. Just do as you're told. Any time I want, that snake'll be gone. Do you understand me?"

Marie bobbed her head and John threw her backward upon the bed. "Get dressed. I want you to be especially good tonight."

"I hate you."

John laughed, slapping Marie lightly about the face and head. Marie flailed, trying to block his hands. When John kissed her again, she lay still. A moan caught in her throat. John patted her bottom; then he abruptly left the room, studiously ignoring the python's box.

Marie punched the bed. She could kill him. Tear his throat apart. Stab him with a knife.

"Too much loving makes you hard." Marie repeated the words. They seemed right—the taste, the feel of the vowels in her mouth. Nattie had said it. She had spoken the truth.

Hugging John's pillow, Marie rubbed her cheek against it. His smell trapped in the down seemed virile. She'd never understood the smell of age that she associated with John. It both repelled and attracted her. It reminded her of plants dying in winter and the capture of a rabbit in a snake's jowls.

Marie rolled onto her back, hugging the pillow close and rubbing it along her groin. In this bed, she felt loved even though she knew it wasn't true. Telling herself that John loved her compensated for the loss of Maman. And the loss of her mother's love made her insecure enough to accept cruelty and false love from John. She was still outside the circle—disconnected, lonely, looking in on herself.

Marie turned her head toward the snake. It was half in and half outside its box. Its texture was like smooth rawhide. Marie smiled. The snake was ugly, yet beautiful.

"What shall I feed you? John? Though he might be hard to swallow. How about a rabbit instead?"

The snake looked amused. Marie laughed. A snake was as good a friend as any. Slipping off her robe and ambling nude toward her dresser, Marie decided playfully she'd teach the snake to talk. A slight noise arrested her and Marie looked at the snake's reflection. Through a trick of light and space, it appeared as if the snake lay coiled upon her shoulder. When she looked around, the real snake was in its crate, its head barely visible. But when she looked back in the mirror, the snake's reflection was draped about her shoulders like a mantle of power. She realized the snake was a sign from Damballah. It was meant to be her hope against John, an essential key in counterbalancing the power between them. All she needed was the will and the recognition of how to use it.

Ribaud was talking to Marie with his drums. The ceremony had begun. Twice, when John wasn't looking, when he was preening like a cock among the crowd, Marie had smiled at Ribaud. Ribaud had chuckled and tapped the bass drum.

The snake was resting in its box beside the altar. Ribaud had fed it a mouse.

The followers were excited, swaying their bodies in time with the drums. They were curious about the box, the way children were curious about promised treats. For many, Voodoo was an escape from the daily brutality of their lives. Marie was their show queen, leading them into realms of imagination. For others, Voodoo was salvation. It soothed them to know that spirits were larger than life, yet subject to desires, hates, and petty jealousies. With gods who acted human, people felt less alienated. With gods who were also aspects of nature, followers could explain some of the randomness, the fickleness of their fate. It was understandable that Ezili, with her many lovers, would be jealous of younger women and could cause a pretty girl's death or rape. Just as it was understandable that Agwé could have an upset stomach and cause towering waves to drown sailors. It was all a part of one's fate, one's *fa*. Sometimes you could save yourself, sometimes not. Saving yourself meant having *loas,* or ancestors, who favored you because of your continuing prayers and gifts. Or else you gained special blessings through sacrifice to the supreme god Damballah.

The worshipers were justly terrified of John. No amount of money or prayer ensured his goodwill. Worshipers recognized the barely suppressed cruelty in him because they'd seen it in their masters. Some respected John's right to be as mean as any slave-holder, as mean as any white man. Maman Marie was warmth and beauty. She was the light to John's darkness.

Tonight, followers were eager to release their passions. John added a new element—a veiled woman with graceful white hands. She was out of place among the perspiring blacks. Yet for many blacks, the woman heightened tensions. They recognized her as an *aristo*. Her presence made the ceremony ahead seem appealingly forbidden.

Marie wished she could see the woman's face. How did the woman see John? Jealousy stirred. John paraded the veiled *aristo* like a prized possession.

Marie felt a deadly, conscious swoon. She was slumped in a chair near the altar.

She focused her emotions.

John began the chant.

> *"Papa Legba, remove the barrier for me*
> *So I may pass through to the spirit world.*
> *Remove the barrier*
> *So I can visit the loa."*

"You be all right?"

"Yes, Nattie." Marie glanced up. Nattie was dressed in a garish costume as well. Bright beads. Bright colors. There was even a red ribbon in her short curly hair. It made her look unattractive, like a Mardi Gras buffoon.

"Do you know who that be?" Nattie pointed at the veiled woman.

Marie looked across the room. The woman's veil fluttered. John caressed the white hand. The blacks were dressed in joyous white; the white woman was dressed in mourning.

"That be Miz Brigette. She shares John's bed. When he tires of you, he visits her."

Marie felt a sharp stab of pain. "Get out of here. You never say anything good."

"What good there be to say when John prefers white to black skin?"

"You're a jealous, interfering woman. We'd be much happier without your lies."

"Who'd be happier? You and John? Foolishness. I don't be the one lying. You lie to yourself all the time. Count how often John stays with you in bed through the long night. How many times in a month? One night? Two? He goes somewhere when he isn't with you." Nattie flounced away, her pantaloons billowing.

Marie bowed her head. It was hard to find joy. Life used to be simpler and more forgiving. Now it was betrayal and lack of trust. She watched John's progress. He was protective of the white woman, maneuvering her through the crowded room with ease. Marie couldn't help noticing John treated Brigette far more tenderly than he treated her. She didn't doubt John's unfaithfulness.

Marie conjured a vision of Miz Brigette and John in bed. There'd be a loveliness to such opposites. Black on white. Fair silken hair against curly black. Soft yielding limbs beneath John's hard, punishing body.

Did John ever beat Mademoiselle Brigette? Marie doubted it.

Marie's hand grazed against the box. The snake was her friend.

"Damballah," someone yelled from the crowd. "Damballah." Caroling voices twisted like a tornado through the crowd. Ribaud intensified his rhythm. A middle-aged man was on his knees, trembling with spiritual possession. "Maman-*loa*. Papa-*loa*. The one true god." His right leg seemed to go limp, and his back rounded with arthritis and age. Marie recognized the man as the spirit Legba. Someone rushed forward with Legba's cane and pipe. Legba got up, surveying the room, then limped to the far corner, his cane tap-tapping. Legba opened the barrier so the other spirits could enter.

Marie drank more rum. She never knew when the gods would succeed in entering her. Tonight, she felt estranged. The white woman was sitting against the right wall, oddly prim and out of place.

John was wringing a chicken's neck, offering sacrifice. When he cut into its body, Brigette screamed. Drops of blood blended with her dark skirt. Marie laughed. Mademoiselle needn't worry about appearing unclean.

Everyone was aroused. The room was hot. Spirits descended like rain. Ezili danced, lifting her skirt above her head. Ogu stomped and sliced the air with his saber. Agwé relived old sea battles. La Croix whimpered, "Why was I betrayed? I died too soon."

Marie felt old. Her self was as tenuous as the candlelight. She kissed the charcoal snake; the crude drawing squirmed on the altar.

"Maman Marie, Voodoo Queen," the chant echoed.

Marie heard voices both dead and alive.

"Maman Marie."

Voices human and inhuman.

Marie doubled over. "Damballah."

"Maman Marie, Voodoo Queen."

Marie rested her head on the snake's box. She could feel the snake inside it calling her.

Marie opened the box and gathered the python in her arms. Some of the followers screamed and retreated. Others hollered "Death" and fell, praying, onto their knees. Some forgot where they were and called on the Virgin Mary and Christ. The majority cried out compassionately for the pretty Voodoo Queen, fearing the snake would bite and release its poison inside her.

Half in, half outside the box, the snake seemed oddly pleased. Marie held its cool skin close, murmuring, "It's all right. Everything is all right." Her other hand reached for the charcoal drawing of Damballah. Damballah had the power she lacked. Marie concentrated, rubbing her fingers along the snake's cool, spineless form.

"Damballah, I'm ready now." Marie felt heat—from the candles, from John, from the rhythm of her own heart. "Come."

Damballah spoke to and through her. All was hushed like the seconds following a storm. Marie was transported to another world. *She became the great serpent.*

To the audience, Marie wriggled like a serpent with its head cut off. Guttural gibberish dropped from her mouth. Curled at her feet was the python, darting its head and tongue at any who dared to come near.

Beneath the veil, Brigette tasted blood inside her mouth. She shouldn't have come. The blacks' passion was too upsetting. The Voodoo Queen seemed like a monster to her, poised at the gates of hell, beckoning. Yet she was also convinced she was hearing and seeing a miracle. In Marie's babbling, she heard the sound and felt the memory of her father. He was promising his baby girl that everything would be all right. She needed everything to be all right.

John fidgeted with his cravat; he didn't believe in miracles. Ribaud was ecstatic, Nattie ambivalent. Later, cynics swore they heard Marie say, "The world will end." Others heard warmth and love. Each follower personalized her sounds: suffering, hope, anguish, justice. Followers wept; some grinned. Her inharmonious babbling translated into a thousand messages.

Marie heard noises from the bayou: the silence of fireflies, the caw of crows. She saw the marsh infused with light and saw herself, swimming. A sable-colored Damballah glided beside her.

"I will show you a tale," Damballah said. Snatches of her and Grandmère rocking; Grandmère lamenting over the broken rocker; Maman spinning rainbows; Maman and herself attacking and being beaten by John; herself, safe in John's arms; John laughing, "Everything I do is real." No pleasure without pain, no joy without sorrow, no love without hate. "I create and re-create," said Damballah. They swam in gradually tightening circles.

Marie relived her dreams, even some undreamt.

Marie saw what she knew she'd always been waiting to see—the snake birthing itself. . . . She yelled, the sound tearing up from her gut. The drums stopped. *Shed skin and the newly alive snake dissolved in the marsh.*

Marie's actions startled John. He wasn't ready to believe any miracle. Instead, he believed Marie was rebelliously trying to manipulate him through the snake.

Marie's yell brought her out of her trance. She was so tired. Still crawling on her knees, she returned the snake to its box. Now she knew animals, too, could be possessed. She'd felt Damballah entering the snake's body just as Damballah had entered hers. Damballah could be in two places, two minds, two bodies. Damballah was omnipresent. She glanced upward. Everyone—John, Nattie, Ribaud, Brigette—was staring at her. Several followers had pressed themselves against the wall; still others were in small groups, awestruck, holding on to one another. Cross-legged, Marie rested on the floor. Strewn about her were chicken feathers, bits of flesh and blood. Someone had sacrificed four chickens while she was possessed.

"Go home. Everybody go home." Nattie shooed people out the door. "Nothing be left to see. Go."

Thoughtfully, Nattie brought Marie a mug of rum.

Lids swollen and soul weary, she said, "Thank you."

"I be able to recognize the great god."

"Is that so, Nattie?" Marie hated the woman's confidence. Marie glanced about the room. A few stragglers were leaving. It was as if, in unison, her followers had sensed her energies were spent and nothing more could be accomplished. No more visiting gods, no prayer requests. So they'd all departed. It was a few hours short of dawn.

John was avoiding her.

Marie wondered how much gold John would count tonight. It never mattered to him how the gold was gained. Many of the slaves risked death by stealing coins, and those who couldn't steal coins stole expensive jewelry—diamond cravat pins, snuffboxes painted and edged with silver or gold. Some were even resourceful enough to steal flatware, gold plates, and French linen and crystal from their master and mistress.

Marie tried to rise but her legs were spent. She sat again and stared at the funereal clothed figure with the slim white hands. Was it truly Brigette? John's lover? As if answering her question, the white woman removed her veil. Marie sharply sucked in air. The Virgin from the market. Nattie hadn't lied. No wonder John preferred Brigette. She was golden and more beautiful than any living soul. Marie knew if she glanced in a mirror, she'd be disgusted at how tired, dirty, and spent she was. Marie wondered, Did Brigette DeLavier recognize her from the Market Square?

Cautiously, Brigette gathered her skirt, moved forward, and stooped until her face was level with Marie's. Brigette was frightened of the brown girl, but her fear didn't dissuade her from hoping the Voodoo Queen could save her.

Marie pinched the white cheek, suffusing it with blood. A crucifix hung in the crevice of Brigette's snowy breasts. Marie was torn between sympathy and hatred. This was the woman who'd saved her and Jacques but bedded John for pleasure. Marie felt jealousy. No, not jealousy but disgust, for they were both sharing John.

"Can you help me?"

"Je suis Marie."

Nervously, Brigette glanced at John. He flicked his hand, urging her to continue.

"Can you help me, Maman Marie?"

Marie cradled Brigette's crucifix in her palm. It was expensive mother-of-pearl overlaid on a ebony cross.

"Why are you here? The Catholic church teaches the serpent is evil." Marie snapped the chain. Brigette winced. A welt raised on Brigette's neck; there was a thin trail of blood. Marie let the cross fall into her lap.

"Please. The church can't help me. I came to you."

"Your hair is lovely." Marie touched it, imagining John's dark head buried in the yellow. She sniffed at the hair and smelled sweet roses. The rose scent turned foul yellow. Brigette was to Marie as Marie was to the Virgin. Estranged. Opposites. Yet Brigette and Marie shared John.

Brigette inhaled, muttering prayers, trying to stop her trembling. She swore she'd repent, do whatever was necessary to end her torment. "Please," she said. "There's someone who wants me."

Marie yanked her hair.

Brigette gasped, falling onto her hip. Her hand skidded in chicken's blood. She screamed.

John cursed, pausing in his counting of the gold.

Nattie shooed Brigette. "Maman Marie be tired," she said nastily, fluttering her hands. "She be done for the evening."

"Shut up, Nattie," answered John.

Brigette, crawling, clutched and kissed Marie's palm. "Anything you want. Money. Jewels. Anything. Only please help me."

Their eyes held: bright blue and soft brown. Marie thought, She doesn't recognize me at all. Marie didn't know why it was essential that she be recognized. She only knew it hurt that Brigette had taken so little notice of her. Brigette hadn't saved her from Antoine or cared about Jacques' life; rather, Brigette had saved herself from boredom and an unpleasant scene in the Market Square. Regretfully, Marie removed her hand from Brigette's grasp.

Brigette sat back on her heels, layering her hands in the folds of her gown and in the space between her thighs. The arrogant, self-assured woman from the Market Square was gone. "I've tried turning him away. He's relentless." Shamed, she lowered her eyes. "Sometimes I encourage him. I can't help it," she said defiantly, then moaned, "I want him."

"Your problems are solved. Marry him," Marie said, her voice flippant. "Isn't that what good Catholic girls do? Marry. Have babies. Raise a family."

"I'm an adulteress." Though spoken softly, the words were powerful and unpleasant.

Adulteress. Marie thought she might smile.

"Marie." John was signaling her. Marie refused to catch his eye. Brigette was fragile. Lovely. Everything John could ever want. She wondered how John felt with his mistress begging for a spell to be rid of him. Or maybe Brigette meant some other lover, a white lover. It was probable. A white woman wouldn't classify dalliance with a black man as adultery. It would be more in the nature of an experiment. Marie felt the urge to laugh. John, an experiment. A rutting beast for a rich, bored woman.

"My lover and I are too close," Brigette confessed. "Much too close. We've committed unspeakable acts."

Marie studied the upturned nose, the silken skin. It wasn't fair that Brigette should look as lovely and innocent as a virgin. Marie felt she looked the demon to Brigette's saintly face. Yet both of them were sinners.

Brigette looked up. Tears balanced on the tips of her lashes. The southern belle was beautiful when she cried. "Maman Marie, what should I do? Please help me."

Jealousy won out over pity. "I could color your hair gray, wrinkle your eyes," Marie said viciously. "I could make your nose a snout. Your skin like an alligator's. Nobody would ever want you anymore." Marie sensed Nattie encouraging her. "I could age you twenty years before your time."

Brigette edged away, wailing. Her dress caught in the mud, feathers, and chicken blood surrounding the altar. She screamed.

"Let's pluck the sin out of you. Tear it out of your heart."

"No, please. Spare me. Anything you want." Brigette was hysterical. Blood drained through her hands, dripped from the edges of her veil.

"What's the matter with you?" John shouted harshly at Marie.

"I don't like her. Get your mistress—"

"She's not."

"Don't lie. Get her out of here."

"Oh, please, John. I want to go. Please help me go."

John escorted the tearful Brigette. One arm was wrapped around her, supporting her waist. Brigette looked like an old widowed crone.

"Should I expect you back?" Marie snapped.

John nodded.

Considerate of Brigette's good name and his own survival, John flung forward Brigette's veil as the two of them went out to meet the dusky morn.

Marie, though dismayed, felt a grim sense of victory. Tonight John would beat her but bruises would fade. Damballah was teaching her about power.

Marie was half-asleep when John invaded the bedroom. He was frightening, framed in the doorway. He looked stark and obscene. He didn't remove his clothes. He moved atop Marie's body, asserting his claim to her. Marie didn't struggle but John acted as if she did. He rode her hard, and she gripped the bedposts for support. She kept her eyes upon the snake's crate, imagining it asleep, imagining Damballah's power. She refused to take pleasure from this coupling. Usually she was guilty of feeling both pleasure and pain. But this time was different. No arousal, no building of tension begging to be released. When she felt he'd never stop, John climaxed. Marie could feel his semen exploding then, wriggling up into the crevices of her womb.

Though she couldn't explain how she knew, she knew her seed divided. A child would be born. Four generations of Marie.

Her last thought before she fell deep into sleep was that the serpent's knowledge balanced souls. She felt a kind of solace.

The serpent balanced the world.

~

Slaves captured from the west African shore brought with them their faith. Gods grouped in hierarchies, dances and music linked to divine possession. Divinities are served primarily by women; they dance for, are possessed by, and clean the gods' sanctuaries.

Damballah is father to all the gods. He enters his chosen priestess: "she writhes, her whole body is convulsed. A goat is sacrificed and the blood collected in a jar." The blood is wiped on the followers' lips, swearing them to secrecy.

·

—The Origins and History of the Voodoo Cults

To prevent Voodoo outbreaks in New Orleans, all blacks, especially Dahomeyans and Haitians, must be baptized and taught the Catholic faith.

·

—Code Noir
(From Louis DeLavier's journal)

La, Marie, not dat way. Here, like dis."

Marie yelped as the curling irons scorched her fingers. Ziti and Marie were alone in the house on St. Anne. Ziti was instructing her in the fine art of hairdressing.

"Why do people abuse their hair so?" Marie slapped the singed wig. "If hair was meant to curl, it would curl naturally."

"All rich white women wear dere hair piled in curls," cooed Ziti. "It gives dem elegance."

Marie giggled as Ziti lifted her skirt, pushed her thick hair forward, and strutted.

John wanted Marie in white people's homes. "You'll learn secrets," he said. "While curling their hair, women will confide in you. You'll gain power over them." The trick was simple: Marie would fix bogus spells for white women's ills—enemies, heartache, money problems. She'd learn all John needed to know for blackmailing their husbands and lovers.

Only yesterday, she and John had been sitting near the altar. Humidity had made it hard to breathe; the wind, lazy, didn't enter the house. Her head propped on her knees, feeling nauseous, Marie watched John carving a Voodoo doll out of wood.

"In a year we'll be ready for Cathedral Square. Imagine, Marie, Cathedral Square!"

"What if Damballah won't protect me?"

John sliced sad eyes in the pine wood. "This is a business. It doesn't matter what Damballah will or won't do. Your power is more inside people's minds than in you." Leaning forward, his tongue sliding across her teeth, he kissed her. "All you need to do is keep people afraid. Your mother was good at business."

That was a lie. Maman hated her audiences. Maman had died brutally and young.

For two months, Marie and John had kept a cautious truce. John still caressed and entered her, but the passion was one-sided. Were women always fools? Exploring her body, John seemed to be searching for Maman. He was always disappointed when he didn't find her.

Truth was one-sided. Marie shook her head slightly and traced the veins in her palms. Snakes lived in her blood. Snakes and the memory of Grandmère. And, growing inside, her daughter—the other Marie.

With a flourish, John presented her with the Voodoo doll.

Marie shook the memory from her head. She enjoyed Ziti's company. They were both eighteen. It was a bright, gay afternoon. Sunlight was making a rare appearance inside the house. Listening to Ziti's clipped speech, Marie forgot about religion, forgot about Maman and John. She forgot about the baby growing inside her.

Ziti was still strutting, imagining herself to be white and handsome.

"I can't believe these white women are all so beautiful," Marie declared, sucking her burnt thumb.

"Tonight you'll see. Rich white women lounge in milk baths all de day. Dey take honey to make dem sweet and put dried lavender in dere bloomers. Dere hair is smooth and fine. Not like my nappy locks." With a frown, Ziti let her hair drop.

"Your hair is beautiful."

"No. It should fall to my waist in waves. Or else be like yours." Envious, she slid her hand down Marie's silken wool.

"Or, best yet, my hair should be blond. Den I'd be de most beautiful woman in New Orleans." Twisting her hair over her shoulder, Ziti poked her face in the mirror. "No," she wailed, "I need blue eyes too."

"You're pretty now," Marie said.

Ziti's brown eyes scowled and rolled. "No. I'm too short. My nose is too flat. My bosom's too small." She touched each offending part of her body, then threw up her hands. "And I'm too black too!"

"How can you say so?"

" 'Cause it's true. No white man wants me for his mistress. I told my mama, my papa should've been white. Den I could be pretty mulatto like you."

Marie wondered. Had her father been white?

"Instead my papa is a house nigger or a sailor. Mama's not sure which." Ziti thrust the curling irons into the embers.

Marie fiddled with Ziti's tray, touching the assorted scalp ointments, feathers, multicolored beads, and ribbons. In the mirror, she saw her face was a caramel brown.

"Does it bother you not to know your father?" she asked, wondering why it had never bothered her.

"La, it don't bother me. Mama explained how she gets de urge. 'It's swift like a swallow.' " Ziti flapped her arms. " 'Like blood rushing downstream.' " She fluttered her hands. " 'Like green shoots pushing up through de earth.' " She stuck a finger up through

223

the cavern of her fist. She shrugged. "So Mama lies with men until de urge passes. Mama says it don't matter dat I don't know my papa. It just matters dat I spring from love.' "

Marie wondered—did she spring from love?

"Each time she do it, Mama says she's in love." Ziti spat the word. "Know what I say? I say less love is best if one's papa is white. All de time, my mama lets her belly swell up. Still we live in dat same old shack."

"Urge" explained what she had felt when she'd met John. All he had to do was look at her and she'd feel desire. A powerful, persistent urging. "Do urges ever come upon you, Ziti?"

"La, yes. But I squash dem like chicken bones. You dink I waste my urges on low-life blacks? Like my mama? I save my urges for white men. Dey pay pretty high for virgins." Ziti smacked her cupid-bow lips.

"Why white? What difference does the color make?"

· "Who else has de money to buy me a fine house? To buy me slippers, a parasol, and lilac perfume? De white man. I'm not wanting marriage. No white man ever marry me. Mistressing is good enough." Ziti turned her head toward the wig. "Marie, it's all in de wrist. You tug gently, like so."

According to Ziti, she'd done it all wrong. Marie snapped the shutters shut; the sky was flaming red, a breeze was stirring dust. To be mistress to a black man was a mistake. But it wasn't John's color that made him a mistake. It was uncertainty about herself, not knowing what she needed.

"White men are funny creatures." Ziti's tongs were poised in midair. "When urges come upon dem, dey never seem to bother dere own women. Dey don't believe dere women have urges. Some white women do say, 'I too delicate.' " Ziti moaned, imitating a languid air. "Others say, 'Birthing babies is more than I can bear.' But most white women want dere husbands. I know. White women say all kinds of dings while I'm fixing dere hair. White women want de same pleasure as a mulatto whore. Funny ding.

"First, I dink white men prefer pretty black skin. But if you be black and ugly as sin, den de white man just takes you. Dey take a black woman in de fields, in de marketplace, wherever she may be.

But den it's no fair exchange. Dey never give dark women any money. Just satisfy dere urge and call de woman scum.

"But if you're light and fine-featured, den dey call you mistress and give you all manner of dings." Ziti threw up her stout hands.

"So I say to myself, 'Ziti, figure dis out.' Know what I figure? I figure white men really prefer dere own women. But dey dink it isn't nice"—she wrinkled her nose—"for dere women to have urges. So dey take whores—coloreds who look almost white. Funny ding. Whole world would be a better place if white men and white women urged togedder." Exhausted by her philosophizing, Ziti plopped down, letting the cool tongs graze her knee. "Mysterious ding!"

Marie rested her head atop the wig. Both girls stared into space: Marie with melancholy, Ziti with frustration. Marie thought she heard thunder rolling over the Gulf.

"Whole world would be a better place if I was white," grumbled Ziti.

If she were white, Marie thought, she'd be a good Catholic. She'd have pleased Grandmère. She could have said her rosary without wondering if Africans gods would try and enter her soul.

"Some of us not lucky enough to be mixed blood like you."

Marie stiffened, surprised at Ziti's jealousy.

"Your fadder must have been white," said Ziti, pricking at Marie. "Your grandfadder too. You're not a mulatto. You're a quadroon. You must be dree-quarters white. How else to account for your hair and skin? Some people be too lucky."

"Lucky! You don't understand," said Marie angrily, toppling the wig.

"I understand you're John's mistress," Ziti snapped. "Plus you got a handsome husband to boot. You live in dis house, but no white man's ever touched you. You wear pretty clothes, but you don't whore."

"Ziti, you're my friend," Marie pleaded. Why did women always turn against her? Nattie. Grandmère. Maman. Or was it she who abandoned them?

"You know what my mama says about you? She says you're an ungrateful child. An ungrateful wife." Ziti bobbed her head. "You

225

left your sweet Grandmère. You left your husband on your wedding night."

"I had to," Marie moaned. Damballah had guided her.

"But you're never punished. You never pay for your sins."

She'd lost Teché. She'd lost innocence.

"You had everything easy," said Ziti.

"That isn't true."

"You have dis house. Two men who love you."

"John doesn't love me."

"You should've been me. I should've been you." Ziti waved the curling iron like a stick. "You don't know how hard my life is. Fixing damn white women's hair. Saying, 'yes, ma'am, no, ma'am, whatever de white ma'am say, ma'am.' I teach you all I know about hair and for what? You don't need money. You're pretty, Miz Marie. You're de mulatto gal, you're de mistress-wife, you're de"—fear settled on her face like mud—"Voodoo Queen."

"That's right. The Voodoo Queen," said John. "You shouldn't forget, Ziti." John had crept softly into the room.

Marie wondered if John had caused the churning wind outside. The sky had lost its light. Cornering herself, Marie rubbed her shoulders between two walls.

"I'm sorry, Master John." Ziti scraped and bowed. "I'm sorry. So sorry."

"You ought to say you're sorry to Marie."

"I'm sorry, Maman Marie." Ziti's face was pinched. But her eyes weren't sorry—afraid, yes, of spells that could dry her scalp and make her hair fall out, of spells that could cripple her hands or blind her by nightfall.

Marie was sorry. "John, Ziti and I were just playing," she said, trying to make amends. "Ziti was teasing. That's all."

John glared at her. Ziti's brown eyes dulled to hatred.

"I'll come for you tonight," Ziti said abruptly, gathering her irons, tray, and wig. "At six. Will dat be all right, Maman Marie?"

"Yes," Marie said dully, shutting her eyes. "That will be all right." Pressed into a corner, Marie wondered, Could she merge with plaster and wood? Ziti rushed out the door.

Marie heard John pace and turn.

226

"When will you ever learn?"

"Ziti's my friend."

"You don't have any friends," he said sharply; then he massaged his brow and sighed. "You're not a child. You're not even an ordinary woman. You are Marie, the Voodoo Queen. Why can't you remember that?"

Marie started crying. She wanted to be ordinary.

"All you have is me," he said.

"You?"

"Yes, me."

"I hate you," she whispered, lifting her head.

"I know," said John, cupping her chin. "I force you to be what you don't want to be. I haven't given you enough time to grow up. But I couldn't wait any longer."

"You're using me."

John hesitated a second. "Yes." He picked her up, bundling her onto his lap. "Sometimes, I'm afraid," he reluctantly admitted.

Marie snuggled into the crevice of his arms and chest.

"I remind myself that life will be better." John held her more tightly, steadily rocking forward and back. "I'm alive. So everything is better."

Marie sighed. She felt a sweet closeness, as comfortable as when Grandmère used to rock her. John seemed so unlike his cold, arrogant self. Now was the time to tell him about the child.

"I love you, Marie."

She peered at him. Was there any truth to what he said? His expression was slack.

John set her down. "Now go lie down and rest. Tonight you must be arrogant."

"Me?" She smiled uncertainly.

He flicked his thumb on her cheek. "No matter what happens, behave yourself."

She shuddered, trying to envision a life for herself, John, and the child. "John, I want to tell you—"

Marie stopped—*the Guédé were peering over John's shoulder*. He continued measuring his potion: seaweed, powder, and oil. *The death gods were wriggling their penises, showering urine.* Oblivious, John savored his drug. "You've made an enemy of Ziti," he said.

Baron Samedi winked. Intuition, bitter as goat's teeth, told Marie she didn't, shouldn't tell John about their child.

"What did you want to tell me?" With a lace handkerchief, John wiped his mouth and smiled pleasantly.

Bile and words caught in her throat. "Nothing. Nothing at all."

The elegant Guédé blew kisses.

Marie stumbled off to bed.

Rain had made the city musty. Marie was afraid of walking city streets alone. Tonight she wasn't alone, but she might as well have been. Stone-faced Ziti was silent.

Marie heard a child's hiccuping cry. Streets veered off from the gas-lit avenues into narrow lanes, dark alleys, dead ends. The air was more stagnant on the side streets. Walking, looking to the left and right, Marie saw cigar smoke curling about a white man's face as his mistress fanned him; a man in soiled underwear, coughing and staggering; a black woman perched on a window ledge, leaning into the night air, open-mouthed.

Marie never had enough air. Sometimes her heart would flutter and she'd feel as though she were suffocating or drowning. Maybe being born with a caul caused the fault. She wondered: When fireflies burned, did they eat their own air? Was the child in her womb less alive since it didn't breathe any air?

"Are white women as good as they are beautiful?" Marie blurted. She couldn't stand her own thoughts. She watched Ziti curl her bottom lip. "Are white men good?"

"White people don't have to be good."

"Then why be mistress to a white man?" Marie prodded. "Don't black women want to be treated well?"

"Black women want to get lucky." Ziti smiled wickedly. Her walk was jaunty. "Dey all hope de rumor is true."

"What rumor?"

"Go to bed wid a white fella and you'll wake up white." Ziti's laugh rumbled.

228

Marie couldn't catch her breath. *She saw the Guédé sadly waving.* Someone was going to die.

"We go in here," said Ziti. They stepped through an open wrought-iron gate and into a city garden. "Remember, don't do anyding unless you're told. Don't even sit. White folks act crazy." A spring gurgled at the base of an ivory nymph. There were roses and honeysuckle shrubs. Marie touched thorns; she recalled Grandmère teaching her how to break a honeysuckle's bloom and suck its dew.

"Remember. Don't do anyding. Don't talk. Don't hear. Dese white women dink a black gal's no better dan a stick of wood. Dey'll say whatever pops into dere heads. But if dey catch you listening, dere be hell to pay." Ziti airily stepped round to the service entrance.

Marie lagged behind. There was an odor the flowers couldn't cloak. Perhaps the baby made her more sensitive: tainted the sweet, sour.

"My mistress has been waiting," said an irritable butler. "She's upset you're late." He was dressed in blue and gold livery. He held his head stiffly; his brows arched and met. A rosary dangled from his pocket.

"La, I'm here now. Your mistress should wait for me. I'm de best hairdresser in New Orleans." Ziti handed him her shawl. "Dis here is Marie."

Marie had seen the man possessed by Ogu. Drunk, he had nicked his leg twenty times with a saber. His name was Jem.

"Maman Marie." The butler glanced about, fearful his mistress or another slave was listening. "Bless me."

Marie cringed. He was a hypocrite. Among blacks, he had faith in Damballah; among whites, he had faith in Christ. John had said it took a Catholic, not an atheist, to believe in Damballah.

"Bless me," insisted the butler.

"La, no time for dat." Ziti shoved her fist between his ribs. "Show me to your mistress. Else I'll say you made me late."

Jem cursed. "You worthless, piddling whore."

"At least I'm a free colored," snapped Ziti. "I'm not a house slave like you."

Jem raised his hand and Ziti squealed. "I'll scream to high heaven if you slap me."

Jem turned his back on her. The three of them formed a processional through the service hallway, then into a grand foyer with crystal chandeliers and marble posts and Italian tiles. Gold brocade lined the walls. Marie had never seen such a display of wealth. She paused at the bottom of the enormous winding staircase. Marie wondered if the seemingly never-ending stairs led to heaven. The foul odor she smelled in the garden was more distinct; it was yellow; it was drifting down the steep steps. The butler and Ziti didn't smell it. Neither did they hear the walls whispering. Ziti and Jem moved forward, squabbling. Candelabras lighted the way.

There was unhappiness in this house, generations layered upon generations. One light touch and Marie was certain the walls would collapse. Perhaps there wasn't any heaven. She heard human voices, one shrill, the other muted, arguing in the room at the top of the stairs. The child was heightening her senses. Marie slowed her steps. She felt the child, no larger than a tadpole, swimming in her womb.

The butler knocked. There were scurrying sounds from behind the door.

"A lover," muttered Ziti. "She's got herself a lover. She couldn't have missed me too much."

The door opened. A putrid odor smacked Marie. She saw the departing man's profile—thick dark curls, a blunt jaw—and recognized Antoine DeLavier. She prayed he hadn't seen her.

Sheets on the fourposter bed were disheveled. Marie noticed a small embellished D entwined with a white, thorny rose embroidered on the sheets.

"It's about time you arrived."

"I couldn't help it," protested Ziti.

Marie sucked in air as she realized whose house this was. Brigette, dressed in blue satin, was terribly beautiful. Marie lowered her head. Why had Ziti brought her here, of all places? Brigette mustn't recognize her. She swallowed curses. John wanted to humiliate her. He was punishing her again for rejecting Brigette. She despaired. She'd never get free of John. He'd always connive to keep power over her. She'd sacrificed Grandmère and Jacques for nothing. John's revenge was even sweeter than he knew. She'd never told him she'd met both Brigette and her brother in the Market Square.

"I have better things to do than to wait for you," Brigette drawled.

Ziti, in mock innocence, widened her eyes. "La, I know. Mistress Brigette always has better dings to do."

The white woman stared at Ziti.

"I couldn't help but be late," Ziti rushed on. "I almost got ate by an alligator."

Ignoring her employer's scowl and Marie's uneasiness, Ziti began arranging her tools. She laid her curling tongs in the fireplace.

"Dis alligator came out of de swamp, snapping, 'Ziti, Ziti, where you be?' 'La,' I say, 'dis alligator is gonna eat me for sure.' Know what I did? I found a big fat drunk. I said, 'Mister Alligator, dis drunk is stewed in rum. He'll taste better dan scrawny Ziti.' Den I ran. De last I saw, de drunk was wriggling his chubby legs outside de alligator's mouth." Enthralled by her own tale, Ziti clapped her hands.

Brigette laughed. "Oh, very good. The best of lies." She sat down on her vanity chair, flipping her blond hair back. "If you're late again, I'll hire Celeste."

Marie stood in the shadows beneath the portrait of the Virgin on the wall. She was furious. John had known she'd meet Brigette. 'Behave,' he had warned. He was probably laughing at her now.

"Celeste is a terrible curler."

"Celeste isn't late," said Brigette, glaring. "Who's this you've brought with you?"

"My assistant," Ziti grumbled, applying the hot iron.

Brigette stared at the figure reflected in the mirror. "Did you meet any alligators too?"

Before Marie could answer, Ziti said, "Yes," and flicked a spiraling curl.

"Let the girl speak for herself."

"She can't. She dumb."

"Poor child."

Marie knew she should be quiet. Yet she couldn't stand this white woman calling her "girl" and "poor child." What had she been doing all these years if not rushing to grow up? Ziti was smug. Marie wasn't stupid. Was it her fault that when she asked "Why?," when she demanded "Tell me who I am," no one answered?

"La, poor child is right," crowed Ziti. "Her pregnant mother saw a spirit, so she was born widout a tongue."

"I'm not dumb," Marie shouted, incensed. "I'm not a poor child."

Brigette turned, nervously drawing her gown closer to her throat.

Shadows made Marie's violet dress black, her eyes hollow.

"Is this some kind of trick?"

Marie stepped into a circle of candlelight.

Brigette slapped Ziti. "Who do you black girls think you are?"

Ziti howled. The hot iron dropped and singed her calf.

"Pick that up. Do you hear?" Brigette slapped her again.

"Leave her alone," said Marie. The carpet was scorched. "Ziti doesn't know anything. It's me you want to hit."

Whimpering, Ziti crouched beside the bed, one hand holding the iron while her other hand alternated between shading her burn and her warm cheek.

Brigette sighed. "You planned on making a fool of me."

"Someone else planned it."

"I didn't plan anyding, Miss Brigette," Ziti whined.

"Shut up," snapped Brigette, never once glancing away from Marie.

"I don't know anyding dat Marie's talking about." Ziti crawled away, dragging her injured leg. "She's sly. Yes, she is. Marie's sly. Ask her about her Grandmère. Ask her about her husband."

"Shut up," said Marie. "I'll hex you for sure. I'll cause your tongue to fall out. Go on. Get out of here." Marie advanced toward Ziti. "I'll make your eyes stick inside your head. I'll make you dead by morning."

"Oh, Maman Marie," Ziti moaned. She scrambled to her feet and fled.

"Oh, Maman Marie," Brigette shrilled. Laughing hysterically, she fell across the bed. "Oh, Maman Marie." Her robe came undone. Marie noticed Brigette's breasts were unusually full, pink-tipped, probably sore. Her belly protruded a bit. Her complexion was drawn from lack of sleep and too much drinking. Marie thought, White women are careless with their bodies. Then Marie paused and studied Brigette again. The second time, her soul saw what her eyes had missed. Brigette and she were both with child.

Brigette hiccuped twice and inhaled. "You made a fool out of me at the ceremony."

Fa had made fools of them both. Marie wanted to lay her head on the golden-haired crotch and weep. She now understood why the Guédé had waved. There weren't any good women. Except for Grandmère.

"I didn't know what you wanted then," said Marie.

"Now you do?"

Yes, she did. Marie placed a protective hand on her abdomen. "You want to get rid of your child."

Dull-eyed, Brigette leaned against down pillows. "Yes. I want you to cut it out."

Marie suspected the babe was John's. She didn't expect Brigette to tolerate carrying a mulatto child. At twelve, Marie had seen a firefly blink near the water pail. She'd tried to shoo it away. But the dumb firefly drowned itself.

"I'm not miraculous," she said.

"Aren't you?"

Flushed, Marie lay down beside Brigette on the unkempt bed. For this moment, it seemed natural. Yellow fragranced the sheets.

"I prayed. Fasted. Nothing helped," murmured Brigette.

The two women faced the ceiling like estranged lovers.

"I came to you. You and your Voodoo didn't help." Brigette seemed drunk. Her words slurred.

Marie strained to hear. What was she doing here, feeling the rise and fall of another woman's chest?

"How could I resist loving him? He's so much like me."

"I don't understand."

"My mother died because of us. The doctor cut and lifted us both out of her womb. Even then we were embracing each other."

Marie pressed her mouth into the pillow. She'd been too blind to see. Nattie—Nattie had made her believe John and Brigette were lovers.

"Twins. Antoine and I."

Twins.

Brigette edged near Marie, her angel face desperate. "Help me."

Could Goddess Ezili tell her how to abort the child? What would it take, herbs? A special chant?

"It's a sin to kill a child," Marie said.

"It wouldn't be a child. It'd be an 'it.' Isn't that why incest is forbidden?"

Incest was the yellow she smelled. "Abortion is a sin," Marie said.

"I already have a husband."

It was Marie's turn to laugh—soft, convulsive shudders. Brigette was a white version of her. Marie's sins were being mirrored by a ghost.

"Damn you." Brigette drew back. She shoved her fingers up her vagina, trying to reach the child and tear it out. Marie fought with her, gripping her arms and preventing Brigette from pummeling her abdomen.

"Don't you care about your soul?"

"Do you?" screamed Brigette. "John's told me about you."

Angrily, Marie swung her feet to the floor. Brigette's nails dug into her shoulders.

"No, please. Don't go."

Marie felt the brush of bare abdomen and breasts against her back. She wanted to turn and smother herself in the warm body.

"What does a snake god care about another child?" Brigette whispered intently. "About incest? Adultery?"

"I care," Marie replied softly. She could imagine someone trying to rip her child from her womb; in her mind's eye, she could see her own daughter struggling to stay attached to her maman.

"If heaven is Christian, we're both damned, Maman Marie."

Marie rose. She'd lost Christ's heaven without knowing it. Had she lost Damballah's too? Voodoo was more forgiving of adultery than Catholicism. Wasn't Mistress Ezili the ultimate coquette? But incest was an offense against nature. Unforgivable in any religion.

"I'm sorry. Forgive me," Brigette pleaded, catching Marie's

violet skirt. "I know you have power. I've seen and heard it. You could curse me. What difference would it make? I'm already terrified. I'm already cursed."

"So am I."

"Have sympathy."

"And make both our sins worse?" Marie stood and looked at Brigette, perched on the bed like a bewildered child. "Why should I have sympathy for you when I don't for myself?" She kissed Brigette's exposed neck, her pale lips. "No religion should tolerate a child's death."

"Damn you. Who are you to give me advice? What about your Grandmère? Your husband? What's your tale? What makes you so superior, Maman Marie?"

Marie walked to the door. A vase of honeysuckle crashed against it.

Marie turned. "We'll both go to hell, that's certain. Maybe fate brought us together. I don't know. But I do know it's inhuman to undo an innocent life."

Marie shut the door, muffling Brigette's screams. Feeling tranced, she started down the stairs. Louis DeLavier was running up them. He stopped, his senses reeling. A miracle had occurred. When Marie was one step past him, Louis reached out and lightly touched her hair. Black silken wool.

"Is she all right? Brigette? I heard yells." He didn't remove his hand. It pleased him to have a wisp of Marie trapped there. "Jem told me one of the coloreds—Ziti, was it?—one of the girls had run out."

"Yes, Brigette's all right."

"I—" Louis looked up the stairs, then again at Marie. He couldn't believe his brown girl was here. In his home. "You don't remember me."

Marie was sick tired. She glanced briefly at him. "No, I don't."

His hands fell forlornly to his sides. He'd made so little impression, whereas she'd become his world.

Marie felt contrite. She disappointed everyone. It was easy now to say, "Yes, maybe I do remember you." ·

Louis smiled brilliantly. Then, urgently, he said, "Look, wait here. I must see if Brigette's all right."

Marie sat on the marble staircase. Where else was there to go? Her legs felt weak and unable to carry her back to John. She gathered her dress between her knees and thought about the number nine. Ignorance had been magical. On her tenth birthday, the unhappiness had started.

Returning, Louis hurried back down the stairs. He shrugged. "She doesn't want to see me." His grin was crooked from trying to stifle the happiness he felt at finding his brown girl. He smoothed his thinning hair. "What's your name?"

"Marie."

Marie—the last detail. She was no longer a ghost, a mere memory.

"In the Market Square. You remember. I tried to save you."

"Can you save me now?" Marie asked bluntly. "I want to be nine. A child again." From upstairs, Marie heard Brigette stumbling, cursing. In her mind's eye, she could see Brigette clawing at the bed sheets, trying to strip away yellow. Brigette might even succeed at clawing the baby out of her body. Marie slumped against the wall; she and the wall were both trembling.

"You're ill." Gently, Louis helped her to rise. "Come."

Supporting her slight form, Louis guided Marie down the steps, across the massive hallway, and into a library smelling of pipe tobacco and wood. In Brigette's room, everything seemed new and brilliant blue, gold, and yellow. Here, everything was used and dull black, beige, and brown. A frayed chair, a sofa, an oak desk littered with quill pens, books, and letters. Even the cameo portraits on the mantel seemed weathered, prim. A fire leaped in the grate. While attractive, it generated an enormous heat.

"No. The chair near the fire is more comfortable." Louis scuttled about. "It's not too hot, is it? Brigette complains my library is too hot."

Marie sunk into leather, unaware of how it enveloped her, making her appear more vulnerable. The room was oppressive. The fire was eating her air.

"Drink this." Louis' voice wasn't southern, it was a soft New

236

England lilt. Nonetheless, Marie obeyed him like a good negress. He was a white male in a world where white and male meant power. The alcohol burned. Marie wanted to drink until she forgot.

Louis stood over her. Though he was slightly built, his intensity made him seem very masculine. His mouth and nose were a bit large, his brows bushy with hair stolen, albeit unwillingly, from his balding skull.

Abruptly, Louis turned back to the shelf of decanters. He fixed his gaze on the amber and clear liquids, not sure how to begin. "Please forgive her. Sometimes she's too harsh with slaves. Coloreds."

"What?"

"Forgive her. My wife, Brigette."

Inexplicably, Marie felt regret. She wasn't sure Louis deserved Brigette. There was too much anger, hatred, and hurt inside her.

Eyes cast down, cradling his glass, Louis watched his swirling brandy. "I favor freedom for slaves. My wife—no, it's her culture—disagrees. I'm sorry. I'm only different because I was raised in the North." He sipped, his eyes like a child's, peering over the glass rim. "I'm sorry."

Louis' shoulders were curved. Marie guessed it was from years of saying 'I'm sorry.' Why was he staring? The heat made her lightheaded. She sipped more brandy and felt an unaccustomed warmth radiating outward. "In the Market Square, you said, 'I'm sorry.' "

"You do remember me." Excitement made him boyish, charming. "You're still the same girl."

The room's only light came from the blazing fire and from Louis' incandescent skin. *A voice whispered warning.* "I must go." Marie couldn't find the energy.

"I searched for you." Louis paced like a trapped bayou animal. "I looked everywhere. I wanted to make sure you were all right." Trying to calm himself, he stroked his head and stretched his fingers toward the fire. "No one had heard of you. I didn't know your name."

"I was new to the city. I lived on the outskirts then, in Haben's Haven."

"That explains it." He caressed the mantel. "I never forgot you. I thought you were so lovely. You're still the same."

"I'm not at all the same," she said softly, her head bowed so her words bounced back from her breasts.

"Still so lovely." Louis knelt beside her, his hair barely rising and curling above her knees.

Marie felt an incredible desire to touch his thinning hair. Grandmère had once said, "Rubbing a balding head brings good luck." She could use a bit of luck in settling her life. A little love.

Marie stared at him. Louis' eyes were huge and brown, his lashes thicker than a woman's. Maybe it was her own 'I'm sorrys' that accounted for her desire to stay. Her own unpleasant loneliness. Reluctantly, she said, "I must go. I'm sorry."

"No. Go if you must, if you prefer to. But I want you to stay. Please stay. Tell me about you."

No one had ever asked about her before. No one had seemed to care. Certainly not John. Not Nattie.

Marie took a deep breath; then, amazingly, sounds slipped from her mouth. She told Louis about the bayou: serene, expectant at dawn; mysterious, unsettling at dusk. Until turning ten, she was happy. She told him how Grandmère could coax herbs to heal and could sing better than a nightingale. How Maman had died when she was young.

Finally, Marie expelled air and said, "I'm an adulteress."

Louis' face was expressionless.

She asked, "When did you marry?"

"August."

"So did I."

"Two years ago."

"Yes." Why did she feel that he, if anyone, could understand her? He'd tried to save her in April, long before summer heat odored the Gulf gray. Or was it yellow? She pursed her lips.

"Is it hell that scares you?"

"Hell isn't elsewhere. It's here."

"Adultery can be forgiven." Louis pressed closer. "Confess. Possibly a priest could absolve you. Cure you." A log shifted in the fireplace.

"I know a Voodoo man who sells charms to cure souls." She smiled wryly. John was more likely to poison her than cure her. Poor Ribaud had no power beyond the call of his drums.

"I'm worried about you." Louis swept Marie's hair forward in front of her shoulders.

Marie shivered. His hands had gently touched her breasts.

"Voodoo is dangerous. The slaves talk about a Voodoo woman. They say she can cure anything. I thought of visiting her once. They call her Marie, this Voodoo Queen."

"Have you seen her?"

"I planned on seeing her to find you. My butler, Jem, wanted to arrange it. I hesitated. I'm a journalist; it's my job to be objective. Yet my family's Protestantism kept putting me off. All those endless hours of listening to strident sermons on devil-worship and the many shapes of evil had taken hold. I haven't gathered enough courage to confront Voodoo directly.

"So I've confronted it indirectly. I've read everything on New Orleans history. Much of the literature suggests Voodoo is nothing more than a primitive exploitative religion. There's one or two exceptions but nothing notable. After reading about Voodoo crimes, murders, possessions, and indecent fornications, I lost the heart to associate with such people. Let alone let them assist me in finding you." Nervous and slightly ashamed, Louis wet his lips and smoothed his hair. He hadn't expected his puritanical streak to be so wide.

"The tales I've heard. She dismembers animals alive. Tortures the unfaithful. And encourages the rape of daughters by their fathers."

"And you believed them?"

"What?"

"The tales. You believed them?"

"Yes. I had had hopes that Voodoo would be more spiritual. Noble. Like the tales of the Indians of the Great West. But all religions seem hypocritical." He angled his face away from her. "I'm somewhat of an atheist. Or at least as much as my Christian upbringing will allow. I believe rationalism, not superstition, is the key to our future. But I support the Christian baptism of all slaves. I'm not certain that Christianity has all the answers, but it provides rules of conduct. It civilizes people who are unable to think rationally on their own." He brushed the tips of Marie's black hair.

"Adultery is an error," Louis continued, "but only a priest, not a devil-worshiper, can correct the sin. See Father Christophe. He appears to be a genuinely good man. Tell him I told you to come."

Marie shuddered and closed her eyes. She was affronted by Louis' words. Part of her recognized he was weak, unable to abide by his own convictions. Part of her knew, too, he was being condescending. Were there any writings on Voodoo written by blacks? She didn't think so. It was illegal for slaves to read and write. During wet bayou winters, Grandmère had taught her how to read the Bible. She knew in New Orleans free coloreds had schools, but she'd never heard of any books written by coloreds. And if they were written who would publish them?

What did Louis know about the world except from a white person's point of view? She wanted to rage he knew nothing of slavery, nothing of the masks free coloreds wore, nothing of the humiliation they endured to coexist with whites.

In Haven, she'd seen poverty. She'd seen neighbors walk the long miles to town for little pay. And when they were cheated, they dared not complain for fear of losing the small change they had. Did Louis know Indians were being slaughtered, enslaved? Did he know that every day thousands of blacks were captured, bound, and dragged into slavery? But Louis looked so gentle, so sweet. He was trying to help her. Was he any less confused than she? Any less naive about life?

Marie shut her eyes. Why did she think Louis wished adultery wasn't a sin? Was it because of the tilt of his head, the tremors in his voice, or the way he reached out to touch her hair? "Sin." The word betrayed Louis as a Christian. From the fire grate, sparks showered like rainbows. "Can a priest correct blasphemy?" Marie murmured.

"What do you mean?"

"I am the Voodooienne. I am Marie."

Stunned, Louis crouched back on his heels. "Voodoo believers boil cats until their flesh separates from bone."

"Cat bones protect against bad luck."

"And 'goats without horns,' is that true?"

"No. We don't murder white babies."

"You make sacrifices."

"Yes. A chicken. A dove. Sometimes a goat. Christians, too, haven't lacked for sacrifices."

"It's not the same."

"Why isn't it?"

"You worship snakes."

"Damballah."

"Snakes are the devil."

"Why?" Marie probed. "Because a snake taught Eve the difference between good and evil? How good is a good without a choice? Voodoo gods are like you and me—they fight, they love, they try to conquer death. They aren't perfect and remote like the white God and the Virgin."

"You don't really believe that?"

She squirmed. "Sometimes. And sometimes I imagine the Virgin one day laughing at me while my soul is sent to rot in hell."

Louis stood, escaping to stare at his somber ancestors painted and framed on the mantel. The family crest hung above the portraits. Trying to calm himself, he stared at the D and the rose. The white rose symbolized purity, everlasting faith, something the DeLaviers had never successfully achieved. Who was he to judge? He shouldn't be disappointed that his beloved was something other than he imagined. If he was honest, he'd admit he'd imagined little about her beyond her beauty.

The midnight chime was unbearably loud. Marie rested her head in her hands. She'd said more than enough for Louis to condemn her. Why now did she have to tell so much truth?

"You don't believe everything you say?" Marie asked tentatively. "I mean, you don't have absolute faith in your God, do you?"

Louis turned, smiling slightly. "No. Professions of Christianity come easily. I use it like a crutch. Often I don't know what to believe. I once thought of converting to Voodoo if it would bring you and me together. I guess I should convert, because you're here now, aren't you?" He looked at her longingly, spread his arms, and shrugged apologetically.

Marie caught her breath. She wanted to run to him and hold him. She'd lay her head on his chest and be comforted.

"Honor," Louis murmured to himself, trying to battle temptation. He wanted to feel Marie—to have her in his arms and feel the weight and shape of her body. But he couldn't ask Marie to sin again. He couldn't ask her to commit adultery twice.

He smoothed his hair and shifted the subject. "I suppose your brother, Jacques, gave you away."

"I married him." Quickly, she added, "He wasn't my brother. Only a rescuer like you."

He eased his grip on the mantel. "I would have done more if I could."

"I believe you."

Louis thought there was still an innocence about Marie, a reluctant sweetness. "Voodoo. You say it isn't evil?"

"No. There are evil Voodoo worshipers. Evil Christians. But Voodoo feels as natural as life. Once you abandon your fears, you can see beauty in it."

"Can you give me proof?"

"Attend a ceremony. Damballah will startle you as He startles me."

He was beside her again, laying his head on her lap. Marie moaned. She stroked his hair. The weight of his head pressed through her merino skirt. It was as though she'd known him forever—known his anxieties, his eagerness to please, known that for years he, like she, had said "I'm sorry."

"Marie," Louis whispered. *Her name reverberated.* He ran his finger along her calf.

Her grip loosened on the glass; a trickle of brandy flowed onto the carpet, staining it like blood. Her head lolled to one side. Didn't Louis have everything? A fine house, wealth, and family? She was certain he didn't know about Brigette's adultery. So why should he lay his head in a brown girl's lap and whisper "Marie" with such bitter sweetness?

"I can't believe you'd lie," he said. "Lying is the worst sin."

Why didn't she notice when his head lifted? Why did it seem his head had always been there, bridging the distance between her two thighs? Why did it feel as though his head was still there, making an impression on her skin?

"Who's your lover?"

"John, the Voodoo priest."

Louis laid his hand upon hers; no color against color, white against brown.

Words came rushing back to her. "White men satisfy dere urge and call de black woman scum," Ziti had said. "They like lovely girls too much," Jacques said. "White men don't pay no mind if a black woman says no," Shad had cautioned. And beyond all this, Marie thought, a white man had the power to make her a slave.

Louis leaned forward to kiss her. Marie wanted him to suck out all her air. Louis drew back, forestalling the kiss, then went to rest his head and hands on the cool mantel.

Marie knew she'd never be harmed by him. *But what about him being harmed by you?* John would use Louis as another way to keep her within his power. "I must go," she whispered.

"Was it something I said? Something I did?"

"No." Something you didn't do, she thought. You didn't sin. Not now. A perfect gentleman. She was weeping.

Louis reached out. He'd hold Marie forever if it would stop her crying.

"Leave me alone. Don't you understand? Everything around me rots. Grandmère. Jacques. Maman."

He held her tight, cheek against cheek. "Hush. It'll be all right."

"Leave me alone."

"Hush."

Marie could feel the silence swelling, demanding her to give in. Silence didn't have any snakes, any guilt, only the touch of this man.

Louis moved against her, tenderly stroking her back.

"Oh, my God," she murmured. *Which God? I don't know.* Then the roaring came, thick with her sins, tangled like bayou vines. She cried out, "I don't want to hurt you." Her words were garbled.

She rushed from his arms, believing she'd never have silence again. Only the roar of guilt and loss. She rushed out the door, across the hallway, and into the garden. Chest heaving, she clung to the

243

wrought-iron gate. How could she save herself? Marie couldn't think of any answer.

She felt a shadow nearby. "Louis? Ribaud?"

Church bells tolled one o'clock. John would be angry she was so late. Heaven knew what Ziti told him. The tree-lined avenue was deserted. Leaves spun, flailing in the Gulf wind. The moon was ghostly. She began counting her steps; she guessed it would take five thousand to reach the house on St. Anne. Left foot, right. Millions of steps if her home was still Teché. Counting, Marie tried to keep her fear at bay. Step 216, 217, 218. She thought she heard a noise behind her. She turned and yelled, "Damn, Ribaud. Come out if you're there. I know John sent you to spy." What was the matter with her? Ribaud was her friend. He didn't spy on her any longer. Fear was making her crazy. Streetlamps cast angry, squiggly shapes. They all stalked her.

Step 401. A hand fastened about her waist; another hand covered her mouth. She smelled yellow, overpowering in its stench. The hand slipped from her mouth to her crotch. Her screams carried over rooftops. Old women and dreaming children shivered in their beds.

When Marie turned and saw his face, she gasped.

"I'm glad you found me," Antoine said, before cuffing her on the side of her head and pulling her into an alleyway.

Now that she saw him and felt his blunt, groping hands, Marie wasn't surprised.

Antoine ripped her bodice, shoving her onto the ground. "You owe me," he said.

She went limp. A part of her thought she deserved this punishment. It would take more than a year to tally her debts, her sins. Screams roared through her veins. But Marie kept silent.

She was outside her body, watching Antoine shoving her legs apart with his knees, biting at her breasts. Her hair fanned prettily in the moist dirt; her palms were arched and exposed like the crucifixion. "Holy Mother of God. Damballah." Her bloomers split away from her crotch.

He thrust like an impotent rutting hog.

Marie laughed, hysterical.

His fist fell on her abdomen. She gasped.

"Colored whore. No-good colored whore." He raised his fist again as Louis came running forward. Bellowing, Antoine twisted while smashing his left fist into Louis' gut. Louis fell backward, stunned, the air knocked out of him.

"You." Antoine stood swaying, both hands pressing against his skull, roaring, "You." Action slowed. Like a felled tree, Antoine's body shifted and crashed down upon Louis. Marie shielded her eyes. Louis groaned. Louis' head snapped right as Antoine hit him on the chin.

Lying on the ground, Louis raised his knee and plunged it into Antoine's groin. Antoine rolled off Louis, gasping in pain. Louis dove at Antoine. Sandwiched together, the two men rolled a few feet. Dirt, sweat, and blood mixed; the air cackled with desperation. On top, Louis pounded his fist down, feeling a cheekbone crack.

Antoine dug his thumbs into Louis' eyes. Tears seeping from closed lids, Louis tried to crawl away. Antoine kicked him in his side, flipped him, and gripped his throat. "Leave my sister alone. Leave her be." Antoine pressed his larynx.

Louis was suffocating.

Marie wanted to lie still and cry. She wanted to say prayers. Instead, she searched in the dirt for something heavy, substantial. Moving forward, she watched Antoine, crazed, pumping his body weight down through his arms into the hands encircling Louis' neck.

"Leave Brigette alone," Antoine yelled, crazed that Brigette was married to a man he hated.

Marie watched Louis slowly dying—his skin parchment white, his eyes bulging. Moaning, she raised the rock above her head. *Antoine's hair became dark, wriggling worms; in the thick roots, she saw Ziti, Maman, and John.* With unnatural force, she crushed his skull. *Blood swamped the worms and faces.* Antoine slumped forward. The rock jumped from her hands. The two men were positioned like sleeping, satiated lovers.

Louis began coughing, his chest straining upward. Tears blinded his eyes. He rolled from beneath Antoine.

"Is he dead?" Marie knew he was but asked nonetheless.

Louis was doubled over, phlegm drooling from his mouth.

She saw a rat dart behind steps, saw a shutter close. Feigning calm, she bent and tested Antoine's pulse.

"Why?" Louis rasped. Guilt was etched on his face as though he, not she, were the monster.

Marie tried to hold him. He pulled away, vicious and sputtering, "What kind of woman are you?" Louis couldn't escape. Marie and Antoine blocked his exit from the alley. "Why?" he yelled, stumbling, his mind unsettled. "Why?"

"He would've killed you."

"He was drunk," Louis shouted back. "Didn't you smell it? You don't murder a drunken man." He collapsed forward onto his knees. "Oh, God, if there is a God, please forgive me. I wanted him dead. Always wanted him dead. I hated the bastard. He made me feel small, weak. Insignificant."

"Hush." Marie cradled him like any mother would. She kissed the imprints on Louis' neck. She couldn't tell him why she smelled yellow or why Antoine had truly deserved his hatred. If Louis knew about Brigette's child, what would he feel then? "Hush," she said.

"My fault," he sobbed. "My fault."

Behind Louis, the death gods huddled, smiling gaily. One of Grandmère's lullabies rose to her throat. "Hush."

"What will I tell Brigette?"

Marie winced at the love reflected in his face. Was it love for his wife or for her?

"Here. Sit here," she said, directing Louis backward to the steps.

Muttering, "You saved my life," Louis folded over, his aching head dangling between his legs. He tried hard for forgetfulness, for an excuse to salve his own guilt. Nothing in his life had prepared him for murder.

Marie looked about her. The alley was dank and dirty. Antoine's body seemed to glow eerily in the surrounding darkness. Blood pooled beneath his bruises. Marie envied Antoine. Surely his soul would feel one moment's peace before being swallowed by hell. Death had to suspend worry and sorrow.

Marie located her weapon. The rock was jagged and rough. She'd never forget the feel of it as it hit Antoine's skull. There had been resistance, a hesitation before it had given way to a softening depression. She placed the bloodied rock on the small of Antoine's back. She knew what she had to do.

On her hands and knees, with the edge of her shoe, Marie drew a circle about Antoine's body. Beneath the circle she drew a snake.

"What are you doing?"

Tearing her slip, Marie twisted it about a bundle of twigs.

"What are you doing?" Louis was hovering, his hands running through his hair, his face perspiring, streaked with dirt and blood. "What are you doing?"

"Making sure everyone knows I committed this crime."

"You're insane." He smacked the twigs from her hands.

"Everything around me rots," Marie yelled. "Murder isn't extraordinary. It's expected of a Voodoo Queen. 'Goats without horns,'" she taunted. "Isn't that what you believed? Murdering white babies. 'Goats without horns.'"

"Antoine and I have been enemies for a long time. Don't you understand? It had nothing to do with you."

Resolute, Marie stared at her muddied lap. Her eyes traced a trail of blood pooling inside Antoine's mouth.

"Damn you. There's no need for this." Louis kicked violently, smudging the circle. "I won't have your sacrifice."

"No," she screamed, scrambling, slapping at his legs, flattening herself on the ground to spare her crude circle. "You'll only make things worse." Knowing she couldn't save herself, Marie wanted to save Louis. He shouldn't be convicted because he was defending her. She didn't want anyone else being hurt at her expense. She felt, too, a strange burgeoning sense of pride. She had done something. Taken vengeance against a man who deserved to die. It was one way to define who she was, and she'd done it on her own, with neither John nor Nattie coaxing her. The responsibility was hers.

"Look, then." Louis was on his knees, pulling Marie upright, grasping her tightly against his chest, feathering her face with kisses. "We'll go to the authorities. A jury would understand. You saved my life."

Marie wanted to relax against him, surrender her cares. It would be madness. She pulled away. "Think of the gossip. The

247

Picayune might run a special edition: 'DeLavier Involved in Murder,' 'Journalist Ruins Family,' 'Christian Found with Pagan Voodoo Queen.' You couldn't stand the damage to your reputation."

"That's not true." He rubbed the veins popping out along his brow. "It won't happen that way. We'd both be set free. People are good."

"Was Antoine good?"

"Don't mock. It isn't you."

"You know nothing about me."

"I know . . . I know you're—" He wanted to say 'sweet' and 'innocent.' But it wasn't true. "God, I don't know anything anymore." Louis sat back on his heels, his hands frenetically rubbing the tops of his thighs. "But there must be good. Someone who would understand."

"White people don't have to be good," snapped Marie. "A white man's rape of a black isn't a crime. You'd be condemned for interfering. I'm not a woman. Just unacknowledged white property. To a jury, you'd be just as responsible for Antoine's death. Not because you tried to help me, but because you threatened Antoine's property, his right to take rather than give, to destroy rather than build." Methodically, Marie began regathering her twigs. "Go home, Louis."

For Louis, the gulf between cultures was too much. Marie was right. He was the naive Northerner. He should just walk away from all his hurt and problems. Walk away from disappointment in love and failed idealism. But could he live with himself if it meant hurting her?

"I'm not leaving you."

"What about your pretty Brigette? She's your wife, isn't she? Would you have her lose a brother and a husband too?" Marie wiped angrily at her tears. "Damn you. Go home."

"Listen to me." He gripped her shoulders. "We'll both leave. The authorities will suspect any number of persons. Antoine wasn't well liked. Many would've paid to have him dead."

"No," she wailed. "It can't be hidden. Someone always sees a crime." Marie shouted fervently, "I did this crime." Dashing, knocking, kicking at alleyway doors, she shouted, "You in there. You saw me, didn't you? I did this crime." She banged a half-closed shutter. "You saw me. Marie, the Voodoo Queen."

Louis caught her by the waist. "Hush," he said. "Hush."

Marie struggled. She was fighting temptation for himself and for her. "Let me go. Let me go!" He held her.

"Why must you believe yourself to be so bad? You needn't take all the blame." Louis smelled hyacinths in her hair. "There must be someplace we can go."

Teché. She sucked in air. "You don't know what you're saying."

Louis lifted her up, swinging her feet off the ground. He kissed her, soft and intimate, gently exploring her mouth.

Marie felt the anger in her yield. Four men had kissed her. Antoine, brutally. John with harsh passion. Jacques, sweetly. But Louis' kiss made her feel innocent and whole again.

He drew her head down to his chest. "I've got to get back to the house. I have money in the house. We'll buy a rail ticket. Wherever the train is going, we'll go."

"They'll track us down."

"You're right. Someplace special then. They'd look for me in cities, in the North. Maybe we could go west. Beyond the prairies and the mountains. Someplace they wouldn't think to look."

Teché. Why couldn't she say it? "You're insane." Marie felt the tension in his limbs, heard the strain in his voice.

"We could do it, Marie." He was willing himself to believe.

"How soon would it be before you ran confessing to a priest? How soon before you realized you were damned?"

"If I could hold you, it wouldn't matter." Louis meant what he said. "Perhaps there isn't a God."

"If you believed that you wouldn't be afraid of Voodoo. If you believe in one set of spirits, you must believe in another. Voodoo is evil; Christ is good. Isn't that how you think and feel?"

"So what if I do believe? I don't know what I believe. I believe I love you." Louis shook her. "That must count for something." He shook her again. "Since I met you, all I've ever done is dream of you. I love you, Marie. I love you."

She turned her head away. If she concentrated on his eyes,

she'd give in. Lurking beneath his tone, Marie heard the uncertainty. Louis was scared. She didn't doubt he'd sacrifice everything for her; she also didn't doubt he'd live to regret it. What did it matter, though? She'd be in Teché. They'd have maybe a year, maybe two or three. The souring would be slow, steady, and imperceptible at first; then it would gain momentum until one day there wouldn't be any sweetness left. But she'd be free of John. She'd only have to destroy Louis' life to buy her own freedom.

What about her child? Could she let Louis take responsibility for raising the child? What about Grandmère? On the run, could she face the possibility of never seeing her again? Wouldn't John kill her if Marie left? What about herself? Could she give up love, no matter how tentatively offered? Marie shook her head. Louis was weak. One day he'd shed his fragile atheism and wake up a righteous Christian. He'd blame her for his seduction.

Without looking up, Marie eased out of the circle of Louis' arms. "I already have a husband and a lover. Besides, murder never hurt a Voodooienne," she said caustically, touching the congealing blood on Antoine. "Killing a white, I'd only be more powerful. A jury wouldn't hang me. They'd be too frightened. Voodoo is criminal. Exploitative. Isn't that what you said? Well, here is a fresh body to exploit."

"You can't do this."

"I do what I want." She placed the twigs in Antoine's palm.

Louis gathered a handful of dirt and threw it at her. "You lied to me. You said Voodoo is beautiful, real. You said you weren't evil. But you are evil. You said you were innocent. But there isn't any innocence in you. I've been in love with a lie."

"You lied to yourself. Louis DeLavier, famed journalist, who hides his faith in a closet. A sniveling atheist but a loyal Christian when it suits him, when he's passing judgment on others. You condemn what you don't understand. Your prejudice is as bad as any Southerner's. It's only different, religious instead of racial. But perhaps it's racial too. Perhaps you wanted me because I have black skin."

Threatening, Louis moved forward to stop her words. He checked himself. He was losing a dream. He'd been looking for a maiden to rescue, someone sweet and naive enough to appreciate his loving and make him the center of her world. Feeling forlorn, Louis mumbled, "I thought you were different."

"Go home, Louis. Did you think because you're white I desired you?" She spat at him. "You're no better than Antoine."

"You'll hang."

"If you stay, you'll hang with me. Or perhaps I'll hex you for a worse death. Fire. Slow poison. Perhaps I'll hex Brigette."

"Don't touch her." He hit her. His hand hit flat against her jaw. Marie tasted blood in her mouth. Covering his eyes, Louis wept wearily, his energy gone. "I'm sorry. I don't know what happened to me. I'm sorry." Louis felt self-disgust. He hadn't any honor. He'd hit a woman, not because she'd spoken the truth but because he was too afraid not to hide behind her skirts. He knew Marie was saving him because he didn't have the strength to save himself.

Marie stared at the sky. Streaks of lavender, orange, and red. The sun was rising. Another day without hope. Louis would have to face Brigette. She'd have to face John. She felt sorry for Louis. Sorry she'd resisted temptation.

She caressed his shoulders, smoothed his tousled hair.

"Is that it?" His eyes were luminous and sad.

"Yes, that's it."

His hand rose toward her face.

"I have work to do," she said.

His hand dropped. "I think I'll hate you for a long time."

Marie shrugged to prove to him it didn't matter. On her knees again, she busily began correcting her circle. She heard the soft crunch of dirt. Louis was walking, desperate, toward the streetlamps. A caretaker had already extinguished their gas glow. When had he done it? When she was murdering Antoine? Or murdering Louis' misguided love?

Of all the times in her life, this was the time to cry. She didn't cry. A cock crowed. Mist rolled in with the Gulf tide.

"I am Marie. The third in a line of Voodoo Queens." *Heartache comes with four.* She brushed her foot against Antoine's body.

"Write good things about me," she called. But Louis had already turned the corner; he hadn't heard.

She stood, massaging her stomach. "My poor baby girl. You didn't want to die, did you?"

Sighing, tottering from side to side, Marie left the dead Antoine.

She imagined Antoine sitting up, mocking her, jeering at her. He couldn't hurt her or anyone anymore.

Marie wandered, humming a disjointed lullaby. Tears fell. She'd do and be anything if she could be nine again. Her heart hardened; her throat closed over tears.

The sky was a sheet of pink. Seagulls circled and cried restlessly. They dived and stole gasping fish from the fishermen's nets. Marie heard curses and groaning from drunks and gamblers straggling out of the saloons. Some vomited in the roadway. A prostitute shifted and turned in her gutter bed. A dog howled after being kicked. Pathetic children begged coins from riverboat captains overseeing the outfitting of their ships. Dockhands swore and, with battered, aching hands, struggled with their loads. Vendors salvaged rotted fruits for resale. A consumptive man coughed, spraying mucus and blood.

Murder made Marie unafraid of walking the city streets alone. The new morning, like the old night, was memorable.

Marie was convinced: no one, anywhere, knew anything about faith.

Those who saw Marie—a black girl peeping from behind a shutter, a drunken sailor weaving back to his ship, a vendor preparing banana fritters for the dawn market—said she had looked wild and pitiful.

"My heart almost stopped," said the girl. "All night I heard scuffling sounds, shouting. I thought I must be dreaming. Then I heard her pounding on my shutter as bold as you please, saying, 'I did this crime.' When I got brave enough to look, all I saw was her and that dead man. Blood was everywhere. She glowed with it. I felt more sorry for her than for him. She seemed like a . . . a child. Sweet. Confused. Yes, that's it. A hurt child."

"She scared me sober," said the sailor. "Crazy, just plumb

crazy she seemed. Like a witch. Like she'd kill anything stepping across her path. She was carrying a black cat. I'm not a weak man. But I stay away from crazy women. Especially them that's bloody and singing to ghosts."

"I knew who she was right away. She asked for a fritter. She didn't have no money so I gave her one. She hexed me. I didn't sell no fritters all that day. I didn't mind. 'Cause I'd seen her like nobody else before had ever done seen her. She looked downtrodden. Hair messed. Clothes torn. Almost naked. Her face bruised. Like a beat-up slave. But she was royal too. Like a queen. Royal and beautiful. I guess I saw more of her breasts and thighs than I was supposed to. Blood prettied her up like jewelry. I guess she hexed me 'cause I'd seen her both ways. Down and lovely."

Half the population of New Orleans claimed to have seen Marie Laveau the morning after she killed Antoine DeLavier.

~

"Louis, sometimes I think regret is the essence of being old. I made so many mistakes, did so many things I would undo."

"We all regret."

"But what I regret most, more than my folly, more than the wrongs I did, is that I never found true love. Grandmère found it, though it didn't last long. But I never got to feel what it's like."

"It's as bitter as anise root, as sweet as summer rain."

•

—MARIE LAVEAU, JUNE 15, 1881, SUNSET
(From Louis DeLavier's journal)

Had she murdered anyone else, it might all have been avoided. But having murdered Antoine DeLavier, a man hated by both blacks and whites—a man who deserved to die—Marie ignited two nights of rampage and looting.

She never fully understood what happened or why. She remembered walking through the city, dazed, as the sun rose out of the Gulf and suspended itself above the wharf. She'd been hungry and asked for a banana fritter. A vendor had given her one even though she had no money. She'd meant to thank him, but Antoine's blood on her hands distracted her. She walked for miles staring at her streaked hands, trying to decide how to wash them without losing hold of her fritter.

Someone yelled at her. She was on the road, blocking traffic.

Maybe it was the sun fanning from behind the rider's back or the sweat-lathered blackness of the horse that reminded her of her first meeting with Antoine. She held up her bloodied hands, screaming, "I did this crime. I murdered him. I did this crime." The horse reared. The fritter fell in the dirt. She darted down the road, along the platform streets, flailing, jutting her hands at people's faces, ranting, "I did this crime. I did this crime. I murdered him. DeLavier is dead." She felt cleaner, less guilty, as faces registered shock. She wanted to take responsibility. She had done something; it wasn't good, but nonetheless she felt strong. She wasn't anyone's victim. For hours, she shouted at people—"I did this crime, I did this crime, I killed him"—until she grew hoarse. Light-headed and tired, she stumbled to the house on St. Anne. She remembered Nattie saying John and Ribaud were out searching the streets for her. She'd nodded, crawled into bed, her arms encircling the child in her womb, and slept a dreamless sleep.

Yet while she was sleeping the world came undone.

Throughout the day, slaves and free coloreds spread the word that Marie Laveau had used Voodoo to kill Antoine DeLavier. How else could a woman overpower a strong man? How else could a man as evil as DeLavier be hurt and killed? And if he could be killed, slaves reasoned, other whites who tortured and enslaved them could be killed as well. Black gods were sending them a sign. Freedom was possible.

White gentlemen spread the word that one of their own had been killed. Even those who believed Antoine DeLavier had been too brutal managed, in the wake of his death, to call him "brother." Whites scratched at the surface of their own fears, remembering that even the most benevolent of them was hated . . . could be murdered. Hexed by black gods. Tortured by maniacal blacks.

So white men armed themselves. An angled head, moments of daydreaming, a whispered aside to another slave were all cause enough for a black to be whipped for rebellion. Some masters refused to feed their slaves and locked them in cellars. Others joyfully, viciously bound and battered slaves for offenses to come. Some owners were merely watchful, insisting on every deference to their authority, from the lowliest bow to instant obedience. Righteous men prayed with their families and found scripture supporting their right to dominate and enslave. Others barricaded themselves behind doors with stockpiles of food and water. Still more paraded the streets in search of blacks who needed a lesson.

Some free blacks went home and fiercely rocked their lovers, believing there was hope for tomorrow—a champion for free coloreds. Some fell into trances, convinced there would be no tomorrow. A slave bludgeoned his mistress's head; a kitchen maid stabbed a family in their beds. A young girl using arsenic laced her owner's sweetened coffee. An old woman sang and recited stories she recalled from Africa, giving voice to memories she'd forced herself to forget when Master sold her last baby forty years before. Black fathers, slave and free, kissed and put their children to bed and armed themselves with crude weapons to wait out the explosive unrest. Bands of slaves and free black men strutted through the French Quarter throwing stones, stealing goods, excited and proud that one less white man was alive.

Whites and blacks fought. Many were scarred and maimed. Soldiers with rifles and bayonets wounded and killed nearly a hundred black men, women, and children. Dozens of others were subdued and carted to prison. Many of these prisoners, when questioned, swore, "Maman Marie. The Voodoo Queen inspired me."

Marie woke to a new day and a new world where everybody believed she'd begun a riot to free the blacks.

~

"I was brought before a judge, Louis. He wore a wig of white curls. The packed courtroom seemed a dream. The judge described murders—throats crushed, abdomens sliced. He accused me of these crimes. I denied them. Yet I saw them as clearly as I see you now, rivers of blood, slippery and pained.

" 'How am I responsible?' I said to the judge. 'I wasn't there, was I?' The white audience in the pews shuffled. The judge called me 'evil.'

" 'What is her sin?' John demanded. 'What are the charges against Marie Laveau?'

"I looked at the prisoners. The prisoners looked at me. Dozens of men and women were manacled together, a heavy-gauge chain twisting in and among their feet. Supposedly these were the worst offenders: rapists, murderers, armed thieves. Many more were locked in cells for lesser crimes. Some of the prisoners I recognized as men and women who danced weeks ago for Damballah . . . for me. Others were complete strangers. Yet every one of them looked to me for salvation.

"The judge shouted, 'These people killed in your name.'

"I screamed, 'No one kills in my name.'

" 'Don't black gods require sacrifice?' the judge asked.

" 'Doesn't Christ?' Ogu, the warrior god, slipped inside me. 'Don't whites sacrifice blacks each day?' Ogu and I stomped and shouted. 'Slave ships kill. Whites torture slaves.' Ogu made me ten feet tall. 'Whites make slave mothers pick cotton in the fields. Black babies shrivel in their wombs. Whites kill our gods . . . erase Damballah from our memory.' With one hand, Ogu and I splintered a chair.

"The judge was terrified. He pounded his gavel. 'Get her out of here. Get her out of here!'

"A white man caroled, 'Goats without horns. That's what Voodoos

257

call the murder of white babies. Goats without horns. They murder our babies.' Ogu and I spun and looked at him; the man sat down.

" 'Get her out of here!'

"The prisoners chanted, 'Marie Laveau. Maman Marie. Marie Laveau, the Voodoo Queen.' Whites shouted, 'Hang her, hang her!'

"It took eight guards to subdue me, subdue Ogu. They dragged me from the courtroom and placed me in a prison cell that was as hot and unclean as I imagine hell to be. I woke from possession lying on dirty straw, watching a chain of ants crawl along my arm.

"John visited me, promising, 'I'll save you. I'll save you. You'll see.' He was excited, joyful even, to see me in jail. 'All of New Orleans. Everybody knows your name.'

"I was a tool to him. Nothing but a tool.

"When John left, I stared stupidly at my bruised hands. I remember thinking I was incapable of violence, Louis. I never wanted to believe my followers' guilt was all mine."

"Hush, Marie."

"But it was *mine. I allowed John to use me. He used me for ill, never for good. All those poor people who believed in me never suspected I knew less than they did about the Voodoo faith. From whom would I have learned it?"*

"Don't cry, Marie," I said.

"Yes, I'm too old to cry. Where is the faith of my ancestors? I was worse than a charlatan. I wasted my gift. I led others to believe in a religion based on lies, on theatrics.

"When the judge called me evil, I perversely believed him.

"It was I who set a crucifix beside a Voodoo doll. I who set the Virgin beside a portrait of Ezili. I who encouraged believers to think Legba was another incarnation of Saint Peter.

"Voodoo and Catholicism merged, and my fame spread. I blasphemed two faiths."

"But maybe it's all the same, Marie. Maybe all religions are a pattern weaving themselves together. One faith is no more 'right' than another. Worshiping two faiths, separately or together, is still worshiping God."

"Louis, you shouldn't tell lies to the dying."

•

—MARIE LAVEAU, JUNE 15, 1881, EVENING
(From Louis DeLavier's journal)

258

Marie thought it was odd that she'd been in prison for seven days and no one had ever accused her of the crime she was truly guilty of—Antoine DeLavier's death. She could still feel what it was like to smash his skull.

Lying awake nights, staring through her prison window at the night sky and stars, she speculated on how Louis had stopped the investigation of the murder and quieted Brigette. Had he bribed officials, then taken his wife north? Did he know yet he was going to be a father? Or was Antoine merely forgotten because of his own legacy of abuse and vindictiveness? Marie thought it was funny that whites were more upset by blacks briefly dreaming themselves free than by the death of one of their own. Antoine's life was ultimately worth less than a black boy's rebellious act of throwing sticks without his master's permission.

She repeated over and over again, "I did this crime. I murdered him." But no one seemed to hear or care. She could accept hanging, but it scared her to think of her child, whether the judge would let the baby be born before she was hanged.

The waiting threatened to destroy her. Each successive night and day, black supporters sat outside on rough cobblestones beneath her cell window. Soldiers surrounded them. Yet there were no riots, no skirmishes. Just quiet protest. They weren't protesting that scores of blacks were imprisoned, they were protesting that *she* was, and it astonished her. She never imagined being anyone's heroine. Every other man, woman, or child in prison, she felt, was more heroic than she'd ever been. They believed in something, and it was ironic that she who was called hero believed in nothing.

Spending endless hours in a small cell without a bed, a chair, or running water and merely a corner hole to collect her body's waste, she felt she'd go mad. She was incredibly lonely, unsure of herself. Yet she was privileged. She had a window, a single cell. The guards were afraid of her and treated her with respect, fearful that she would hex or kill them when she was possessed. Marie quickly learned to encourage fear. She mumbled dire nonsense and twitched her legs and arms when guards were near. She insisted on milk and fresh foods, a blanket and a pillow for her head. But the guards' fear never extended to her requests for other blacks. She did not have the power to change another's misery. And because she didn't, she felt she had no right to complain.

There were eight cells in all: two singles at diagonally opposite ends. The other single cell was used for beatings and rapes. Over a hundred souls were crammed in the other six cells. Barely enough air: stifling heat by day, cold at night. The larger cells were twelve by twelve, without windows, with a dirt and plank floor. Bodies were intertwined, the living layered on top of the wounded and ill. Like a slave ship, except they were moving toward another kind of death. Instead of death at sea or a lifetime sentence as overworked slaves, a rope would snap their necks as easily as Grandmère snapped the gullets of chickens. The lucky ones died earlier, drifting away in their sleep.

Sometimes Marie dreamed she'd gone back in time to blue water and a ship loosened from its moorings, proud of its billowing sails, ferrying black gold. Grandmère said she'd been born a slave. *Blood veined from the line of an African queen.* Grandmère's mother had made the sea journey. How had she survived the trip? Marie, confined against her will, had sympathy for the woman forced to cross the water. When Marie most feared her own death, she reminded herself of the freedoms she had had (even to love the wrong man) and how death by hanging couldn't compare with the deadly and deadening sea journey made by her great-grandmother.

Everyone dies anyway. But Marie hadn't expected her path toward death would be so frightening and the conditions so ugly. Sometimes Marie dreamed of walking on water—the secret desire of every slave ever bound in a ship's hold. Waking, with her dreams still raw and vivid, she could taste sea salt and feel the dampness about her ankles as well as any Christ. She felt desperate to make miracles for her fellow prisoners. Each and every one of them had descended from Africans who'd survived the sea; each and every one of them was likely to die one sun-drenched morning, swinging their feet through air.

But Damballah sent no miracles.

At night she was thankful there weren't any candles. When the guards set themselves to drink and play cards behind the door, the prisoners had a kind of privacy within the heavy, rank darkness. As though by mutual consent, everyone slept in the day when what little light there was exposed horrors: dead slaves, insects, vomit along the walls. During daylight hours, blacks were most often taken to the single cell near the guardroom and beaten. If Marie was lucky, exhaustion claimed her and she didn't hear the screams.

At night the prisoners awoke and whispered among themselves, intimate and confiding. In the darkness, you could see your own soul clearly. Some confessed their past sins, others their most secret desires. Some souls, hours before death, murmured their life histories, asking listeners to witness that they had lived. Very few complained of their imprisonment. Time was too important to waste on what everybody knew.

"I meant to love my wife better. She worked so hard. Bearing babies, sewing lace on ladies' dresses. She cooked and cleaned for me. Helped me in my carpentry shop. I never had a kind word for her. She was a good woman. A good mother. She died of fever while I was at work. She locked the children in the bedroom—the oldest not even four—and lay down before the fire and died."

"Like a dog," a voice somewhere else whispered.

"Yes. I've been drinking ever since, unable to forget or forgive myself."

A cracking, whispery voice spoke. "He kept me chained by his bed and used me like a dog. I loved him. I told him so over and over again. But he was convinced blacks were animals, that they had no finer feelings. The night after Maman Laveau killed DeLavier, I killed him. I bit him on the throat like a dog."

"I think I'm forty-eight," someone announced from the nearest cell. The voice was raspy, disrupted by hacking coughs. "I've been a slave for as long as I can remember. My owners were all right. They could have been worse. I taught myself to play music on a piano. That was how I lived. Nights I stole out to hear players in the bars or ballrooms of grand houses. I learned new songs that way. During the fighting, soldiers found me and brought me here. Now I'm dying and I keep hearing a sweet melody. I'd give anything for keys to play

261

it." He hummed, his baritone swelling, cutting through the night's despair until he fell into a fit of coughing.

Night after night Marie wept, privileged to hear the tales.

And like it or not, she'd come to believe there would have been no rioting, no one would have suffered or been killed or been imprisoned, had it not been for her. She'd spoken a lie to the judge. Some had killed in her name.

So she ministered to them. These were her people: loyal, faithful to their dream, and in need of her. She was loved in a way she had never imagined. And because she felt loved, she told great and necessary lies. She told them she could save them. She told them yes to whatever they wanted to hear.

"I'm worried about my babies. Are they all right? Will they be taken care of if I don't go back?"

"Yes, yes," she would say to lonely and weeping mothers.

"Who will care for my children?" a bewildered soul wanted to know.

"Someone who loves you very much." And Marie's heart gladdened when she heard a soft sigh.

A voice cried out, "When I die, will I fly across to Africa?"

"Yes."

"My pap told tales of a beautiful black African who could chant and make you remember *home*. He'd chant and you'd sprout wings. Pap said he saw him. Saw him sing his song in a young girl's ear. Saw her sprout wings. When your time comes, drop your hoe in the fields, the skillet in the kitchen, and—"

"Fly. Yes, you'll fly from this prison and swiftly across the sea."

"Home."

"You'll fly home." For nights afterward, Marie listened for the hearty voice sweet with awe, but she never heard it again. She imagined he'd found his way home, across the sea.

Most nights she heard fears about dying, about the afterlife, if there was one. Everyone was afraid to miss salvation.

"The snake god isn't like the Christ god. He'll love my black skin. He'll forgive my sins."

"Yes. Damballah loves your black skin."

"The Virgin Mary believes in me. She'll save me."

"Yes."

"I pray to all—both white and black saints."

"Damballah isn't a jealous god," Marie soothed the whining voice.

"I don't pray to any god."

"Damballah believes in you anyway."

"Will I be saved? I'm afraid to die by hanging. Will I be spared?"

"Yes."

Swearing "yes" made everybody happy. She even said a rosary—"Hail Mary, full of grace"—for those who wanted one. And she shared, as she had shared with no one, how it felt when Damballah was inside her. She whispered across the darkness, "It is sweet peace. Nothing dies. Nothing is gone forever. Everything about nature is teeming with life. Stare at a leaf and you see it. Even the killing swamp has life. Mud and soil oozing with creatures, insects. Everything is resurrected. A miracle."

"Like raising Lazarus."

"Like Christ walking on water."

"Yes, but Damballah is more. Different. Christ walks and triumphs over the water. Damballah makes you part of it. You are in and within the water."

"Miracles."

"Yes. Both of them. Each different. But Damballah makes me feel part of the miracle. Like being inside the water, part of something too big to imagine. Connected to everything, to the slightest thing, the texture of a falling leaf, the sand churned by the tide."

"Praise be." Someone hummed, and the melody sounded like mourning. Someone began a syncopated clapping. At first one pair of hands, then ten, twenty, a host of hands clap-clapping, transforming the message into one of insistent joy. Harmony was added, and soprano cries of "Yes, Lord" and "Praise be!" seemed to lift the ceiling, to enclose even the people keeping vigil before the prison walls. The sound was echoed back. Glorious sound pressed its way into stone crevices, warm hearts. A rumbling and swelling bass matched the rhythmic hands: "Damballah, Damballah." And Marie shouted, "Yes, Damballah. Yes!" They were singing the healing sounds of a village after disaster.

Guards burst in shouting, "Quiet down, quiet," banging their sticks against cell bars. "Quiet. Damn niggers. Shut your mouths." The rhythm tightened, speeding up, buzzing like a trillion bees, demanding space, seeking escape; then, abruptly, it died. Their emotion drained, one by one the singers and prisoners closed their eyes, rested their heads against the wall, or covered their faces and wept.

The twelfth night, by pressing herself close to the wall, twisting her hand through and to the left of the bars, Marie was able to hold on to the hand of a young boy as he died. He'd been curious the second night of the riots. He wanted to go see "some black mens fight white." He saw nothing. Instead, a couple of soldiers startled him, beat him, and Marie could only guess he suffered internal wounds. She held on to his hand until daybreak, when the guards came with stale *beignets* and water. They carted him away and she got to see his face as he passed, slumped over a guard's shoulder like a sack. No more than thirteen, skin like chocolate, yet rail-thin. In his final moments he'd kept calling for a mama he never remembered seeing. She dared to murmur she was his mama and he needn't fear death for he was becoming spirit. She sang the song she remembered of childhood and love, "Mon píti bebe. Fais dodo." She stroked his tight curls, the curve of his cheek, trying to make her hands as gentle and strong as Grandmère's.

That day she'd stayed awake, her hands smothering her mouth, weeping but not wanting anyone else to wake and know she wept. She didn't know if she'd been right, consoling the boy; she didn't know if what she said was true. She waited for a sign, some message that she was fulfilling what Damballah expected of his Voodoo Queen. Her only sign was dysentery: racking pain and bowels she couldn't control.

Because she was awake, she got to see a lovely woman, a few years older than herself, dressed finely in peach-colored silk and white lace, carrying a parasol and a black Bible with the word "holy" written in gold script. She looked like an *aristo,* though the guard hurrying her along called her "negress." Marie inhaled the scent of gardenias and for a moment, squatting over her dirt hole, she felt relief from stomach cramps, nausea, and trickling diarrhea. She wanted to stand and address the woman. She wanted to move toward the bars and touch her hand. But she couldn't. Instead the woman stopped at her cell, murmuring, "Maman Marie, Maman Marie. You did a great thing, killing him who deserved to be killed.

"My master said he loved me. I bore him two children. Two children whom he sold. Now he does this to me. I wish I had your strength. I would have killed my monsieur long ago. It is all my stupid fault for believing if I was kind enough, gentle enough, sweet enough, he would value me and my children. I should have done like you."

The guard hit her.

"Leave her alone," shouted Marie, squatting over her hole. The guard looked away, muttering.

Tears swept down the woman's cheek; she brushed them quickly away. "I fool myself. I couldn't have hurt anyone. Remember me. I'm Marianne."

"Hurry along." The guard shoved her forward.

Marianne quickened her pace, passing out of sight.

At night, when the screaming began, nobody knew who the new prisoner was. Everyone knew it was a woman, but the agony was detached from any visual image. Marie, though, had a clear picture of Marianne's upturned nose, her delicate hands fringed with lace and silk cuffs. Marianne was a porcelain figure imbued with life.

Marie could well imagine what the guards were doing to Marianne. There could be no reason other than power. The guards had waited for darkness, gone against their own pattern of daylight brutality. They must have known the degree of their own degradation and couldn't stand to see it reflected in one another's eyes. Acts so unspeakable they didn't even want slaves in the neighboring cell, slaves whom they considered less than human, to see. This was more than rape, more than intimidation of blacks. It went beyond the guards' need to satisfy themselves, reaching to the men's desire to torture and humiliate women.

Marianne lasted three nights. All confidences stopped among the other prisoners. No one spoke during the long nights. Instead everyone was praying, finding the means to rein in their own grief and hysteria. During the days she was alive, Marianne slept and sang hymns.

A voice calling himself Cholly hurled accusations. "Aren't you going to save her, Maman Marie? You've been promising everyone else you'd save them. Why not save her?" The taunt was unrelenting, a disembodied voice that echoed her own self-doubt. Marie hated it. She didn't control when the gods entered her. She desperately wished she was Ogu, able to tear through iron bars to battle the men. She said her own prayers to Damballah and to the Virgin. Yet each night amid the screams, Cholly would still call, "Aren't you going to save her?"

One night there was a moan, soft yet piercing, which seemed to carry the weight of Marianne's soul. Then there was nothing else. Silence. Then, the shuffling of feet, the sliding of a weight across the floor. The door of the guardroom opened, and a shaft of light stretched the length of the prison. Marie never saw Marianne's body and she was glad. But Cholly and the other prisoners in the cell across from Marianne's did. He called, "You should be proud of yourself, Maman Marie. You used your power well."

Marie collapsed in her cell like a useless marionette, her body weak, dehydrated, powerless. Marianne had been the only one brought to jail not because of the riots, yet Marie felt guilty for her as well. When she was finally gone, no one spoke of her. It was as if she had never been. Cholly said nothing more.

If she could have stood, Marie would have yelled down to the growing street crowd, "I'm a charlatan. Fake." But then the people within the prison would overhear. She'd take away their comfort, their need to believe. Except for Cholly, the prisoners implicitly believed that because she'd been possessed by a spirit, because she'd killed a white man and not immediately been killed, she could do anything and everything. Her being in the same prison with them, they believed, kept them all alive. While it was true some prisoners died and guards tortured others, no one built scaffolds and took them all to be hanged. This, too, was one of her miracles.

She'd been imprisoned for sixteen days.

"Maman Marie, can you help me, please?"

"Yes." And she immediately thought to herself, Liar.

"Don't forget you promised to save me."

"Yes." Liar.

Yet what was wrong with telling lies to the dying? And all of them in the cells were dying, including her.

Hallucinating, Marie dreamed Brigette's baby was hers, the twin of her own child. Once she dreamed Marianne was her baby—born full-grown from her body, bathed in red. The sweet caramel boy came back, half skeleton, arms outstretched, calling "Mama."

Marie felt her baby low in her abdomen, felt with each explosion of diarrhea and blood that the baby was suffering, losing the very life force she needed to survive. This was her worst fear—failing a daughter of hers the way she felt her mother failed her. No miracles, no walking on water. Just her own incapacity to nurture and protect her own child.

Damballah, send me a sign, she prayed. She held on—eating when she felt she couldn't, breathing deeply through unbearable cramps, resting when she felt driven to slam her body against the cell's metal and stone. She patterned circles on her abdomen, trying to see her daughter within the water inside her womb.

By the eighteenth day, she was full of self-pity. Where was her comfort? No one, not even John or Nattie, came to visit. She wanted someone to touch her; she wanted the pleasure of someone with her . . . now. She wanted a healthy baby in her arms.

One night, Marie swore she saw a firefly cutting across the moon. It blinked once, then twice, and lying on her back, Marie reached for the firefly, trying to catch it in her palm and hold it close to her stomach so baby Marie could see the glimmering light. But she was too weak, the firefly too fast. Even the moon seemed to loom and mock her. Marie cried. She'd lie on cold stone and die. She'd never see Grandmère or Jacques. She'd never see her baby.

Stars formed the image of a snake.

"I won't die."

The voice was light, touching her soul from within. Marie felt her baby's presence speaking to her, felt love radiating as the star snake radiated and circled the full moon.

"We are Marie."

This was her sign, her restoration of faith. She mouthed the words to herself: "We are Marie."

This was her miracle—holding and hearing life inside her womb. Rocking her stomach, listening to her heart and the faint drumming of her daughter's, she thought she heard whistling, clear and steady, trilling like a nightingale's evening song. Her fever abated, the cramps ended, and her spirit lifted, knowing beyond any doubt that she and her daughter would survive.

The next morning John and Ribaud came for her. As she leaned on them, her legs weak, John was babbling. "Judge set you free. He set you free." Ribaud was muttering "Blackmail." John was gleeful.

Marie wanted them to be quiet, for she was searching for Cholly, scanning faces, trying to find a face to match the voice of the only one who derided her, who pointed out her weaknesses, who wanted her to be accountable.

Faces were pressed against the bars, happy for her, chanting "Maman Marie," reaching out a hand to touch her. The noise was deafening.

A young man was pressing forward through the stampede of bodies and arms. "Let me through. I must get through. Let me through." He was down on his knees, clutching bars, his face distorted, trying to squeeze through the tight space. "Maman Marie." She inhaled sharply. Was this him?

Marie slapped John's and Ribaud's hands away and knelt, her fingers wrapping around the young man's.

"What's your name?"

"Lee. Don't forget you said you'd save me. You swore you'd save me."

"I'll save you." She stroked away a small river of tears on his cheek. His expression lightened. He gave her a toothy grin.

Others, who had been silent for the seconds she consoled Lee, now shouted, "Save me!" waving their arms at her, grasping at her, pulling her off-balance into the metal bars. She felt like screaming. John and Ribaud were untangling her from a sea of arms, propelling her forward. She looked back. She saw fewer faces, only black and brown arms waving to the left and right of her. She could distinguish

Lee's voice above the shouts, "Save me!" She never saw Cholly, the one who knew her best.

The room was spinning, the floor rising up to her face. John scooped her up and held her. His face was triumphant as he carried her in her arms out into the street.

~

Voodoo is a form of ancestor worship. Souls survive after death. It is a family's responsibility to see that these souls rest easy. Offerings should be made to the family ancestors and to the family's spirit guardian.

Souls who are shown the proper respect by their families join in harmony with the other spirits of the world. They roam the earth, frolic, and possess family members when necessary to convey guidance and advice.

Beware those ancestral souls who are dishonored. These souls take every opportunity to wreak revenge on the family line. The sins of a mother can haunt a great-granddaughter and beyond. No one dies. Just as tree, water, and earth spirits exist forever . . . so, too, does the human soul go on.

The most feared evil in Voodoo is a zombie. Resurrected mindless, soulless bodies are controlled by a priest, an evil houngan. *Souls from resurrected bodies roam the earth in torment.*

To prevent zombies, "Make sure your loved ones are indeed dead and their bodies do not go warm to the grave."

•

—The Origins and History of the Voodoo Cults
(From Louis DeLavier's journal)

P rison taught her that whether she liked it or not she had a congregation—Creoles, quadroons, black slaves, free coloreds—all of whom wanted a little hope. Marie was determined to offer it. Prison taught her that the desperate didn't care whether hope was Christian or African, Catholic or Voodoo, only that it existed.

Marie set the Virgin Mother beside the coquette Mistress Ezili. Legba, holding the keys to the spiritual world, was placed beside a gruff Saint Peter. Saint James brandished a sword beside the warrior Ogu. Ulrich, cradling a fish, swapped tales of ships and storms with the sea god Agwé.

For many, the Christian symbols affirmed Marie's power. The Christian God didn't strike Marie dead. No curses rained from heaven. For others, the symbols appealed to their titillating interest in blasphemy. They relied on Marie to entertain, beguile, and lift their lives above the ordinary. They carried rosaries while praying to Damballah. Everyone was mesmerized, and business thrived. Father Christophe condemned Marie from the pulpit. John lost count of the gold and stolen jewelry bartered for Marie's spells and charms.

Ceremonies followed a pattern: first, homage and tribute to both white and black gods, then the sacrifice of goats and chickens (occasionally a calf). Dancing would begin. Ribaud made love to his drums, building rhythms slowly, methodically, to a frenzy. People were possessed by the minor gods.

Marie danced with the python, then Damballah arrived and prophetic visions flowed through Marie's mind. Her trance would last for minutes or for hours. Awakening, Marie counseled the love-lorn, the vengeful, the jealous. Nattie and John would sell holy water, scented candles, love potions, and charms—charms to conquer an enemy, to bring good luck, bad luck. The religious script was always the same, and Marie was always amazed by its popularity.

The more popular she became, the more Marie doubted herself. No blinding light revealed to her the rightness of her course. Whenever she looked at the Christian saints, she felt ambivalence. She believed in them because she was too afraid of not believing. But she hated them for having no black saints. The black gods she still believed in because, remarkably, they still believed in her.

The baby was growing larger. Marie often felt it shifting in her womb. Gracefully. Sweetly. It was only a matter of time before her pregnancy was discovered. Her breasts were dark and tender; her stomach was stretching; she wore shapeless shifts. Another four to five months, her baby would arrive and John would dominate her daughter just as he dominated her. She felt powerless to stop it.

Today, Marie sat in the enclosed courtyard behind the house on St. Anne. She preferred spending her free hours in the garden. Curling vines, riotous bushes, wild roses, and lush honeysuckle grew unchecked. She was reminded of Teché's wildness. John thought it a waste of energy and money to tend a fruitless garden. Marie was pleased. The courtyard was one place where John didn't rule.

Marie often wondered about the family who had rented the house before them. She imagined them to be modest, retiring, and loving. A daughter. A son. A dedicated father. A mother who tended the garden. Not at all like the discontented family John had made, distorted by his greed.

It was cool in the garden. The snake was nearby. Li Zombi. Her Damballah god. Why Damballah continued to possess her, she didn't know. The python inched its head upward. Marie envied the snake's calm. She still wasn't certain it was supernatural. The snake, though, kept John away, and for that she was grateful.

Ribaud sat cross-legged in the dirt, scraping clean a cat's hide for his drums. Once it was clean, he would dry it and sew it together with other skins to form the head of a bass drum. Marie never asked Ribaud how he killed his cats. Maybe he suffocated them. Broke their backs. Maybe he knocked them unconscious before skinning them alive. Marie only knew Ribaud kept dozens of cats in cages along one side of the house. The cats seemed to know when Ribaud intended to murder one of them; they scratched and howled and threw themselves against the wire mesh. She could listen calmly to them. Funny, she used to feel guilty about the death of a firefly! But since Antoine's murder, it seemed natural to be involved with death, with a dubious snake, and with a skinny spell man named Ribaud who knew no spells. She still recalled Ribaud, years ago, carrying his pail of writhing snakes and screaming in the square, "Fear me. All of you, fear me!"

Ribaud was no one to fear. Except for killing cats, Ribaud was gentle. Loyal to her.

Once Nattie, in a vindictive mood, had declared Ribaud had killed his own daughter. The three of them had been in the kitchen eating chicken when Nattie launched her attack.

"Ribaud found his daughter lying with a man, he did. Pretty

nude body sweaty with love. Ribaud cut off the man's cock. Let him bleed to death. 'Tis true. John helped Ribaud get rid of the body. The daughter went crazy, killed herself. Slit her own throat." Ribaud hadn't denied it. He'd kept eating as Nattie had cooed, "I no say what don't be true."

Now Marie watched Ribaud dismembering a cat. "Ribaud, remember when we first met?"

Lifting his gray head, Ribaud smiled his crooked grin. "You were de prettiest sight I ever did see."

Pretty was a word for virgins, innocents. "And now, Ribaud?"

"You're de famous Voodoo Queen."

"Famous for murder, brutality. People think I commit the worst sins. Killing white babies. Poisoning rivals. It's amazing. I'm more powerful than ever. The judge didn't dare convict me of Antoine's murder. All because John swore a hideous revenge. Funny, killing a man was the only thing I've done that made John truly happy." Marie buried her face in her hands. "All my life, I've just wanted to know myself. I don't know anything about me. And what other people know of me is lies. Even if I died, the lies would live on."

"Don't, Miz Marie." Ribaud scuttled near. Stroking Marie's hand, he tried to comfort her. "Don't be dying. You always hurt who's left behind. No way for anybody to earn your forgiveness. No way for you to learn to forgive."

"I'm covered with filth," she said, shuddering. "John has made me as dirty as he is."

Ribaud wanted to hug away Marie's hurt. He slipped his arms about her waist, then snatched his hands back. Marie gasped. Ribaud had felt the swelling of her abdomen.

"Miz Marie?"

She laughed hysterically. "Yes, yes."

"Miz Marie, stop. Dey'll hear." Helplessly, Ribaud flailed his hands. He kicked aside his drum casings and slippery entrails.

"Isn't it funny?" Grasping her stomach, shoulders trembling, Marie laughed as she cried. "So funny. So funny."

"John and Nattie, dey'll hear."

"Ribaud, how can I raise my daughter here? Nattic as god-mother. John as father. What chance will my baby have?"

Marie moaned and burrowed her face against the unyielding chair.

Ribaud stroked her hair. Seeing Marie crying, he saw his daughter's tears. His daughter had once needed his understanding and he'd failed her. Yvonne had been as sweet and beautiful as her mother, who'd died birthing her. Maybe it would've been different if his wife had lived. He'd watched Yvonne falling in love and he, stupid Ribaud, had kept treating her like a child. He'd called her a fool and stirred rebellion. He'd locked her up and fed her rice, finally driving her to disobedience.

Ribaud screwed his face tight. Fifteen years and he still felt murderous rage toward the man. But his rage was best aimed at himself. He'd driven his only child to death.

John had found him gathering courage to jump off the dock and into the Gulf. But he hadn't really had the courage for suicide. He'd been too afraid of the water washing over him and pouring into his lungs.

John helped him bury both bodies. Yvonne's pretty head wouldn't sit right in the coffin. Before long, John was providing shelter and calling him "friend." But John's friendship became blackmail, and it didn't take long before Ribaud became an accomplice in blackmailing others. He'd surrendered his will. John became his punishment. A lifetime of despising himself as John's lackey seemed more fitting than death by drowning. But since knowing Marie, Ribaud had glimpsed redemption. Some spirit in Marie reminded him of his daughter. No, it was more—it was Marie's relentless loving of John (even when she knew loving him was misguided) that reminded him of Yvonne. Yvonne had kept dreaming Zack would leave his wife and children. Ribaud had overheard them arguing the day before Zack's death. He'd heard Zack insisting, "A wife keeps me free from other women's traps." John was just as selfish. With his greed for money and power, he could be no more faithful to Marie than to anybody.

If he defied John and helped Marie, maybe he could make peace with his little girl. Yvonne's spirit could feel good knowing he'd saved someone else when he couldn't save her. He'd be a man again. These thoughts rushed through Ribaud's mind, creating a deep-felt need to help Marie survive. The "girl" in Marie needed compassion and understanding; she probably needed it more because she was the great Voodoo Queen.

Ribaud believed in *both* Maries more than Marie believed in herself. Drums were his calling, and he felt the magic and mystery of helping Marie be possessed by Damballah. It made sense to help her now as he'd always helped her, since the first night Damballah possessed her. Ribaud's faith was pure. It seemed fitting to him that Marie could be extraordinarily and ordinarily human. He accepted everything about her. And because Marie wasn't his daughter, he was free from worrying about his own shortcomings or fearing how her actions would reflect upon him. He was freer to love her.

"Jacques be back," Ribaud whispered, his head turning to see if John or Nattie were near. "Now. Here. In New Orleans."

"Why didn't you tell me?"

"I was afraid for you."

"And now?"

"I could take you to him."

Marie felt suspended. Her breath came in short bursts. "You don't know what you're saying. If we're caught—"

"He's been wid Grandmère. I done seen him. He's been back. One, two months at least. He takes good care of Grandmère."

"Did he ask for me?"

"Naw."

Marie schooled her emotions. She dried her tears.

"But dat don't mean he don't care," Ribaud went on. "You should've done seen his face," he improvised. "Each time I seen him, all tore up he was. He wanted to ask for you. I know he did."

Hope flickered in Marie's eyes.

"Jacques don't want to push where he's not wanted. He's got pride. But Sailor Jacques would do anyding for you." Ribaud's voice was like a caress. "Anyding at all."

The words hung in the air, tempting Marie with possibilities, escape. She stared past Ribaud. All the colors in the garden blended in one vibrant, lush, overflowing green. Jacques was her last hope for redemption.

Her spirits fell. Did Jacques still love her? Would he hate her bastard child? Would he help her out of duty to their marriage vows?

"In sickness and in health. . . ." Her soul was sick. "For better or for worse. . . ." Marie trembled. Perhaps Jacques would help her out of love. That was her wildest fantasy. Jacques would willingly rescue Grandmère and herself; Marie would spend her life paying him back.

Marie turned to Ribaud. "Yes," she said. "Yes."

The spell man grinned, his gold-capped teeth glinting in the sun.

Marie was nervous. She promised herself she wouldn't beg. Jacques would either want her or not want her. Simple as that.

All day she'd been on the verge of fainting. It was Ribaud who'd given her the courage to plan the one-sided rendezvous. They'd decided to wait until Sunday evening. John was fond of sinning on Sundays. He liked to drink whiskey, whore, and talk in shorefront bars. Usually he didn't return until Monday. Tuesday, if he met a woman he liked.

No, Marie decided, she wouldn't beg. She'd ask Jacques what she needed to ask and that was that.

Marie dressed carefully, stepping into a loose cotton dress with a square collar, hoping to hide her swelling abdomen. She twisted her lush hair into a bun. She didn't know what stories Jacques had heard about her. Rumors ran wild. Not even nineteen and she was already a legend, an accused "murderous demon."

Maybe Jacques wouldn't want to see her. The last time he'd been in port, they'd made love and then she'd left. Ribaud had kept carrying her gifts to Grandmère, but Marie had never asked him to carry any message to Jacques. She'd felt a clean break was fairer. Ribaud had never brought any message back. After a few weeks, Marie assumed Jacques had shipped out to sea again. Each morning from her bedroom window, she'd stared at complaining seagulls in the harbor sky, hoping Jacques had forgotten all about her. She even hoped he hated her if it would mean less pain for him. Ironically, now she was praying beyond hope that Jacques still had enough love left to help her and her child.

Marie washed her face and hands again. She wanted to be clean when she saw Jacques. She looked at herself in the mirror. She still felt as if she were covered with prison filth, rat droppings, and spider bites, as she'd been on the day of her release. When she left the prison, her hair had been matted, her clothes torn and grimy, and her undergarments and legs stained with excrement. Feeling filthy and being filthy had sometimes merged. She believed her soul matched her appearance. Marie reached out to touch herself in the mirror. What a desperate mission she was planning. Jacques would have to be a fool to find her beautiful.

Ribaud tapped lightly at the door. His head jutted round the corner. Breathlessly, he said, "Now. Right now. John's whoring. Gone for days. He's found a new gal. Nattie's left, shopping for bad wishes and secrets. De old bitch don't suspect a ding."

"I'd given up expecting you." Jacques was squinting at Marie standing in the doorway. His breath was hurried and shallow. Marie was carelessly beautiful. Jacques wanted to raise his hand and strike her.

"I'm here now," Marie said harshly. Nervousness made her defensive.

"You've been gone a long time. I had time enough to sail to the Bahamas and back." Jacques turned away and lit a candle. Dusk was settling in the sky, and a vivid streak of orange cut across the dirt floor and the litter of empty bottles on a table.

Jacques was pale. Living on land didn't agree with him. He was weathered, weary. The skin around his eyes was stretched and dark. He smelled of rum. Marie noticed he was thinner, too, like an alley cat, and just as cautious and beguiling. "I've been busy," she murmured.

"I heard."

"What did you hear?" Poised on the threshold, Marie could feel her neck reddening, her skin swelling, itching with nervous hives.

Jacques stared hard. Marie held her breath. His eyes undressed her like she was a whore. Ribaud shifted uncomfortably beside her. Marie whispered to him and, nodding, the spell man shuffled down the steps toward the riverbank, pausing every few feet to glance over his shoulder and wonder if he made a mistake bringing Marie and Jacques together again.

"May I come in?"

Jacques stepped aside and Marie softly closed the door.

"Does Grandmère know? About the things you heard?"

"No."

Marie scanned the room. Sparse. Tidy in the kitchen area. The floors had been swept. Only the dining table had been spared cleanliness. Empty jugs and bottles of island rum were like trophies, a testament to Jacques' hard head and iron stomach. A half-empty glass beckoned on the table. Marie averted her eyes. Grandmère must be in the bedroom. "How is she?"

"Better. Clean at least," Jacques answered sarcastically.

Marie settled her package onto the nearest chair. It was outrageous coming here. Since the trial, wagging tongues had commented on her every act. Some she'd committed; some she hadn't. All of New Orleans spied on her for John.

"I brought food. A gift for Grandmère." Her hands were trembling. She lifted out a pound of sugar. "I would have brought a gift for you. I didn't know you'd be here." She smiled fleetingly. Jacques didn't respond. She felt despairing. Jacques wasn't giving an inch. Cowardly, like a schoolgirl, she lied, delaying what she'd come to say. "I didn't know you'd be here."

"I'm here."

"Beans. Crayfish. Rice," she said, poking her face into the bag. "Enough to hold you and Grandmère, don't you think? Grandmère loves crayfish. They're easy on her teeth and gums."

"Tell me about it."

"What?" Had he guessed what she wanted to say?

"About the trial."

Avoiding him, she moved toward the bedroom. Jacques stole behind her, whispering, "She's sleeping." His lips brushed her ear.

"I don't want her upset," murmured Marie, cracking open the door.

The bedroom was dark; the shutters were closed. A thin blanket covering her, Grandmère lay on the bed like a corpse. Her hands were crossed over her hips; her fingers clutched a rosary. Her white hair in two long braids, Grandmère was breathing torturously through her mouth. Vials of herbs and medicines cluttered the nightstand. Horrified, Marie twisted and looked at Jacques.

"I've done the best I could," he said, defensive. "You needn't look at me that way." He stumbled backward into the chair. "When I got here she was ill."

"Why didn't you let me know?"

"What do you care? Who the hell are you to care?"

Hushing him, Marie shut the bedroom door and followed him to the center of the room. "You could've at least let me know. Don't I deserve that?"

"No."

Marie reacted as though she'd been struck. Her cheeks heated and she felt off-balance, stunned.

"Every day I kept expecting you." Jacques swallowed his rum and poured another glass. "I'd wake excited each morning and feel disgusted by evening. You never came. You sent your slave, Ribaud. He left food or coins to soothe your conscience. On the doorstep even. He'd knock and be gone. But where were you?" Swallowing, Jacques emptied another glass, then poured another. "I did the best I could," he repeated stubbornly. "What've you done? Were you here when Grandmère coughed all night? When she spit up blood? Were you here? Did you feed her? Clothe her?" He emptied Marie's groceries onto the table. Pink crayfish shuddered on ice; dry kidney beans rolled and scattered across the floor; white rice cascaded off the table. "This isn't enough food for three days. You think Grandmère can survive on this? You don't care. The things I've heard must be true. You're a monster. You don't care about Grandmère. You don't care at all."

"I do care." Marie rounded on him. "And don't tell me your conscience kept you from eating the food I sent with Ribaud. I paid good money for others to look after Grandmère. All you bought and cared about was rum. I only have to look at you to know drink has gotten the better of you. You're nothing but a drunk."

Jacques slammed his fist into the wall. "Don't speak to me like that. You've no right. No right at all." He was shaking with rage; he wanted to hurt Marie. He might even be capable of killing her. Staring at the floor, Jacques wiped sweat from his brow. He wanted a drink badly. He felt disgusted with himself.

"I'm sorry." Marie brushed a strand of hair from her eyes. "I've no right to be mean and selfish. But it's too dangerous for me to spend time with Grandmère."

"Six months, I figure," Jacques said, astonished. "You haven't seen her in at least six months. Don't you know she's waiting for you? Hoping for you?"

"Villagers were supposed to look after her. I paid good money. Halo, Ziti, and others. . . ." Her voice trailed off. "They were supposed to tell me if she was ill. If she needed any help. They were supposed to provide for her. Cook, clean, and care for her."

"Since I've been here, no one has come. Only Ribaud, prowling like one of his cats."

Why hadn't Ribaud told her? Marie ignored this question and focused on the villagers. "I'll fix them," she murmured to herself. Unconsciously, she drew herself tall. She dwelled on thoughts of "die away" spells and torture. She envisioned Halo crippled, unable to satisfy her paying lovers. How would Halo live then? She saw Ziti disfigured with scars and bleached more white than she'd ever desired. "Whole world would be a better place if I was white," Ziti had grumbled. Except no man, let alone a white man, would desire her as a mistress when Marie was done with her. All of Haben's Haven would experience blight—plants would die, animals would become diseased, and any hopes the villagers had about life, about love, would shrivel like forgotten dreams.

Amazed, Jacques was staring at her. Another Marie—hardened, bitter, and vengeful—seemed to fill the room. Marie turned away, embarrassed. Could Jacques guess how filthy her mind had become? How bloodthirsty her heart?

"Jacques, I wasn't criticizing your care of Grandmère. You've loved her better than I have. I'm just sorry she's so ill. I can be sorry, can't I?"

"Sorry never helped anything."

"I know," Marie said dully, curling her fist in her hair. "I should've expected Grandmère to grow worse. But I thought . . . I wanted to believe if she was clean . . . if I paid people to keep her clean . . . to care for her, everything would be all right. I should've known better." Tears spilled onto her face. "But I did what I thought was best. I thought it better for Grandmère to be cared for by strangers than to die because I came to her." Woeful, she shrugged her shoulders; her hands swayed limp at her sides. "John said he'd kill her if I came, but today I had to risk it."

Jacques slapped his chest. He would give anything to make Marie smile and be happy again. But he had his own pain that needed curing. He'd lost a carefree life. He'd lost the daily mindless peace he found in sailing, exploring ports, and seducing pretty girls. Marie had changed everything. He'd become entangled in two lives, hers and Grandmère's. Entangled in Voodoo. He hadn't realized what the high cost of loving her would be.

"Grandmère has nightmares. You should hear her screeching, hollering." Jacques exhaled, making the sign of the cross. "She sees ghosts. Goblins. 'Perching on her stomach, scratching her,' she says, 'trying to keep her from Teché.' Sometimes the ghosts draw blood." He slid into the chair and poured more rum. "I've seen welts on her, red and swollen. I don't know what to believe. But her blood flows as red as mine."

Jacques continued more quietly, his voice rough from alcohol. "I don't know whether she's insane or not. She says she'll die when the ghosts start scratching her from the inside out." He looked up. "She doesn't want to die here. She wants to go home. To Teché."

"So do I, Jacques." There—she'd said it. The room seemed to shrink in size. The air stilled in her lungs.

Marie heard yelps carrying from the shoreline; children were playing on the waterfront. Jacques was still morose. He angled his head away from her, toward the cold grate. Old half-burnt logs seemed a reproach. Her eyes stung. Marie had counted on him to want to rescue her. She stooped down, scooping the spilt kidney beans from the dirt floor into her palms. The rice was already scattered and nearly buried in the dirt. Nothing was ever easy for her.

Jacques handed her the straw broom.

Marie whisked and stabbed at the beans, their color reminding her of dried blood. The white rice turned a sooty gray.

"Did you kill a man?"

The broom was poised in midair. In one word she was going to lose Teché. Marie wanted badly to lie but she couldn't. "Yes," she said. She stepped on the mound of beans, cracking, splitting them open. "You must hate me." She smacked impatiently at the air. "I'm Grandmère's ghost. I must be the one who draws blood."

"I figure if you killed a man, he deserved it."

"He did. Antoine DeLavier."

Jacques whistled softly. He held open his arms. The broom fell as Marie rushed forward, hurling herself against him.

"Marie," Jacques whispered. The pain in him lightened like an early morning sky. The two of them held each other, swaying.

"Murder isn't hard," Marie said wonderingly. "The hard part comes afterward. The only way to live with it is to *be* hard, *feel* hard. I don't cry anymore. I've given it up."

"Confess."

"To a priest? In prison they sent me a priest. Father Christophe. He said there's a mark on my forehead, Cain's mark. 'Black people, the evil children of Cain.' " She shuddered. "I don't believe that. I don't believe I'm evil because I murdered a man who deserved to die. I regret killing him. But I can't repent."

"You're not evil." He pressed a light kiss on her brow.

"Father Christophe said Voodoo was my evil, my pact with the devil. At times he sounded so sensible, so sympathetic, I wanted desperately to believe him. If I could believe the priest, I wouldn't have to struggle to make sense of my life. I wouldn't have to worry about right or wrong. Yet I couldn't do it, Jacques." She pulled out of his arms. Her hands flattened against the window. "Belief in Cain's mark is an excuse for slavery, a burden for blacks to carry."

Marie felt forlorn. She needed Jacques to understand part of what she was feeling.

282

"They kept me in prison for almost three weeks," she went on. "Outside my bars, I saw black people praying, believing in me. Hundreds of them. Calling me a saint."

"Are you?"

"I'm too miserable to be a saint." She laughed ruefully. "No, I don't know. Maybe in people's minds. Maybe that's all a saint ever is—someone made special by others' belief. Maybe, like Grandmère, I'm crazy. I invent visions. You *see* welts on Grandmère. I *feel* Damballah in me. I know so little about this faith I practice. John won't or can't tell me what I need to know. Grandmère refuses to help." Shifting her weight, rubbing her head, she sighed.

"Do you know who's in prison, Jacques? Poor coloreds. Slaves. Quadroon mistresses. There was one woman, Marianne, just as white and delicate as you can imagine, but because she had a drop of black blood, because her lover abandoned her, the guards did horrible . . . cruel. . . ." Marie closed her eyes. She could hear echoes of Marianne's screams. She smelled the press of bodies, the yellowing filth. She was back in her cell again, terrified, living by her wits, threatening the guards with her Voodoo power. Any moment she'd expected to be found out, to be proven a charlatan, but the moment never came and she'd survived.

"Prisoners were treated horribly. Most were beaten, forced to lie in excrement. One man's legs were broken for no reason. Another was shackled, spread-eagled, to a wall." Her tone flattened and her words sounded distant, as though spoken from far off.

"The prisoners looked to me for guidance. Comfort. They shouted across bars, 'Maman Marie,' 'Maman Marie!' In the night, when the guards were sleeping, they'd whisper their stories. Often I didn't know which voice came from where or from whom. Their stories were gruesome. One had been lashed a hundred times. Another had been castrated and survived.

"Those who held on to their sanity never gave up hope. I learned something about the will to live, Jacques. You can still hope, even when it's hopeless.

"In the middle of the night, these people begged and pleaded with me to spare them. You know what I said, Jacques? I said I'd try. Can you believe it? I'd try.

283

"They were happy, so certain that when I was freed, I'd save them from the hangman's noose." She was breathing heavily, almost choking in her effort not to cry. "Maybe prison was Damballah's sign. I serve all those people Catholicism has forgotten. I'm a saint to them because I've survived. They saw the guards afraid to touch me. They saw me acquitted. They saw me walk away from prison dirty and foul, but alive. My survival brought them comfort. My promise meant salvation to them. Even if there is no Damballah, if Damballah is the devil, is what I did—do—so wrong, so evil? My promise gives them hope."

"I don't know." Jacques doubled over and let his head fall forward into his hands. Rocking in the chair, his head covered, he wrestled with his conscience. He murmured, "Blasphemy. You forget I'm a Catholic. I'm poor. I'm black. Almost a slave."

"But you aren't a good Catholic, are you, Jacques?"

"You don't know what you're saying," he said, angry and hurt.

"Every time you cross yourself against Voodoo, you betray your belief. You're called to Voodoo just like I am. It's in your skin, your blood."

"That's not true." He flung himself out of the chair.

"Prove it." Marie held out her hand and began to chant: "Legba, remove the barrier. So I may pass through. So I can visit the *loa*." Louder. "Legba, remove the barrier. So I may pass through. So I can visit the *loa*." Still louder. "Legba, remove the barrier. So I may pass through. So I can—"

"Stop it. Stop it." Jacques was retreating, tensing his arms, trying to avoid blessing himself.

"What do you have to fear?" Marie demanded, advancing. "Catholics should scoff at Voodoo. What harm is there if a slave or a colored believes I can protect him? What's wrong with a few lies? Or maybe it isn't a lie." She spoke softly. Her hand plucked nervously at her skirt.

"I sometimes hate the people who attend my ceremonies. Some followers want an excuse to discard inhibitions. They're skilled at pursuing their own pleasures. Some attend because they think everyone else attends. They're like pack rats. It doesn't matter where I lead them or what I ask them to believe in. It's the group, the sense of belonging that's important. Others are interested in me failing. The more spectacular my fall, the better. And we play a waiting game until the day I'm unmasked as a fraud.

"But others, Jacques, are truly searching for more. They're looking for spirituality, a kind of peace. I never realized that until prison. Some just want a champion to speak for them. And some remember the tales of their parents and grandparents, praising the land of Dahomey and its black ancestral gods." There was an inch of space between them. "Touch me, Jacques. Go on. I'm not the devil. I'm Marie, your wife. How can I be a devil? 'Devil' is a word white people made up for Cain's children."

He was crying.

"Oh, Jacques. I'm sorry." She pulled his head to her shoulder, stroked his hair, and cooed, "I'm sorry."

"Nothing is as I expected it to be. Nothing turned out as I planned." Jacques' reserves were gone; up came all his woes, his complaints. "I just wanted to be happy. Decent. To live free with my family. I wanted to breathe air like any other man. I wanted joy. Love. Once free, I didn't expect life to be so hard. Nothing is as I hoped. Sometimes I think it would've been better if I'd remained a slave. Ignorance would've been less painful."

Marie cupped Jacques' face in her palms. "I'm disappointed too." She saw his weariness, the lines of strain etched on his nose and mouth. "I didn't plan on my life being this way. Don't you see, Jacques? It's much easier to be angry with you. I worry all the time God will condemn me to hell. I can't let go of Christian gods any more than you can. I thought I could. But I can't. Maybe to be free of them . . . to love Damballah with all my soul, I would've had to have been African. But Grandmère baptized me Catholic. It makes all the difference in the world."

Embarrassed, Jacques tried to smile. For the first time, Marie felt intimate with him as his wife.

"Why do you take care of Grandmère, Jacques?" She traced his brow line arching in surprise.

"You and Grandmère are the only family I have."

"Just by marriage." Marie repeated it, her tone hinting at

another unspoken question. "Only by marriage. Not blood ties. Is it enough?"

"Yes." Jacques was smiling full out now, regaining some of his handsomeness.

"Jacques," she said tentatively. "Don't you wish you'd never met me?"

He lost his smile.

"The truth, Jacques. Please. Just the truth."

"Yes. All the time. But I did meet you, and everything is changed. Just as I bought myself free. I can't go back. In slavery, I was desperate to have a family—a wife, sons, and daughters who couldn't be sold like cattle or bartered for bales of cotton. Free, I was content but alone. I never thought I'd find the right woman. But I did. The dream was fulfilled. I was free to love and take a wife. Now, which is better? To be free, but alone and without love? Or to feel the joy of loving you and aching for the moment when you would learn to love me as much as I love you?"

Marie started to cry.

Jacques cupped her face in his hand. "Isn't it worthwhile trying to have freedom, happiness, and love? Isn't it worthwhile to create a family rather than living alone? Marie. Oh, Marie," he murmured, "I was trying for it all. Though I've failed, it doesn't mean I regret loving you."

"I love you, Jacques."

Their mouths came together, gently at first, then more demandingly as Jacques explored Marie's mouth with his tongue. Marie slid her arms behind his back and pressed him inward to close the space between their bodies. She lowered his hand from her face, guiding it down her neck, shoulder, and breast until it rested on her swelling abdomen.

She shifted her lips away from his. "Could you act as father to another man's child?"

Jacques' hazel eyes looked at her, yet beyond her.

Marie watched him struggling with the idea. So close to Teché. Yet she couldn't lie. What good would it do to save herself if it meant her child would grow in a home unloved?

Tenderly, Jacques stroked her abdomen, spiraling outward

from the center. *Marie felt the baby move, swimming toward the caress.*

Jacques held her, pressing his teeth against her neck, gently biting into brown skin. "Yes," he said softly. "Since the child is yours, I'd treat it as my own."

"Then take us home, Jacques. Me. Grandmère. Our child. Please take us home."

She moaned as Jacques' hands moved over her. He unbuttoned her dress and slipped the cloth to her waist. He massaged her breasts, holding them in his palms, luxuriating in their fullness. He captured one breast in his mouth, tickling the tip with his tongue. His hand kneaded and stroked her buttocks; his fingers strained toward her crotch. Both hands moved up her skirt and down inside her undergarments. He touched her until she was moist and yielding. Marie stepped out of her undergarments and helped Jacques release the clasp on his pants. His skin felt hot against hers.

Sitting on a chair, Jacques turned her a half turn, then guided her down onto his cock. Marie gasped as he entered her. They rocked slowly. Jacques' hands made feathery strokes along her belly and clitoris. Sensations welled inside her, and she felt explosions of longing and satisfaction radiating throughout her body. He moved faster inside her, holding her hips, twisting them, pulling her hips against the rhythmic rocking. He kissed her back, sucking her skin into his mouth. Time passed sweetly. And when it was done, they cradled and soothed each other. Marie had hopes that the marriage would work. They talked and planned like newlyweds. Jacques was gleeful, amazed that Marie knew the unborn child was a girl. "She'll look just like you," he said, freckling Marie's nose with kisses. "A real beauty she'll be. A rare beauty. We'll name her after you."

Secure on his lap, Marie stroked his chest. She felt renewed and grateful. In her thoughts, she swore over and over again that she'd do anything to please Jacques.

"I'll have to go sailing. We'll need money."

Astonished, Marie looked up. "No. Take us now, Jacques. There's nothing to buy in Teché."

He slid her off his lap, stood, and kept speaking as if he hadn't heard her. "I was thrown off ship for drinking. I lied about sailing to the Bahamas."

"Oh, Jacques, no." Her knees buckled and she reached out, lowering herself into the chair.

"I couldn't face being alone." Embarrassed, he was circling the room. "I acted a fool. I picked fights. Reported late for duty. I was drunk too much. I drank all the time." Jacques slapped his chest; his eyes were wide and guileless. "But I've reformed now. I've got my wife back, my family. It makes all the difference in the world. I won't take another drink again." He was on his knees before Marie, his head on her abdomen, his hands gently squeezing her waist.

"I only have to explain things and they'll take me back. I'll be sailing on the *Marie-Thérèse* before you say 'tomorrow.' The sea breeze will wrap around me. I'll taste salt in the air." He buried his head in the folds of her skirt. "They've got to take me back."

Marie wept. Sailing was Jacques' craft and livelihood. She hadn't meant to hurt him this much. Yet wasn't she asking him to forswear sailing by taking her to Teché? Wasn't she asking him to cut away a part of himself in order to save both her and the baby? Love was never perfectly given. Wouldn't he regret his choice?

"The captain owes me. Just a few words in private, and he'll know he can rely on me again."

"If you go, we'll lose our chance."

"Nonsense. A man's got to provide for his family. Marie, Marie." He sighed. "Don't you understand?" He brushed his lips against her cheek. "A short journey. No more than three months."

"No."

He gripped her hand. "One day we might be grateful for money set aside."

Marie felt dread, afraid of *fa,* her fate. When did anything she dreamed turn out right? She imagined all that could go wrong on a sea voyage. A storm. Man overboard. A rigging accident on ship. Marie felt herself trembling, a chill swelling and settling in her limbs. Away from her, Jacques could change his mind. He'd realize there wasn't anything special about her. She was incapable of unselfish love. Even now she was trying to manipulate him to *do* and *be* what she wanted. What about him? She'd never really cared about him. Escape meant survival. Given time she'd learn to love him as he loved her. Wouldn't she?

"I'll be back, little one. Ma petite, I'll be back—I can tell what you're thinking. You're thinking I don't love you enough. But I do. You're thinking you don't love me enough. But you do. That's why you'll let me go. You'll let me take care of you in my own way. You'll let me be a man on my own terms."

"No, no."

"I'll be back, Marie. The ship is set to sail for the Indies. First Barbados, then Haiti. Afterward home. Only three months. I'll meet you back here. On Mardi Gras Eve. Then we'll leave for Teché."

"Won't you miss me?"

"I always miss you. Except when you're in my arms." His kissed her brow, her eyelids, her cheeks and nose. He feathered kisses down the length of her neck. Marie moaned.

"My last voyage," he swore.

If she seduced him, would he change his mind?

"Imagine me." Weariness had slipped away. Color rushed to Jacques' face. "Sailing waters as green and as clear as emeralds."

Marie could feel his excitement, bubbling like air pockets rising to the surface. Jacques leapt to his feet again, strutting proudly on an imaginary deck. The room seemed strained, smaller, trying to contain his energy. Jacques paused, fixing his gaze on the clear blue horizon.

You couldn't sail the swamps of Teché.

Bowing her head, Marie tensed her hands and knees together. "I could get money. Worshipers pay John." She'd stolen gold to pay for Grandmère's care.

"No!" shouted Jacques.

She exhaled. "It's my money too. I earn it." With lies, theatrics, and fervent prayers to Damballah. "I'm not entirely in John's keeping."

"Leave him now."

"I can't."

Distrust crept into Jacques' eyes. With his shoulders sloped, his hands stuffed deep in his pockets, he seemed diminished. Hurt.

"If John knew what we were planning—" Marie shrugged. "I don't trust him not to hurt us. Or Grandmère."

Jacques tilted his head.

"I love you, Jacques," she said sincerely. "But it's safer to do nothing until you return."

There. She'd given him permission. He could take years sailing to and from the coral reef and she'd as much as admitted she'd be waiting. She must love him. Why else risk destruction? She wanted to reach up and smooth a stray curl from his forehead.

Jacques slapped his chest. "Fair. You're doing something I don't like, and I'm doing something you don't like. It's even. Fair. But it won't happen again, Marie. Not when I come back. We won't do anything the other disapproves of."

"Yes," she said meekly. She'd driven him far enough.

"Smile," Jacques said.

She did.

"Jacques, Jacques, where are you?" The call was a dreary whine.

"It's Grandmère. See? Everything will turn out right." Jacques slipped behind Marie's chair, stroking her head once before calling, "In here, Grandmère."

"We should go to her," Marie said, starting to rise.

"No. She likes to believe she can still do for herself. These few steps help her keep her pride."

Marie felt the baby shifting in her womb. She hadn't noticed the heat before. The room was stifling, humid. She smoothed the creases in her dress. "Do I look all right?"

"You look fine."

Grandmère was framed in the doorway. There was a long pause. A suspension of movement. In her mind's eyes, Marie could see the dramatic tableau. The guilty and penitent granddaughter and the sickly Grandmère.

"It's you," Grandmère said, tottering forward like a bird toppling from its perch. Her white hair and gown stuck to her skin. "It's you," she shrilled, staccato. "The ghost. It's you who's scratching at me."

Marie blanched.

"Grandmère," admonished Jacques.

"You'll keep me from Teché." Grandmère flared her nails to

scratch Marie's eyes. "The devil's ghost." Grandmère was about to rip and tear at Marie's skin.

Marie couldn't move. She was shocked; she was Grandmère's demon personified. Her confidence waned and she felt her own self-hatred returning in force. She was worthless, and in time even Jacques would realize she was unlovable.

"No, Grandmère." Jacques was holding her, but the old woman was looking round the side of his head, her arms still flailing.

"It's Marie," said Jacques.

"The ghost."

"No. Your granddaughter, Marie."

"Save me. I'm dying." Gripping his cloth shirt, Grandmère tried to burrow her head into his chest. She would've crawled and hid inside his body if she could. "I'm an old woman dying."

"Quiet now. You'll live longer than I will." His voice soothed; he rubbed his scratchy chin against her head. "Let me take you to bed. I'll bring supper. Crayfish."

"Crayfish?"

"Yes. Off to bed with you."

"I like crayfish." Grandmère stumbled forward, smacking, sucking her gums.

Jacques glanced back over his shoulder. He winked and smiled crookedly. Marie knew he was telling her not to worry. Nonetheless she slumped down in the chair.

Grandmère chirped excitedly about crayfish tentacles wriggling out of her mouth like worms. "My granddaughter used to make crayfish. Crayfish and rice."

Jacques was murmuring, "Yes, yes," while tucking her in bed.

Marie reflected on ghosts and hell.

"Don't blame her, Marie."

. She lifted her head. "I don't." She bit her nails jagged. "You take good care of her, Jacques."

He brushed the air, awkwardly shifting his weight.

To dull her pain, Marie stifled her emotions, swallowing a wail. "I've a gift for Grandmère." She rose suddenly, opened the door, and signaled to Ribaud, squatting on the shore. The spell man nodded and headed toward their wagon.

"What's he doing?"

Ribaud was removing a canvas cover from their cart.

"What's he got?"

With a gold-toothed smile, Ribaud was dragging a rosewood rocker. Its size overshadowed him. He banged the rocker up the steps and onto the slim porch.

Marie, caressing the wooden arm, stilled the chair's violent rocking. "I owe Grandmère this. Tell her one debt is paid."

Ribaud, his birdseed and feathered hat clutched in both hands, stepped aside as Marie started down the steps.

"Marie," cried Jacques.

She turned. "On the eve before Mardi Gras, Jacques. Don't forget."

"I won't." He lowered his head and she stepped up to kiss him. Their passion was special and sweet. For extra comfort, she placed his hand on her abdomen.

"I'll ask Shad to look in on Grandmère," said Jacques.

"Yes. Do that."

A breeze was roaring in off the Mississippi; she heard the rocker behind her, creaking on the planks. "I'll come to see Grandmère more often myself." Damn John. Marie looked back, shading her eyes. "I promise, Jacques."

Moonlight highlighted every line, every particle of tension in Jacques' face. He was doing his best not to grab Marie, not to hold her, love her, and never let her go.

Softly, she asked, "Must you go to sea?" She was nearly begging; any moment, she'd be on her knees.

"I want to be remembered as a sailor—not a drunk."

Marie relaxed her squint and stepped down onto the cushioning earth. She was the Voodoo Queen of New Orleans. Ribaud, her escort and fool, followed after her. He skipped to keep up with Marie's long strides.

Ribaud wanted to know what had gone wrong. But a side glance told him Marie was crying, bravely and silently. Her head was high and she ignored the few villagers who were foolish enough to gape from their porches or else stare, heads thrust out, from cottage windows. Ribaud shook his fist at them.

Then, suddenly remembering his one moment of prophecy, Ribaud pitied Jacques. He turned around. He remembered saying, *"You'll leave a fine widow. The Widow Paris."* With his floppy hat, he waved goodbye to the lean sailor standing yellow and sad-faced beside the red rocker.

~

"You did right by me, Marie. A true act of charity."

"Christian? Christian charity, Louis?"

"You saved my life—from Antoine, from adulterous sin."

"You've converted in your old age. Are you religious now, Louis? Have you thrown off your doubts?"

"I believe there's human goodness as well as men and women who take perverse pleasure in keeping others from doing good."

"That's no answer. Do you believe in God?"

"As much as any act of kindness can be considered God. You've been a kind of God to me."

"Nonsense. I was never kind to you. I was trying to save my own life, my soul."

"Did you?"

"I don't know, Louis."

"If we'd run away, we would've been happy, wouldn't we?"

"Maybe."

"I've always loved you."

"Once you hated me."

"Maybe. Some. I don't know. When I told Brigette about Antoine's death, she went wild. I sent for a doctor. He said she was pregnant. I always suspected you knew and that's why you sent me away. Did you know?"

"Hush. I want to rub your bald head for luck. I'm dying, you know."

"The judge freed you for the wrong reason—fear of your power. He didn't know you deserved to be free because of your charity. If you

294

had been convicted of Antoine's death, I would have come forward. You
believe that, don't you? Don't you, Marie?"
    "Louis, where do souls go?"
                    •

—MARIE LAVEAU, JUNE 16, 1881, SUNRISE
(From Louis DeLavier's journal)

Success is its own reward. Crowds grew so large that the
ceremonies were moved from Congo Square to the shore of Lake
Pontchartrain. John's staging became more elaborate; he added
more drummers, nearly nude dancing girls, and countless animal
sacrifices. Marie felt disconnected, an insect clamped inside a jar. She
was expected to dance, sing, glow brilliantly with spiritual fire.

Rainbow people came to see her—rich whites, poor blacks,
half-caste mulattoes. At times, the spectacle almost became a riot.
John paid young men to patrol the crowd. They'd whisk away
unpleasant, raucous drunks. They'd sometimes maim ardent heck-
lers.

It was still illegal for blacks to gather for "Voodoo night dancing." Yet the DeLavier trial had raised Marie above the law. John
bribed local officials with a percentage of the profits, and those
resistant to bribes were converted with threats. Everyone came to
Lake Pontchartrain to see and be seen. Everyone came to say they'd
been there.

Black-frocked priests documented Marie's blasphemy, and if
they felt more saintly afterward who was to blame them? *Aristo*
women came, gathering gossip for drawing room parties. It was a
vicarious thrill if one of their class overcame inhibitions and danced
with a black; it gave them someone to both condemn and envy, the
morning after. Often it was the plain girls, the lonely women, who
drank too much and shed their clothes during Voodoo dances. And
if these lonely white women secretly enjoyed their subsequent repentance and the status of having been possessed by devilish spirits,
who could fault them? Everyone deserved one moment, one memory
of glory.

Other whites were notorious cynics who gleefully scoffed at Voodoo ritual and mockingly shuddered at the "terror" of it all. Cynical women found fame during needlepoint sessions and tea parties while gently preaching Armageddon and the second coming of Christ. Doubting men found fame during port-laced debates, pontificating about scientific method and rationalism.

Most *aristo* men, however, came to be entertained, to clutch rum bottles and pretty black girls or poor white girls. If a rape occurred, there was always Voodoo to blame. Quite often such screams were never distinguished from the crowd's titillating roar; quite often the crowd shifted its position or maneuvered around a rape-in-progress. Sometimes members of the crowd joined the rutting scene.

At a Voodoo ceremony, there was a superficial equality; coloreds and whites conversed, master and slave behaved like friends, and everyone felt free to lose control. Marie doubted there were many true believers. Nonetheless, she often glimpsed a few who seemed to glow from a bright light within. Invariably, they were possessed, and afterward they'd weep and pray fervently. Usually, it was the slaves and ex-slaves who'd heard bits of African history and legends from their parents who believed Voodoo was authentic. Marie began systematically questioning them. Sometimes days, weeks afterward, she'd have Ribaud bring these rare believers to her home on St. Anne. Marie became skillful at not revealing how little she knew while gathering scraps of information from them.

Marie heard echoed again and again that the world and nature were infused with spirits. The world and nature were one. Spirits influenced everything: birth, life, death, and the afterlife. Ancestors would either hurt or protect you, depending upon how often you sacrificed and sent burnt offerings of food and wine. She discovered that, in life and in death, the battle between good and evil continued. Except there wasn't any devil. Every spirit or aspect of nature had the potential for both.

Marie's education was piecemeal and confusing. She knew Mistress Ezili was also Erzulie, or the Virgin of Voodoo. Ezili was the goddess of love, beauty, and fortune as well as the goddess of vengeance, jealousy, and discord. Marie heard tales of how Damballah impregnated the earth with rain in springtime, how Damballah was lord of the rivers and marshes, and how Damballah rested in trees. Damballah once loved Ezili and gave her the title Serpent Goddess.

Marie learned there was a hierarchy of gods. She understood that Africans had different languages and so different names for gods who represented the same thing. Even slaves born in Haiti or the West Indies had different names for similar spirits. Marie's head often ached from trying to sort out the stories. But it seemed clear Voodoo itself was like a snake—twisting and turning its shape and substance to suit place and people, not minding that it shed an old identity and rebirthed itself. Perhaps that was why Voodoo had survived. It incorporated and modified traditions. The Catholic church claimed to have all the answers, preaching certainty and ritual, whereas Voodoo seemed flexible and constantly changing.

Marie knew of no other Voodooienne who had willingly and boldly placed the Christian God beside the snake. Yet she was increasingly convinced that Voodoo was and could be a "mixed blood" stew, the right faith for a New World and a New World Voodooienne. Had it even been called Voodoo in Africa? Or was it descended from another faith that was transformed as the slave trade went from Africa to the Indies to the Americas, transformed as Africans themselves altered in color and language?

Ill at ease, Marie stared at Lake Ponchartrain, imagining swift currents blending with the Gulf Stream and sailing Jacques home. She said a "safe voyage" prayer to whatever god would listen: Damballah, Jesus. A crucifix and a clay snake were both deep in the folds of her pocket. Marie remembered how John had praised her desperate actions. "Shocking," he'd said when she told him her plans to make friends of Damballah and Christ. "Two gods are better than one. Better for business." John didn't understand she was balancing her soul.

Tomorrow she'd be nineteen.

Marie inhaled. In an hour, she'd begin her ceremony. Through the dusk, she could see burgeoning stars. The moon was not quite full, the sun not quite gone. Over fifty feet away, she could hear the murmur of her followers assembling. Marie felt as though each one of them was pummeling his or her way forward, trying to reach her. Besides aggressive guards, barriers of cord and hemp and a half-dozen bonfires separated her from overeager disciples. Her skin itched. She wanted to run away from her audience, her responsibilities, just the way she'd run away from her troubles and into the swamps as a child.

The horizon was entirely silver; stars created a pool of light mirrored in the currents of the lake. Marie bent and let her hand touch the water. The surface plopped and gurgled. She could see the shape of her hand, the moon's reflection, and a mirror image of the stars. She couldn't see the water's depth.

What kind of creatures lurked within the dark, shifting water? What was their nature? Evil, good, or both? There were fish. What did they feel when a fisherman caught them by a line or net? Were they startled when their ceiling opened and they saw sky, sun, and clouds and died upon the shore? What did it feel like when they took air into their gills? Did the other fish mourn, flutter, and dive when they lost one of their own?

Marie looked behind her. The bonfires were raging and several goats and sheep were being tethered in a makeshift pen. The crowd had swelled. Marie felt the urging, restless audience. It was her largest audience yet, probably more than a thousand people. The crowd smelled nervous, like a flock of backyard chickens. Or were they fish?

It had become a ritual for Marie, preceding a ceremony, to stand alone on the shoreline. She didn't always think about religion. Most often she thought about the child upsetting her balance. Her layered petticoats and ruffled skirt hid her pregnancy well. But it was hard to control bodily functions. The seven-month baby was already rebelling, kicking her stomach, eager to be out. Marie wondered what her baby girl was expecting to accomplish. How could she explain that other people, other happenings, controlled what one did or didn't do? Maybe that's why she wanted to hide in Teché. She'd forget about everything and keep her child younger than ten. She'd teach the girl about honeysuckle, porches, and rocking, about avoiding strange men and the soft, sucking swamp. Would the fourth Marie need to know anything different? Want to know anything different? Wasn't the fourth Marie controlling her now?

The child sank like a deadweight to the bottom of her womb.

Marie blanched. John was strutting confidently toward her. He looked like one of the Guédé in his black formal-dress suit. Shoulders squared, chest thrust forward, and thighs straining against silk threads made John appear both threatening and seductive. Earlier she'd watched him take a double dose of his potion and rub palm oil over his face. The effect was startling. John seemed years younger. Too young. She sniffed the air, searching for yellow.

"Marie, it's time."

Obstinately, she dug her toes deeper in sand.

"Don't you feel it? The crowd will explode. They're waiting for you."

"Let them wait."

"It's time now." John jerked her arm, rocking her off-balance. "What's the matter with you?"

"Nothing." She slipped out of his arms, covering her expanding waist. It'd been easy to keep him from touching her, from discovering the hiding child. He'd wanted Maman. Five months they'd lain in bed facing opposite walls. Some nights John caressed himself. She'd hear him groan and sigh. He did it to annoy. Other nights he stayed away, thrusting inside whores who were probably sly and selfish like Maman. But she knew it wasn't Brigette. It hadn't ever been Brigette.

It was nights when she upset him, when her ceremonies went too well, that John became amorous. His hands wanted to roam over her. Control and demean. She'd stay awake concocting stew in the kitchen, using Ribaud, jambalaya, and the python as shields.

"I've been feeling tired lately. That's all, John."

He selected a stone and skipped it across the lake. "Sit down," he said, laying his jacket on wet sand. "Don't look surprised. I can be courteous to my Queen, can't I?"

"I suppose you can." She heard someone cry "Maman Marie." Echoes swept through the crowd, then died abruptly to tense murmurs. She sat facing the water.

"I was wrong."

Marie raised her brows. What was he talking about? His mood was strangely light.

John squatted beside her like a child in grown-up dress, resting on his haunches, dangling his arms between his knees. "If the crowd was ready for your performance, everyone would be chanting, 'Marie. Maman Marie.'" He paused. "Pretty Marie."

"I don't perform," she whispered.

With a lost tackle stick, John drew spiraling circles in the sand. "Did I ever thank you?"

"For what?"

"This." The stick pointed at the crowd, the altar, Ribaud and his small band of drummers, and the banners of white silk hung upon rods. "I never imagined our plans would succeed so well." Tipping his head forward, he chuckled low, slyly peeping at her. "It's only a matter of time before Cathedral Square."

She'd never seen this John, the boy, playing, flirting. *"Our* plans," he had said. Yet John manipulated everything and everyone. Marie drew her feet closer to her body.

"I've never been happier." John touched the parallel scars on his cheek. "When they cut my face, they said it was because I was royal. I never cried when my father and the priest gripped me. They held me down like an animal—a chicken before its throat is cut, a pig before it's disemboweled. Instead of screaming out loud, I screamed inside my head. I would have withstood anything to be royal. Special.

"Nights later, though, I wept for their betrayal. I wept because I didn't feel any different. I did the same chores—clearing land, skinning meat, filling my father's pipe. I had had all that pain and for what? I hated the priest and my father. Especially my father. I looked forward to his death so I could rule. And when his death did come, it was a surprise. A rebellion led by the high priest." The stick, pressed too hard, snapped. John kept staring into the sand, hoping to find understanding there between the particles of seaweed, rock, and shells.

"My own people sold me into slavery," he said disbelievingly. "For what? So I would suffer. They could have killed me as easily as they killed my father. A chief's death—one slice at the heart. A royal death."

Marie watched his neck muscles tightening, rippling like the water. Eels were crawling out of the lake.

"Tonight I feel royal."

The moonlight above John's head flickered off, then on. Was it her imagination?

"Marie, we should marry."

She gasped.

"I vowed I'd be everything. Father. Husband. Son. Say yes, Maman Marie."

The crowd exploded, "Maman Marie." The chanting was savage, laced with need. "Maman Marie."

"Don't you see?" John was gripping her shoulders, compelling her. "Father to a new royal family. Husband to the most powerful woman in New Orleans. Son to the mother of our faith. Say yes."

"Maman Marie. Maman Marie." The crowd was demanding her, needing Marie's performance. Now. "Maman Marie."

Her tongue thick, Marie flexed soundless words. She staggered upright. John's face was jutting, darting at hers like a plucking seagull.

"Say yes," he shouted above the din. "The crowd expects it."

His palm oil made her nauseous. The child was clawing at her. Terrified, Marie was stumbling, trying to get away. Her feet kept sinking in sand. John kept trying to clutch her waist.

Ribaud, seeing the two shadows struggling on the beach, signaled his drummers. Four young men began pounding cats' gut, wooing Damballah. The sound was deafening. The crowd went wild.

Marie fell to her knees. Sand grated on her skin. She raised her head. Ribaud was flagging her, hopping up and down. He seemed miles away. She struggled upright, with both the sand and the baby making it difficult. "It's time," she said, but John didn't react as if he had heard her. His face was screwed in an expression Marie couldn't understand.

"Answer me, Marie. Say yes."

Terrified, she repeated, "It's time."

"Marie Laveau. Maman Marie," the crowd raved.

She curtsied to her audience. The sentries strained, trying to keep the crowd in place behind the air-thirsty bonfires. Marie saw one guard club a man. She averted her eyes and saw Nattie, off to the left of the altar, staring intently at her. Marie trudged on. She didn't know whether John was following her. To calm herself, she concentrated on Nattie. After a few feet, she realized Nattie was staring at her bulging waist. Marie shook herself. She couldn't worry about the crow woman now. She had to get on with the ceremony and, at all costs, avoid John.

Ribaud stepped forward. Marie had a moment to smile and scratch his nappy head. She whispered, "Thank you," and he grinned, his head bobbing, before he swooped on his pigeon-feathered hat and turned to his drums.

Six female disciples dressed in white began dancing. The audience swayed like a massive snake. Marie could see persons shuddering and swooning. Alcohol, the heat, dancing, and drums quickly undid inhibitions. Marie wondered how many persons would be trampled before the night's end. How many dead. People made the lakeside ugly.

John was brandishing his blades. He dragged a ewe. Nattie carried a cage of doves. Nattie and John grouped about her, forming a trinity. Why did John insist on so much blood?

> Make way! Make way for li Grand Zombi.
> Eh, yé, yé, Mademoiselle Marie,
> The power is yours to weave spells.
> Marie Laveau is a snake.

Unnoticed, John had slipped behind Marie. His hand drifted under her hair, clamping her neck. He kissed her. "Say yes." The crowd yelled, "Papa John. Maman Marie." Nattie laughed. And Marie jerked angrily away, tossing her hair like a mane.

John sliced the ewe's throat. The animal cried once. Its body convulsed as it died. One by one, Nattie handed John the doves. He wrung their necks and carved out their hearts. A red-white mound formed at his feet.

Marie felt a sense of unreality. Everything was theatrical. In each ceremony she had to fight her way to spirituality. She fought for some sense that her life wasn't corrupted. There was a Voodoo that existed beyond John's interpretation and influence. The sand was soaking up red blood.

Marie moved through the weaving dancers and toward the altar. She laid her head down on Damballah's image. No longer a crude charcoal drawing, the snake was fashioned with gaudy oil colors. Behind the painting was the real snake, her python, spiraling around itself, as quiet as a lull during a winter storm. Marie prayed, "Make me special. Make this world of mine better. Bearable."

She always worried what would happen if Damballah didn't come. She'd be like Nattie. John. Bereft.

She compressed her lips. Why should Damballah bother to come? She cried, spilling tears onto the altar. She was the weakest woman. She failed love. She couldn't even hate John properly.

Minutes seemed like hours.

She had to find faith among sinners and thrill-seekers. Why didn't she have the power to lead them to something better? Shouldn't a Voodoo Queen have found peace?

Nattie and John were directing the crowd. Building upon their intensity, they threw animal hearts. Women shrieked. Chants merged with curses, screams. People were trying to outdo each other's possession. Disciples danced like drunken whores. Only the music seemed authentic. Ribaud found rhythms suggesting a long-ago past, a world more ancient, more innocent than Teché. A world where being and self-discovery were the same.

If Damballah didn't come, what would she do?

Marie concentrated on the drums, pressing the painting of Damballah close to her heart. The python had unfurled itself and inched forward. Marie pressed her lips against its cool skin. "Forgive me." Her body was drenched in sweat. "Feed my spirit." On the edge of consciousness, she could feel a flicker of something, someone. She moaned, slumping forward.

The crowd stilled abruptly. Delayed reverence. They watched as Marie stood, unsteady at first, then confident in each step as she moved from center stage and walked toward the lake. She walked as water swirled about her ankles, drenched her skirt and knees. When the water was waist high she paused and bowed her head, as if in prayer, before diving into chilling blue water and disappearing into its depths.

The crowd broke past the guards and roped areas and spread along the shoreline, trying to sight her. The crowd wailed and the drums fell silent.

One minute passed. Two.

Ribaud stopped breathing, imagining Marie holding her breath beneath water. Finally, he coughed, gasping for air. A woman fainted. A man spoke aloud their common thought: "She's dead."

The audience was bewildered, uncertain. John was up to his chest in water.

"She's a witch," crowed one of the priests. "A body should float."

John raged, kicking at waves. Marie was dead, he thought. A suicide to spite him.

"A devil," said another. "I knew she'd come to no good end." Ribaud smacked the man's mouth.

On shore, Nattie began a dirge. Like a rippling wave, the harmony flashed through the crowd. Slaves and faithful coloreds, gripped in an enchantment, sang.

> *"My soul walks free.*
> *Death awaits me,*
> *Guédé, Guédé, have mercy,*
> *Don't let me lose my way."*

A reedlike soprano answered the musical phrase:

> *"O Mary, don't you weep, don't you mourn.*
> *One of dese mornings, bright and fair,*
> *Take my wings and cleave the air.*
> *O Mary, don't you weep, don't you moan."*

Dozens of slaves sang the reassuring Christian song. There was an afterlife. Christ sacrificed on the cross would rise again. So too would Marie.

At first, the two competing songs cracked with a painful dissonance but gradually they became a rhythmic counterpoint, then blended into a new, powerful hymn. Those who didn't know the words sang vowels or hummed the music in their throats. Wails shook the sky. Stars fell. The song stretched to the ends of the earth. Women fainted and men trembled. In New Orleans, residents quit whatever they were doing—sleeping, dancing, loving—claiming angels were crying. Seamen sailing far beyond the lake's mouth and up beyond the coast of the Carolinas thought sirens lured. Grandmère stirred, vividly dreaming of her enslaved African maman, freed and guiding her home. In the mourning song, John heard his own impending death.

Tears filled Ribaud's eyes. His Marie was dead, just like his pretty daughter. Nattie, in her funereal wail, felt both sorry and angry at herself. Through Marie, she'd hoped to find her blessed pathway to Damballah. She'd foolishly lost her chance. She'd never gone beyond jealousy.

Louis DeLavier wanted forgiveness. When he'd first seen Marie enter the water, he'd begun beating his way to the forefront of the crowd. He couldn't bear to believe Marie was dead. Winded, he'd ripped off his boots and jacket and run to the water's edge. He'd dived and nearly shouted from the shocking cold. He'd swum, crazed and erratic, calling "Marie!" until his strength gave out. He hadn't see any signs. No floating body. No piece of clothing rising to the surface. His lungs ached from successive dives beneath the dark and chilly water.

Damballah had taken her to a quiet place.

Marie felt cocooned. Damballah was her best lover. She felt secure, happy, rooted in an African tradition she sensed rather than knew. Damballah wanted to go to sea. She couldn't feel anything other than the desire to be immersed.

She and Damballah dove. They were free, sinking low and deep. She breathed the thick, heady water. Damballah liked plankton tickling His belly. A school of fish swished by. Giggling, Marie stroked a turtle's back and kissed a sleepy-eyed catfish. The world was cool, vibrant with blues, greens, and specks of yellow and red in the gentle, overwhelming darkness. They swam to the center of the lake and sat.

Damballah was whispering from inside Marie's head. The language was strange, clicking and rhythmic, and Marie recognized it as an African dialect she'd heard among newly captured slaves. Gradually, she began to understand.

"You belong to me," said Damballah. "You always have and you always will."

Agwé, the sea god, appeared, pulling a ship as big and wide as a whale. Black people were on the ship, all different shades of black. Some were slaves dressed in coarse cotton and chains; others were free coloreds dressed as blacksmiths, shopkeepers; others were lovely mulatto and quadroon girls dressed in ball gowns and silk tea dresses. All were beckoning Marie. Grandmère was in the stern, shouting, "Home. Let's go home."

"Home," said Damballah. And Marie was rushing forward, stumbling on the ocean bottom, slipping on shells, upsetting the pace of seahorses and schools of fish.

"Marie." Grandmère was waving. Marie felt indescribable joy. Beside Grandmère, steering the rudder, was a majestic black woman in brightly colored robes. "You are me," she said. On Grandmère's right was Maman, beckoning Marie aboard. And on the deck was a small child with long black braids.

"These are all who you are," murmured Damballah. "Mixed blood. But your blood flows because of and through me, Damballah. The god of your ancestors. We sail toward Africa. Home."

The women and child formed a circle with Marie in the center, its heart. And around their circle, the other passengers formed circles around circles until they all clung together weeping and singing and praising the core of their multiplying circles—Marie Laveau possessed by Damballah.

The whalelike ship arrived home. Agwé, on his broad back, carried passengers ashore. Africa. Off the ship, everyone became a wondering, awestruck child again. Marie cried. Africa was Teché magnified. Every particle of her being felt reborn. Love was in the lush foliage, the caw-cawing of birds. Rebirth was in the fertile black soil and among animals poised in the shade and on the limbs of trees.

"It's time," said Damballah.

"No," Marie mouthed.

306

"It's time." The landscape and people and animals became spirit. And through her eyes, the spirits flew into her soul, and she cried out at having so much history inside her. "This is who you are." At first, Marie thought it was Grandmère singing; then she realized it was her own voice crooning. "This is who I am."

Up she flew, through ageless and ancient waters, bursting into the air. Marie was convinced she could pluck the moon. Then her body lowered to the wet surface. Damp, tangled hair clung to her face and back. Her yellow skirt and blouse outlined her curves, the soft swelling of her abdomen.

She walked on the surface of the water as if it were earth.

DeLavier, resting, floating on his back, was the first to see Marie up close. He flipped onto his stomach, disbelieving as she walked, her feet steady on the tips of waves. A rainbow guided her path. There was no hesitancy, no awe; only a sense of labored sadness, disappointment, about her. Louis couldn't speak. Childhood prayers flooded his mind. There has to be a God, he thought.

Marie walked past him, focusing on her followers. In the water, Damballah had shown her how to reconnect herself to both a past and a future. Time spirals outward from the center, and the center was Damballah, who could make spirits—and the spirit in her—whole. And though there was still so very much to do and so very much to consider, though she felt tentative and insecure, Marie felt a new lightness of being. She wasn't a firefly burning her own air. There was a light inside her, guiding her, if she let it, to peace and safety.

The crowd cried out in amazement as they saw Marie walk across the lake toward them. Some of the people fell to their knees, chanting "Damballah"; "Miracle"; "Resurrection." John was screaming unnecessarily, "Back, back." He couldn't allow himself to grasp the significance of Marie's miracle. He had to be asserting himself, exercising control. So he kept pushing and shoving, lashing out at whoever was near his imaginary line of safety for Marie.

None of the stunned audience was moving toward her. The crowd was still, except for incoherent murmurings and soft prayers.

Marie felt grit beneath her feet as she stepped onto the shore. The sand seemed as foreign and insubstantial as the cresting waves. Ribaud, dragging and splashing through the tide, his small body loping lopsidedly forward, met her and offered his cloak.

"Thank you." Marie didn't feel cold or wet; what she felt went beyond ordinary sensations.

"How did you do it?" Ribaud whispered intently. Eyes wide with awe, he hesitated to touch her.

"I don't know, Ribaud. I don't know."

Her legs gave way and she stumbled. Ribaud offered his body as a crutch. Marie leaned against him. She was astonished and glad that Ribaud loved her. With his drums, Ribaud procured the one thing that made her feel special. His drums brought her to Damballah. His drums brought her to herself.

From beneath her lashes, Marie saw John, standing a few feet away, apart from the crowd, his fists clenched. Marie shivered. Ribaud led her onto the beach.

They formed lines: herself and Ribaud, their backs facing the water; Nattie and John, facing them. Two against two. The moon cast four shadows.

Ribaud's hand settled on the arc of her back while Nattie, her dress soaked with doves' blood, mumbled, "I don't believe it. I don't believe it." But she did believe. Jealousy hurt her again. She wanted to scratch out Marie's eyes. Envy was consuming her, and there was nothing she could do to stop it.

John, stifling his rage, hung his head and tugged at his open collar. His veins were constricting. He wanted to kill Marie and Ribaud. The two had planned his humiliation. He struggled to compose himself. Involuntarily, his fingers touched the scars on his face. He felt cheated again. He didn't feel royal.

"We should get Marie home," said Ribaud.

"Don't tell me what we should do," cracked John, advancing, his fury focused on the spell man. "What do you know about what we should do? You're nothing, do you understand that? A man who kills his own daughter is nothing. Nothing."

"Let him be," Marie said, unveiling more hate in John. His expression was wild, indecent. She drew back. "What should we do then, John?" she asked, soothingly. "Where should we go, if not home?"

Marie watched as John raged, struggling to find the means to best her possession. She almost pitied him. All his animals had been slaughtered.

John smiled slightly, turned toward the audience, extending his arms for silence. "Marie and I will marry," he exclaimed. There were soft calls of approval. "We will marry." A few cheers. "Don't you hear me?" he demanded. "We will marry."

The crowd was staring beyond him—amazed that Marie, risen from the dead, had walked on water like Jesus. Blacks and whites were dumbstruck. Each person was wondering how to claim a personal blessing, a blessing to soothe old wounds and hurts, a blessing to comfort fears or cure ills. Even priests were trying to rationalize Marie's miracle as one of theirs. Everyone was convinced they'd witnessed the supernatural. Whether good or evil, they didn't know. For most in the crowd, it didn't matter. Marie Laveau represented power.

"We will marry," John asserted again.

Ribaud shrieked, "Marie Laveau! Voodoo Queen! Marie Laveau!" with the full force of his lungs.

The audience started shouting, surging toward them. Marie gripped the cloak tightly about her as bodies pressed forward. Hands pulled and tugged at her; she swayed precariously. Hands formed a throne that lifted Marie in the air.

"Marie Laveau. Voodoo Queen. Marie Laveau." There were calls too of "Bless Jesus"; "Praise God"; "Devil"; "Damballah is all."

Ribaud whooped and slapped his hands down on his drum. Other drummers imitated him: lashing drums across their chests, weaving among the crowd, transporting the feverish, riotous chant into an infectious celebration. "Marie Laveau. Marie Laveau." It was a procession of marching, giddy people. They would carry Marie across sand, along the dockside, through the French Quarter, and all the way home. Marie let herself feel exalted. For once, she'd bested John. She was a Queen.

Marie turned and, above bobbing heads and flailing, seemingly disembodied arms, she saw big-hipped Nattie treading carefully to the lake's edge. Her butt up in the air, Nattie was bending, touching the iridescent water. All the while Nattie, disbelievingly, shook her head.

To the left of John, Marie saw Louis, a ghostly figure, smiling and waving. Twisting around to the left for a better view, Marie realized Louis was soaked. Water dripped from his hair down to his bare toes. He looked comical and pathetic. Louis must've followed her into the water. No one else among the hundreds had. Only Louis. Marie blushed to think he still cared enough to save her. She'd never tell him his attempted rescue was misguided.

Marie looked beyond Louis, searching for John. The bonfires were casting monstrous shadows. Dismembered doves were gaily floating on the water. John had disappeared. Marie refused to worry. Something wondrous had happened to her beneath the lake. For the first time since she was nine, she knew joy. Damballah had given her a glimmering of who she was, and tonight she felt even the stars above were within her grasp.

Stragglers from the lakeside ceremony were outside the St. Anne's house, conducting a vigil in honor of Marie Laveau's powers, while Marie was inside, facing John and feeling powerless. They were alone. Nattie and Ribaud were overseeing the crowd's devotion. John had ordered them both out of the house. Nattie had gone willingly; Ribaud had needed to be beaten. John had cruelly battered Ribaud's head, scarring the skin about his eyes and bloodying his nose and mouth. Marie had begged Ribaud to leave. The spell man had conceded, but not before he'd made a great clatter of settling his drum in the far corner, then hurriedly whispering in Marie's ear, "Python be in de drum." And those simple words had uplifted Marie and given her a filament of hope and courage.

Sitting primly, almost like a child, her hands clasped in the weave of her skirt, her back erect, Marie concentrated on appearing daunted and defeated. She watched John warily. He was pacing like a cat. She didn't dare speak first; she waited for John to break the awful silence. She wished she held the python on her lap. Or better yet, she wished it was curled up beside the sleeping babe in her womb. Strength could only come from centering herself. She needed guile to defeat John. Damballah had shown her salvation was possible. If she survived this night, she might outwit John and triumph.

The house was disordered. Covertly, Marie studied the debris. Chairs were overturned, dishes shattered, and shelves littered with broken jars of beans, rice, and spices. Marie guessed John had been desperately searching for something. He'd reached the house an hour before she had. The damage was considerable. The feather mattress had been dragged from their bed and ripped. Her trunk had been emptied. Clothes and makeup jars were scattered. The mirrored vanity was smeared with candle wax.

Marie sighed, stroking damp strands from her face. She was unable to quench her nervousness completely. The heady lake smell had settled in her pores. She'd been allowed to change her damp dress for a cotton shift. But her hair still hung wet and heavy. The hearth had never been lit.

"You made a fool out of me."

Marie couldn't think of a safe reply.

"A fool." John was pressing his brow against the wall, slamming his open palms against the grain. "A goddamn fool."

Marie winced at each strike. Dawn wasn't for several hours. Perhaps, at dawn, she'd be allowed to escape to dreams of lying forever at the bottom of the lake.

"Nothing I did was meant to hurt you," Marie murmured. It was true. Like a passive fool, she'd accepted whatever John did to her. She'd never once sought revenge.

"Liar."

Marie blinked.

John swallowed rum. He no longer seemed young and healthy. There was a horrible tautness about him, like straining cat's gut stretched across the bass barrel drum. Slight tremors shook his body. John resembled one of Ribaud's thrashing alley cats before its slaughter.

He sat across the table from Marie. He kept his eyes on his glass, on how the amber rum absorbed the light. His blunt fingers stubbed at pools of spilled alcohol on the table. Now that Marie was here, John seemed distracted, oddly uncomfortable with his anger.

He spoke suddenly. "Where's my herb case?"

"I don't know. It's where you left it, I suppose."

"If it was, I'd be able to find it," he shouted, shaking his fist. "Where is it? My herbs!" Distraught, he ran his fingers down his face, stretching his skin and pulling his features out of proportion. "I've searched everywhere. I need my case. The powders are what I need."

"Yes, John." Marie was certain he was toying with her. Why didn't he beat her and get it over with? Maybe he didn't have the energy. John looked pale and sick. Streaks of gray lined his temples. That was odd. His hair had been brilliantly dark a few hours ago. It must be a trick of the light. Everything about him now was strangely misshapen and slow. Worry added years to his face. His body seemed to collapse in on itself as he bent forward, hiding his face in his hands, cursing. "I need my case."

"I need to sleep, John," Marie responded quietly, rising and edging like a crippled hare toward the bedroom. John looked like an old man. Perhaps she'd find safety in their room. Perhaps, by some miracle, John didn't intend to hurt her. Self-absorbed, he seemed to have forgotten she was near. Marie continued treading lightly. Her hand reached for the door.

John lunged, sending his chair toppling, his rum glass diving toward the floor. "I need my herb case. You've hidden it, haven't you?"

"No, John." She could feel his hot breath on her face, his fingers digging into her skin. She wanted to scream because his face was twisted with something more than anger. He seemed mad, irrational. He was having trouble focusing his eyes.

"We both need to sleep, John. We both need rest."

"Don't order me." He slapped her with his open palm.

Marie gasped and fought away tears. She couldn't stand it if John saw her cry now.

"How did you do it?" John demanded. "How? Tell me how or I'll beat it out of you."

"How what? What are you talking about?" The shift in attack disoriented Marie.

"When I met you, you knew nothing. Stupid and ignorant you were. Stupid and ignorant. I," John said, drumming his fingers on his chest, "I taught you your lessons. I didn't teach you tricks with water. Who taught you, Marie? How did you do it? How did you survive the water?"

Her back against the wall, John's arms entrapped her on both sides.

"Faith," Marie said stubbornly. "Weren't you the one who taught me to have faith?"

His fists slammed into wood. "Don't preach. I'm not mindless and ignorant like those outside. Do you think I'm one of your followers to bow and scrape and say 'Yes, Maman Marie'? Everything has an explanation. Even why you're lying."

"I'm not lying," Marie screeched. "Damballah guides me. I don't understand any more than you do. I don't."

John jerked away, weaving back to the table for more rum. "Your Maman sometimes did more than we planned. She knew how angry it made me. Like you, she lied by claiming gods called her. What gods? There aren't any gods." He swallowed from the bottle; rum dribbled down his chin and neck. "Sometimes I believed she was special. Like your Grandmère." His hands were trembling. "But I'm too old to believe in such miracles. Over forty years, I've been serving this god called Damballah. Selling snake charms. Selling His image for gold. Forty years ago, I met your Grandmère. She was the only one to make me believe in miracles."

Forty years. Marie had always assumed John was forty. At most forty-five. Yet he hadn't met Grandmère and Maman until he was a man. She shook her head with wonder. John must be sixty, perhaps sixty-five, much older than Nattie. How naive she'd been. Now she understood what his herb potion meant. Evidence flooded her memory: the sudden bursts of energy, the despondent lulls, skin tone that alternated between wan and glowing, his motions sometimes fluid, sometimes stiff. The evidence had been there. Herbs kept him young. How could she have been so blind?

John paced, his words slurring. "Your Grandmère could walk on water. She could sing, just sing, and followers would fall upon their knees to her," he said, amazed. "Words didn't matter, only the sounds." His pace slowed, then stopped.

"After all these years, I would've felt something, don't you think? If Damballah was real, he would've come to me. Who says a woman is the key? Why should she be?" John was puzzling, rationalizing to himself. "I'm the one with royal blood. I should've been king. It doesn't make sense. None of it makes sense. No matter how small, how insignificant, I should've felt something. Some spirit. Some power. Some god." John's eyes were bewildered. His palms were outstretched like a beggar needing alms.

"No *loa* has ever possessed me. Why not me?" Piteously, John was staring at Marie, waiting for some response.

Marie exulted at seeing John vulnerable. All this time John had been jealous because Damballah visited her, her Maman, and, before that, Grandmère. Marie wanted to shout. Glee was cresting inside her. John was jealous and in an odd way powerless. He was waiting for his answer. Careless, she murmured, "Perhaps Damballah doesn't believe you're worthy."

He was upon her, pounding her with his fists. Her head reeled and hit the wall. "Leave me alone," she cried as he hit her again.

"You're to tell me everything, you understand? Everything you plan or dream of doing." He twisted her hair; her neck arched. "No surprises, Marie. I want to know every ceremonial step. Every action you plan with Damballah."

"I don't know beforehand." Blood spotted her mouth.

"Then you'll have trouble, won't you, Marie?"

"You're asking the impossible."

"You won't trick me again." John clutched Marie's throat; her feet lifted off the floor.

Marie was whimpering, gripping John's shoulders, trying to prevent her neck from snapping, trying to stabilize herself so she'd have enough air. John's hands were a hangman's noose.

"It's tricks, not miracles, isn't it?" John demanded. "Stupid, childish tricks to fool an audience. But you don't fool me."

Pain radiated through Marie's lungs and chest.

"Grandmère taught you, didn't she? Taught you to walk on water."

"No," she rasped.

"I know you've been seeing her."

"She's old. Sick." Smelling the stench of alcohol, Marie felt consciousness draining.

"Grandmère's been turning you against me."

It isn't true, she wanted to say, but she couldn't speak, couldn't shake her head no.

"You used to stand me well enough. Since visiting Grandmère, you don't want me to touch you." He forced his tongue inside her mouth. "You think you're better than me. That's it, isn't it?"

315

Rather than fighting, Marie thought it was easier to let John kill her. One of his hands grabbed at her crotch while the other pressed against her larynx. John was crazy, obsessed by her powers. He envied Damballah. He envied her sex. Marie stopped struggling, feeling a darkness spreading down and through her limbs. She was going to sit at the bottom of the lake.

"John, you drunken fool," Nattie shouted from the doorway; then she was cursing, shoving, pulling at John. "Can't you see the girl be pregnant? You'll kill both her and the babe."

At first the words didn't connect. They scratched at the fringe of John's consciousness. He barely felt Nattie and Ribaud battering at his back and tugging at his arms.

"Do you want to murder your own child?"

John's brow furrowed. His grip slackened and Marie inhaled sharply and collapsed. Wonderingly, John stroked the scars on his cheeks. "There isn't any child."

Coughing, Marie doubled over. Her throat inside and out was bruised and raw.

"Let her pass, you fool man. Let her go."

John stepped aside, dazed, his eyes straying to Marie's abdomen. "A child," he whispered.

Tenderly, Ribaud guided Marie to a chair. It was Ribaud's tenderness more than anything else that caused Marie to clutch his shirt, bury her face on his shoulder, and begin crying out her pain. Clucking soothingly, Ribaud stroked her hair, her back. He rubbed the knotted veins on her arms.

John stumbled to the table and drank. His breathing was ragged. Wrinkles lined his face, and each passing minute the weblike network seemed to be multiplying. "How far along?" he asked.

"Marie be six, seven months gone. Maybe more. Like her Maman, she be carrying the babe in the hip. Her show don't be normal."

John felt less drunk. Fingers pressed to his temples, he was figuring, planning. In his child he sensed new potential, perhaps more power for himself. His depression seemed to be rolling back like a tidal wave. "A daughter?"

"Too soon to say," Nattie answered, waspish. "But most likely be a girl. Girls run in the family. Four generations of Marie." Nattie's tone grudgingly hovered between awe and envy.

John exhaled, feeling his world righting itself. He flung wide his arms, then just as quickly closed them about himself, exulting in this second chance, an unexpected miracle. "Then we'll certainly marry."

"I'm already married," Marie blurted.

"Who cares what you say?" John swooped in front of her like a vulture toward its carcass. He pushed Ribaud aside. Protectively, Marie covered her abdomen.

John seemed to have regained his old power. Reality was what he chose to make it. And though he looked older, ghoulish, Marie could feel his influence burrowing into her. John cast his spell by violence and by sheer force of will. Marie hadn't yet succeeded in fortifying herself against him.

Suave, manipulative, John stated, "You were abandoned." His voice was soothing, assured. His dark eyes seemed to fill his face. He was impressive. Royal.

"Jacques died at sea. Don't you remember?"

"What?" Marie felt light-headed, susceptible.

"He died at sea. After abandoning you. Isn't that right, Nattie?"

"Yes, 'tis so." The black woman looked at Marie scornfully.

"Abandoned?" Her emotions were haywire. Marie was bewildered. This night's living had been too intense. She'd died and been reborn; she'd walked on water; she'd experienced reverence, abuse, near death, and rescue. Where did reality begin and visions end? Tonight she'd seen spirits on a sunken ship. Perhaps Jacques had been one of them. John's voice was so certain, so confident. Perhaps all the passengers were dead. The ship was underwater. Maybe she herself was dead. She almost believed John. John was here, clutching her shoulders, watching her. Jacques had been gone longer than Marie could remember. She was sick, afraid. "Yes," she said, "Jacques died at sea."

John pulled her into his comforting arms.

Over the crest of John's shoulder, Marie saw movement. Ribaud was shaking his head, staring at her, hopping from foot to foot.

Marie frowned. What was he telling her? Ribaud gathered the python in his arms. Seeing the animal, Marie could more clearly see John. She drew back. "You're lying, John. Nothing you say is true."

"I might produce Jacques' body." His hand tightly clasped her throat. "Bloated from lying at the bottom of the sea. You wouldn't want that, now, would you? Not a pretty sight."

"I hate you," Marie said, coughing again, her head falling between her knees.

John tenderly stroked her hair. "The child needs a father."

"The child isn't yours," she yelled fiercely.

John slapped her and Marie's head flung backward. She saw a shower of stars.

"What do you mean the child isn't mine? If you've been unfaithful—"

"She be lying, can't you see that?" said Nattie, swatting at John's arms. "She wants you to be angry. Have some sense, man."

"I'm not lying," Marie shouted. "The child isn't his." It's mine, she thought. Mine alone.

Enraged, John twisted Marie's head unnaturally far to the right.

"Shut up, child. Can't you see I be trying to save your life?" Nattie pressed forward. John kept forcing Marie's head farther and farther to the right as though she were a doll whose head spun in circles.

"Think, John," Nattie insisted. "What time has Marie had to take a lover? What time has she had when you, I, or Ribaud weren't there? You don't think she be unfaithful in public? Simple foolishness. Everybody know Marie Laveau, Voodoo Queen. She wouldn't rut like a hog."

John laughed. "Yes. Yes. That's right." He eased the strain on Marie's neck. But his fingers dug in and around her vocal cords as if, in arresting her voice, he could command her obedience and null all the unflattering truths he didn't want to hear.

"You be plenty man for one woman," Nattie cajoled, straightening the flap on his collar. "Marie has sense enough to know that what's good for you don't be good for her. A virile man should have plenty of mistresses. A woman don't dare be unfaithful." Black lips parting, Nattie chuckled. "Besides, Marie not have the nerve. She be but a child herself. She not know yet what it means to be a woman. She not know the power between her thighs."

"Yes, yes, that's right." John stood, chuckling, serenely accepting Nattie's words as evidence to explain Marie's lies and salvage his own vanity. Marie's head fell forward. "I barely tolerate her myself. She's a cold stick in bed. Yes. What man would want her? Her Maman was a different story."

"That's right, John," Nattie said encouragingly. "Marie be too innocent. How can a man pleasure himself with her?"

Marie couldn't believe them: Nattie, butting John with her hips; John, swigging and spilling rum; the two of them laughing, bobbing their heads like silly crows. "I hate you both," she rasped.

"Be still, girl," warned Nattie. "John's been good to you. You should be grateful he be willing to marry such a cold stick. Lucky you don't have to bear a bastard child."

"I'd have been lucky if I was never found."

Nattie yanked Marie's arm, whispering hoarsely, "Don't try his anger. Simple foolishness."

Marie ignored her. "I'd have been lucky if I'd stayed in Teché."

"Your child won't be like you," shouted Nattie, "a white man's bastard daughter. Your Maman couldn't even remember who she lay with. Any white man could have fathered you—I think a pig merchant did."

"At least I'll have my own daughter. I'm not a dried-up crow like you."

Nattie raised her hand to strike Marie. "Foolishness." She couldn't remember when she'd given up thoughts of a child of her own filling her up. She used to be young, pretty, and convinced her future held both big and little glories. But striking Marie wouldn't make her young again. Striking Marie wouldn't make John love her.

John leaned over Marie, grabbing her hair and yanking her head back. "You're lucky I've been so gentle with you. You've still got something coming to you for tonight's tricks. The child doesn't get you out of that."

Nattie fixed her gaze on John. "Your face," she said softly. "What's happened to your face?"

John looked stricken. He'd forgotten. He touched himself and felt the wrinkles, the folds of skin on his neck, the lack of resilience in his skin. He staggered to the hearth and fell on his knees in front of the tub basin. The dull metal added more distortion. John felt cowed. Carefully keeping his back to the others, he studied himself disbelievingly, touching his skin, then snatching at it, pricking it as though he could uncover his real face, the face that matched his pride. What struck him was how much he looked like his father, humbled and worn, when his father, aware of his own defeat, had been only moments away from his enemy's blade.

Nattie was glad she'd pierced John's self-assurance. She couldn't see his face, but from the way he sprawled on the dirt floor, she could tell he was in anguish.

"I need my herb case," John rasped, unmoving. "I need it now."

Nattie cursed herself for not guessing John's magic long ago. Simple foolishness. But then she'd always been a fool about John.

Looking across the room, Nattie caught Ribaud gloating. She was surprised. She didn't think the spell man had backbone in him. But it made sense for Ribaud finally to lash out at John, to give as good as he got. Ribaud more than anyone knew John's secrets. But why did Ribaud choose this time to expose him?

Ribaud sensed Nattie watching him. He looked up, his gaze steady, and challenged Nattie to betray him.

"Find it, Nattie." John stood swiftly, and Nattie was taken aback by how skull-like and hateful he seemed. "Find my herbs and you'll share my secret. I promise."

"Yes, yes." Nattie smiled with satisfaction. Ribaud took refuge by lingering near his drum and the python. She'd make Ribaud tell her where the herb case was. Yes, she would. She'd only have to threaten his Marie. Then she'd delay giving the herbs to John, heightening his anxiety and increasing his dependence. She'd have to think of an appropriate payment. An image flashed through her mind of her and John, both apparently young, entwined and making love.

320

Recovering himself, John settled in a chair. He looked like a diminished Legba, his hair eerily white, his bones arthritic. "Find my herb case, Nattie. I'll share my secret. I need it now."

Part of Nattie wanted to shout that there'd be no bargaining. John's power was as much of an illusion as his extended youth. Watching him act as though he had power made Nattie want to spite him. She wanted him to stay old, ugly, and gray. Yet her own vanity couldn't let her resist a chance to restore the small beauty she'd had when she was young. Only fleetingly did she think of making herself youthful while John stayed withered and dry. Simple foolishness. It was a fact that if she withheld the herbs from John, he'd murder her. Besides, in time he might be able to duplicate the potion anyway. She'd gain little either way.

Nattie smiled at Marie. "Simple foolishness. You should be in bed making that baby grow big. Goat's milk three times a day. Kale will grow healthy limbs." Nattie still believed she'd live long enough to see a Voodoo Queen behave with appropriate regal arrogance. None of the three Maries she'd known had had it, but she hoped the fourth Marie would. The fourth Marie might appreciate Nattie better, especially if Nattie was the only one to mother her.

Nattie turned to John. "I'll find your herbs, John. But you'll have to think long and hard about what you'll owe me. It wouldn't do to forget like you've forgotten before." Smiling serenely, Nattie left the room, feigning a renewed search for herbs and youth.

"Poor Nattie. She accepts promises so easily." Giddy, John scuttled forward and pinched Marie's cheek. "I'll have two Maries. Two pretty Voodoo Queens. My own daughter."

Marie jerked away.

"Come say hello." John was pulling her toward the window.

Marie couldn't stand John's touch or the memory of the times when he'd loved her. An old man, veiled by magic, had caressed and hurt her body. Illusion was crucial to his powerful performances. No wonder he believed reality was inside people's minds. "Reality" was often wrong.

"Wave. Your followers want to see you. Us. Papa John and Maman Marie." He laughed cruelly.

People were camped in front of the house. When they saw

Marie, they stumbled, clawed over one another in an effort to be near her. Hands and noses pressed and flattened against the pane.

Marie heard, "Maman Marie. Bless me. Maman Marie."

"Wave," said John. He gripped her arm and flapped her limp hand. Marie felt she was a marionette. "Wave."

Waves were sweeping Jacques home.

Feeling John's chest against her back, feeling his arm drawing her stomach and baby up into her ribs, feeling his hand causing hers to wave, Marie felt lost. Over the tops of her followers' heads, she saw the sun rise. The sky was pale blue. The sunrise was too late. She didn't believe Jacques was coming anymore.

John dropped her hand and turned from the window. "Nattie," he called. "Damn you, Nattie." He shuffled slowly to the chair, a wheezing noise tickling his throat.

Staring at John's reflection in the pane, Marie could see him, in all clarity, for the monster he was. His charm and beauty, his tools to seduce and beguile, were gone. She started laughing, hysterical and high-pitched. She began to comprehend she didn't owe John anything. No special allegiance. She began to understand that John owed her. He'd used her. He'd manipulated her, and she'd fallen giddily into his trap. All because of lies and appearances.

"You know, women are nothing," said John, drinking again, rocking like a grandfather in the harsh morning light. "Absolutely nothing, Ribaud."

Ribaud was as still as a man without a heart. He was grinning sympathetically at Marie, feeling he had trumped John just this once. John's herbs were in the python's cage in the garden.

"I sometimes think women are Damballah's whores. It explains why He uses their bodies for prophecy, visions. But the power is male. Always male. Don't you think so, Marie?" John smiled crookedly. "It well explains why Damballah chose you. Just as you've been my whore, so you've been Damballah's. I control you just as He does." His laugh turned into a racking cough. "Nattie. Damn you, Nattie, have you found it?"

Stripped of his youth, his bones frail, John didn't seem invincible. In an odd way, Marie realized John was stupid. His herbs were the secret to wealth and power. Yet he'd been too selfish to share his fountain of youth. He'd had more pleasure abusing and controlling her.

"Yes, women are absolutely nothing. Worthless and stupid."

Marie's anger swelled, enlarging and enveloping her with a need for vengeance. She couldn't count on Jacques to save her. Last night, Damballah had demonstrated his confidence in her. It might take slow-gaited steps to re-create herself, to steady her hand and find courage, but now it was clear to her. She'd have to fight her way free. She'd have to kill John.

But right now she needed to sleep. She was so cold—so cold. And a warm lake of dreams was waiting.

~

Special editorial by Louis DeLavier, rejected for publication in the Daily Picayune, *November 30, 1821.*

Last night on Lake Pontchartrain, Marie Laveau, the self-proclaimed Voodoo Queen of New Orleans, performed a miracle. It was beyond belief. Yet it happened, it was real. This reporter was not drunk. Indeed, this reporter was an eyewitness to the fact that Marie Laveau remained submerged underwater for nearly ten minutes. No mortal being can survive that length of time without air. Marie Laveau did; she survived.

It was a clear, humid night. The Voodoo ceremony, with its music, dancing, and animal sacrifices, was at its peak approximately at midnight. Laveau prostrated herself in front of the altar honoring the snake god, Damballah. After several minutes, she stood and made her way to the lake's edge. Her followers, intensely excited, broke through the bonfire boundaries and ran after her. Screams filled the air as Laveau walked into the water. Followers were stunned as the water continued to rise, higher and higher, to Laveau's waist. She paused, then dove forcefully, deeply, beneath the chilling water. It seemed the act of a madwoman, a suicide. I took it upon myself to attempt a rescue. I swam but could find no traces of Laveau, no traces of chicanery or trickery that would have made her feat possible. Exhausted, fearing for my own safety, I rested, believing beyond doubt that Marie Laveau was dead.

Then, with a vast explosion, Marie Laveau rose out of the lake and walked. This reporter saw her, haloed in lights, walking on the waves like the Fisherman Christ.

Who is Marie Laveau? Is she a functionary of the devil or a

*messenger of God? Such a miracle, in imitation of Christ's, cannot be
summarily dismissed as a barbaric, primitive ritual.*

*Priests, pointing out that the Voodoo deity is a snake, argue for the
imprisonment of Laveau. Can bars hold such a woman of miraculous
powers?*

*Marie Laveau's miracle suggests an authentic form of worship.
Certainly slaveowners have the right and the obligation to care for their
slaves' souls; indeed, Catholics may feel impelled to instruct their slaves in
Christianity. But possibly free blacks deserve the latitude and the right to
worship whomever they please, even if it be the snake god Damballah.*

*Satan as the snake in the Garden of Eden was God's creation and
ultimately served God's ends. Because of the snake, we're thought to have
"free will" and the blessings of Christ. Could it be that Laveau is another
disguised gift from God?*

*Marie Laveau has stirred public controversy. Military and political
leaders are silent. Their silence can be interpreted as fear. Or could it be
that the authorities are judiciously awaiting more evidence regarding the
nature of Marie Laveau? No court has yet convicted her of any crime.*

*Time will tell the possible greatness of Marie Laveau. Time will tell
the good intentions of her soul.*

•

—LOUIS DELAVIER
(From Louis DeLavier's journal)

Marie leaned back in the rocker and rocked. The motion
was soothing, but it lacked the power of sitting in a strong and
confident Grandmère's lap, letting her legs swish against Grandmère's skirt. Marie realized Grandmère's lap had been an enveloping
world where fears were kept at bay and cuts and scrapes were
soothed. She'd been kept warm and shielded from the elements that
battered body and soul. In Grandmère's lap, she hadn't had to worry
about monsters lurking in the bayou, the squeal of a field rabbit
clenched in a coyote's jaws, or the unsettling, shifting shapes of
shadows. She'd been protected from dark strangers who trapped her
in the sticky marsh, muttering threats in a ten-year-old's ear. Marie

realized it had been when she slid off Grandmère's lap, when her feet touched the porch floorboards, that trouble had begun. Heartache had stirred when Grandmère yelled "Marie, you come back here!" and Marie hadn't listened.

Feeling the rocker's rosewood spine on her back felt odd to Marie. She should've been feeling the shuddering of Grandmère's ribs, the rise and fall of her breasts, and listening to the gentle pounding of her heart.

She should be small again and Grandmère powerful. They should be watching the sunset, counting orange streaks piercing the bayou's humid haze. Grandmère should be singing a joint lullaby to the sun and a welcome song to the new moon. Their arms and legs should be entwined, feeling the sweet texture and heat of each other's skin. Whereas now Grandmère was inside the shanty, dreaming. And Marie was alone on the porch, rocking and staring at Haven's bleak landscape. Grandmère was no longer whispering in her ear about mosquitoes searching for blood or bats uncurling from their daylight sleep, ready for hunting.

In her rush to grow up, she'd lost so much that was precious. On Grandmère's lap, she'd been loved, secure and protected. Grandmère had always thought her worth protecting.

Marie sighed. She was nineteen and already feeling like an old woman. She was tired and swollen pregnant. She'd already ruined much of her life wrongly pursuing the one she thought was herself. Maman was not her. She was not Maman. Despite the wind and the cold, Marie liked sitting on the porch rocker. Rocking helped her perspective.

Power between her and John had shifted. She was no longer in awe of him. Yet she stayed with him. She was certain he'd left the miniature coffin on Grandmère's doorstep. If John was challenged directly, who knew what he would do? But she visited Grandmère openly now. John said nothing. Eight months pregnant, how could she leave? All she could do was bide her time, hoping Jacques could rescue her.

John was handsome again, but whenever Marie looked at him, she never failed to see a skull beneath his face. Nattie grew increasingly bitter because John never shared his youthful tricks. Nattie looked uglier than a lost soul. Only Ribaud seemed at peace. He cared for his drums. He ate. He slept. He helped her feed the snake.

Wrapping her shawl tightly about her, Marie rose. The January weather was rushing her back inside the cottage. Once inside, she moved forward to Grandmère's bedroom door. Marie smiled. Grandmère had fallen back asleep. She'd come to visit Grandmère, bringing food, clean clothes, and candles for her Catholic altar. She'd even brought a vial of holy water; Ribaud had stolen it for her. She'd fed Grandmère okra and hoppin' john, and, after eating, Grandmère had fallen asleep. Marie had gone outside to the rocker. She realized now she'd lost track of time. The candles were half gone and the lengthening evening shadows were reminding her that she lived in shadows, a world without reality or truths.

Marie stretched out her hand to make sure Grandmère was warm enough. It unnerved her to see the small brown face amid so much white—white hair, white gown, white sheets. Grandmère was surrounded by statues of whites: Mary, John, Jesus, Peter. The plaster figures were on the shelves, the walls, scattered about the dirt floor. Grandmère's collection had miraculously grown as if the Virgin Mother had birthed scores of baby saints. Grandmère's rosary was clasped fitfully in one hand. Marie wondered, Did the old woman worry about heaven and hell as much as she did? She settled in the stiff-backed chair beside Grandmère's bed.

Mardi Gras would begin in a week. Everyone would sin as much as they could, only to repent during Lent. Excess, then redemption. Confession on Ash Wednesday, and all the good Catholics could rest easy about heaven—at least until they sinned again. Did Grandmère need to be redeemed? Marie still didn't know whether a black heaven or hell existed. She only knew that the Voodoo dead would roam the earth if their families neglected to honor them with prayers. When she was dead, would her child honor her or desert her as she'd deserted Maman and even sweet Grandmère?

Grandmère reached out to her from the bed. "So long ago, you kept asking me the same question and I never answered. I was wrong not to tell you, but I can answer now: Yes, you do look like your Maman. You're as lovely as she was. You're old enough now to know your history," whispered Grandmère, her fingers tracing

Marie's protruding belly. "You were old enough when we first came to New Orleans, but I was too much of an old fool to know it." She pressed Marie's fingertips to her lips. "I'll tell you who you are. I'll tell you about me, about your Maman, about yourself. About your growing daughter."

Marie nearly wept, for Grandmère sounded as comforting and consoling as she had when they lived in Teché.

"Yes, yes. It'll be a girl," said Grandmère, smacking her gums with satisfaction. "A fine, squalling girl. Women in our family have always birthed girls. They've all been named Marie. Except for your great-grandmother, my Maman."

Marie felt the baby shift and turn. She swallowed to hide her nervousness.

"People called your great-grandmother Marie. But white folks gave her that name. Her African name was Membe." The old woman struggled to sit up; the coverlet tumbled to her waist. Her flannel gown creased about her sagging breasts. Grandmère's body was bent sideways like a broken reed.

Grandmère was dying. Listening to her, Marie could pretend otherwise, for Grandmère's voice was strong and melodic, but the body was visibly wasting. Weathered skin draped over brittle bones. Marie was overwhelmed by the time lost between them, the years of neglect and anger.

"Aw, Grandmère," she moaned. Marie was on the bed, her arms clasping the old woman's neck and supporting her back. She smelled Grandmère's sweet scent and felt childish trust again. She and Grandmère held tightly to each other, crying, rocking away all the pain between them.

Tears pooled on Grandmère's cheeks. In the tears, Marie saw a snake swallowing a field mouse, a fox stalking a rabbit. All natural deaths in Teché, nothing like the slow drain of New Orleans.

"We should've stayed in Teché."

"Hush, child. Stop this foolishness," said Grandmère, wiping her sallow face, pushing Marie away. "Both of us whining like babies."

Marie laughed. Her smile faded as she stared at the million new creases on Grandmère's face and arms. The hands that had slapped her bottom and tossed her in the river were barely recognizable, they were so gnarled and wrinkled. She felt responsible for Grandmère's lines. She'd begun etching old age and death when she'd demanded, "Tell me who I am."

"No need for feeling sorry."

Marie's eyes widened.

Grandmère cupped her face. "I've always been able to see inside your mind. Don't you know that, like any child, you had to slip off my lap or die trying? The fault was mine for holding you too close, not yours for wanting to go." Then, in a whispery, singsong voice, Grandmère said, "Who's my baby? My oh-so-pretty baby?"

"Me. Always me, Grandmère." The candles cast a warm glow. Their shadows entwined, flickered on the wall. Wind howled outside.

"Blood ties bind. That was my mistake." The old woman clicked her gums. "Believing blood wouldn't tell. Believing it would roll upstream rather than down. I betrayed my own mother. Damballah. You."

"You don't have to tell me anything. It doesn't matter anymore."

"Oh, but I do. I have to tell you everything. For the child." Grandmère's fingers poked Marie's belly. "I'm in that child. Membe. Your Maman. We're all inside you, kicking, waiting to be born. It won't be an easy birth. 'Cause we'll all be with her, struggling out. You'll be struggling too." Grandmère paused, then whispered fiercely, "We live forever."

Grandmère sang:

> *"Carry me back to Guinea,*
> *Let my soul find the shore.*
> *Carry me back home.*
> *Let my heart be buried in Guinea,*
> *My African home."*

Bittersweet notes conjured images of a world more perfect than Teché. Rampant grasslands. Sun. Cool water. Peace in animal sounds: the trilling of birds, hyenas' laughter. Marie was reminded of the place where Damballah took her.

"Marie. In the chest by the door, bring me the package from the bottom."

Marie waddled, balancing the baby's weight. Her hands dove into the deep trunk, sifting through parcels and scraps of memorabilia. She lifted out the package and returned to Grandmère.

Fingers plucked at ties. "Your heritage is in here," said Grandmère. "I should've told you years ago, but I was too frightened." Grandmère lifted out a sheaf of indigo cotton. The texture was worn to a gleaming silkiness. On the deep blue was a pattern of repeating skies filled with a sun, moon, and stars colored in red, white, and gold. A gigantic snake coiled itself about the hem.

Marie was awed by the cloth's beauty. The creases and folds still held a wetlands scent. The shapes and images reflected a simplicity and beauty.

"This was Membe's dress," said Grandmère reverently. "She wore it on the slave ship, all the way from Africa. When I was born, my mother wrapped me in this dress. Your Maman and you felt it too. It was your first protection against the cold. When your baby is due, spread this cloth beneath you. Let the bloody baby be swaddled in this cloth. She'll remember Membe. Me. Your Maman."

Marie buried her face in the cloth, sensing, feeling the heat, the blood of so many Maries. She felt the need to recapture everything that was lost. She spoke urgently. "You'll be here, Grandmère. You can wrap the baby in the cloth."

"Hush, child," Grandmère intoned. "Let me tell you the legend of yourself." On the bedspread between them lay Membe's dress. The story began.

"Damballah is father to all the gods. He lives in springs and swamps. All of Africa's children know and love Him.

"White people across the sea tell lies about Damballah. They don't know Damballah made the land fertile, caused the world to grow. White folks don't believe Damballah gave women secret knowledge: clues to see into the past, the future, and the spirit world. White folks don't understand the world is full of more gods than one.

"One day, Damballah raised His head and looked across the ocean.

Ships were stealing His dark children; white men were battering and enslaving them. Damballah's children wept in a New World. Their souls were dying. Memories of Africa and Damballah were being lost.

"Damballah searched for Membe. He found her washing clothes against the bedrock of a clear stream. Membe was a young, pretty girl. Tall and very black. Damballah slithered upon the rocks. 'Membe,' He said, 'I want you to mother my lost children.' Membe bowed her head, overcome with feeling His spirit possess and strengthen her.

" 'Go to the seacoast. Be taken as a slave. When you get to the New World, teach my children to remember their faith. Tell them the tales of themselves and their creation.'

" 'I'll have to leave my parents,' said Membe. 'My brothers and sisters. I shall be friendless in a strange world, wandering without my ancestors.'

"Damballah said, 'I promise your soul will split in two. When you die, part of you will return to live with me in Guinea. Part of you will live forever in a line of daughters.' "

Grandmère coughed mucus and blood. Marie gave her water.

"Membe prepared for her departure. She ate white foods. She wove this cloth. She said goodbye to her village. For a week, she walked toward the sea. Damballah guided her path with rainbows. She allowed herself to be captured as a slave.

"Three months she was chained, feverish, in the hull of a ship. Damballah sent her visions to comfort her. She sang of Damballah. In New Orleans she was sold to Monsieur Laveau. She worked his fields from sunup to sundown. Still she sang of Damballah. She learned a new way of speaking and shared her stories with the other slaves, who added their stories and tales of spirits. Membe spread the words of her faith. Master said she was Laveau property and Laveaus had to learn the Catholic faith. Membe learned it but kept true to Voudon, the Dahomeyan religion.

"For each evening ritual, for each bit of faith Membe stirred in the slaves, the Master made her pay. He said he didn't believe in Voodoo. Said he loved to see Membe dance. After each ceremony, for payment, Master spent the night in Membe's shack. She sang of Damballah."

"What about you, Grandmère? What about you?"

Grandmère tried to focus. "I was trouble, child." Her hand

clutched convulsively at Marie's. "There's no beauty in my story. No legend." She stroked Marie's hair.

"In time, Membe's body was broken by field work, too many stillborn babies. I began conducting the ceremonies. Slaves came to me for healing. One night the Master came for me to pay. It was the night after your grandfather, Sachwaw, died. He was a Muskogean. Strong and kind. I was grieving for him, enraged that my Master, my own father, had killed him.

"I think Master always wanted to rape me. Never mind that I was his flesh and blood, his daughter. I think he purposely delayed raping me, but discovering I'd lain with Sachwaw enraged him. I think he'd wanted to be first.

"When Master came for me, he was cold sober. I always thought he'd need a drink before he could bring himself to touch me. I was wrong. Master insisted I was his for the taking." Grandmère slouched forward. In her mind's eye, she could see Membe, majestic and beautiful, gathering her strength for one final stand.

"Membe killed Master that night. Master killed Membe too. They fought like two men and I crouched in a corner, bawling my heart out. Master hit his head. Membe lost her strength. She died bleeding from her eyes and nose. Before she died, she handed me this cloth and reminded me of my oath and loyalty to Damballah.

"I was a coward. I ran off and hid among the Indians. Two years I was gone. The first year I birthed your Maman and ignored the meaning of her caul. I knew I had to keep faith with Damballah. But I was scared. I didn't have Membe's strength. Her certainty." Grandmère sighed. "Membe was Membe. I never thought of her as my mother. Do you understand? She never seemed real."

Marie caressed Grandmère's brow. Until now, Grandmère had never seemed real. She'd pictured Grandmère in the same strong, self-sufficient shades as Grandmère had pictured Membe.

"Time came when I either had to marry or leave the reservation. The Muskogeans didn't think it right for me to have just one child. I decided to leave. There was nobody I loved. They weren't my people. Damballah was calling, and I was worried that Membe was resting uneasy.

"I'd heard stories of free coloreds living in New Orleans. I thought I could be happy there. Walking with my burdens, I made it as far as Haben's Haven."

"It must've taken weeks."

"Months. I carried your Maman in a papoose and worried about fever and finding enough food for her. I had to stop for days at a time to hunt and fish. I had to rest and let the child be a child. I worried about being ill. I collapsed one day on the coast. Nattie found me and brought me to this cottage. She nursed both your Maman and me. She fed and clothed us. And when I recovered, I shared, in the middle of the night, my history with her. She'd worshiped Damballah in Haiti. She was the one who encouraged me to practice and teach. She called us sisters of the same faith.

"I was scared. Weak. Not much older than you." Grandmère cried out, fluttering her hands, remembering. "But with Nattie's help, I was determined to fulfill Membe's hopes. I thought Membe had purposely led me to Nattie. I thought Nattie was my sign. Yet each time I conducted a ceremony or passed herbs to worshipers in New Orleans, I was terrified whites would discover I wasn't free. I believed they'd sell your Maman and me back into slavery. Sometimes I was afraid to venture out the door. Then one day Nattie brought John."

"Nattie brought John. Not Maman?"

"Yes. Yes. It was a relief to hide behind a man. For a time, I felt secure, protected. John got me forged papers. John made it possible for me to feel free. It was a heady, wondrous feeling. Then, one day, everything changed.

"John wanted to collect money. He said it didn't make sense that we were so poor. 'New World thinking,' I kept saying. 'Not African. Membe never took money.' John kept saying I was a fool. We fought many a night but he always backed down. Never pushed but so far. John was charming when he wanted. He reminded me of Sachwaw. So strong, seemingly invincible. John fell in love with my baby girl. He couldn't keep his eyes off her. He was twenty; she was eight."

Marie was angry. Nattie had lied again. She'd implied Maman had found John, when it had been Nattie who'd brought him among them.

"Your Maman adored John. I encouraged it. I was lonely and frightened that my girl would grow and never know the attentions of the right man. It took me a long time to realize that John was really interested in Marie as something he could sell." Grandmère slumped forward, her shoulders trembling. "I taught John how to slow his aging."

"Seaweed, coconut oil, grave dust mixed with cat's blood and eye," Marie said, not realizing until she said it that she'd learned the secret. How many mornings and nights had she watched John mix and blend his potion?

"Yes, yes. My baby was free, black, and a Voodooienne. White folks would always be scared to death of her. She'd always need someone to keep her safe."

"Just as you felt I needed Jacques."

Grandmère nodded. "I was a fool. I thought I could teach John wisdom and experience. I never once guessed he was manipulating me, waiting to use my baby girl. He was handsome. I thought if I kept him that way, if your Maman fell in love—"

"Like you did? With your Indian?"

"There's never been anyone else." Grandmère turned her face into the pillow.

"The birthday chant you sang. 'Muskogean warrior veined to make the stew wield power. Mulattoes veined from the line of an African Queen.' The warrior would be Sachwaw. The African Queen would be Membe, wouldn't it? 'Creoles veined from the line of French royalty.' That was your master."

"Yes." Grandmère paused. "My Indian had his own faith and spirits. Gods of sky, fire, and wind. Similar to Damballah and the other *loas*. He was a sensitive man."

Reminiscing, Grandmère looked beautiful. All these years and Marie realized she'd never thought of Grandmère as a woman. Never thought of her as desiring a man. Never thought of her as being young.

Grandmère inhaled, pinching her skin. "Master drowned Sachwaw before your Maman was born. White men and white gods have always been more powerful. Sometimes I believe I sacrificed everything for nothing."

"Rest now, Grandmère. There's no more to be said."

"There's lots more," said Grandmère, her skin flushing. "John kept urging your mother to test her powers in New Orleans. I blamed him for your Maman's revolt. They loved too much. Fed on each other like animals: yelling, screaming. Your Maman was to blame too. Proud, like John. She stumbled on the fact that Nattie and John were lovers. Your Maman was still a child. Barely fifteen. Nattie was John's age, a woman waiting, needing loving, while John needed an outlet like any other man.

"When your Maman was sixteen, she and John were supposed to be married. I didn't know John had already seduced her into his bed. So she went wild when she found out about Nattie. Your Maman never did marry John. She never forgave him or Nattie."

Marie understood better now. Nattie had lied to sanitize her own sins. Nattie hadn't wanted to admit to her part in finding and loving John. Nattie, who claimed to love Damballah's faith, had in a sense started its destruction. Nattie must've always loved John. Even now her behavior hinted at the sexual. Poor Nattie. It must've galled her to see Maman and then herself, Maman's daughter, bedded by John.

"Who was my father?"

"I don't know." Grandmère squeezed Marie's hand. "John was unfaithful whenever your Maman wouldn't do or say what he wanted. He forswore Nattie, but there were others. Scores of women. I think it satisfied him to dominate and taunt women. Love had nothing to do with it. I'm convinced he never loved your Maman.

"One night your Maman, riled, went off and came back with the seed of you. Your father was white. I don't know who he was. I made it my business not to know. Your Maman only said her lover was someone rich and powerful. He gave her a silk dress. The chest, child. Go back to my chest. You'll find a package wrapped in white tissue. It has the gift your Maman received when you were born."

Marie tore into the package, causing wafts of tissue to fall to the floor. She stared at a lovely yellowed satin-and-lace christening gown.

"Your Maman and John both took lovers. I quietly kept trying to teach the faith." Grandmère lowered her eyes. "I disappointed myself in raising your Maman. I wanted to do better with you than I did with her."

"You did your best, Grandmère."

"My best wasn't good enough," she said sharply. "I couldn't convey the dignity, the sacredness of Voodoo to your Maman. I was too afraid, too tentative. John and your Maman both wanted spectacle. Power. They both felt the seduction of the world—New Orleans and the New World beckoning with all its falseness. Voodoo became a contest between them. Who commanded the most loyalty, devotion, the most flourishing of prizes and gifts?

"John dared your Maman to lead a ceremony in Cathedral Square."

"John did?"

"Right in front of the Roman Catholic church. I was terrified. White people, white gods, were—*are* dangerous." Grandmère's eyes bulged. She twisted the bed sheets. A spot of blood crept out the corner of her mouth.

"Your Maman danced. She was beautiful. Whites of all kinds—nasty drunks, rough sailors, decadent gentlemen—crowded about her. Your Maman was pleased, enjoying herself. The center of attention. John was passing an unfinished drum, collecting money. His greed was remarkable.

"For a while, I thought nothing would happen. Your Maman would finish her dance and all of us—John, your Maman, and I—would go home.

"Then the cathedral doors opened. A priest, red and scrawny, came out screaming, 'Savages! Devil worshipers!' He waved a rosary. 'In the name of Mary, repent, repent.' My baby danced, her skirt twirling, swaying, her limbs covered with sweat. White folks were hooting and yelling like it was carnival. Men started touching her. One tore her dress. I couldn't get through. Too many hands kept pushing, shoving me back. My baby was slapping, kicking, crying out. The men got angry. I prayed, 'Damballah, save her.'

"I saw my baby rise from the ground. Damballah was going to save her. My heart fluttered. Everyone fell back, frightened, 'cause my baby was walking on air. I sang a chant to the Guédé. I saw the spirits—Barons Samedi, La Croix, and Cimetière—bearing sabers, attacking the crowd. Several white men fell back with blood spurting from their chests. But the crowd kept coming. I called on Ogu, the warrior god, to help me. He used a broadsword, but his strength wasn't enough. For every man slain, there were a hundred more. The scrawny priest yelled, 'Devil. Crucify the devil!' Everyone listened. Weak, stupid men pulled my baby down. She took a long time to die. They tied her to a tree. Whipped her. White people, white gods, were more powerful. Damballah wasn't strong enough to save her." Grandmère sang, "Were you there when they crucified my child?" The melody was haunting. "Were you there?"

Grandmère went on relentlessly, hypnotized by her own story. "Nothing I could do to save her. I was afraid for my life. I hid inside the cathedral till it was over. I hid in a confessional, believing no one would look for me there. My baby girl was dying outside."

"Oh, Grandmère." Marie rocked herself, her hands covering her swollen abdomen.

"White gods mocked me all night. Spirits flew through the cathedral. Jesus. Peter. Where they touched me, my skin burned. Only the Virgin Mother smiled, making me feel peace. She knew what it felt like to lose a child.

"Father Christophe found me there in the confessional. He listened to me, and his words of Jesus, of Mary, stilled my weeping. He was so quiet, so different from that scrawny priest.

"At dawn, I heard Nattie calling for me. I went outside to meet her. The square was empty, except for a few drunken stragglers and the crucifix where they'd lashed my baby's body."

"Nattie wasn't with you or John? She wasn't with Maman at the ceremony?"

"No. She'd been at home watching you. Nonetheless, it was Nattie who cut your Maman down. She had brought you. You were there, toddling, squealing, playing in your Maman's blood, among her scattered and torn clothes. Don't you remember? Nattie and Father Christophe helped me load your Maman into the wagon. Nattie was incensed that I'd let a priest touch my daughter's body and prepare her for burial. But in the end we were afraid to bury her. Afraid the mob would terrorize us too. So we put your Maman's body in the ocean, hoping she'd swim back to Guinea. All I had left of her was the snake and rose brooch I'd given her for her birthday. The same one I passed on to you. Don't you remember?"

Yes, Marie remembered. She'd thrown the brooch away because she'd been furious at Grandmère.

Grandmère caressed Marie's hair. "After your Maman died, all I could do was sing. It was like I was singing every emotion, thought, and feeling. I was singing myself dry.

"When my voice wore out, I gathered you in my arms and placed you on the wagon seat beside me. I drove until I found Teché, a place to hide. I had given up my faith in Damballah. Damballah had given up faith in me. I prayed to the Virgin. I swore you'd never be a Voodoo Queen. I failed Membe."

"Where was John?" Marie whispered.

"I lost him at the ceremony," Grandmère said gently. "I never saw John again until the night twelve years later when he came for you."

Marie cried. Her shadow seemed to shrink on the wall. "John just left her to die, didn't he?"

"Child, I've always been a weak woman."

"Not true."

"A weak, stupid woman. I'm not sure where my soul will go. Maybe to Guinea. Maybe to heaven. Hell. Maybe no place."

"You'll live a long time."

"No. A crow will kill me. But I want you to live. I want your child to live."

"I've got to kill John, Grandmère."

"Hurt anyone and I'll disown you."

Marie sucked in air.

Grandmère's head fell back, cushioned by pillows. "I didn't sacrifice so you could throw everything away." With a burst of passionate energy, she leaned forward, tapping her finger into Marie's chest. "Survival is what matters. Live and let live. And you live by following the rules. Whatever world you live in, you live by following the rules. Don't you see these white saints about me? They're part of our world. See how serenely the Virgin stares? See how Saint Peter smiles at me? They know I'm doing the right thing.

"Black gods can't survive in this world. White folks have too much power. You, who should teach and know the Voodoo faith, know nothing about the faith. I don't have time to teach you the lessons Membe taught me.

"Be a good Catholic, Marie. As a Catholic, you'll survive in this New World. It's been so long since Damballah made His promise to Membe. Maybe He's forgotten. Maybe Damballah is dead in Guinea."

Marie could feel her baby crying, hiccuping water in the womb. She felt herself dissolving. In the well of her soul, Marie knew, Membe was crying. This, then, was the sadness behind the generations of Maries. Because of Grandmère's decision, the course of Membe's pact with Damballah was forever altered. Marie wept. She felt a stirring, too, of compassion.

Marie didn't know Membe, but she knew Grandmère had always tried hard to do what she believed was right. What did it matter if Grandmère was not the Grandmère of her childhood memories? What did it matter if she'd been fallible, sometimes weak, and wrong? She had done her best.

Grandmère clutched Marie's hand. "When I'm gone—"

"You'll be here a long time yet."

Grandmère shrugged, shook her head. "Christian charity. Do acts of Christian charity for me." Closing her eyes, she fell back exhausted.

Marie leaned forward to kiss the dry, cracked lips. Grandmère threw her arms about her. Her grip was unexpectedly strong and bruising against Marie's back. Their lips pressed; they shared each other's air. Her tears and Grandmère's intermingled and tasted salty on Marie's lips.

Still gripping her tightly, Grandmère whispered into Marie's ear, "I worry that I've made a mistake. What if the white gods desert me when I die? What if they don't accept such a fake as I? I know Membe will scorn me, Damballah whom I've betrayed will forsake me, and I shall wander in nothingness. No Guinea. No heaven."

Straining, Marie heard beneath the words a quaking desperation. Staring at Grandmère's slight shadow on the wall, she whispered as though she were telling a great secret to a child. "I think the Virgin and Her Son will kiss you. I think Damballah will smile and embrace you. I think Membe will welcome you as a daughter of her blood. I think all the gods will make a new place for you with both the pleasures of Guinea and heaven."

Hazel eyes opened. Some of the fierce sadness was gone. "I'm tired, child. So tired." Grandmère lay back on the bed, rolled to one side, and drew her legs toward her chest. She curled a fist beneath her cheek and, breathing softly and evenly, quickly fell asleep.

Marie stared at the relaxed face. Confession had eased Grandmère's soul. Marie tucked in the bed sheets, blew out the candles, and gathered Membe's indigo cloth in her arms.

The night had been filled with revelations. Marie knew without a doubt she'd have to murder John, just as she'd murdered Antoine. She stepped out the front door and walked toward the riverbank, letting the wet spray cleanse her wounds. Charity of any sort seemed beyond her.

On this cold night, the villagers were shut inside their houses, remaining warm, snug, and protected. Marie was trying to outwalk nightmares, despair, and contradictions. She wrapped the indigo cloth about her shoulders. The lost snake brooch would've held it snug.

Marie heard a piercing, bell-like whistle. Maybe it was her own fears or guilty conscience that made her start suddenly. Maybe she hadn't heard anything. Just as she convinced herself she was imagining things, she heard the whistling sound tearing through the trees, the wild shrubs, and entering her soul. *It was unlike any other sound she'd ever heard. It was clear, steady, and sweet. It trilled into a harmonic pattern like a nightingale's evening song.* Marie realized she'd heard faint echoes of this sound in Grandmère's singing. But this sound was much purer and pregnant with emotions far greater than any notes conjured by Grandmère. But the *quality* of sound was related. Then Marie realized it was Membe, ephemeral and shimmering in notes not unlike one of Grandmère's loveliest, most heartfelt melodies. But the effect was overwhelmingly, achingly, generous and kind. *Marie reached out to snatch the sound from the air. It disappeared.* She cried out. She hadn't heard nearly enough. Membe's spirit distilled into music was beyond anything she could imagine. Marie stopped, her ribs and chest heaving. She wanted to know more, but she sensed Membe wouldn't come again. The phrase of music was just a whisper to prove Membe existed in spirit somewhere.

Marie realized that part of who and what she was she'd never quite know. Like the tantalizing sound, which couldn't be called back no matter how hard she tried, part of her culture and history was forever lost. An ocean voyage, slavery, and the New World had ripped away parts of herself and distorted what was left. The legacy of Damballah was frayed and tattered. Even Membe must have felt the loss of her family and village. Perhaps she'd forgotten some of the rituals, the ancient cures, the names of her ancestors. Membe never had the opportunity to learn any new expressions of faith, just as she never had the opportunity to learn the faces and names of new nieces or brothers or sisters. Membe must have felt the strangeness too of learning a new language and then using that language to praise Damballah. Voudon became Voodoo. Membe became Marie. Who knows what was lost?

"Who am I?" No wonder that simple question had been so painful, Marie thought. All the confusion she'd felt had been part of her tradition, part of Membe's mission to teach the faith to those who'd been disconnected from their past. No one had accounted for Membe's children going astray.

Mixed blood; mixed legends and faiths. This, then, was real and crucial to survival. Marie felt she had to keep on doing what she had been doing, blending white and black saints, not choosing one over the other as Grandmère had done. Exclusion had been the mistake. It was the blend that kept remnants of Membe's faith alive.

Marie would pray to African and Christian gods because there wasn't a single truth, a single people. Voodoo wasn't African anymore. But, in some form, Voudon had survived. Black peoples had survived. Damballah didn't say to Membe, I am the one true and only God. He said, Mother my children. Tell them tales of themselves. Surely Damballah would have realized how His children would change in a New World into a new race of people. Confusion, pain, and loss were all part of their survival, embedded in the memories of Africa and Damballah. For if you kept alive the African ideas, you kept alive the memory of freedom and the security of villagers who shared your blood and skin.

If Damballah mistrusted Membe's children, He would have deserted them long ago. But He hadn't deserted the Maries. Damballah still whispered secrets to her . . . He still showed her miracles of another time and place . . . Damballah loved her, the third Marie, still. And Marie already knew her daughter also would be born with Damballah's caul.

Marie turned and stared at the Mississippi flowing beneath the moonlight's grandeur. If Jacques returned, she'd ask for his help to fulfill the legacy of Membe. She'd explain to him that she couldn't just be his wife or anyone's wife. She needed to grow and take responsibility for herself and her child. She needed to offer hope for all those who didn't have hope: slaves, indentured servants, prisoners in the city jail, the residents of Haven. "Who am I?" translated into learning to serve others, offering the remnants of faith so all Damballah's children might prevail in this frightening New World. Marie rubbed successive circles on her swollen abdomen. With practice, she could learn to shed some of her selfishness. And she'd remember to tell her child everything. To hold nothing back. She'd explain that life was harsh, unfair, and real.

Maybe, in time, she'd return the kind of love Jacques deserved. They'd be a happy family: Jacques, baby, and Marie.

Marie picked up a smooth stone and with a flick of her wrist sent it slicing, skipping across the churning water. Rippling circles of water spread outward from the stone. Then the stone sank with a soft plop.

"Come home, Jacques," Marie murmured, her voice lifting like a siren's across the Mississippi and down through the currents leading into the Gulf Stream and the open sea. "Come home." She needed someone who had a little faith in her.

As she walked back toward the village, her feet crunching in soft, gritty mud, she heard a clear, glorious bell-like sound shadowing her heels. She saw snakes rising out of the ground and striding upright toward the water. Marie shivered, and Membe's dress flapped in the wind.

~

"Brigette died. Did you know?"

"Yes, I knew. It scared me terribly, because I thought if she died then I'd die giving birth too. It's a fearful process, having life tear itself out of you."

"She killed herself, you know. She refused the midwife and the doctor. She murdered two innocent babies. I helped."

"Hush, Louis. There's no need to talk."

"Brigette wouldn't accept that she was pregnant. She kept to her room, mumbling about having killed the babies. She said they'd died with Antoine. Even when the weight of the babies made it nearly impossible to move, she still denied them.

"I'd been working late at the newspaper. It was past midnight when I returned home. The house was in an uproar. Brigette was in labor, screaming. Her maid, Clara, was in tears. I sent for a doctor and Brigette fought him like a she-devil. I couldn't reason with her. Finally, it took four of us to hold her down while the doctor examined her. He said the twins were breeched. The only hope for the children was to cut them out. He wanted my permission, since it would kill her."

"Hush, Louis."

"I kept delaying. I didn't want the responsibility. At dawn, the doctor said, 'Now or never.'"

"Don't cry, Louis."

"Brigette wasn't dead. She was weak, drifting in and out of consciousness. I can still see the bloodied sheets. She bled for hours. Blood on blue satin, can you imagine? But she wasn't dead. She was like a beached, bloated whale. I could see—I still see—vague outlines of the babes on her abdomen. A straining hand, a foot. But I couldn't say yes. The babies died with her."

343

On the evening before Mardi Gras, Marie sat on the dock, her feet kicking at the free space between land and sea. This morning, she'd risen from her bed, looked out the paned window, and had known Jacques wasn't coming. The sky didn't have any sun. Haze colored the world gray. Cathedral bells tolled sluggishly. When Marie tried to light a candle, the match blew out though there wasn't any wind. A street beggar's plea caught in his throat, and when Marie rushed to the window to throw him a coin, the beggar, empty-handed, had already shuffled by.

Marie dressed in her finest clothes, packed a basket with cold yams and smoked hocks, and swung Membe's dress, sewn into a shawl, about her shoulders. Uninvited, Ribaud accompanied her, and at daybreak the two of them rambled through the nearly deserted streets down to the smelly docks.

Now Marie could see Ribaud a few yards away and to the left of the tall merchant ships, lowering a trap to catch crayfish or shrimp. He'd been at it for hours without any luck. The tide was too low. Seagulls circled restlessly, unable to find the morning's catch. Just as she was unable to find Jacques.

The sun reached its zenith, but Marie still felt a bone-chilling cold. Sitting on the exposed wharf, her feet swinging haphazardly, her back grew rigid, her hands numb. She tried to ignore the spiraling contractions that spread outward from her belly. She concentrated on praying to Damballah. "Bring Jacques home." For good measure, she said the rosary, pretending that the stones on the wharf were pearl beads in a rosary chain. Marie played the sailor's wife, performing an ancient waiting ritual, dreaming of rescue, hoping her man wasn't lost at sea.

She watched full-bellied cargo ships, slave ships, fishing boats, dinghies, and triple-masted naval ships set sail. She watched ships return, scarred by rough seas, hurricane, and rebellion. But no *Marie-Thérèse,* Jacques' ship.

"Miz Marie, we should go. Be here any longer and John go crazy."

Marie squinted against the glare of the setting sun. "He said he'd come. He'll be here."

"But he's not here. We should go. Don't make no sense to be here," Ribaud said insistently, scratching his head, pacing back and forth like a hungry bird. He was sorry he'd ever tried to reconcile Marie and Jacques. One big heartache was all he could see in Marie.

"I'm going to wait, Ribaud."

Marie didn't doubt the uselessness of her waiting. False confidence and pride, perhaps. Yet there was a sweet sadness in waiting for Jacques even though she knew he wouldn't come. She would wait until night; she owed him that.

"Stubborn," Ribaud said. "You're more stubborn dan a dead mule."

Marie smiled slightly.

Ribaud walked away, muttering.

Marie indulged herself in being lovesick, forgetting the hard need for shaping herself, forgetting her desire to escape John, forgetting everything beyond an intense longing to comfort Jacques and begin anew with their marriage vows.

The sun lowered. The moon made its steady, unhurried rise. Dusk settled over the harbor and billowy waves rose, battering the wharf, rushing senselessly forward and back from the shoreline. Marie ate all her yams. Jacques never came.

"Tell her. Tell her like you done told me."

Startled, Marie saw Ribaud prodding, shoving a man forward, slapping him about the head and neck. The man's belly strained against his wine-stained shirt, with flesh spilling over his leather belt, blocking the view to his feet. His face was damp and flushed. He had a drunkard's pockmarked nose and wore a familiar and common naval overcoat with brass buttons. It was comical, spying Ribaud herding a sailor twice his size forward, but it was also frightening because the sailor was white and no black man was supposed to treat a white man the way Ribaud was treating him.

"I done told him you're de Voodoo Queen. Told him you'd hex him to death. Cause his heart to shrivel and his balls to fall off. Told him you'd make him sorry he'd ever been born."

"Ribaud, no." Marie wanted to laugh because Ribaud was so foolishly, unexpectedly fierce.

"Told him he'd better tell de truth. Told him he'd better tell you like he done told me, else I'd kill him myself."

Marie rose awkwardly, the baby shifting in her abdomen, and stared frankly at the sullen man, wondering what on earth he had to do with her. Her first impression had been wrong; he wasn't a sailor exactly. A merchant or clerk of some sort. Rough hands, a general caginess, fish oil and sea smells typed him as a man wedded to the docks. He was a man who slept in a cheap and sparsely furnished boardinghouse, and when he wasn't working he was drinking or visiting prostitutes.

"Dis here man knows about Mister Jacques."

"Is this true?"

"He keeps lists of all de ships. He knows everything. Knows all about de cargo on de *Marie-Thérèse*. All about her men. His name is Chestnutt." Ribaud shoved the man forward.

Marie's breathing was rapid and shallow. "His name is Jacques Paris. He's on the *Marie-Thérèse*. Do you know what happened to his ship? Why isn't it here?"

"You're not what I expected." Chestnutt's soft tenor was at odds with his slovenly appearance. His voice suggested southern courtesy, gentility. "The Marie Laveau I heard about was staunch, sturdy, and black as sin. Rumor said her neck was as wide as a man's arm. I didn't expect anyone half as pretty. But I suspect pretty witches are best for the devil's work."

"And ugly men are shaped in God's image," Marie snapped.

Scowling, Chestnutt planted his feet and, squaring his shoulders, thrust out his chest.

Marie was furious, her face skewed with bitterness. "I'll do everything Ribaud said. I'll summon demons to eat away your cock. I'll torture you with your worst nightmares, your failures and dreams. I'll see you buried alive. I'll haunt your mother if I have to and curse your sons. Tell me. Where is Jacques Paris?"

Chestnutt cocked his head, measuring Marie's fury. He didn't seem to be afraid. "Does it mean that much to you?" he asked softly.

"Yes," Marie said, captivated by his change in tone.

Chestnutt let his hand rest on the weathered posts. Six feet down, the wooden supports plunged into the sea. A wind tugged at his coat, and he snapped his collar to offset the chill. His belly was still exposed. A new moon reflected off his tarnished buttons. He spoke to the horizon.

"When I used to sail—oh, yes, I did sail, coasting over the waves in a tall, brave ship—I'd think of my young woman waiting for me in port just as you're waiting for Paris. It was hard on her. She never told me so, but I knew it was. I'd see relief and despair sweating out of her pores when I'd return after months, sometimes years at sea. I'd see new lines in her face, coarser hair and dulling eyes. The young girl in her went away. Her aging didn't make her any less beautiful to me. But it made me feel guilty that she was giving up so much on my account: a home, children, life itself. For several voyages more, she waited, until finally I couldn't stand it anymore— her waiting. I told her to go. Told her I hated her. I hated myself because she was capable of loving so much better than me." Chestnutt turned to Marie and said colorlessly, "I know Jacques Paris. But I haven't seen him. Not since he was fired from the *Marie-Thérèse*. He couldn't stop drinking."

"They took him back. I know they did. He sailed on the last voyage. Somewhere in the West Indies."

Chestnutt slowly shook his head. "No, Ma'am." He'd known several women like Marie, abandoned, pregnant with bastards, and lovesick over a lying sailor. He straightened his neckcloth, patted ineffectually at his wild, strawlike hair. "I don't go to sea myself anymore. You can't count on a drunk when there's a typhoon. And drunken sailors are famous for hiding rum aboard ship. Funny, when my woman was gone, I took to drink. When I was landlocked, she'd already left and gone west with someone else. Now I just keep charts and ledgers for Baker and Moore. They don't trust me with any ships."

"What has that to do with Jacques?"

"I'm coming to it," he said gently, scratching his ear, delaying bad news. "I take an interest in drunks like me. I knew Paris when he was the best bosun's mate a captain could ever want. But something happened." He looked curiously at Marie, then continued after clearing his throat. "I would've known if Paris was back. I would've been glad for him, nigger and all. I mean that. I know what it's like to lose the sea."

Marie's air whistled out of her body like a hiss out of a snake. She wanted to attack the spindly-legged man, because she'd already guessed what he had to say.

"But Paris never made it onto the *Marie-Thérèse*. I had a payroll warrant for him. But when time came to sail, he wasn't on board. We figured he'd drunk himself into a stupor. Someone else took his place."

"I don't believe it." Marie looked out over the harbor. But she did believe him. Signs had told her Jacques wasn't coming. Her bones ached. The beggar went empty-handed. Birds didn't feed. High tide was tinged blood-red while saltwater churned, threatening to hide and erase. The shoreline was diminished. Fish dove beneath the raucous waves, and treasures from sunken ships burrowed deeper in the sand. Marie couldn't stop herself from saying, "When the *Marie-Thérèse* docks, I'll know you're lying." Disgruntled seagulls circled overhead, screeching.

"Harm me if you want, but I'm telling you as I'd tell my own daughter: Paris is gone. You're better off without a drunk in your life. No good ever comes of it." Brushing past Ribaud, Chestnutt had the sensation he was strutting a gangplank. He thought Marie or Ribaud or both would snatch and curse him. He walked gingerly, not knowing what to expect. He believed in Voodoo as much as he believed in evil, but he wasn't clear about the limits of its power. He'd go to mass tonight. He'd drink until he was unconscious. If demons came to claim him, he'd be oblivious. Recalling his wife made him want to drink too. He hadn't allowed himself to think about her in years. Something about Marie had disarmed him. It was evil that any woman should make a man feel so vulnerable.

"Madame Laveau," Chestnutt called, when he felt he was at a safe distance, "the *Marie-Thérèse* has come and gone. She anchored a week ago and is already two days bound for Antigua. You can wait three more months for her to return, if you care to."

Marie felt she was seeing Chestnutt through a telescope, his face filling the limits of her vision. "Get out of here!" she screamed, clenching her fists, wanting to destroy Chestnutt's enjoyment of the bad news.

Walking backward, Chestnutt doffed an imaginary cap. Marie stooped and threw her rosary stones at him. The pebbles landed short and rolled crazily: some plopped into the ocean, others slowed and stuck in the dirt, while still others got caught between the boardwalk crevices. "White bastard. You filthy white bastard," she screamed again, stumbling forward, tripping on her dragging shawl.

"Maman Marie, it's no good," said Ribaud. "He spoke de truth. Truth don't always have de best face. Sometimes it slaps you hard and dere ain't nothing you can do but slam de door and get on with it."

Marie extended a hand, flailing for support, for something to grasp and hold. "He lied. Why did Jacques lie to me?" She'd been prepared to hear that Jacques' ship had been sunk or stranded by a typhoon. She could even entertain thoughts of his falling overboard or dying of a tropical fever. But for him to just leave her, she didn't understand.

"Come now, Miz Marie." Ribaud gently touched her shoulder. "Let's go home. We need to get ready for Mardi Gras. Mardi Gras be tomorrow. You got to prove dat you're de great Voodoo Queen."

Disoriented, her head bobbing, Marie set off, her back curved, staring blindly down the wharf. "Jacques. Jacques."

Gripping her elbow, Ribaud supported Marie for the long walk home. He made soothing, clucking noises as if herding a chick. "Home ain't de best to be, but it's *someplace*. It's all we got. Dere be many ain't got dat. Ain't got no place to be."

They were an odd couple, but few turned to stare. There were other sights more startling and spectacular than a distraught, moaning woman and a trembling, small-boned man.

The farther away from the wharf, the more frenetic and crowded were the city streets. Ribaud tried to hire a cab but none were in sight as waves of bodies, pulsing with a desperate energy, filled the avenues. People were celebrating Mardi Gras early. Whining harmonicas and twangy banjos seemed both grating and uplifting. Ribaud cursed and tried to propel Marie safely through the swarming revelers. He jabbed with his elbow and at times kicked viciously with his foot.

Time was lost. Marie felt a roaring in her head. Place receded. She knew she was moving because she could feel Ribaud's hot hand urging her forward. Her legs moved, but it no longer mattered where she was going or where she had been. If it hadn't been for the baby inside her, she probably would've crouched and tried to dig a hole in the swampy dirt. She would've buried herself beneath dirt and false hopes. But the baby settling itself, head down in her womb, caused Marie to take notice of the world.

Marie saw hell. Moonlit shadows stalked. People were screaming, giggling, shouting boastfully. Strangers danced, embraced one another, and fought. One man wore a goat head of wire and paper; he rammed and butted the crowd. A woman wore chicken feathers instead of clothes. There was a hobbyhorse, gangly and squat, with mismatched legs and linen sides. A woman, pouncing and purring like a cat, had broom needles attached to her nose. She leaped on a soldier's back. Torches made the sky flare a violent red.

Monsters speckled the crowd, their bodies glistening with sweat-streaked dyes of blue, yellow, gold, and purple. Some had extra limbs: a creature shook hands with three persons at once while another dragged a spare leg. A grinning mulatto, walking on sticks, towered seven feet high. The city was preparing for carnival.

Marie felt she'd stumbled into madness. This morning, the world had seemed somber yet calm; this evening, the world was awry with lunacy. It all made sense. Jacques wasn't coming.

"Through here, Miz Marie. We're almost dere."

Marie and Ribaud ducked through an alleyway. Six men dressed in pirates' costumes were swinging swords and whacking a skull back and forth. Moaning "Save me," a decrepit man held up a noose slung about his neck.

Marie shivered. Tomorrow night she'd be in the midst of this. John had declared Mardi Gras as the time to stage the ceremony in Cathedral Square. "It'll be your chance," he'd said, "to succeed where your mother failed. This time, my timing is right."

For weeks, she'd watched John sitting at the table drawing up plans, sketching ideas. He was always careful to hide his bits and scraps of paper. But time and again he'd punctuate his scribbling by saying, "I'm going to get you under my thumb and keep you there." This new John (and he *was* new) was unkempt and more frightening.

"The child's mother has to be worthy of the child."

Each time John repeated this, Marie felt a violent tremor inside her. As though she were worthless and the baby inside her was everything.

Crazed. When John looked at her with his lips dry and parted, his eyes holding that same terrible expression he had before a climax, she thought, He's crazed.

How like a crazy man to want to risk her life in the same place where her mother died. How like John to risk both her and the child. She'd ignored John's plans because she'd hoped that by Mardi Gras she and Jacques would be gone.

"We're here." Ribaud stroked his chin and looked speculatively at Marie.

She winced. Touching her finger to her nose, she said, "I'm all right, Ribaud. I understand Jacques isn't coming back." She scraped her fingers against the door. "It doesn't change that I desperately want him back. But he's off somewhere," she said flatly. "He's off somewhere drunk. Self-pity doesn't mean a damn thing."

"I'll open de door," Ribaud murmured. The door squealed open and they saw disorder and clutter. *Gris-gris,* candles, liquor jugs, and insects clamped inside colored jars littered the floor. Nattie and John were at the table shrouded in lamplight.

Marie sighed. She had to strike a bargain with a crazy man. With the baby almost due, Marie couldn't hide.

351

A woman with green skin, green hair, and a green robe paraded, stealing garish costume jewels from fellow revelers. The woman called herself Envy. Gluttony wriggled his immense belly while stuffing beans in his face. He called, "More food. More food." Flies hovered about his bare, dirty chest. A black boy dressed outlandishly as a French page carried Gluttony's supplies of fat-filled sausages and fried bananas. Trailing behind him was a band of red devils stabbing pitchforks at one another and swaying their limp tails.

Mardi Gras.

Everyone switched identities. Whites painted their skin with black tar and pretended they were lustful slaves. Slaves painted themselves with rice flour and slapped and kicked like outraged masters. Rich men played the beggar. Beggars played the gentleman. Virgins acted like wild whores. Whores behaved like gently reared ladies. Everyone was drunk. Stragglers vomited in gutters. Several men and women collapsed, unconscious.

During Mardi Gras, everyone took risks and shed inhibitions. It didn't surprise Marie that John would choose this time to assert the growing influence of Voodoo in New Orleans. Yet it left her breathless and anxious. Standing on her platform stage, Marie could see St. Louis Cathedral. She could imagine Grandmère hiding in the dim church, cowering there while Maman was dying. She could see Grandmère burying her head in her hands, covering her ears, trying to block the shouts and screams and trying to rationalize that it was all right for her to want to live too. She could see Grandmère listening, separating her daughter's voice from the din, and shivering when she heard the frightened, defiant howls and the moans when they lashed her daughter's back. Marie felt sorry, especially for Grandmère. She felt sorry for her Maman. The white men who'd applied the lash had stolen from both Marie and her Maman an opportunity to love.

Marie turned to the indigo box that held the snake. *Fa* was a strange and wondrous thing, she supposed. Still, she wished that Maman had lived. She wished she'd been a more obedient girl. She wished John had left her alone. She wished she hadn't so relentlessly pursued her own fate.

Ribaud, solicitous, passed by, whispering, "Keep faith. Everyding gonna be all right. Keep faith."

Marie smiled gratefully, watching Ribaud weave his way toward his drums. She bowed her head low, trying to shut out the noise of the crowd. They wanted sensationalism, not religious miracles. What did any of it matter? She inhaled and felt a lingering wind caress her hair.

"It be a great thing you're doing."

Marie stared. Nattie, complex and strange, always seemed to want too much from her. Looking at Nattie's drawn face, Marie felt compelled to be honest, to attempt again an understanding between them. Maman dead, Grandmère ill; there wasn't another woman to reach out to. Membe was a ghost.

"I'm not certain I can do it, Nattie. Perform miracles tonight. What if Damballah doesn't come? This carnival feels so far removed from Africa. I can't work miracles on demand."

"You'll work one tonight. Else John—" Nattie slapped her hips. "Foolishness. You know what he'll say and do. I don't need to tell you. You know better than me."

There were violent shrieks. Off the platform, Marie could see two grease-slicked men among the crowd, shoving at each other, pecking like strutting, prideful roosters.

"Look." Nattie pressed her face close. Marie could smell garlic and cayenne. She saw shadows between Nattie's softening gums and teeth. "Illusion be necessary sometimes. Nothing be quite real. That be the essence of Mardi Gras—Voodoo. It makes sense to believe in what makes you feel good. The trick be not believing in what don't make you feel good. But trust be needed too. You got to trust sometimes that the things that make you feel bad might turn out good. Sometimes, horrible things be necessary. You got to trust that strange things can serve Voudon."

"You're scaring me, Nattie. Every time I've trusted you, I've ended up hurt."

"I be hurt too," Nattie said bitterly. "But not like you. Not saddened like a chick needing its rooster or its mother hen. I feel twisted in my gut all the same. In my head. In my heart. Simple foolishness."

"Then leave it alone, Nattie." Marie hated Nattie's conniving, her need to manipulate. "You've lied to me too often."

"No, I be warning you. I must say this before John comes. I've found out some things. Strange things. Illusions." Her words were coming faster. "Death be not always real. Zombies have special grace." Nattie choked, feeling overwhelmed. In Marie's face, she saw Grandmère. "Remember to trust. All things serve Damballah."

"It's time," said John, shouting above the noisy crowd, wedging his body between the two women. His body blocked their view. His face painted a deadly white, John stroked Marie's chin and fastened his hands on her shoulder blades. Nattie stepped aside.

Marie, brows raised, tried to search Nattie's face for meaning. Each time she moved to get a better glimpse of Nattie, John's body blocked her.

"Leave us," said John, never once glancing away from Marie. "I don't want you here, Nattie."

Unnaturally subdued, Nattie turned tail and moved forward to give instructions to the dancers.

"Are you ready, Marie? You're not feeling cowardly, are you?"

Marie sighed. Each step she took, John seemed to mimic like a shadow. On the altar was an indigo box painted with half-moons and herb seed. She opened its lid, reaching in to touch the sleepy, dreaming snake. John edged away. "I'm as ready as I'll ever be," she said.

"There'll be a surprise tonight."

The snake was clammy, smooth.

"A reminder that it's best to obey me."

"What more do you want from me? I'm here, aren't I? I'm risking my life. Like Maman."

John just smiled, his skin resilient as a baby's.

Marie composed her face. John fed on seeing her hurt. Grand-mère was safe. Ribaud had checked before the ceremony. What more could John do to her?

"You think too highly of yourself, Marie. Too highly indeed." John's hands made spiraling motions on her abdomen. Marie concentrated on not flinching. "Once this baby is born, we'll marry. After tonight, you won't be the Queen anymore. You'll be my servant, my slave. Like Ribaud. You haven't begun to find out the things I can make you do."

"If the spirits don't come tonight, the crowd will kill me."

"Then you'll have to make sure the spirits come, won't you? Or fake it. You've no other choice. That's the point."

Furious, Marie lowered the box's lid. "And will you prove you're a coward, John? Will you desert me like you deserted Maman? Will you leave me alone to die?"

"It's time," said John, gripping Marie's elbow and jockeying her toward the platform's edge. A sea of bodies surged. Marie stepped back. "See. All the wise and unwise citizens of New Orleans are here. A mayor. Somewhere, my spies say, a governor. The spiritual and the blasphemous have all come to see a sensation. Look, there's Father Christophe. I wonder what keeps him quiet on the church step? He wants to see how you've put the serpent in bed with the Virgin."

"You're damned, John."

Marie saw the frail priest and felt like waving. She felt giddy. Beside the priest was Louis DeLavier. He was nearly bald. She wanted to touch his scalp and imagine they were lovers. John didn't seem to recognize Louis.

Marie murmured, "Father Christophe knows better than to be threatened by charlatans like us."

"On the contrary, he's enormously threatened. Threatened by the will of the people. Why shouldn't he be? His religion hasn't had a miracle in a thousand years. The New World wants and demands new things. The people want and need us.

"Just do what you did at the lake, Marie." John ran his tongue along Marie's ear. "A miracle. That's all that's needed. A little bit of magic. And so you won't feel alone, I've got a miracle as well. It's not true that I'm a coward. Tonight I'll show you *my* miracle. I made it specially for you." John laughed, and beneath the grating sound Marie heard the threat. Damn John, anyway. But he was right, it was time. The nightmare crowd was impatient for its spectacle.

Marie pushed herself forward and began to dance. The huge Mardi Gras crowd applauded. Ribaud played his drums. His beats seemed like a death knell, sluggish beyond imagining. Two other drummers were a frenzied contrast, their calloused hands beating a fast calimba pattern. Marie danced, carefully balancing her baby's weight, alternating between the two rhythms. Fast, then slow. She felt degraded. She glanced at Father Christophe. Beside him on the church steps altar boys were swinging canisters of burning incense. She wondered if it was Louis who kept the priest from yelling out that she was a devil. Or was the good father loyal to Grandmère? Or maybe he was counting on her martyring herself.

Nattie lit torches on the rough-hewn stage. It was dusk. The moon was creeping over the horizon. Squealing, screaming people pressed against the stage. Marie was entertaining.

She swayed left, then right. Whites leered, copying the swing of her hips. Others thrust their pelvises forward, pretending they were mounting her. One woman let fly her billowing blouse while cupping her exposed breasts. What more did they want from her? Sin: exotic and dark. She could see it in their rabid faces. The crowd wanted to believe she was the devil's mistress. Marie lacked the courage to spit at them. A similar crowd had killed her mother. The stained-glass window above the massive cathedral doors, depicting Christ arising from the dead, was illuminated by the moonlight. Tomorrow, Ash Wednesday, this hungry, sinning crowd would go to mass and receive Father Christophe's blessing. Such good Christians, Marie thought sarcastically. Tonight, hardly anyone was sober. People would commit deeds they'd spent all year dreaming about.

John made obscene gestures at the white women; any other day he would've been lynched. But not tonight. Anything was possible. From a wheelbarrow, John passed out Voodoo dolls. "Zombies," he called. "Turn your enemies into the undead." He let a painted whore kiss his palms.

Marie kept dancing, waiting for Damballah to come.

Scattered throughout the white crowd, blacks were chanting, "Maman Marie, save us. Maman Marie, save us." Some held lighted candles. Some had their eyes closed, their lips murmuring fervent prayers. Others linked arms and seemed to sway back and forth, singing strains of gospel melodies.

Marie winced. Her faithful followers were raggedy black men, poor mulattoes and downtrodden slaves, and a sad bourgeoisie of free coloreds. What did they expect? For her to whisk them back to Guinea? To make white Christians disappear? She was terrified. Terrified the whites would crucify her like Maman. Scared, too, that she couldn't reach out to the audience that needed her the most. Membe might've known what to do. Nonetheless, Marie felt a strange, unfamiliar pride that among the white sinners her own people were reaching out to her. She felt a deep joy that black people seemed to be needing and loving her.

John was wringing chickens' necks, slicing out their hearts and spraying blood. Women swooned and men cheered. Ribaud grinned as he caressed his drums, building his own rhythms, encouraging a breathless insanity.

John filled a cup with blood. People in the crowd surged forward, fighting among themselves to drink it.

Nattie was dancing, twirling her skirt above her head, exposing bowlegs and a wide pelvis. Her motions were erratic and seductive, her breathing slow. Nattie was pretending Ezili possessed her. She stroked John's cock. He batted her away.

Marie swallowed mucus. She was still waiting for Damballah to come. She danced. Sweat stuck her yellow skirt to her thighs. Pains swept through her abdomen. She laughed harshly. Her baby would be born during carnival. Why didn't Damballah come?

Did it matter to anyone that she was scared? Drunken strangers were reaching for her, plucking her skirt. John was watching. Someone might grasp her skirt too hard. Did it matter if she toppled? If she fell among the crowd? Would they hang her? Kill her? Did it matter that at any second Father Christophe might shout from the cathedral steps, "In the name of Mary, repent"? Did it matter that she might have used up all her miracles? She wasn't Membe.

Someone yelled, "Charlatan. Fake." Marie turned her head. Two devils were helping a woman undress. A boy with purple headgear was blowing a horn. A man in silver pants whooped and threw a torch into the air. He clapped his hands as the flame fell, igniting the lamé train of a make-believe king.

Maybe Damballah was angry at her. Hadn't He ignored her prayers for Jacques? Maybe the fault was John's; he'd conceived this pathetic ceremony. Maybe there were too many people in the crowd who didn't believe in Voodoo, too many leering whites eager only for spectacle. Had Maman, before she died, thought similar thoughts?

There were more curses. Chants. "Charlatan. Cheat." Her dance was sluggish. "Where's the great Voodoo Queen?" Ugly murmurs slapped her and made her feel more disconnected, a firefly burning its own air.

Two beggars dressed like clownish gentlemen were climbing onto the platform. Marie could feel a shift in the crowd's emotions. High spirits became fury. In her mind, she suddenly beheld Maman, faltering and frightened, as Marie herself faltered in her dance.

"For God's sake, get the snake, Marie," John shouted. "The snake." He kicked the two men in the chest; they fell backward, spread-eagled into the crowd. If everyone hadn't been so drunk, there might have been more ire against John, a black man kicking whites. But the two men, with scarred arms and hands, looked poor, and who really cared? They might've been dockworkers or sailors. The crowd cheered as the men fell inelegantly, bruised and bleeding. Men with thick boots harshly kicked the sprawled men. Soon a circle formed as dozens of masked revelers beat them with sticks, stones, and pitchfork handles.

A scared Nattie was murmuring "Foolishness," her body prostrated on the altar. The dancers flanking Marie tried to run away. John slapped one of the girls and cowed them all into remaining, huddled against the crowd's onslaught. John was shouting orders at the drummers. Marie couldn't hear him, but she saw Ribaud's shocked face, and the drummer, Cecil, climbed off the stage and disappeared. John turned to protect her. He swept a torch in a wide arc near the platform's edge. Though she saw fear in him, she also saw a strange exhilaration. John was enjoying himself. He grinned at her. He looked the demon. Night clouds floated above them. Marie kept dancing. It was senseless to pretend there was any way for her to escape. She might as well dance until the crowd came for her like they'd come for her Maman.

She saw Louis moving toward her in slow motion, trying frantically to get through the pressing barrier of bodies, legs, and arms. Poor Louis, always intent upon rescuing her. Beyond him, Father Christophe was pacing the length of the church steps, making the sign of the cross. The crowd continued to sway between mob violence and pleasure.

Small groups were fighting: black against white, men against women, the righteous against the dispossessed. More people danced. Ribaud's tune was frantic. John patrolled the platform. One of the dancing girls managed to run away. Bodies pressed nearer, threatening to overwhelm the small stage. Marie cringed. She heard Nattie screaming, "Save us! They'll crucify. Crucify." Nattie was pressing her buttocks against the altar. "Do something, Marie."

The horror had always been there. But Nattie's cry touched a nerve in her. In the back of her mind, Marie heard Maman's screams.

"Do something." Nattie had dropped her defenses. She was old and scared. "Do something."

So she did. Marie dropped to her knees, babbling. She pitched her sounds low, then high. Her eyes rolled upward. Her limbs shook. She staggered toward the altar. Feigned trance. What was it Nattie said? Illusion.

She opened the box, coiling the python about her throat while crying, "Damballah. Damballah." The snake darted out its tongue.

"She'll die," some people screamed. Some shuddered and drew back; some leaned forward expectantly; most assumed the snake was poisonous.

Marie wanted to laugh; instead, she moaned. She was afraid to die.

"Who else but Marie Laveau," John proclaimed, flailing his

arms, smiling like a ghoul, "can dance with a snake? Who else has the power?"

Marie cooed and tenderly held the snake. Nattie was shrieking, stomping; she scattered dust from the altar over the crowd. Ribaud was grimly pounding his drums. They were all performing, Marie thought. It was easier than she imagined.

Boldly, she walked to the edge of the platform. She rubbed the snake's mouth against hers. "Try," she called. "Try Damballah's kiss." The crowd encouraged her; their fear and her power over them were addictive.

Blacks dressed like French royalty were jerking, twisting their bodies, calling, "Damballah. Marie Laveau. Damballah." Were they possessed or pretending?

John was urging Marie to swallow a chicken's heart.

Nauseous, she turned and saw Louis, elbowing his way through the crowd. He was smiling idiotically, waving to her. She turned back to John; blood spotted his mouth. "Give me your knife."

"What?"

"Your knife. Give it to me." She smacked her palm.

"No."

"Damn you." Marie slipped the knife from his belt. John was too surprised, too wary of the snake to stop her.

Marie faced Louis. The crowd's clamor dulled. From far off, she heard Nattie bleating, "Salvation be here." Then she heard John's angry shout at the drummer, Cecil. "What were you about? What took you so long?"

Sounds receded. Marie was transfixed by Louis, by her belief that he was mocking her. Before Marie knew what she planned to do, she was sliding the knife down her arm, leaving a trail of blood. She dropped the knife. The snake coiled about her wounded arm. Louis' concerned face kept her from crying.

Louis' hand was outstretched and Marie could feel herself desperate to take it. She wanted to leave this nightmare. Her head lifted. The audience was silent. She could hear shuffling, nervous coughs, and the fluttering of hands and cloth, but otherwise the crowd was silent. Something had happened. The tenor of the air had changed. It was oppressive, clogging her lungs. Something told her not to turn around. She remembered John shouting, "What were you about? What took you so long?" Cecil had brought something back. And whatever it was, it was enough to stun thousands into silence.

Marie blinked. The warm night turned cold. She was afraid to turn around.

Louis had stepped backward from the platform's edge. His gaze was focused beyond her, his face twisted with revulsion. Ribaud's drums were silent.

John was whispering behind her ear. "So it begins. So it begins." He reeked of foul yellow. Marie could feel herself gagging, feel tremors where John's fingertip traced the hairline on her neck, but still she couldn't turn around. Horror was awaiting her.

John began chanting.

> *"If you see a snake*
> *You see Marie Laveau.*
> *If you see a snake*
> *You see Damballah.*
> *Marie Laveau is a snake."*

Marie looked at the python curled about her arm. Her blood covered it. Staring at the snake's eyes, Marie thought she saw tears.

John was stomping, shouting. "Ribaud, the drums." The wooden planks trembled beneath Marie's feet. The rhythm was somber, dissonant in its intensity.

"See here," John was calling. "Witness a miracle." Then he was chanting again, his voice screeching and wailing:

> *"Zombie. Zombie.*
> *Marie Laveau makes zombies.*
> *Walking dead. The undead.*
> *Marie Laveau makes zombies."*

Thousands echoed John; the freak audience danced. Some shouted "Miracle!" Others insisted "Witchcraft."

Zombie? She had to think. Marie tried to calm herself. Nattie said you could make souls disappear. Cause someone to join the dead early.

"Zombie. Zombie."

Nattie once told her that evil *houngans* in Haiti knew the trick of making the living appear dead. They could slow breathing, pulse. Loved ones mourned. People were buried alive. The lucky suffocated, while the unlucky survived only to be dug up to become mindless slaves.

"Marie Laveau makes zombies."

Nattie was unfurling the snake from Marie's arm, lowering it back inside the box. "What's he done? What's John done?" Marie asked, nearly hysterical.

Nattie picked up the knife and laid it on the altar. Solicitous, she wrapped a cloth about Marie's bleeding arm. "Remember to trust in Damballah."

"What's he done?"

"I couldn't stop him," Nattie screamed over the tumult. Her face was twisted with anguish. "It be *fa*. Necessary." Then, she shrugged. "He would've done it anyway. With or without me."

"So you helped," Marie whispered, feeling her knees buckle. Horror was behind her. Louis DeLavier raised himself onto the wood planks. He was coming to help her. Just as she stepped toward Louis, John gripped her, turning her around.

"Surprise, ma petite." He tightly clasped her shoulders. "Surprise."

Torch smoke and flames blurred Marie's vision. Focusing, she saw Cecil standing languidly with his hands on his hips. In the shadows someone, something, was beside him.

Cecil pushed his charge forward. It shuffled like an old man. Marie screamed. John held her upright.

The crowd chanted, "Zombie. Zombie."

Marie screamed again, vomit filling her mouth. "No!"

Jacques stood dull-eyed, center stage, in a filthy sailor's uniform. His clothes hung loosely. Having lost his soul, his body seemed shriveled. His skin lacked color and his hair was matted and tangled. His arms dangled. To the crowd, Jacques was the bogeyman come to life. He was the ghost who'd haunted their childhood dreams.

Soulless, spiritless, there was nothing in the world more horrible than Jacques.

Marie kicked and squirmed. John wouldn't let her go.

"Did you think I didn't suspect?" he whispered. "Did you think I didn't know you wanted to run? Hide. That you wanted to escape with Jacques. To steal from me my child?"

Marie whimpered. It was useless to struggle. There was no place to run. She looked across at Ribaud. He was weeping.

Nattie crept up beside her, standing taut and staring at Jacques.

"How?" Marie asked.

"The gills of a fish. Skull powder and grave dust. A simple spell. We sent all the way to Haiti."

"Why did you do this? How could this be necessary?"

Nattie shrugged. "You wouldn't understand."

Marie crooked her neck, staring up at John. His hands were latched onto her skin. "Why?" she asked.

"Because I don't trust you," he said, pinching her nose. "I never trust women named Marie. Besides, I didn't want you to be unfaithful like your Maman. Jacques never made it back to his ship. I captured him outside Grandmère's house."

Marie watched her motionless, deadened husband. To John and Nattie, she murmured, "I wish the crowd had killed us."

"Look," said John, "look at him. Jacques has disappeared. That's my miracle. A miracle as spectacular as Marie Laveau's. The audience loves it."

It was true. There were whistles, shouts, chanting, and applause. The remaining three dancers, sensing the audience's acceptance, pranced, poking at Jacques' face and abdomen. Someone from the audience threw a stone. The sailor rocked off-balance.

One dancer, named Yvette, singsonged, "Maman Marie makes souls disappear. Makes souls disappear."

Marie shuddered. Yvette reminded her of Ziti, just as careless and jealous. Marie spat.

Yvette wiped her cheek on her red sleeve. "La, you don't have everything now, Miz Marie." Her hand brushed a stray curl. "You got nothing." She picked up the knife that Marie had dropped.

Skipping back to Jacques, Yvette cried gaily, "Watch. Watch, Widow Paris."

Yvette grabbed Jacques' palm and stabbed it. Jacques didn't flinch.

Ecstatic, the audience roared.

Marie lowered her chin to her chest; she stared at her swelled belly, crying.

"Don't worry, Marie," Nattie said softly. "He can't feel anything. Can't even talk. He be already dead."

"What kind of woman are you?"

"Same as you. I do what has to be done." Grunting, Nattie stroked the snake inside the box. "Pity. Jacques was a handsome man. A shame he loved you."

Marie forced herself to look at Jacques. Yvette had angled his face toward hers. Marie would've felt better if Jacques' eyes were accusing; instead they were wide, dilated. Could he think? Did he know what was happening to him? Where had his soul gone?

Yvette, lowering Jacques' pants, flapped his cock.

John was laughing; Marie could feel raucous tremors through his hands and arms on her shoulders.

Everyone's life was forfeit. Hers. Grandmère's. Poor Jacques'.

She had to help him. Maybe if she could get him away from John, she could restore his soul, find a spell that would bring her husband back. Louis could help her—if only she could find a way to distract John.

Marie twisted her torso. Louis was sitting on the edge of the stage, watching her. Wordless, she implored Louis with her gaze, straining every particle of her will: Help me to help Jacques. Louis must have understood, for he nodded. Marie tried to smile, but a spirit was entering her. Her neck arched. *Her body felt weighted, pulled down toward the ground.* John was struggling to hold her up.

"No," she moaned. "Not now." Marie could see the floor rushing to meet her. She vaguely heard chanting. Why did spirits have to enter her now? Why now, when she wanted to be in possession of herself? When she needed her wits about her to save Jacques? John released her. Her words slurred. "It isn't fair."

Damballah—"li Grand Zombi"—Damballah, the snake god, was taking possession.

When Marie next opened her eyes, she was stretched out on the platform, seeing Jacques in two dimensions, two depths of being. She saw the surface Jacques, hollow-eyed, fleshy, and limp. His limbs seemed unrelated, as though no spark connected them with motion. He was a perfect puppet or slave.

John had continued with the performance. He was ordering Jacques about: "Left . . . right . . . two steps forward . . . two back." Indiscriminately, John would hit Jacques and the frail body would stagger back, then right itself. John would hit him again. Catcalls of "Let me hit him," "He'll feel my fist right enough," ballooned out of the audience. "I'll knock sense into him." "Give me ten of him for my fields." Shrieks rent the air.

Marie rose.

"Maman Marie. Marie Laveau."

Marie saw a faint light seeping out of Jacques. As she moved forward, the others fell back. John didn't bar her way. She rested her hands on Jacques' shoulders, and through and beyond his eyes she saw the man inside, weeping. Jacques was conscious of everything around him. He'd felt each of John's blows. He felt shame at his nakedness. "Oh, my love," Marie murmured. She hugged Jacques, and Damballah let her glimpse and feel the tragedy of a soul without will, a mind without power. Jacques was like a gull clipped of beak and wings. He was like a fish stranded onshore, gasping while the sea was visible. Marie moaned and pressed her lips against Jacques' chest, his cheek. She stroked his body, tenderly, lovingly. With her touch, she tried to make him feel the way a wife should make a husband feel. With her touch, she begged his forgiveness.

The crowd was silenced. Awestruck. Women wept openly. Men envied the romantic display. Marie's kisses were both erotic and maternal. Ribaud's drums had softened.

Marie felt a sweet glory inside her. Membe was guiding her, offering Jacques salvation.

"Sail across the River Jordan. Sail across the sea."

"Yes," Marie whispered, understanding. Jacques' death was an *illusion. Killing him now would set him free. He'd be beyond John's power.*

"Lead him to the water, Marie. Lead him to the shore. Take him beneath the waves."

Membe and Damballah left her, and Marie was in full possession of herself. She glanced covertly at John. John still believed she was possessed. Marie kept sliding her hands down Jacques' body, pretending to be entranced. Nattie had lied. Jacques saw, felt, and knew everything. He was trapped in his body. Dirt streaked his face. His nails were broken, and dried blood was on his hands. She could imagine him trying to scratch himself out of his coffin, trying to overcome the terror of being buried alive. She held him close and whispered in his ear. "I know what to do, Jacques. I'll take you home to the sea." Calculating, Marie guessed the harbor was a quarter mile at most. The hard part would be maneuvering Jacques off the platform, away from John. Once in the crowd, she and Jacques would be relatively safe. She felt confident she could use the crowd's energy to propel her and Jacques to the harbor. Once on the shoreline, the crowd would expect her to walk on water again; she'd take Jacques with her. Jacques would sink, drown . . . find peace at the bottom of the sea, and his spirit would fly to another world where spells weren't corrupted. Marie felt a strength of purpose. Her eyes signaled Louis. He rose expectantly. Guiding Jacques slowly toward Louis, she kept murmuring, "I know you can hear me, Jacques, I know it. To sea . . . we're going to sea, Jacques." Jacques' steps were sluggish, as though he were already walking through foam-capped waves. Marie prayed their luck would hold. If only Jacques could move faster. She waved at the crowd. They cheered. Ribaud increased the rhythm of his drums.

John was shifting his weight from foot to foot. He was furious, stunned. He didn't understand what Marie was doing. He'd expected her to be cowed, and here she was using his trick against him. Using Jacques to win the crowd.

Marie could feel John's confusion. "Come along, Jacques," she murmured. "Hurry, dear Jacques." She concentrated on getting Jacques to Louis. Louis would help them down into the crowd. The audience would gather round, claiming Jacques. Marie could picture the processional, thousands helping her to lead Jacques into the water, where drowning would set him free. John's plan would be thwarted. He wouldn't be able to manipulate and torture Jacques. "Yes, yes," Marie nearly shouted. This would be her greatest miracle.

"What do you think you're doing?" John was yelling at her. Marie kept walking, tugging Jacques across the stage, praying, "Dear God . . . dear God . . . dear Damballah God." The few feet might as well have been miles. "Membe help us. Please."

"What do you think you're doing?"

John blocked their path. Marie was trembling. Jacques stumbled to a stop, his shoulders rounded, his gaze transfixed on his feet.

"You're trying to steal him from me, aren't you?" He raised his fist.

"Don't hit me, John. The crowd wouldn't like it."

"You're threatening me." His hand fiercely clutched hers. "Don't you understand, Marie. Making Jacques my slave is your punishment. When you misbehave, I'll torture him. His torment is your fault. You should've obeyed me. You shouldn't have cheated me."

Marie slowly raised her eyes.

John saw Marie's defiance. He saw a woman before him. He realized that the girl, Marie, had become a Voodoo Queen, but he hadn't become a King. Before thousands, she was stealing his triumph, his power. He wouldn't be able to use Jacques as he'd planned. He could see Marie was immune to that now. And worse, he felt she was on the verge of another triumph.

And then John knew what he should do. With a huge shout, he cried, "You won't cheat me again," and lunged for the knife on the altar.

Louis rushed forward too late. Marie moved too late. The audience roared too late. John plunged the knife in Jacques' heart. Blood squirted everywhere, splattering John's face and chest, staining Marie's gown. Without making a sound, Jacques slid to the floor.

It was a still-life tableau. The body was oddly crumpled, blood draining onto the wood and off the stage. John looked menacing, his knife glinting, dripping red in the firelight. Marie raised her hands high in supplication. The crowd misinterpreted her gesture as triumphant. No one heard Marie's desperate plea, "Damballah, help him. Please."

The crowd, thrilled by the sensation, went wild, chanting, "Maman Marie, Voodoo Queen. Marie Laveau, Voodoo Queen."

~

Who would have thought that I, an old white man, would be sitting at the bedside of a black woman watching her die? My wife, Brigette, if she were alive, would say I was a voyeur, preparing myself for my own death.

I sit here writing, turning now and again to check the gentle rise and fall of her chest. She is sleeping. I am in love.

When she wakes, she will rub my bald skull for luck again. Many times she offered to give me a charm. "A full head of hair you'll have," she said. I refused. Stroking the top of my head gave her so much pleasure.

When she wakes, she will tell me more about her life, and I will write it down.

Truth is in the imagination, and in my imagination I have been everything and everyone to her.

She's dying. She tells me she's immortal. But what good does that do me?

She is my own. My lovely Marie.

•

—LOUIS DELAVIER, JUNE 16, 1881, AFTERNOON
(From Louis DeLavier's journal)

F or weeks, Marie slept. She drifted in and out of dreams.
She dreamed Jacques was a bird, a seagull sweeping before the crest of a tailwind. He was feathered a light gray, screeching uproariously and gliding briskly through a cloudless summer sky. He sailed east over the

369

Atlantic while below him slave ships sailed west. Sailors shot arrows from the top mast. He dove and skittered through the air like a startled albatross, then pressed on with amazing speed. His wings were touched with the kiss of a rainbow. He landed on the Dahomeyan coast and thousands of snakes slithered down to greet him, as his wings became arms and he rose up from the sand, a man.

Another time, Marie dreamed Jacques was a fish diving among green foam-capped waves, his scales glistening like diamonds and his eyes bright and searching. He moved nonstop, swimming beyond sunken derelict vessels and swirling octopi and escaping the gaping mouth of a white whale. When he reached a shimmering pink reef, his fins turned into legs and he stepped onto an African plain. Membe and two lions stepped forward to greet him.

In another dream, Marie had a raft and Jacques was beside her, pressing light kisses on her forehead as she blew air to fill up the sails—air sweetly scented with hyacinths and all her love for Jacques. She blew and blew until finally Jacques became part of the sail, his spirit billowing ahead of her. And as they approached the shore he became ever lighter, less substantial, until he was but a gossamer wisp waving before her. And when their raft touched the beach he cut loose from her, soaring away over the treetops of his domain.

Damballah was inspiring her dreams, and when she wasn't dreaming she was sleeping, lulled by a satisfying forgetfulness. Often she heard voices swirling about her. Several times she woke and heard Nattie and John in the next room, arguing. A chair toppled. A door slammed. But always the dreams overtook her.

Once Nattie and John were beside her bed.

Nattie was whispering, "She's been through too much. Why must you be so hard on the girl? She's done all you've asked. Foolishness to demand what she can't give."

John clutched Marie's arms, shouting, "Wake. Wake." His hands were hot, leeching like a fresh parasite. Marie whimpered in her sleep and pulled away.

Finally, her dreaming came to an end—Jacques waved goodbye, and she woke.

"Pretty Marie. Pretty Marie."

Ribaud was bending over her, placing a moist compress on her head.

"Where's—?" She raised herself onto her elbow, searching.

"Dey gone," he said softly. "John's wid a fancy woman, I suspect. I don't know where Nattie be." Tenderly, he lowered her onto the pillow. "Maybe she spelled herself dead. She ought to, if she know what's good." He tucked the covers neatly.

Marie wet her lips.

Ribaud gave her slivers of ice. "You been ill," he said. "Had me worried good."

"Jacques?"

"No need to talk now. Rest. Gain your strength." His feathered cap was lopsided and dirty. One candle flickered on the bedstand. Rows of shadow feathers lined the ceiling.

"What happened, Ribaud?" Pleading, Marie pressed his hand against her cheek.

"Well, I guess it won't hurt to say it all now." Eyes cloudy, Ribaud cleared his throat and removed his hat, fingering and staring at the sweaty brim.

"Damballah hit you hard. Sudden. You were squirming, wriggling like a fish on a tackle line. Nattie and John tried to hold you. Dey were afraid you'd be hurt, I guess." He pointed at her abdomen. "Or else de child. While dey were struggling wid you, a white man took Jacques."

"Louis?"

"Yeah."

"Did John see?"

"Naw. I don't know. If he did, he decided it didn't matter."

"I dreamed Louis was here." She remembered him pressing a sweet kiss on her cheek and feeding her thin soup.

"He been here almost every night, sneaking in after John's gone. He'd cajole you into eating. You'd purr for him like some kitten, but you wouldn't talk.

"Louis wanted to know what to do wid Jacques' body . . . didn't think you'd want a Christian burial . . . went ahead anyway. Father Christophe helped. De body was rotting. Dey put him in St. Louis Cemetery. In one of dem tombs." His brows contracted. "Dat all right. We figured when you were well you could say words over him. Father Christophe did Catholic rites. Dat all right?"

Marie sighed. The objects in the room lost shape. Jacques was all right. He would have wanted a Christian burial. Yet it didn't matter where or how he was buried. Jacques' soul was across the sea and it had been she who, dreaming, guided him there.

Marie closed her eyes, swallowing tears. "I'm tired, Ribaud."

"Do you want me to find DeLavier? I'll do whatever you want."

"I want to sleep."

"You're sleeping your life away. De baby's too."

"What if I am?" she murmured into the pillow. "Sleep is good."

Marie settled beneath the covers.

Ribaud applied another compress. "You'll come awake soon. See if you don't, pretty Marie." He sat, crossing his short legs over his bucket of writhing snakes. "I'll keep an eye on you. Hurt don't quit just because you sleep."

In another day, Marie's body reasserted itself. Whimpering, she stirred. Her head felt thick.

Outside, she heard the whir of a robin and a blue jay's cry. She stumbled to the window, thinking she'd spirited herself back to the bayou. She flung open the shutters and shivered with disappointment. Same dirty streets and cobblestones marked with mud and horse dung. Same low-slung city shacks, rotting together.

She heard a flutter of wings. Twisting her head, she saw a crow with a wide head and black beak perched on the roof. "Get," she shouted. "Go on, get out of here." The bird cawed and flew. Cathedral bells bellowed.

Marie heard scuffling and turned.

Ribaud was digging himself out from under his makeshift bed in the corner. "Now you gone and done it. Nattie and John heard you for sure."

"Let them hear."

Ribaud cocked his head.

Marie blushed. "What day is it? Sunday?" The bells were howling like spiteful ghosts.

"No. Friday."

"How many Fridays have I been asleep?"

"I don't know," grumbled Ribaud, removing his hat and scratching his head. "Four. Dis would be four."

"So long it's been." She turned back to the window. "It's Good Friday then." The sky was clear blue, and sunshine streaked the cobblestones. "Christ's crucifixion."

"I don't know 'bout Christ." Ribaud plopped on his hat. "I know dey're planning to hang de last two men from de trial. Someding about thieves and saints."

"What are you talking about?"

"Two of dose men who figured you wanted dem to murder whites, to lead a revolt. Crazy folk." He clicked spit between his teeth. "Deserve to be hanged. Everybody knows a rebellion don't work if whites have all de guns."

Marie cursed at herself. She'd promised to help them and she hadn't done anything. Were they all dead now? "The women? The children? What happened to them, Ribaud?"

"I don't know." He fixed on his toes. "De children I heard were sold to plantations in Georgia and Alabama. Most of de women were sold as cooks on merchant ships."

Marie trembled. She had no doubt the women were mainly "cooking" on their backs.

"All this happened when I was dreaming?"

"Some of it. Some happened before. Dey been killing dose folks for months now. Dey just got dese two left."

Moaning, Marie covered her face with her hands. She hadn't helped any of them.

"So you're up," said John, sailing into the room.

John's wide smile hurt her. His goodwill snapped at her bones.

"We thought you were a zombie. Didn't we, Nattie?" John chuckled. "All in fun," he said. "All in fun, Marie. I'm glad you're up and looking well. Your followers were worried. Silly people thought you were cursed."

"I am."

"In your mind. All in your mind. Pregnant women are given to fancies. Need coddling." Solicitous, he led her back to bed. "Rest, that's all you need," John crooned. "Rest. Nattie thinks the baby's almost due."

Marie looked at the woman. Some of her spirit was gone. Her skin was parched and her hips thinner. Marie almost felt sorry for her, standing lost with her back against the door. John radiated health.

"Of course, we're only guessing about the babe," said John. "Ribaud fought stubbornly to nurse you. Says he fed you well enough. Wouldn't let us near you. I admire loyalty." Grinning, he knocked off Ribaud's hat. The spell man scowled. "Nattie's loyal to Damballah. She just can't figure out why Damballah isn't loyal to her."

Nattie pinched her lips shut.

John sat at Marie's bedside. Marie flinched. "I'm not angry, you know." John's mood and hands were expansive. "Well, perhaps some. But I clearly showed you your place. Now, didn't I? You won't be running off with Jacques anytime soon. Quite impossible, isn't it?"

"Yes, John."

His hands caressed her thighs. "The entire city is outraged by us. They love us. At least for now. I can't go anywhere without someone recognizing me. It's quite remarkable."

"Women fling demselves at him," said Nattie sarcastically.

"Yes. Murder stimulates desire."

"Ribaud says two men are to be hanged."

John was caught off guard. He leaned back and crossed his arms over his chest. "Yes. In Cathedral Square."

"I want to go see them," Marie said hurriedly. "I know them. At least I think I do. In prison, several of the men made me promise to save them."

"You can't save anyone."

"I know." Marie curled her feet beneath her. "To say goodbye, then. That's all."

John chipped hard wax from the base of the candle. "You'll raise their hopes. You'd do better to ask Nattie for poison. Cheat the hangmen." He cupped her chin.

Marie shifted away.

"Nattie learned all she knows about roots and such from your Grandmère. She learned well, didn't she?"

"Grandmère never taught her how to hurt. Grandmère never taught her about zombies."

"How would you know?"

Marie set her lips stubbornly.

"It be true," said Nattie. "You know dat, John. A man in Haiti taught me."

John leaned forward and nuzzled Marie's neck and shoulders.

Marie dug her nails into the mattress. "The men believe in me. Let me go."

"Ah, comforting your flock. Good deeds." He reached out and snapped the candle in half. "I don't want you to go."

"It doesn't mean anything."

"I won't beat you. It might hurt Damballah's littlest Queen."

"This once." Gently, she reached out and touched his lace cravat. "I won't ask another favor."

"What do you think, Ribaud?" John called over his shoulder, bemused by Marie's audacity. "Should I let her go?"

"Besides, this journalist"—she stuttered—"DeLavier, wants to talk with me. Print my story."

"Why didn't you say so before?"

"I forgot."

"Bring him here."

"Yes, yes. I will. But I have to meet him first. In Cathedral Square. For the hangings. I promised." She knew John knew she was lying. Marie buried her face in her hands. There were more outrageous tones from the bells, a biting cacophony.

John thought how much like a child Marie looked in her white cotton gown, lying in the middle of the bed with her legs nestled under her, her hair, black silk, fanning beneath her and across her breasts. Sleep had drained some of the harshness out of her, made her skin rosy and flush. Her Maman, occasionally, had had the same innocence. The same inept lies. Marie's hands were so small, so delicate. Everything about her seemed breakable. He could see the young girl peeping out of the woman. He hated it; it stirred yearnings in him, was stirring desire in him now. The longer he stayed with a woman, the less he saw the girl. He wondered why.

"I know about DeLavier being here too. Visiting while you slept. Touching you. Feeding you," he said bitterly. He pressed his finger against Marie's larynx, choking her unexpectedly. Then, just as abruptly, he released her.

"Go," John said, moving away from the bed. "Go. Ribaud, go with her. Keep her safe." He brushed past Nattie, out the bedroom door.

Marie shuddered, swallowing against the pain in her throat. Ribaud stroked her hair.

Nattie, shaking her head, followed John.

"Why did you do it?"

John was pouring himself a drink. "Publicity is good. Newspaper men are influential. Especially if they're called DeLavier. I think he's in love with her." He drank. "Or maybe he just hated his cousin." John poured more rum.

"Why?" Nattie wanted to know what charm she was missing. She'd seen John's hatred, seen him ready to snap Marie's larynx, then seen his face suffused with love. His expression had been fleeting yet tender. Nattie was envious.

John looked at Nattie. Seeing her wrinkles, the crepe neck, swollen fingers, and cloudy eyes, he knew he'd look the same without his drug. Nights when it was quiet, when he let himself, he could hear his bones and flesh, dying.

"Why?"

"I pitied her. I pitied her innocence. Does that answer your question?" John slammed his bottle down. "I pitied her because in ten years she'll begin to look just like you. An old, ugly crow. In ten years, she'll act like you. Sly. Frustrated and angry because she's guilty as sin."

Nattie stepped forward and slapped his face.

They stared at one another, wrestling silently with their eyes like old souls. Finally, Nattie collapsed in the chair, hitching her knees toward her chest. Innocence was seductive. She'd lost all her innocence long before she met John. Poverty had destroyed it early.

John swallowed another drink; the liquor was much too rough

and hard on an empty stomach. Scowling, he felt his insides burning. He seemed to have lost satisfaction. This past year he'd accomplished more than he ever imagined. He had power and loyalty because people feared him. He enjoyed their fear, liked the smell and sweat of it. Yet he wasn't satisfied; if anything, he felt a wider chasm within him. He felt the need for *more,* more anything, something. As a slave he'd learned not to expect happiness. Yet he always expected satisfaction and pleasure when he achieved his goals. That would be fair, wouldn't it? Instead, the boy in him felt betrayed again. He'd grown old without being young. Now he was helping leach the youth out of Marie. John took another swig, using his tongue to wash the rum against his teeth and sting his gums.

"In ten years," John said, "Marie won't have any innocent dreams. Not a single damn one."

"In ten years, Marie will have forgotten how to dream." Nattie rocked herself and moaned. "Won't be no hope. Won't be nothing left in her. You'll have stolen everything."

John smiled. "In ten years, my daughter will be almost grown. Almost a Voodoo Queen."

Marie was glad to be out of the house. John's tangled emotions unnerved her. Right now she felt good, like a newly born butterfly. It didn't make sense. Trudging alongside Ribaud, she rejoiced in the sun warming her brown skin and watched seagulls circling in from the Gulf. Not a cloud: only yellow sun, blue sky, and white birds. She didn't even mind people stopping and staring, whispering tall tales and lies. Or the children hooting and hollering, dodging in front and in back of her. Ribaud chased them away. But the children always dared one another onward, thrilling at the danger of being so near Marie Laveau.

An almost perfect day. "Almost" because she was going to a hanging. She felt an almost perfect happiness. "Almost" because she expected to fail at saving the condemned men's lives. She hadn't saved her own life. Or Jacques'.

Marie pressed her face into the breeze. She wouldn't want to have to die on such a crisp, clear day. Christ had done it. "Sky didn't get ugly," Grandmère once said, "till His spirit started seeping from His bones, rising like smoke to the heavens."

Good Friday.

She'd never understood what good it'd done for Christ to die. Or why His Father made the dying hard. Didn't make sense. How could someone else's hurt make you happy? Maybe all religions were strange. She didn't understand Damballah either. She just wanted to do a simple act of Christian charity for Grandmère. For Jacques. Make the black men feel better before they died.

She stopped, feeling pain in her womb.

"You all right?" asked Ribaud.

"Yes. Let's go on." Nervously, Marie glanced back.

Curious people were tracing her steps. Shopkeepers had closed their doors, men emptied saloons, whores stopped haggling, slaves quit working, all hoping they'd witness another Voodoo sensation. Marie felt a tearing in her lower abdomen. The child was scratching herself out.

"Look," said Ribaud, somberly slipping off his hat.

Cathedral Square was slightly less wild than it had been during carnival. People wore their Sunday best, but they pushed and shoved for better vision. They all wanted to see a dead man's face up close. Boys and girls were perched on their fathers' shoulders. Families stood in wagons. Men and women on horseback trotted ruthlessly ahead, while enterprising mulattoes sold lemonade and fritters. The Catholic cathedral was background for the scaffold.

"Ribaud, find Louis DeLavier. Tell him"—she crinkled her brows—"tell him Marie Laveau wants to see the prisoners."

"You going to be safe?"

"Yes." People were still keeping their distance. But a few were itching, restlessly excited. "I'll be safer when Louis is here." Her foolish good humor slipped away.

The scaffold was painted black. You couldn't tell there was a false bottom. Two T-shaped poles, resembling dead, branchless trees, pierced the scaffold. The two nooses swaying from the poles looked harmless, oddly abandoned. A child could've left them after tiring of the game of leaping and swinging from one rope to the other.

She waited.

It was hard to breathe. Marie wiped sweat from her neck and head. She was crazy to come. She knew nobody was going to be resurrected. Not the two prisoners. Not Maman. Not Jacques. Was Christ more powerful than Damballah? Did that account for white people's power?

"Marie."

"Thank you for coming," she said.

"It's nothing." Louis reached for her cheek, then guiltily lowered his hand. "Come, let's move away from here. I have my carriage."

379

He propelled Marie through the crowd, elbowing away the curious, the vain whispers of "witch," "nigger lover."

"We'll have more privacy here," he said gently.

Marie hesitated, remembering the first time she'd seen the DeLavier carriage. She almost expected Antoine to step out, arrogant and bold, and for lovely Brigette to lean out the door. Louis offered his hand; supporting herself, she stepped inside. She smelled stale lavender perfume. Curtains shut out the world; sounds were muted. Marie felt her tension lifting. She settled back against the soft cushion, folding her hands over the baby. Louis was across from her, watching. She wondered if he still thought her pretty.

"I—"

"Thank—"

They both laughed. "You go first," he said.

"No, you." She smiled.

He touched her abdomen. "You're more beautiful than ever." Louis stroked circles on her belly, and Marie felt enormous comfort. "When's it due?"

"Soon."

"Brigette was pregnant, you know."

"I know."

"I always thought you knew." Earnest, he leaned forward, his hands clasped between his knees. "I thought that was why you sent me away." He paused. "Was it? Was that the reason?"

"Yes," she lied. "That was part of it."

He leaned back in his seat. "I thought so. You really are kind."

Marie nodded absently. No one should be allowed to have such brown eyes as his. Their glancing sweetness wounded her.

Louis grabbed her wrist, holding her cool hand, tracing the wrinkled design in her palm. He could feel his heart beating in the center of Marie's hand. Slowly, she pulled her hand away. Louis sighed. He ran his fingers over his skull.

"Thank you for saving Jacques."

"But I didn't. There wasn't much I could do." He shrugged. "I'm a failure at rescue."

"That isn't so." Marie felt anger welling again. "You saved Jacques' soul. Damballah explained it to me. Jacques wasn't dead, but his will was stolen. By murdering him, John only freed Jacques' spirit from his body. Without a proper burial, Jacques would've gone on wandering, lost from his ancestors. Now he's home in Guinea. Damballah told me in my dreams."

"But we buried him with Catholic rites. There wasn't much else we could do. You were sleeping, and Father Christophe and I had no idea what you would want."

"It didn't matter. You were burying the body for me. John would've let Jacques rot. His spirit would've been in torment. You and Father Christophe were demonstrating love and charity. You made the proper homage to his soul. You connected his spirit to loving. It was enough. Damballah did the rest."

"I wanted to save Jacques' life. I didn't know I was helping to save his soul."

Marie leaned against the squab cushions, murmuring, "Damballah kept his promise to me. Jacques returned home safely. I always dreamed he'd return home to me . . . I never dreamed home to mean Guinea. It's a shame that black folks can only be free in a spirit world."

"You're free."

"Am I? John's lunacy holds me. And when the citizens tire of me or are no longer afraid of me, they'll enslave me or kill me. There's never any freedom when people need you to work miracles and you feel you have to try."

"Is that why you're here? To save these men?"

Marie laughed harshly. "You don't believe in me, do you?"

"Yes," he said simply. "I do."

"Don't."

Louis looked down. It hurt him to think that Marie had lost her innocence. But he'd already guessed that someone with her outrageous powers couldn't remain innocent for long. The audiences, with their sins, conspired against it. Even Christ had been racked by flaws: doubt, guilt, anger. Marie could be allowed her bitterness and cynicism. But he missed the girl. "Do you want to see Jacques' grave?"

"No. He isn't there." Marie pressed her fingers to her eyelids.

"I want to see the two men. The prisoners." Her eyes brimmed with tears. "They believe in me too. They shouldn't, but they do."

"I'll arrange it, then. The prison's not far. We could walk but—"

"Let's ride." She wasn't feeling well. The sun was too bright. She didn't want to be among a hostile, curious crowd.

"We'll just make it. They're due to hang within the hour." Louis called out, "Prison gates," to the driver and Ribaud leaped up beside the colored coachman.

Louis turned back to Marie. "Hush," he said. "There's a little time. Lean back. Close your eyes."

"Thank you, Louis. For everything," she murmured, syncopating the horse's *clip-clop* with her heartbeat. Her body felt drowsy; her legs seemed weighted with stones. For a few minutes she fell blessedly asleep.

Louis hated to wake her. He caressed her face and resisted the urge to kiss the pulse beating in her throat. Though the prison was only a thousand feet to the right of the cathedral and behind the scaffold, the coach made slow progress. The entire city seemed to have flooded into the square, anxious to see the men die. Louis heard Ribaud and the coachman, Samuel, yelling at the pedestrians. Their curses had no effect. Louis felt a glad guilt. Isolated in the carriage, he was free to imagine a life with Marie. He could imagine her always beside him, sweetly sleeping. Yet when he'd seen her walk on water, he realized what a fool he'd been. It seemed right that no man should have her. She was powerful enough alone. Louis could only guess what hold John had over her.

The carriage jolted to a stop. Louis wondered if Marie had had time enough to dream as they traversed the square. Did she dream of him? Louis called her name; Marie stirred.

"The scene won't be very pretty," he warned.

"You forget—I've been here before." Marie straightened her blouse and skirt, trying to look important instead of scared.

Two military guards shielded the prison door. Louis spoke softly to them. Then he put his arm around Marie, whispering, "Don't say anything. Nothing at all." The guards let them pass.

Marie shivered as she walked back into the prison. Light-headed, she closed her eyes. All the sensations of being a prisoner came back to her. She remembered the rats, the stench of urine and excrement, the bitter taste of death. Eyes closed, Marie pretended she was elsewhere, sleeping, dreaming.

Some guards were playing cards; a florid gentleman sat in a chair with his feet upon the desk.

"Captain," said Louis, "this woman wants to see the prisoners."

"Isn't she—?"

"Yes."

"No visitors. The mayor—"

"I had dinner with him last night. He's a compassionate man."

"Look here, DeLavier. You're not going to cow me." The captain sputtered with indignation. "Just because your family's rich—"

"Of course not," said Louis amiably, "I wouldn't dream of telling you your job. But if those two men were Catholics, you'd let them see their priest."

"Of course."

"Well, then. Marie Laveau has come to administer last rites."

The captain was livid. "Get out of here. Before I have you thrown out." Two guards positioned themselves behind Louis.

"I'm a reporter," Louis said, still amiable, flicking imaginary dirt from his nails. "You can't throw me out."

"Security."

"Security be damned!" Louis shouted. "How would you like your name in the *Daily Picayune*? 'Captain of the Guards Fears Reporter and Pregnant Girl.' Interesting reading."

"She's not an ordinary girl."

"Are you telling me you believe in Voodoo, captain? Why else would you refuse my request? What harm is there in allowing Marie Laveau to visit?"

The two men looked at each other. Louis kept his hands at his side; the captain rubbed his thick neck. "Five minutes. They're going to be hanged in five minutes."

"I appreciate it, captain." Louis touched Marie's arm; startled, she opened her eyes, then followed at his side.

The prison was as dark as she remembered it. On the right wall of the cell hung a wooden crucifix. A plate of untouched grits on the floor was crusted with ants. A hole dug in the dirt floor held an overflow of excrement.

One of the men was flat on his back on the cot, looking already dead. The other man, looking like a much-abused field hand, was standing near the barbed window, eyeing the distant scaffold. He was quite young. Maybe eighteen.

The young man at the window saw her. "Maman Marie." He moved forward, reaching his hands through the bars, touching Marie. He was dirty, wearing the same clothes he'd worn during the trial months before. He was the one named Lee; she remembered him.

"You came to save me. I knew you'd come." Crying, Lee slid his hands down the prison bars. Marie knelt, caressing him between the bars. He rubbed his head back and forth against her hands like a scared pup. Marie felt she should've brought poison.

"Is it true?" The man from the cot was sitting up. His clothes were loose; his body seemed shrunken, collapsed in upon itself. He couldn't stand. "You've come to save us?" His head was gray, his skin yellow like Jacques' had been. His tone was restrained, skeptical.

The youth had stopped crying. Eyes wide, squeezing Marie's hand, he repeated, "Say it be true. Say it. Please say it."

The older man cackled. "I don't believe in no God or Damballah. I killed myself a white man 'cause things white deserve dyin'."

"Shut up, Cholly," screamed Lee, pounding his head against the bars. "Shut up." He kissed Marie's hand. "Say it be true. Say it. Please say it. Master Winslow, he was good to me. I didn't kill nobody. I took his rum to the harbor."

"Both of us did," said Cholly.

"Every Saturday," said the youth. "I never drank any. Ask Master Winslow, he'll tell you. I never killed nobody."

"A big dumb slave. That's all he was. Both of us goin' to die."

"It was his fault. Cholly's fault."

"Shut up, boy."

"Cholly's been like a stone round my neck ever since. I'd a been treated better if not for him."

"Kissin', yes sirrin' up to white mens," Cholly growled. "Holdin' up your backside for dem to prick. You ain't no kinda man."

"But I didn't do nothin' to die for."

"You ain't done nothin' worth livin' for either. You low-down meat."

Marie wanted to yell at Cholly to shut up. She remembered his taunting during Marianne's torture. She stroked Lee's head.

"But you'll die with me if I have to kill you myself," said Cholly from the cot. "You hear me?"

Lee was blubbering. "He's crazy. He's crazy."

Marie reached out to Lee, saying, "I'll save you."

"Damballah will give you the power," he replied wonderingly.

"Yes. Damballah will give me the power."

The older man snorted and lay back down in the sun. "Save your powers. No use savin' two niggers when neither one of us believes in you."

"I believe," said Lee fervently.

"You didn't before."

"Don't believe him, Maman Marie. Don't believe him."

"You don't believe in me, Cholly, yet they say you killed in my name."

"I didn't kill in nobody's name but my own." Cholly had moved so fast, Marie felt breathless. He was pounding his fist against the metal bars, pounding and choking, shouting. "Yes, we were watching your ceremony—"

"We were running late. It was Cholly's idea to see you. I knew it'd turn out to be no good. I knew Master Winslow be angry."

"Shut up, you." Cholly was on his knees, twisting his face, trying to get his whole being to squeeze through the bars to Marie.

"Here, now," said Louis.

"Shut up." Cholly's fingers were tearing at Marie's skirt. "I wanted to see a black woman who could get away with somethin'. I wanted to see a black woman who wasn't a slave or a whore. I wanted to see the woman in you, not some Damballah. It made me proud just to watch you, singin', dancin', and not any white person stoppin' you.

"White folks stopped me often enough. I was born free, here in this city, but it didn't much matter when Master Winslow needed another slave. I had me a business, shoeing horses, making reins. Had me a free wife too. A daughter. Winslow said he'd claim they were runaways unless I stayed with him and never tried to see them again.

"You riled up folks good with your snake and babblin'. I thought I heard my daughter callin', and I knew I had to see her. She was sayin', 'Daddy, come home. Daddy, come home.' "

Lee interrupted. "Cholly said we'd say we were stuck. Say the crowd wouldn't let our wagon through. That's how we was gonna explain to Master why we so late."

"Yes," said Cholly, without looking at Lee, still staring at Marie. "We drove to the colored quarter and I saw another man puttin' his hands to my livery business like I'd never been there. Like I'd never built that business with the sweat of my own two hands. When we got to the house, my own house, it was boarded up. I peeked between planks and nothing was inside. Not my chair. Not my wife's sofa. Not the carriage for the baby."

"He was hootin' and hollerin' awful."

"My wife wouldn't never leave."

"We went back to the stable," Lee droned.

"We went back to the stable and I asked that black bastard handlin' my tools, stokin' with my fire irons, where was my wife?"

"And child," said Lee.

"And he told me they'd been sold upriver." Cholly was trembling, sobbing his soul out, banging his head against the bars.

Marie stooped down. "Hush," she said, stroking Cholly's face, wiping away tears, crying herself and pressing her forehead lightly against his.

"You poor man," Louis murmured.

"Don't you say anythin'. Not anythin'," said Cholly, glaring at Louis so venomously that Louis stepped back from the shock of it. "I'll kill you. I wanted to kill somebody then. No sense killin' the blacksmith. He was black, same as me. Tryin' to make a living. I wanted to kill Master Winslow, but I couldn't wait."

"So he killed another white man. First one we saw," said Lee, shocked anew. "Jumped down from the cart and hit him. The man fell hard and split his head open on a trough handle."

"I ain't sorry for it," whispered Cholly. "You understand me, don't you?"

Marie's two hands fitted over his hands, grasping the bars. "I'm sorry. And, yes, I understand."

Cholly's shoulders sagged. "I wouldn't have done it. But the bargain wasn't kept. I'd been a free man. White man was supposed to leave me alone. When the bargain wasn't kept, I still went along, tryin' to be a good nigger. Shoein' Master Winslow's horses when all along he was breakin' another bargain with me. I shoulda killed him when he first came for me."

Lee scuttled over to Marie, extending his hand. "Save me. I ain't done nothin'. I don't plan to do nothin'. Save me, Maman Marie. I know my master, and I don't plan on hurting nobody never. Cholly deserves hanging. He's a crazy man. One no-good nigger."

Marie pulled away. Louis was beside her, helping her to rise.

"Maman Marie, save me. You got to save me. I didn't do nothin'. Nothin' at all."

Marie felt pity for Lee, twisted and ugly though he was. Cholly stirred her sympathy and compassion.

"It's time to go," said Louis, and Marie held on to him gratefully.

Lee was smiling and foolishly grinning. "I'm gonna be saved. Maman Marie," he called. "I'm gonna be saved."

Cholly had already gone back to his cot. He was lying face down, with the sun streaming on his back. He turned and tilted his head. "Save Lee, if you can. Don't worry about me." Cholly took a huge breath. "I don't mind dyin', I guess." He flipped onto his back, staring at the ceiling. "If your snake god wants, tell Him I'll be waitin' on the other side. Lee"—he sneered—"already told me he's gonna see Christ."

"Naw. That's a lie. I didn't say it. I don't believe in nobody but you, Maman Marie. I swear. You're still gonna save me, ain't you?

You're gonna save me. Ain't you, Maman Marie?" Lee's voice echoed in the stone walled chamber, snapping at Marie's heels like an angry dog.

"Can you do it?" Louis asked Marie outside the prison. The air was clean again, the sky bright.

"No."

"Then why'd you say it?"

"Christian charity," she mumbled, walking away.

Louis grabbed her arm. "I don't understand you. I've seen you walk on water. I've seen your miracles. Why can't you do something for those men? You promised Lee. You've got to do something. Why can't you, Marie? Why can't you save them? Why didn't you do something for—"

"Jacques?" Marie snapped, her chest heaving. "Don't you think I'd have given my life if it would've helped? I would've done anything for Jacques. Damn you. I'm just a woman. Do you think I understand what happens to me? Do you think I can control it? I'm just a woman, I tell you. Just another human being."

"Forgive me." Louis stroked his head. "I'll see you home."

"No. I owe them. At least I can watch them die." Marie laughed ruefully and wrapped her arm through Louis'. "I can pray. It might do some good. Might not. Maybe Lee's spirit will whisk back to Guinea. Maybe not. He's as two-faced in the faith as I am."

"I don't understand you."

"That makes two, Louis. But I can't blame Lee for needing both Christ and Damballah. Though Cholly in his lack of faith seems the better man. It's Cholly I'd really like to help."

Ribaud was swinging like a monkey on the carriage door. The coachman was muttering disapproval.

Ribaud jumped down when he saw Marie and Louis. "Gonna see a hanging?" he asked.

"Yes. Bloodthirsty fool." Marie smiled. She couldn't be angry with him. Ribaud's judgments were always harsh and spectacular.

"Let's wait inside the carriage," said Louis. Marie murmured her assent. The crowd's emotions were unstable and bloodthirsty. She'd seen this hunger for violence again and again; it never failed to startle her. She trembled and rubbed her palms over her belly.

Louis bowed his head. Samuel jockeyed the carriage forward for a better view.

The wait was short. The crowd cheered as the two men were led out in chains. Metal links connected their arms and legs. Where would they have run to? Marie wanted to know. The show of force seemed inhumane. The mob would easily have beaten them senseless.

Cholly, composed, came first. Lee, howling, trailed, his chin pressed into his chest. Cholly stared at his audience as avidly as they stared at him. Six stone-faced guards walked beside the two men. The captain guarded the rear.

A soldier played a snare drum. The sound was different from Ribaud's drums, more wrenching and erratic. It prophesied bones snapping and breaking. The noonday sun was intense. Marie, leaning out of the carriage, crooked her arm over her forehead for shade. Miraculously, Cholly saw her motion. He shouted something to Lee. Lee looked up, shouting randomly, "Maman Marie. Maman Marie." He tripped and finished stumbling up the scaffold steps with the captain kicking at him from behind.

Louis was watching Marie, willing her to do something. He shifted his body a little, so their shoulders and arms touched. Marie still smelled of hyacinths. Sweat beaded her neck. Louis felt tempted to bury his face in her sweet mound of breasts pressed against the ledge of the carriage door.

The chains were removed from Lee and Cholly. Riflemen pointed guns at their backs. Cholly didn't flinch when they put the noose about his neck.

Lee screamed, twisting and wriggling his bulk with such force that he had to be hit twice with a club. Shouts sailed up from the crowd. "Coward. The nigger's dancing. Watch him hang." Even Ribaud did a mocking, imitating jig. Marie forced herself not to flinch.

Finally, the noose was adjusted tightly around Lee's neck. Each hanging tree had been adjusted in height so that both men had to stand on tiptoe. They couldn't move forward or back or side to side without killing themselves; the balancing was so fine, they couldn't speak any last words.

In French, then in English, the captain read a document detailing their crime of "murderous rampage" and their punishment of "death by hanging."

His head angled to the right, unblinking, Cholly looked at Marie. She admired his courage. She prayed.

"O Damballah, Father to all the gods, save your sons from death." Self-conscious, she spoke slowly, her words sticking in her throat. "Have mercy. Innocent, your sons deserve to live."

Louis cupped her elbow. She inhaled.

"Damballah. I am unworthy. I don't ask for myself. I ask in the name of your sons, Cholly and Lee." *She could feel Him—feel Damballah coming.* Her voice rumbled, gaining momentum. "And in the name of their ancestors who were stolen from Guinea. O my god, my Damballah, help us to live now." She beat her hands against the door, pounding and making a furor like a bass drum. Ribaud, seeing the power touch Marie, sympathetically smacked his palms on his thighs. The horses shied, and strangers who heard the awful voice from within the carriage moved away.

"Damballah. Come from the earth. The sea. The sky. Damballah, speed to me from Guinea. Save all the lost sons, the daughters. Save us from this New World. Damballah," she cried, crazy with unnamed grief. *Her womb contracted.*

Mesmerized, Louis watched her body flush, then sweat thin streams of tears. Eyes closed, Marie seemed transported to another world.

"Damballah, in the name of Membe." There were small tremors beneath their feet—people screamed. "In the name of Membe, save your children." The earth rumbled again. "Keep your promise to Membe."

You owe her, Marie wanted to say. You owe me.

A flock of seagulls swarmed in from the harbor, buffeting the guards and crowd, swirling like a mad wind. Horses shied and bolted.

Her water broke, dripping beneath her skirt to the rich leather flooring. Marie felt the water draining from in and around her child. *The fourth Marie wanted to be born.*

"Now," bellowed the captain, beating helplessly at the birds. "Hang 'em!"

A guard pushed a lever, opening the platform. Both ropes broke simultaneously and the men fell to the ground. Lee lay unconscious; Cholly's leg was oddly twisted.

The ground stilled and the screeching gulls scattered as quickly as they'd come. The stunned crowd was silent.

Louis cradled Marie protectively. "You did it," he whispered. "You did it."

Gasping, she said, "The child is coming." She buried her face in Louis' cravat while another contraction rocked her body.

The captain of the guard called out, "Hang 'em again!"

Marie spun back to the window. "No!" she shouted.

The six guards were soon clustering about the two men, dragging Lee's unconscious body up the steps. Cholly raged as they bullied him forward on his broken leg. Within minutes, nooses were fitted once again around the men's necks. Since there already was a gaping hole, the two men were pushed forward until they fell through it. For good measure, the captain ordered two guards to throw themselves on the bodies, adding weight and insurance that they were "well and truly hanged." Lee never woke up. Marie saw Cholly's surprised expression, a fleeting moment when the rope hadn't quite finished him, then his sudden shock as a guard grabbed his body and hung with his hands clasped about Cholly's chest and exploding lungs.

"Get me out of here," Marie said to Louis.

"Samuel," Louis shouted. "Get us out."

Samuel clicked his gums. "Hear yah," he cried. The carriage jolted forward.

Ribaud shouted, "Make way. Make way." The crowd easily parted. They'd seen an almost miracle.

Marie huddled in pain.

Inside, Louis was consoling. "Lee died believing you'd saved him."

"It's Cholly I'm worried about. Cholly needed some faith restored."

"You did your best."

"You can't hang a man twice. Isn't there some law?" She moaned. "Louis, the baby's coming."

"Come home with me. Ribaud too, if you want." He held her as the pain crested. "I'll make a place for you. You can raise your child in peace and safety. You needn't return to John."

She shook her head. Contractions eased. "No. To the house on St. Anne."

Louis embraced her. "Stay with me," he whispered insistently.

"I almost saved them," Marie murmured, eyes wide. "Damballah didn't fail me." Her contractions were punishing.

"You did save them. It's against the law to hang a man twice."

She gurgled and moaned, then turned her frightened face toward his. "I'm afraid of dying."

"You won't die."

"What if I die giving birth? Brigette died."

"You won't die."

"Let me rub your skull for luck."

Louis pressed her to him and lovingly murmured, "Marie."

The carriage picked up speed. Louis shouted, "To St. Anne. We go to St. Anne."

Marie clawed at Louis' jacket as another pain seared her abdomen. She said, her voice touched with a gentle wonder, "I did save them. Did you see it? Damballah listened to me." Staring at Louis' waistcoat, she saw snakes shedding their skins.

~

"I don't remember how you got me home. No, to the house on St. Anne. The pain was so great. My own child was ripping the life out of me. Making me pay for my sins with blood.

"I couldn't stand anyone touching me. I yelled at Nattie, 'Get away from me. Keep your hands away from me.' A killer crow. I wanted to birth the baby myself.

"I labored so hard. Then, one moment, everything just stopped. All the contractions, all the hurt. It lasted so long I thought little Marie had died inside me. Decided not to enter this world. I remember thinking, Take me with you.

"For a time, I lost my mind. I was a child again, snipping off the lighted abdomen of a firefly, screaming when the light stuck to my palm. I was hot. Terrified that I couldn't make a whole life. Feeling my baby would be deformed, ugly and blue. Remembering Grandmère calling, 'Who's my baby? My oh-so-pretty baby?' "

"I was beside you, Marie. I never left."

"But it didn't matter. Nothing mattered except the blood running down between my legs. The blood spoke. It talked to me. Membe, Maman, Grandmère were spirits in the blood—coursing down my legs, then (I swear) coursing back inside me. They were telling me it was all right. Telling me blood binds. 'Blood is life, a link to all the dead.' And, then I moaned, scratched at my face and eyes. Because I knew, you see: I knew Grandmère was dead. When my menstrual cycle first began, she'd spoken those same words. Now I realize she'd been talking about a dead Maman and Membe, talking about ancestors. When I heard the three voices, I knew Grandmère had crossed over. She was talking through my blood, and she was dead. I saw my prophecy fulfilled. I saw three bodies, three women. Grandmère was stretched as dead. Another woman was

393

crucified on a tree, her face and breasts pressed against rotting wood; scars striped her back: Maman. Then I saw myself, older, rising out of the lake, three lighted candles waxed to my head and palms. The vision changed. Four. I saw my baby girl sucking at my teat while her chubby fingers tried to grasp the candle's flame.

"My contractions started again with vigor. They were washing over me, sucking me under like the swamp. Filling my eyes, nose, and mouth. Suffocating me. I didn't care anymore. Living had lost meaning. It was dark and I couldn't breathe.

"Grandmère wasn't there to save me. Yet she was there to save me. I saw her in the red blood; I felt her warmth layering me. Heard her singing to wake the dead. They were all there, three Maries—Grandmère, Maman, and the baby, telling me to go on. One generation would get it right."

"And you woke to Easter Sunday."

"Yes. Marie was born. I ripped the caul from her face."

•

—MARIE LAVEAU, JUNE 16, 1881, EVENING
(From Louis DeLavier's journal)

Marie opened her eyes. Her body felt light, lost in the soft bed. It was dawn. Pale sunlight made the room hazy. Ribaud was asleep. One arm was thrown across a pine cradle; his other arm was curled about his bucket of snakes.

Louis was in the chair beside Marie's bed, watching her. He squeezed her hand. "Thank God you're all right. This habit of sleeping is becoming too much."

Marie pressed Louis' hand on the coverlet. "Grandmère is dead," she said, raspy and weak.

Louis shifted his body onto the bed and gazed into her shadowed face. "Are you sure?"

"Yes. She spoke to me." Trembling, Marie stared at the ceiling. Today of all days she must trust her feelings. Her intuition *was* good. A gift from the gods. "Yes. She died this night. It was her voice calling me to wake up." Roaring up through Marie's belly came her pain. Her regret.

"I'm sorry, Marie." Louis tenderly brushed her cheek. "She must've loved you very much."

"I don't think I loved her enough."

Louis gathered her close, his fingers sifting through her hair, whispering "Hush" during the rushing then subsiding tears.

Marie caught his hand and pressed a kiss within it. "Why did you stay?" She laid her head on the pillows as Louis flushed.

"I wanted to make sure you were all right. Besides, John didn't mind. He liked you having a white man as midwife." Self-consciously, he rubbed his head. "You were quite rude to Nattie, you know. I think she felt you owed her to help birth the child. She was quite insistent. She wanted to kill me. She wanted to kill Ribaud too. He helped a great deal."

"I don't remember much. Damballah must've wanted it this way. Was the baby born with a caul?"

"Yes. You ripped it off. You made us wrap the baby in a blue cloth with stars and a snake."

"Membe's dress. I thought it was a dream." Abruptly, Marie asked, "Where's John?" She could feel danger seeping under her skin, chilling her.

"Drinking in the front room. You don't think—? He's been here all night. You don't think he murdered Grandmère?"

"I don't know what I think yet."

Louis rocked his body forward and cupped her hands in his two hands. By degrees, he began a nervous rocking, shifting the weight and balance between their arms. "You know, you terrified me. I thought I was going to lose you like Brigette. You wouldn't let me call a doctor."

"Poor Louis."

"Marie, let me care for you. Let me love you. I'd do it well."

"I know you would. But don't you think I need to learn to care for myself? My child?"

"I'll support her too."

Marie hooded her eyes, saying almost too softly, "I can do it."

Louis felt the hurt keenly. He pulled back, twisting slightly away in the chair. He'd have to reconcile himself to never having Marie. He realized he wanted to treat her like the white women he'd known. He'd failed to see her as anything but helpless, sweet, and weak, when on each count she'd surprised him with evidence of a far different order. Thinking about it now, he realized Brigette hadn't fit his pattern of virtuous, ineffectual womanhood either. Only when Brigette was dying, when he knew her as an adulteress, did he glimpse more of the real Brigette. Given time he wondered if he would have liked her.

"And Nattie?" Marie raised her voice. "Where's Nattie been tonight?"

"I don't know. I mean—"

"She's gone," piped Ribaud, stirring from his awkward sleep, crawling to the foot of the bed. "She slipped out de door when de baby came slipping out of you."

Louis, embarrassed by his lovesickness, went to gaze out the window. Ribaud scooted closer to the bed.

"Find Nattie." Marie clutched the sheets. "Find her, Ribaud."

The spell man cocked his head, noticing how Marie's lips, thin and tightly pressed, made her less pretty.

"Find her."

"I will, Miz Marie." Solemn, he waved his hand over the pine cradle, lightly kicked his bucket beneath it, then left the room.

Louis stayed at the window, watching Ribaud slip out the front door and turn left down the deserted street. Ribaud loved Marie too. Unceasingly, Ribaud had murmured nonsense and applied moist towels to Marie's head during labor.

Louis said with forced heartiness, "Do you want to see the babe?"

"Yes. More than anything."

"She's really remarkable," he said, tenderly lifting the baby. "So alert. I swear she sees, recognizes faces. I caught her eyes following me." He handed the baby, wrapped in indigo cloth, to Marie. "You must think I'm crazy. But she's an unusual child."

Marie held the infant with a wealth of feeling. She wanted to cry, laugh, and caress the baby all at once. It astounded her that everything about the baby was in miniature. Such perfect fingers and nails, such delicate features and wriggling toes. The baby didn't cry but seemed to be basking in her mother's closeness and warmth.

Marie murmured, "Who's my pretty baby? My pretty girl?"

The baby touched her mother's face. Her fingers felt like silk, like the light, fluttering caress of a butterfly.

Marie kissed her child's fingertips and heard, *Do I look like my maman?*

Black curly hair, black eyes, caramel-colored skin.

"She looks just like you," said Louis.

Heartache comes with four. The words unbidden, resounded in Marie's mind. She didn't believe it. She swore she'd love the child better than Maman had ever loved her. She'd be the best maman.

Baby Marie smiled. Marie bared her breast, encouraging the child to suck. Pressing her closer, Marie felt the stirrings of her blood. She felt the tiny mouth enclose her.

"Who's my baby? My oh-so-pretty baby?"

"Me," the child said.

Marie laughed until she cried.

The child pulled away from the breast and cried long staccato wails. Marie bundled the baby closer, whispering, "Hush, pretty baby. Fais dodo."

Seconds before John entered, the baby's head turned toward the door.

Marie tensed, watching the jovial John swaying toward bed and baby.

"Come to Papa," he called, slightly drunk, his arms thrust forward, ready to grasp.

Marie hated to give the baby up. But what defense did she have? Louis inched closer, but Marie hated the thought of Louis being harmed.

"Smile, ma petite. Smile for Papa." John scooped the baby up, swinging her toward the ceiling, making her laugh and gurgle. Marie felt jealous. Father love. The baby was fascinated by John's lace collar. Marie remembered: it'd been John who cut the ropelike cord connecting her and the baby. His knife, bloodied, still lay on the nightstand.

"She looks just like me," John crowed. Marie shuddered.

Pregnant, she'd thought hard about John being the father of her child. She'd have to minimize the effects. She knew how (there really was only one alternative), but now she wanted to discover who killed Grandmère. And someone *had* killed her. Marie was trusting the instinct in her bones.

"Where's Nattie?" she asked.

"I don't know. *Wheeee,*" John said, swinging his child through the air, pressing a kiss on her brow when she was close. *"Wheeee!"*

"Grandmère's dead."

John stopped. "Are you sure?"

Marie studied him, searching for any clues of guilt. The baby was pressed against John's shoulder. His face was expressionless, his facial scars smooth.

"I had nothing to do with it, Marie." The baby cooed, her fingers batting John's face.

Marie lowered her eyes.

"Believe me," said John. "I've got what I want. You and the child."

Marie could feel Louis tensing beside her. The baby made John look almost honorable. She'd expected the baby to hate her father; instead, she could already see glimmers of their closeness. In her mind, she could weave images of them playing together, of the little girl being seduced easily by her father's charm.

"I thought we'd name her Antoinette Claire," he said. "It sounds royal, doesn't it? Aristocratic."

"Not after Maman?"

"Or you?" John scowled. "Marie is so common."

Marie wanted to hit him. John was already asserting his claim of ownership. She hated him, lightly tapping on the baby's back, comforting the child as though all his life he'd carried a child in his arms.

"Damballah might not know how to call Antoinette. It sounds strange. He's quite skilled at calling Marie. He's had three generations of practice."

Marie watched John thinking, weighing power and advantage.

"It makes sense for her to be named Marie. In honor of Grandmère. Damballah says we should honor our ancestors, our dead. Will your guilt allow that, John? After all, one soul was leaving as another one was coming."

Startled, Marie heard Jacques' voice carrying from the grave: *"She'll look just like you. A real beauty she'll be. A rare beauty. We'll name her after you."* Marie started to cry, and Louis put his arms about her.

John said patronizingly, "It's too soon after the birth for you to be discussing anything logically. Maybe you hallucinated Grandmère's death. Why wouldn't I be loyal to my daughter's family? It doesn't make sense. 'Foolishness,' Nattie would say. I say, look to Nattie if you want any answers."

Her head ached. Marie cried harder. Louis was pressing her back against the pillows. She wanted to sleep again. Escape. John was right; it didn't make sense for him to kill Grandmère. He didn't need to. He'd used her, a too-curious child, to hurt and manipulate Grandmère. Now she'd taken Grandmère's place. It was tragic and funny. John could now use the fourth Marie against her.

Nattie entered the bedroom and Marie struggled upright, alert to a new tension. She sucked in air, waiting for a sign. At first glance, Nattie seemed poised.

"My, my," Nattie said softly. "The baby be born. Let me see. Let me see."

"Why should I let a crow handle my child?" demanded John. "I doubt Marie would like it."

"Foolishness. What be the matter? First, you won't let me birth the child, then you won't let me hold it. You must be crazy in that thick head of yours."

Nattie stood impudently with one hand on her hip, but her brow glistened with nervousness. Her eyelids creased with hurt.

Marie smelled a yellowish odor of discontent. When she looked at Nattie sideways, she saw an impression of blood gurgling through Nattie's skirt. "Where've you been, Nattie?"

"Let me hold the child, John," Nattie sputtered, ignoring Marie. "The child should feel her Aunt Nattie's arms. It be only right." She stepped forward, and the rising sun splashed her outstretched arms with light.

"Where've you been, Nattie?" drawled John.

The atmosphere was charged. On one level, Marie knew she was using Nattie to divert her from confronting John's paternity, yet she also knew Nattie's guilt. People changed (as she well knew) when blood was on their hands.

"Where have you been, Nattie?"

"Walking. Praying to Damballah." Nattie tilted her head left, then right. "You all seen a ghost? That why your eyes be popping from your head?"

"I saw a ghost. Grandmère," Marie said flatly.

"Birthing mothers always see things." Nattie moved toward the cradle. The bucket was stuffed under it. "Foolish Ribaud's left his pail. You all seen him?"

"We sent him searching for you," said Louis.

"What for? I wouldn't be no place but here. This be my home too. Ain't it so, John?" Her toe stubbed the pail.

"Let it alone, Nattie," said John. "My future's in that pail."

"Your future?" snapped Nattie scornfully. "It isn't yours. The future, Damballah's power, belongs to Marie and her child."

"I don't want you stealing what isn't yours."

Nattie countered viciously, "You do so all the time, John. You do it well."

"What's in the pail?" asked Marie, straining to see. "What did Ribaud put in the pail? His snakes?"

"No. The afterbirth and caul," said John. "I asked Ribaud to protect them. Nattie knows spells to hex a child. Don't you, Nattie? Make a baby grow extra limbs. Turn blue. You know how to destroy second sight by burning a caul."

"You think I'd do such a thing?" Nattie demanded.

"I'd kill you if you dared," said John.

"I don't have to stand for this. I be faithful to Marie and her child. Faithful to Grandmère. Damballah."

"Shut up!" yelled Marie.

"Everybody mistreats me. Everybody mistreats Nattie." The black woman was raving, frantically pacing. "Everybody thinks I have no feelings. When have I ever done anything that was not in the best interest of Damballah? Voodoo? I've been faithful to three Maries. There be no reason for me not to be faithful to a fourth."

400

"Liar," growled Marie. "Liar."

Baby Marie started crying, hiccuping for air. John rocked her violently against him.

"I tell the truth. I no be lying. I be telling the truth."

"You killed Grandmère!" screamed Marie.

The baby stopped wailing.

Nattie buried her face in her hands. Then, entranced, she edged closer to John and the baby, muttering, "Let me see. Let me see." She touched the child's cheeks. "Such a lovely child, she be. Just like her Maman."

Nattie turned toward Marie, her hands open in appeal, whining, "John told me to. He ordered the death of Grandmère long ago. He said, "Wait and see if the baby survives. If it does, kill Grandmère."

"Liar."

"He knew when it happened. I tell you, he knew." Nattie looked pathetic, her hips ballooning, her hands limp at her sides. "He knew, Marie. I tell you he knew."

John collected his knife from the nightstand. "You're a pitiful crow. Trying to lie away your guilt." He spoke to Nattie's back. One hand held the baby while his other hand held the steel blade.

Seeing the knife, Louis edged forward.

"Let her be, John," said Marie. "I want to hear Nattie's story."

"I tell you he knew." Steadfast, Nattie stared at Marie without flinching. The two women were watching each other, synchronizing their breaths.

"I'm talking about you, Nattie. Not John."

"You be so smart," Nattie retorted. "You blame everything on another woman. You always let John blind you. Like he blinded your Maman."

"Listen to her," whispered Louis. "She makes sense."

Ignoring Louis, Marie murmured, "I want to talk with Nattie alone."

John looked chagrined. Nattie straightened her spine, hopeful and alert.

"John, get out of here!" screamed Marie. "You too, Louis. Everyone get out of here."

"Marie," said Louis.

"Let us be." Her head sank into the pillow; she closed her eyes.

Rocking his daughter, John enclosed his fingers around the back of Nattie's neck, "You'll pay," he whispered in her ear. Then, to Marie, John said, "I don't approve of this."

Louis, pausing at the door, asked, "Are you sure you'll be all right, Marie?"

Marie didn't answer. Louis closed the bedroom door, shutting him, John, and the baby out.

Nattie guffawed and sashayed to the chair. "You be getting sense now, Marie. No more foolishness. The power be passed down through the generations. Special women. Mother to daughter. Us two can stop John. Stop John from using you like he used your Maman. I be your new Maman. John don't know nothing about babies; screaming in a child's ear like that don't make sense. Foolishness."

"Shut up," Marie said fiercely, opening her eyes. "Shut up. Sit down, Nattie."

Nattie stood over her, wavering. It galled her to have Marie ordering her about.

"Sit down. You hate me as much as I hate you."

Nattie, her skirt flouncing, stuffed her expansive hips into the chair.

Marie turned her head on the pillow, staring at the round black face jutting forward. Nattie had said they'd been friends when she was a child. They'd played together for hours.

"Funny," Marie said. "I can't see myself hiding beneath your skirts. Ever."

"You be small then. A child."

"Yes. I'm not a child now, Nattie. It's time for me to stop hiding."

Nattie frowned. She wondered if she'd miscalculated. Propped up by pillows, Marie looked remarkably like Grandmère. "Say what you got to say, Marie. Be done with it."

Smiling, Marie dug her nails into Nattie's wrist. "You believe Damballah has given me power?"

"Yes."

"You believe, then, I'm the Voodoo Queen? That my power will always be stronger than yours?"

"Yes, yes," clucked Nattie, nervous.

"If I sleep facing the wall—"

"Somebody die. Simple, simple foolishness."

"Tonight I'll sleep facing the wall. Understand me?"

"You don't know what you be saying."

"I know this," said Marie gathering her strength, whispering intently. "I'm going to kill you. One way or the other. With or without Damballah's help." Marie saw she'd hit home, using Nattie's own superstitions against her. Nattie seemed to be withering before her eyes. John always said her power was inside people's minds; seeing Nattie afraid of her, she believed him.

"You be hard, Marie."

"Yes." There was a sore inside her. It was easier to concentrate on Nattie than on her own pain. She couldn't sing her pain like Grandmère.

"Tell me how you did it," Marie insisted. "How you killed Grandmère and why. Grandmère was a friend to you."

"I no hurt Grandmère any more than you did." Nattie lashed out viciously. "Don't play false with me. Don't act as if you cared. In spirit, your actions already be the death of Grandmère. I only made it fact. I tell you this, Grandmère was ready to die. You'd already broken her heart."

"I'll kill you now, Nattie."

"You no scare me, Marie. You think you do. But I don't scare." Plucking her skirt, hysteria crept into her voice. "In Haiti, I done seen more powerful women than you, your Grandmère, and your Maman. More powerful than the three of you together. There be nothing special about you. For three generations, I watch Damballah come to your family. And each time I wonder, 'Why not me? Why not me?' "

Nattie grimly pounded her chest.

"One day the power will come to your child. The fourth Marie. There be so little reason for it. You have so little to recommend. Especially you, Marie. I hated teaching you. You don't even know the faith. An accident of birth. History made you Voodoo Queen instead of me. If there was any justice, you should've been me. I should've been you."

Marie shuddered, remembering Ziti having once said the same thing.

"You've been a child too long. I be pleased you're finally behaving like a woman. Pleased you're acting like a Voodoo Queen. It be good to feel righteous anger. But it be an act, it not be truly in you. Not in your heart, like it be in mine.

"Your Maman was no better than a whore. Shaking her tail after John. You no better. You want to kill me, then kill me. But I don't believe you have the power to do it. You lack the courage. Your Grandmère was worthy of respect. But she, too, failed Damballah by creating you. Someone with no self. No faith. No history."

Marie was stung by partial truths; she pinched at the blood beneath her skin. "I didn't ask to be here, Nattie."

"That don't matter. It don't be fair. You be dragged to Damballah unwillingly. I would go willingly, would even go further if Damballah blessed me with power of possession and sight.

"Religion be ruthless. You think the white God be all about love. That be a lie. An eye for an eye, a tooth for a tooth, that be the white God. Like themselves, white people need a god who can be righteous in anger. Destroy if need be. Even His son. Even black folks. All week, folks been celebrating Christ's beating and death—"

"No, His resurrection. That's the salvation."

"No, it be the destruction that has the power. Gods destroy in order to build. And that be what I did. I destroyed to make way for life."

"You don't understand."

"No, you don't understand, Marie. Black gods need soldiers to fight the influence of the white God. They need to rely on someone strong. You've never been strong. You be too softhearted. Damballah should've blessed me. Over and over again, I pay the price. I've done things I don't like, but I did them because they had to be done. I be sick watching you wallow all the time in self-pity because you hurt Grandmère. I loved her too. Admit your religion be demanding. I killed Grandmère for Damballah's sake. Grandmère be a sacrifice." Nattie, satisfied, slapped her thighs and leaned back in the chair.

Marie looked at her pityingly. "Voodoo isn't death. It's life. I feel it. You'd feel it too if Damballah was in you."

"But He's not," said Nattie, glaring, "so it be His fault if I be wrong. I serve Him the best I can."

"No, that's just what you tell yourself."

"I be a true believer. I learned spells in Haiti. From Grandmère. All my life I be preparing, making myself worthy of Damballah. You don't know anything. I taught you potions but you hardly ever use them. Your Grandmère taught you nothing but white folks' lies."

"Spells aren't needed," said Marie. "Damballah is located in the heart." For the first time, Marie realized she knew this. It was as though Damballah's attempt to spare the hanged men had made things clearer to her.

"Christian corruption. Filth." Nattie spat. "I killed your Grandmère. I've been killing her, and you never knew. I kept her weak, kept her crazy. John asked me to. Just like John asked me to persuade your Maman to dance in Cathedral Square."

"What are you saying?"

"Humpf. You and your Grandmère, the great Voodoo Queens, never knew nothing. Your Maman was scared. It be the one time she didn't want to go along with John's plan. Cathedral Square scared her. John talked to me. I talked to your Maman. I told her I'd seen a special sign from Damballah." Nattie clicked her gums, then stretched her mouth into a self-satisfied smile.

Marie said, "And it was you who found John, wasn't it? Not Maman. You were the one who brought John into the family. You were the one who started our destruction."

Breathing deeply, Nattie continued. "He'd been my lover. Six months before. Later, I understood he used me to get to your Grandmère. Your Maman. When your Maman turned fifteen, he left my bed. Always the younger, prettier woman he wanted."

"Yes," Marie said, feeling again her utter helplessness in the face of John's cruelty.

"Marie." Nattie reached out and stroked her leg. "Set aside

our differences. Do what you want with me. But don't let John live. He'll go on hurting you for sure."

Marie stared at the ceiling. *Grandmère was floating, dead.* She could almost hear Grandmère's ghost whispering in her ear, "Christian charity." Grandmère had always turned the other cheek. If she'd wanted, Grandmère could've killed John long ago. Marie plucked at the bed sheet.

"Fool," said Nattie.

"Voodoos don't kill."

Nattie laughed hard and loud. "So. Who be the bigger hypocrite? You or me? You think to kill me, but when I speak of John you say, 'Voodoos don't kill.' Ha. I think you still care for him. Else the space between your legs itches to have him."

Marie wanted to slap Nattie's face.

"How many Catholics have killed, kill every day? Hypocrites. Your Grandmère believed what she was told: 'Christian charity.' There be no charity in this world. Any person kills when they must." Nattie paused, overcome with pain. Bending forward, she rested her head on her knees. Grandmère's face, contorted with pain, rose in her memory. She'd forced herself to watch Grandmère until her body stopped writhing and she lay still.

It stunned Marie to hear Nattie's version of the truth. If her truth hadn't been so obscene, she could've admired Nattie's loyalty.

"I would've let Grandmère live," Nattie said, so quietly that Marie almost didn't hear her. "I would've defied John. But tonight I couldn't stand your arrogance. I couldn't stand you not letting me birth the babe. You let a white man, not even a believer, do for you. You let John, who has no power, do for you. Ignorant Ribaud runs for the sheets and the baby's salve. Ribaud be entrusted with the caul." Tears rapidly slid down Nattie's cheeks. "I *had* to say the last spell over Grandmère. You forced me to do it. Grandmère knew what I was doing. She understood. Grateful, she ate my poison mixed with ground glass."

"You're the hypocrite," Marie screamed. "You killed Grandmère because you hated me, not because you loved Damballah."

"That be a lie." Then Nattie shrugged. "I be confused. I don't know what I mean anymore." Her eyes glazed.

"You could've done it painlessly. Why'd you make her suffer? What were you building by destroying Grandmère?"

Nattie remained silent.

"What were you planning? Would you have stolen the caul?"

"Yes, I would've stolen it," Nattie said fiercely, her attention riveted. Compelled, she slid over to the cradle and stooped down, looking into the tin bucket. The caul was a bloody, slippery sheath; the afterbirth was a deflated, gritty, blue-red thing. Nattie was transfixed.

"I dreamed that if I ate the caul, visions would come to me. I'd be a great Voodoo Queen. Failing that, I would've used the caul and afterbirth to make baby Marie mine. Make the baby dependent upon me. Tie her to my blood just as the afterbirth and cord tied her to you."

"You would steal what isn't yours, just like John?"

"Yes. She should've been mine."

"Then you'd get rid of me."

"Yes. I'd be the baby's maman. I'd love her very much. I'd be the best maman."

"Too much loving makes you hard," Marie whispered, echoing Nattie's old words.

" 'Tis true." Nattie's voice had taken on a strange lilting quality. She seemed entranced, talking to herself, rationalizing, picking apart her own bewilderment. "After all my love I felt so little when Grandmère be dead. I didn't understand it. So much had become nothing."

"And if the baby hadn't brought you closer to Damballah, you would've hurt her."

"If I had to, but only for Damballah's sake."

"Like you hurt Annette's baby, the blue misshapen child everyone blamed on Grandmère."

"Yes. All for a good cause. A sacrifice. How else would you have broken from Grandmère and gone with John?"

Marie felt she was confronting a great evil. Murder was never logical. And Nattie's logic was as twisted as her own.

"I'm going to kill you, Nattie." She leaned forward, her nails digging into Nattie's thigh. "Look at me."

Nattie, her face impassive, stared back.

"I'm going to tell you the truth about yourself. Then I'm going to kill you. Do you hear?"

"There be nothing you can say."

"Shut up. You want to know why the gods never visited you? I'll tell you why." Marie couldn't catch her breath. Words and air were rushing out of her, vengeful and furious. "You're evil, Nattie. You haven't been building Voodoo, you've been destroying it. You've been hurting the very god you claim to love. Why should spirits possess you? What did you have to offer besides petty hate and jealousy?

"Nattie, it was you who introduced John to Maman. You who placed the viper in the garden. It was you who convinced Maman to do the ceremony in Cathedral Square. It was you who sent Maman to her death. Just as it was you who helped turn me from Grandmère and who introduced me to John."

"No. It not be that way."

"Yes. Yes. You tried to destroy us, didn't you? You've been killing Damballah's Queens—Maman, Grandmère. You nearly killed me with your twisted hate, your passion for John. Why did you never recognize that John was the greater evil? Why didn't you destroy him? If it hadn't been for John, Grandmère never would've run off to the bayou. She would've quietly practiced the faith here in New Orleans, and taught her daughter the joy of Damballah, and her granddaughter, great-granddaughter, and so on, and so on. Thousands of people would've been touched by the spirit. It would've spanned generations." Marie was crying. "You ruined all that. Voodoo would've thrived. Mother to daughter."

Nattie was dazed. She stumbled out of the chair. "I not be what you say I am. I not destroy the faith. I be helping Damballah."

"You destroyed Jacques. How did his death help the faith? You helped murder him because you're a jealous, spiteful old crow."

Nattie's mouth puckered wordlessly.

"How many times did John make love to you? How many years ago? Was it so good, so special, Nattie, that you'd betray yourself and everything you believed in?"

"You should talk. You're no better than me."

"Maybe." Marie fell back against the pillow. "But I never let John use me to murder. And it didn't take me—how many years has it been? thirty? forty?—forty years to discover that John's cock couldn't make up for being a traitor to Damballah. Yes, John is evil. But there is a point where John ends and you begin. You had a thousand choices." Marie sighed, her energy spent. "You believe you always served Damballah, but you used Damballah for your perversion. You defiled the faith with your own jealousy and hate."

Everything about Nattie had dulled. She resembled a zombie: her eyes fixed, her skin blanched, her movements sluggish, haphazard. She seemed to have willed herself dead. "I be tired, Marie. Can you understand how many times I waited for Damballah's touch while nightly He rode your Grandmère, your Maman, then you? Gods be cruel. All I wanted was some vision, something to fill me up. Something other than bitterness. Damballah paid me no mind. Foolishness. I would be happy with so little. The slightest touch."

Nattie stooped and reached into the bucket beneath the cradle. The caul and afterbirth were still warm. Nattie reveled in seeing the blood stain her hands and arms. "Do you think Damballah will reward me?"

Marie didn't answer. Her bare feet slipped to the floor. Her gown hung loosely. There was no swelling baby to throw her off-balance. She towered over Nattie. "Did John ask you to kill Grandmère?"

"Do you plan on killing him?" Nattie asked.

"Yes."

"Good. The Maries finally overtake him. John has a coward's faith in Damballah. He believes he doesn't believe, but he does. Fear be his belief. You scare him. Your miracles make him feel like a rooster without a cock. He be frustrated that he can't harness the power. We be alike. Except I be better than him. I know Damballah only grants visions to women. John be a fool."

"Answer me, Nattie. Did John ever order Grandmère's death?"

"Yes. He ordered me to kill her. But he didn't expect it to happen tonight. My hate made it happen tonight. He saw me leave.

I don't doubt he knew where I be going. He be glad, I tell you. Glad to see Grandmère gone."

"Will he kill me?"

"Probably. You be too strange, unpredictable. A child raised can be shaped. His vision be power, you know. Faith be just a tool to him to cut out people's will and heart." Nattie was burying her face in the caul, inhaling resilient flesh and blood. She seemed to be drunk with possibilities.

Marie's rage crested. It was an affront that Nattie would touch what so intimately belonged to her and the baby.

As if hearing Marie's thoughts, Nattie looked up, her face streaked with blood and salty tears. "I be sorry you never wanted the gift you had. I always wanted it. Visions from gods be glorious."

"Here's your death, Nattie," Marie whispered, then cried out, "Nattie's stealing the caul!"

The door swung open. John had been waiting on the other side. Marie had only a second to see Nattie's stunned face before John plunged his knife in her back. Nattie hadn't expected Marie to have the courage to destroy her. Nattie's mouth shaped into a small O. She toppled forward like a crow off its perch. The caul slid to the floor.

Ribaud's face peeked around the door.

Marie asked Louis to bring her her child. The infant was beautiful.

John was smiling. Murder simplified his life. Nattie and Grandmère were two less women to worry about.

Louis looked mournfully at Marie, wondering where the innocent young girl had gone.

Murder was never logical, Marie thought. She bared her breast for baby Marie. The child suckled greedily. Staring at Ribaud's grinning face, all Marie could think to ask was, "Ribaud, whatever did you do with your snakes?"

THE MIDDLE:

Eighteen Hundred and Twenty-two

~

"You understand, Louis? Stories should begin at the beginning. But in this story, the middle is the beginning. John's death became a vortex. My life propelled me to murder him, and my life was propelled by his death. Everything for me spirals outward from this center. Lies, pain, and loss haunt the future as well as the past.

"I've forgiven Nattie. My daughter hasn't forgiven me. She doesn't understand why I had to murder her father. Unlike Grandmère, I never kept secrets from my daughter. But without a father, Marie grew up idealizing a father's love. I sometimes think I should've lied and told her Jacques Paris was her father. Then, I think, her hatred of John would be as strong as mine.

"I never returned to Teché. I think of that time in my life—the only time when I've been truly happy—as an aberration. It's not part of the spiral; rather, it's displaced in time.

"Damballah has stayed with me. Even though I feel undeserving, He still possesses me. When I fall asleep now, I can see Him waiting in my dreams, surrounded by hyacinths and roses. I have no idea whether I'll go to Heaven or Guinea. I might even go to Hell or wander without a home if my daughter, Marie, fails to honor me with sacrifice. I no longer know where she is.

"Life is a spiral. The only protection is to become disembodied—to see the self as other. Immortal. Grandmère, my mother, my daughter, and myself—we were all named Marie.

"The generations are overlapping. Women hand sight down through the generations.

"One generation will get it right."

•

—MARIE LAVEAU, JUNE 16, 1881, TWO HOURS BEFORE HER DEATH
(From Louis DeLavier's journal)

413

They were in the garden, trying to stay cool in the afternoon sun. Willows and jasmine vines with a cloying scent arched overhead. Marie was rocking in the rosewood rocker she'd given Grandmère shortly before her death. She didn't believe Grandmère had ever had a chance to rock on the cottage porch. Marie had such bittersweet regrets, but rocking brought a measure of comfort and reminded her of life with Grandmère in Teché.

Ribaud was whistling and skinning cats. Blood pooled at his feet, and muscle and bone were piled high in a bucket. More than once Marie had almost implored Ribaud to stop. But since Grandmère's death, Ribaud had been especially sweet to her and she didn't have the heart to ask him to stop doing what he enjoyed so much. It had been Ribaud who'd gathered up Grandmère's belongings and brought them to her when she'd been still confined to bed, weak after birth. She'd cried when she'd seen the rosewood rocker. She'd stumbled out of bed and sat in it, feeling enormous comfort. Then Ribaud had stunned her when he'd handed her the wedding brooch Grandmère had given her. She thought it lost when she'd thrown it into the brush in Haven. She wore the brooch now, and the snake curling about the rose never failed to remind her of both Grandmère and Jacques. Yes, Ribaud could gut as many cats as he wanted. Besides, rationalized Marie, Ribaud making skins for his drums was like a mother sewing clothes for her children.

Baby Marie was sleeping in the cradle. Rocking, Marie could see her daughter's sweet face and the pretty and perfect brown hand curled beneath her chin. At five months, baby Marie was fat and healthy and had learned to gurgle and smile hello. Marie envied the baby's calm, her innocence. The baby didn't know the evil in the world. The baby loved John indiscriminately.

Just outside the garden, yellow fever was raging. It was August, and poor and colored people were dying by the hundreds. Marie did her best to guard the baby's health; camomile and thyme spiced with salt were fed to her daily. Marie bathed her each night.

Damballah hadn't come to her since the baby's birth. Marie had had no visions, no dreams, no omens. She worried that murdering Nattie had put her beyond Damballah's grace. Perhaps Damballah had finally given up on the Maries, given up on the New World. She wondered whether her sins had now become too great for either Damballah or Christ.

Perhaps as penance, she'd taken to aiding Father Christophe nurse the fever victims and prisoners. Father Christophe had sent her a missive, saying he was sorry for Grandmère's and Jacques' deaths. His sincerity had touched her, and she'd offered to help him. She still didn't believe that torment and suffering were blessings that paved the way to heaven. But she helped because she felt Grandmère would've liked it. Christian charity could be a blessing. It made her feel good to nurse the ill and dying. It helped mask some of her sorrow. And she didn't have to feel like a fake, a charlatan pretending spirituality. If the dying wanted to hear the rosary, she said it. If they wanted to hear prayers to Damballah, Marie said them too. She asked both Christ and Damballah to spare her daughter from the fever.

John approved of her nursing the ill. He said, "It's good to be popular. Good for business." Citizens heralded her in the streets.

John also liked it that, since the birth, neither Damballah nor any other god had possessed Marie. Her ceremonies were a farce, but to her audiences it didn't seem to matter. Streams of visitors needing money, love, vengeance, health, always something, came to the house on St. Anne and to her ceremonies. Marie hated it, since she had nothing in her to give, and often what audiences demanded of her was petty and hateful. John's elaborate network of spies uncovered the vulnerabilities and incriminating secrets of most everyone, from a field hand to a slaveowner, from a cook to a white mistress. Briberies, threats, and violence accomplished great things. This was now the sole power behind Marie Laveau's spells—not spirits but manipulation. Many charms worked well without elaborate threats, because people believed they'd work. Illnesses were cured; lonely souls found happiness. If only people would realize it wasn't necessary to pay John outrageous fees.

"I like you as an ordinary woman," said John. "It complicates business to have a faith healer believe in the faith." Perversely, John became more amorous. He'd tease her with the thought of having a dozen children. Late at night, after carousing, he'd come to her without much warning. He'd move inside her until he arched and shuddered. Always, he sighed, "Marie. Marie." Sometimes he smelled of another woman, a musky, heavy odor if the woman was lower class and a sweet floral odor if she was a daring *aristo*. Other times he smelled of catfish and rum.

John seemed to have grown in stature while Marie felt herself diminished. She didn't quite know why she accepted John's attentions. Partly because it was too much of a struggle to fight them. Partly because her body no longer seemed to belong to her. It was someone else's. The changes the baby had wrought had distanced her from full milk-leaking breasts, from a soft yielding abdomen, and from ragged stretch marks along her thighs.

Marie did know her emotions had dulled. She hadn't cried since the night of Grandmère's death. Damballah's abandonment had left her too insecure and uncertain to leave John. And if she left, he'd track her and the baby down, and when the chance beckoned, he'd murder her.

Murdering John was the only course. But how? John wasn't a fool. Often after his loving, his rapes, she'd lie in bed trying to think of ways to destroy him. Every method—poisoning, hiring assassins, trying to cast a spell—seemed too impractical. Dangerous. But it'd also taken her all these months to realize that having killed Antoine, Nattie, and, unintentionally, Jacques and Grandmère, she couldn't stand the thought of having more blood on her. If murder were a good thing, she reasoned, Damballah would've sent her a sign these past months.

Marie despised herself. Only the baby filled her with any love and happiness. But it wasn't enough.

"You need someding? Food? Someding to drink?"

Marie flushed. She didn't realize Ribaud had been watching her. "No, I'm all right, Ribaud. Just thinking."

"I bet I guess what." He looked both frightening and comical with his feathered cap on his head, his hands and his arms up to his elbows covered in blood, and with yards of cats' guts stretched before him. "You want me to feed de snake?"

Beside the rocker, the python rested in a straw-lined box.

Marie lifted the lid, reached inside, and stroked the python's head. Its body spiraled in tight circles.

A few months ago, Ribaud had started feeding the snake cats. He enjoyed the spectacle of watching the snake trap and squeeze its victim to death. It took minutes for it to swallow the sinewy cat, and for days there would be a lump in the snake's belly until the cat was digested.

"Not now, Ribaud. Later. When I'm not around."

He cackled. "If you say so."

The baby wailed and Marie smiled, lifted her baby, and pressed her nose into the sweet folds of skin on the infant's neck. She smelled so clean. Pure. The odor was a lovely summer green. The baby's head was covered with black curls and her eyes were brown.

"She looks just like you," said Ribaud. "Same eyes. Same nose. Same mouth."

Marie uncovered her breast and let the baby suck.

"My, my, what a lovely picture."

Marie tensed as John stepped out into the garden. She could feel her milk drying up.

John looked handsome today. His skin was firm, his coloring robust. How long could John manage to stay young, forever? He'd outfoxed Nattie. He'd even seemed younger, more buoyant, since he stabbed her.

"What are you doing here, John?"

"Don't fret. I won't disturb your sanctuary for long, Marie. Don't look surprised. I'm well aware you hide here. Everyone needs a private place."

"Then why don't you leave?"

"Ah, the kitten has claws. Mind your manners. It doesn't pay to berate a father in front of his child." John towered over her and, with his finger, traced where the baby had latched onto her breast. He caressed Marie's skin and the edges of the baby's mouth. Marie felt a tingling sensation and hated to admit to herself that she felt a contraction in her vagina. The baby sucked harder.

John stepped back. "I've got good news. Ribaud, you'll need

as many drums as you can manage to make. You'll wear them out soon enough. We'll have dozens of ceremonies."

Saying nothing, Ribaud quietly gathered up his dead cats. John cuffed his head, knocking off his feathered cap.

"I've bought a house. Halfway between New Orleans and Haben's Haven. It's a bit remote but not too remote for your followers to join you, Marie, for special exclusive ceremonies."

"What are you talking about?"

"Don't you see?" He was stooping before her and the baby. His hands covered Marie's knees. "We'll create an elite. Up to now, our ceremonies have been open—anyone can come for free. With this house, we can conduct private ceremonies. We'll charge outrageous fees. Don't you see? It's genius. Everyone will be afraid they're missing something. So of course they'll pay. Whatever I ask."

He was heady, drunk with his idea. For the first time, Marie wondered what John might have accomplished had he been white.

"What about the slaves? What about the poor who can't afford to come? Voodoo serves them too."

"Nonsense." He stood abruptly. "Besides, if they want to come, let them beg or steal. I want power, fortune. This is the way to get it. Just as New Orleans wants more of you, we'll give them less."

Appalled, Marie let her palm graze the snake. John stepped right, in the opposite direction from the snake.

He bent forward. "Let me see my daughter. I haven't held her all day."

Reluctantly, Marie gave the child up.

John swung the baby through the air. *"Wheee, wheee!"* His face was suffused with love as baby Marie squealed and squirmed with laughter. "One happy family," said John, turning, surprising Marie with a huge smile. "One rich, happy family." The baby batted his face and John caught her tiny hand and kissed her fingers, running them through his mouth and between his teeth. A couple of yards away from Marie and Ribaud, he sat down on a bench with the infant, cradling her to his chest. He puckered his mouth, popped wide his eyes, and made cooing nonsense sounds. Baby Marie loved it and snuggled deeper into his chest.

Marie couldn't help feeling resentment. The snake was unfurling itself. Marie clenched the rocker's arms to keep from screaming, Give me back my baby! Give me back my baby!

The python inched its flat S-shaped head outside the box and stretched toward Marie in the rocker.

Ribaud rested his hand on Marie's shoulder. From time to time, his fingers pinched her skin, reminding her to stay in control.

John was happy. Having a child was more wonderful than he'd imagined. In each of the babe's features, he saw signs of his parentage. He believed his daughter to be a mirror. Her beauty reflected his, yet with the feminine difference. His mind fixed on the idea that they were twins, complements of a sort. Having never once thought of children or of being a father, John had been caught off guard by the intensity of his feelings. He reveled in the idea of having someone to teach so effectively, so completely. He could mold his heart's desire. His vanity encouraged him to unwrap the baby's light cotton bunting so he could better see her toes and light, moon-shaped nails. "My, what a pretty girl," he exclaimed. "A princess you are. A royal princess." And so excited was he by her kicking arms and legs, he unwrapped the tie to her gown, so he could better see her chest and stomach and caress her legs and thighs. The baby was delighted and seemed mesmerized by her father's face.

The python had shifted itself onto Marie's still lap. Slowly, it formed concentric circles, fitting itself against her. Marie's breath was coming sharply. She hated to see John touch her baby girl.

Sun and shadow leaves shimmered across John and baby Marie. John wished the enemies who'd sold him into slavery could see him now—soon to be rich, already successful and powerful in New Orleans, and holding in his embrace the start of a dynasty. His eyes and hands couldn't get enough of the baby. He wanted to smell and taste her, appreciate fully the miracle of his daughter. Everything, except for the images of power in his own mind and the shape and feel of the warm, silken baby, receded. He untied the cloth from between his daughter's legs and delighted in seeing the baby stretch and arch on his lap. His hand could almost cover her entire body. His palm came down, stroking baby Marie in slow, easy movements from her head to her toes. The baby was babbling contentedly as his hand reached under and stroked her back and buttocks, the flat soles of her feet.

Marie felt trapped in the rocker. Ribaud's two hands were pressing down on her shoulders. The python's weight was centered in her lap. She felt she was going to suffocate. She couldn't catch her air. She was ten again in the bayou, waking from a deep, dream-ridden sleep to John's caressing hand. Marie moaned softly, feeling her own body squirm and stir restlessly with the memory. She could feel John again as he'd teased her immature nipples. Just as she could see John now drawing circles with his fingers on her baby's chest.

Father. Husband. Son. John, in the bayou, had promised to be everything to her, and in a sense he had been. The punishing father. The demanding husband. The petulant son.

The baby's arms flailed up toward her head, her legs bowed open. John marveled at how sweetly, sensitively formed were the folds of skin between the baby's thighs. How ripe, how glistening pink. His index finger ever so gently touched the exposed skin.

Marie felt ill; sweat formed along her neck and brow. She could feel the memory of John's hands between her childish legs, making her feel both pleasure and shame. A damp wetness had seeped into her bloomers then. Now Marie tried to scream, but the sound choked in her chest. The snake was cool between her legs and she could feel the python's head rising up toward her chest.

John was rising, swinging the baby again. *"Wheee, wheee!"* Then he was kissing her, holding her close, softly touching her round, firm buttocks as the baby's head turned right and her hands explored the interesting texture of the scars on his face. *"Wheee!"* John shouted. *"Wheee!"* he called again while the baby, nude in the sunlight, laughed gaily.

And Marie's emotions crested. All her rage and hatred came back in force. John, playing with her daughter—so happy, so young, so full of life—was standing in the afternoon sun, his cock pulsing and raining semen into his pants.

Marie averted her eyes.

The python was gazing steadily up at her. Marie conceived her plan.

It was evening in the new house—it was little more than an abandoned shack, really, set in a marshy landscape. But Marie understood why it appealed to John; it was isolated enough that anything could happen and no one would be the wiser. The private ceremony was a success. Marie was tired. For over two hours she'd been manipulating the crowd, and through the crowd she'd been manipulating John.

"Saint Marie," the crowd was shouting, begging to be infected with the spirit. "Saint Marie." Bodies clamored forward, heedlessly stumbling, trying to touch Marie and be part of the miracle. They were clamoring for the snake's kiss. They wanted to feel Damballah enter their souls. "Saint Marie."

Trembling, Marie headed toward the altar. The trap was sprung.

"Marie." Clutching her hair, causing her chin to tilt upward and back, John kissed her. "How does it feel to be a saint?"

"You may join me." She offered him the snake.

"I'm already joined with you."

Marie thought of all the nuances—joined by his plunging into her, by the fears he inspired. Together they'd made Voodoo a religion of lies and horror.

"Yes," she said demurely.

"Then why should I want more?"

"Not more." She stared at the scars on his face. "As much as due you."

"I'd rather be kissed by you."

"Why not two kisses for my King?" She offered him the python again.

John edged away. "You're trying to trick me, aren't you? It's dangerous when the conjurer believes she conjures."

"Or perhaps—," Marie said, cradling the snake—"the gods taught me more than you know."

He paused. "I don't believe you."

"Try," she crooned.

John opened his arms. "I'm not afraid, Marie." *The snake slid across her arms to his.* "Not of this. Not of you. Any power you have still comes from me." *The snake's tail drifted down his chest.*

"I made you," John said harshly, "Queen of the Voudons."

"Thank you," she said, *as the snake squeezed, choking him.* His nostrils flared in surprise; his hands clutched and unclutched as he tried to untangle the animal from his lace collar.

Marie remembered John saying, "Spells work because people believe." Did John believe? The snake, a tight fist-sized spring, was wrapped about his chest and throat. His raspy breathing unnerved her; spasms racked his body; his arms were pinioned to his sides. He fell with one leg twisted beneath him, his tongue swelling, his eyes popped wide.

Her head lifted. *The child ghost at the windowpane began a high-pitched wailing.* Marie wanted to cover her ears, but no one else heard what she was hearing so clearly. The audience was silent. Marie realized John had ceased struggling.

In a loud, clear voice, Marie shouted, "Dahomeyans praised the serpent. For Eve came into the world blind. A snake gave her—a snake gave me sight. I am," she added vehemently, "Marie Laveau."

"Saint Marie." Chanting again syncopated the drums. Marie looked up. *A sorrowful Grandmère was floating across the ceiling.*

Followers bowed before her; one by one, they shyly kissed her hem. "Marie . . . Marie est Voudon . . . Voudon." She felt like crying.

John, alive, would have destroyed their daughter—the fourth Marie—as surely as he'd destroyed all the others.

"The blood is alive," Grandmère whispered.

"Yes." Marie closed her eyes.

When the room was quiet, her followers dispersed, Marie lifted a candle and crossed to the pane. Red mosquitoes banged against it; the startled child was gone.

"Assassine."

"Yes, Ribaud. Murderer."

She saw his reflection grin.

Soon afterward, she heard him slide a heavy weight across the packed earth floor while she stared into a night alive with owl squeals, wind moans, and her own whisperings.

"Women hand sight down through the generations. Mother to daughter."

Marie turned and watched as Ribaud crossed the room, carrying the baby wrapped in the silky cotton of Membe's dress. She didn't ask him what had become of John's body. She didn't want to know. Gratefully, Marie cradled the sleeping baby in her arms.

"You need some food? Drink?"

Marie smiled. "No, Ribaud. I'm all right."

Ribaud shifted from foot to foot, hopping nervously. "You did fine tonight. Just fine."

"You can feed the python, Ribaud. Any cats?"

Ribaud grinned. They both looked at the snake curled in front of the altar. "I'll see what I can do," said Ribaud, turning to care for the snake.

"Ribaud," Marie called softly. "It wasn't all illusion tonight. Damballah sent me signs."

His face was arrested. "Your powers be coming back?"

"Maybe. I think Grandmère has forgiven me."

"Dat's good. I knew she would. She loved you more dan anyding," Ribaud said fiercely.

They stared at each other.

"Ribaud, I—"

"No, don't say it. No need to say it. I only do what family would do."

"Yes, family," Marie murmured, watching the spell man turn and glide toward the snake.

"Dis snake is getting bigger. Maybe I'll feed it two cats." Ribaud grinned, half dragging and half carrying the animal. "We'll be waiting in de wagon for you. No hurry. Come when it's time."

"Thank you, Ribaud. I won't be long."

Marie turned back to the window. She kissed the baby's brow. Baby Marie sighed and stirred slightly. Membe's dress fit perfectly as a bunting and made the baby seem especially lovely. On the indigo blue was a pattern of repeating skies filled with a sun, moon, and stars colored in red, white, and gold. A gigantic snake coiled about

423

the hem. The sleeping child seemed connected to the universe. Membe must've have felt such wonder when she beheld her own newly born daughter wailing, proudly announcing her entrance in this world.

A hoot owl called. Some animal was rustling in the weeds.

Marie realized now that the child at the windowpane had been the spirit ghost of her daughter. Someday her child, in a vision, would see the murder of her father. Baby Marie would become, in a sense, the child at the window. She'd probably be ten.

Marie didn't expect her daughter to understand why her mother had killed her father. Just as she'd struggled with Grandmère, her daughter would probably struggle with her. Marie wasn't sure how the struggle would end. She could only love her daughter and do her best to help her grow.

Marie was exhausted, a little frightened. She wanted to go home. She didn't believe she belonged in Teché any longer. She'd go to the house on St. Anne. It might be pleasant now that John was dead. There'd be no one to intimidate and oppress her.

Marie stepped up to the altar. The Virgin and the plaster baby Jesus were next to drawings of Ezili and Damballah. Most of the candles were melted down to their stumps. They flickered erratically. She lifted the lid on a rosewood-and-pearl box. Inside were four perfect white-tallow candles wrapped in velvet. She placed them each inside golden holders shaped like budding roses. She arranged them into a neat row and lit them slowly, one by one. "Blessed be the Virgin. Take care of my Grandmère. Blessed be Damballah. Take care of my Grandmère." Two candles sparked into flame and glowed.

"This third candle is for you, Grandmère." She lit it. "To let you know you're not forgotten. You're not unloved." Her hand hesitated above the fourth wick. She lowered the lighter, then raised it again. "This fourth candle is for all of us—you, Grandmère, Maman, myself, and my daughter. Heartache doesn't have to come with four. We're all Maries. We're all loving daughters." The four candles glowed brilliantly. "If I could sing, Grandmère, I'd sing a song of love." Though there wasn't any wind, the flames elongated, shining brighter.

Marie blew out the other dying candles, left from the ceremony. She prayed for a bit, watching the four flames illuminating and tinting rose-pink the Voodoo gods and the Christian saints.

What was she going to do with her life? Live. Be generous, good to others.

What was she going to do with her faith? Keep it alive.

Marie turned to go. *She heard a piercing, bell-like whistle.* Marie sucked in air and held the baby close. Had she imagined it? Was she so desperate for forgiveness that she'd hallucinate spirits? She turned and looked out at the empty room. It was desolate.

Marie kissed the baby's brow. "It's time to get you home."

The whistle was clear and steady; then it trilled into a harmonic pattern like a nightingale's evening song.

There was a lightness in the atmosphere, a sweetness of being that was remarkably soothing. Marie smelled sandalwood, lush greenery, and honeysuckle. Moonlight was spilling into the room. The flames of the four candles had merged into a single incandescent light. Marie turned and saw the statue of the Virgin smiling, holding her baby as tenderly as Marie held hers. The charcoal-colored Damballah was slithering across the drawing paper and encircling the ankles of Ezili.

"I am here."

Marie spun around. Before her was a young woman dressed in another blue African robe of sun, sky, stars, and moon. The woman looked like Grandmère in features but was much darker in tone. Her skin was the purest black.

"I be Membe." She held out her hand.

Marie touched it and felt joy. This was her ancestor.

"There don't be any way to stop the river, the stream and flow of blood."

"Yes."

Membe seemed both substantial and insubstantial, both flesh and spirit. Strong and wonderful. Dead yet vitally alive.

Marie fell to her knees. She felt soiled by comparison, insignificant, ashamed of herself and all that she'd done. "I'm so confused. So lost. Forgive me."

"Never be no need for forgiveness among family."

"I've sinned against both you and Damballah."

"*There be no sins. Only life. Mistakes be a part of life.*" *Membe stepped forward and cupped Marie's face in her hands. Marie could see herself reflected in Membe's brown eyes. She could also see, beyond her own image, an African landscape of fertile plains and lush foliage, restless animals, and a community of blacks working, playing, loving. It was startling. She could see herself in the foreground of an African village that felt like home.*

"I hurt Grandmère," Marie whispered. "Hated Maman. Betrayed Damballah. You."

Membe stroked Marie's hair. Marie shuddered and rested her head in Membe's palm.

"*People make mistakes because they feel so much. Hate. Anger. Loneliness. Love. Black people be lost, friendless in a strange world. So Damballah sent me—sent us, all the Maries—to remind black people of themselves, their history and creation.*" *Membe blew air across Marie's face.* Marie could feel the sweet wind filling her up. "*Black people don't stay the same, they have to grow to fit into changing lives, new worlds. It be only right.*"

"But I've prayed, pray to white saints."

Membe laughed and spun until the snake on the hem of her gown became a swirl of rainbows. "*Damballah not be a jealous god. Damballah be a celebration of life. Birth, rebirth, respect for one's family, for all people. Do you feel good when you pray to the Virgin? Christ? Damballah has many names. There be many paths. Nothing diminishes the Voodoo faith. Voodoo always be a reverence for life.*"

"I murdered tonight."

"*Sometimes life be hard, ugly. Even the spirit* loas *fight and shout. All be not goodness. Being a Voodoo Queen means fighting one step at a time, to live as much goodness as possible, to help others live as much goodness too. Now you know who you be—your history—it should be easier.*

"*The light and faith be right here.*" *Membe's finger pointed at Marie's heart.* "*And here.*" *She kissed the sleeping baby's forehead.* "*And here.*" *Blood was trickling out of Membe's fingertips.*

Membe stepped back and began to dance, her body lilting and swaying through the air. From far off, Grandmère was singing.

"You be the New World Voodooienne."

"Wait . . . wait. There's so much more I need to know."

There was a brilliant burst of rainbows. The room seemed unable to contain the light. For a moment, Marie was blinded. Then, the rainbows began to fade; yellows, blues, reds shimmered, blended, and lightened. As the colors were fading, Membe's spirit was fading, disappearing, leaving behind a field of fireflies.

"Membe!" Marie called.

"Life be a celebration. No need to be more than a woman. Being a woman be just fine. Being Marie be . . . just fine."

Then Marie heard a soft admonition, echoing across the darkness. "Feel good. You be a New World Voodooienne. Love and trust yourself to be just fine."

Marie wept happy tears.

EPILOGUE:

Eighteen Hundred and Eighty-one

~

Marie is dead.

She'd been sleeping quietly, her chest gently rising and falling. Then shortly before midnight she turned to me and asked me to light candles for her. "In case my daughter doesn't hear of my death, say prayers for me, Louis. Tell her I missed her. If you see her, tell her to have faith in herself and Damballah."

I said I would.

Her eyes closed, and then they opened for what would be the last time (though I didn't know it then).

"I'm so scared, Louis," she said. "Dying scares me. I don't want to be damned. My life seems to have been filled with so much bitterness. So much loss."

I leaned forward and clasped her hand. "Don't be afraid. Remember what you told me. Life is a spiral. Everything starts over, spiraling outward from the center. Your center is good. You are good."

"I've committed the worst sins. I don't want to die."

"What did Membe say?" I said patiently to her as if she was a child again. "Membe said life would be hard. But she never said anything bad about dying. I think Membe, Grandmère, Maman . . . they must all be waiting for you. Jacques too. There must be a Guinea."

Her eyes lit up as fear washed out of her face. She looked so beautiful.

"My own, my pretty Marie," I whispered.

"You've become a faith healer, Louis."

"If I have, Marie, it is because you've taught me how to have faith—in life and in love."

She stared at me intently. "Say prayers for the dying, Louis."

Just once I wanted to lie down beside her and feel her body against the length of mine. I wanted to bury my face in her hair. My love was leaving.

"Louis, you've become part of my family. You've been good to me. I'll be waiting for you."

Then she expelled air and died.

•

—Louis DeLavier, June 16, 1881
(From Louis DeLavier's journal)

~

Special to the Daily Picayune
By Louis DeLavier

NEW ORLEANS, June 17, 1881—Marie Laveau, who preferred to be called the Widow Paris, died last night of natural causes. She was one of the most colorful personages of New Orleans. Reports about her age vary: 70 to 103. The attendant doctor, M. Reims, estimates she was in her late 70s.

Some remember Marie Laveau (particularly during the latter half of her life) as a sainted Catholic woman who nursed yellow fever victims and gave solace to prisoners. Many remember her acts of Christian charity throughout the city, helping orphans, the poor, and all who had need. Others say she was a witch, an evil Voodoo worshiper who never repented of consorting with the devil.

Many New Orleans residents thought she had died earlier. The last eight years of her life, Laveau was a recluse. Reports of her death are also confused because her sole child and daughter (also known as Marie Laveau and a practicing Voodooienne) often told people she was her mother reborn.

The funeral was a spectacular blend of Catholic ritual and Voodoo drums and dancing. She was buried in a crypt in St. Louis Cemetery, but already rumor has it that Marie Laveau was buried at sea. One woman claims she saw Laveau, after her death, walking east across the Gulf waves toward Africa.

•

—Louis DeLavier
(From Louis DeLavier's journal)

Author's Note

I first came across a reference to Marie Laveau many years ago in a Time-Life book on Creole and Acadian cooking. As an African-American and a feminist, I was intrigued by this historic figure of a black woman thriving amid slavery and oppression. Then the "signs" came. For over a year, without effort, I stumbled time and again across mentions of Laveau, in a song, in a text. I became convinced I was being "haunted" into a subject far removed from my experience.

I began writing *Voodoo Dreams*, and long-suppressed memories of my childhood and my own forgotten conjuring grandmother, Ernestine, were unleashed. *Scratch a wall, somebody die. If a bird makes a nest using hair from your brush, your hair will fall out. Put a glass under your bed, a letter under your pillow, say the words, and the one called will arise from the dead.* My quest to know about Laveau also became a quest to account for why I had suppressed and dismissed the power of my grandmother.

Little is know about Marie Laveau or her introduction to Voodoo. Folklorists seem to agree on certain facts: she was once a hairdresser and a Roman Catholic; she married a man named Jacques Paris (who later disappeared); and as the "Widow Paris," Laveau transformed herself into a flamboyant and powerful Voodooienne. She comforted the condemned and yellow fever victims, often working alongside Catholic priests. There was indeed a Voodoo Doctor named John, a contemporary of Laveau, though it's unclear whether any relationship existed between them. According to newspaper accounts, two men did in fact survive a hanging under curious circumstances attributed to Laveau, only to be hanged again moments later.

Apparently Laveau's daughter, also named Marie, carried on the Voodoo tradition, often claiming to be the original Marie Laveau, much to the consternation of folklorists trying to distinguish between the two. Some folklorists suggest that the daughter imprisoned her mother during her declining years as a way of stealing power and claiming immortality. Beyond this, the history of Marie Laveau is obscured by time, legend, and conflicting opinions.

As I uncovered bits of Marie's past, I became more and more fascinated by her. I wondered how a woman who had been Roman Catholic could transform herself into a Voodooienne. And I wondered why the miracles of a black woman should be dismissed as chicanery while miracles attributed to white men become evidence of sainthood. I began to see Laveau as a heroic character and, drawing on memories of my grandmother, I wove into Laveau's story a matrilineal line of knowledge and power. Gradually, Laveau's quest for rediscovery of self became a metaphor for a larger process of rediscovery of lost traditions and lost vision.

Most of this story sprang from imagination, from my vision of Laveau as a woman of power, and from my sense that Voodoo has been and continues to be a spiritual well that is far richer than American media and popular stereotypes allow. My newspaper articles and journal entries are fictional, as are all my character portrayals—Grandmère, Maman, Nattie, John, and the DeLaviers. Yet I feel that Laveau's spirit would approve of this tale of her legend and legacy.

All women are conjurers.

The power be passed down through the generations.